Captivated

Book 1

To: Shawna

Fall in love with
Romance
Big Hart Festival
9-30-23

Captivated

Book 1

Jessica Rooker

Captivated (Book 1) Identifiers
ISBN 978-1-961101-00-5 (eBook)
ISBN 978-1-961101-01-2 (paperback)

Cover design by Lynn Andreozzi
Cover photographer © Wander Aguiar Photography LLC
Cover model Andrew Biernat

Edited by Elise Hitchings

Author photographer © Evermore Photo Co.

Printed in the United States of America

Dedication

For Christy, you believed in me before I believed in myself. And for my husband, for helping make this book possible.

Table Of Contents

Chapter 1: Amelia

I'm sitting here thinking about my marriage. I hear stories all the time of abusive relationships ... physical abuse ... emotional abuse; but what is the difference? Emotional, physical, it's all abuse. Both have physical and emotional impacts on the abused. I'd love for someone to argue with me on that point. I live everyday with physical scars, yet they're unseen to the naked eye. Maybe those are the worst kind of scars, I don't know. Is a scar just a scar? Can physical abuse exist without emotional, or can emotional abuse exist without physical?

I'm Amelia Johansson and I have a story tell, but no one is listening. Who would I even share it with? My secrets have ruined any ties to my friends; I have no coworkers because I've allowed myself to be manipulated and my family has passed on. Sadness feels my soul remembering my sweet daddy, laying in the hospital alone and dying. I couldn't even be there to hold his hand in his final hours. Yet he's the man whose hand always held mine. He made me a strong independent woman. Today he wouldn't recognize the shell that once hosted the soul of his only daughter.

The anxiety is almost overwhelming at times; it's usually worse when we've just had another typical day of screaming, doors slamming, furniture kicked across the room, and, oh yes, my personal favorite: watching a grown ass man throw his cell phone or the remote control across the living room in a fit of rage. Yes, that's what I find most attractive about my husband—his ability to single-handedly demonstrate what a true ass the male population can be.

He is the true epitome of why I never wanted to marry. He wraps up the very essence of what a bad marriage is with a big pretty bow! Boy he's a great player; master manipulator. I see glimpses of my true self, yet only glimpses remain.

I look up when I hear a car pull in. I've got to pull myself out of my self-loathing pity party; it's time to play the perfect hostess. One of the many masks I wear nowadays. I plaster on my hostess smile, and as I make my way from the back of the house, my grandmother's antique oval mirror catches my reflection. I stop and turn, looking at myself. I don't have to worry about smile lines, because I'm never overly happy. Just pleasant I reckon, looking at my complexion, and I smooth my flyaways. As I reach my hostess desk, the door opens.

"Hi, welcome to Amelia's." I recognize my repeat guests: Marty and Jeanette Compton. They come every year for the Isle of Eight Flags Shrimp Festival. This is one of my busiest weekends of the year, with the festival attracting more than one hundred thousand visitors; and the pirate parade is always a highlight. We're usually booked in full by this time, but this has been a slow season.

12

"Hello darling." Marty's long southern draw makes me laugh. He's such a sweet man who adores his wife; I'm envious.

"Hey sugar, aren't you just a vision," Jeanette sings. Her brimming toothy smile is quite charming in a southern belle kind of way. Sometimes I wonder if she can actually not smile or close her mouth completely for her teeth. "Isn't she just a doll, Marty?" She grins, taking me in with her hand clutched over her bosom like a proud momma bear.

"She sure is. I reckon she's still off the market." I smile at his joke. He's hinted I should meet their eldest son since they first started visiting my inn, four years ago. "She's as pretty as a ripe peach on a hot summer day."

I'm laughing on the outside, eyes rolling on the inside. "Yes, I'm afraid I'm still off the market. You might as well find that boy of yours another catch." I take their credit card and swipe it to complete their payment. "Okay, you two are in your usual room."

"Tell me, peaches, are you booked up for the weekend?" Marty inquires as he slides his card back in its rightful spot. Smiling, he tucks his leather wallet in his back pocket.

"Not yet, it has actually been slow," I say fanning my hand through the air, "but I'm sure some procrastinators will fill the rooms."

"Are you making those delicious cinnamon rolls?"

"Marty, they're already rising." I wink. I watch them walk towards their room, laughing and talking about the lovely décor of my quaint bed and breakfast.

Yes, I suppose areas of my life aren't dark and dreary. Eric did buy us a turn-key establishment in the historic sector on Amelia Island four years ago. He told me 'we' were going to run it; truth be told, I'm running it … pretty much alone. The only real change we made was to the third level of the home—now our private quarters, consisting of three bedrooms, two bathrooms, a living room, and office area. The former owners used the main level bedrooms as their private quarters. Of course it is the least he could do, for what he caused to happen in the first place. I hate to go there; it will only bring my sour mood back with a vengeance.

I glance at my book. "Hmm, only one more booking for this weekend." I don't recognize the name: they haven't stayed at our establishment in the past.

My timer goes off in the kitchen, pulling me from my thoughts. We don't serve dinner but we do offer evening appetizers. The savory aroma permeates my all-white gourmet kitchen. Tonight I'm serving goat cheese asparagus tarts, cream puffs, and a charcuterie board. I take the tartlets out and set them on the counter to cool when the door chimes. "Looks like my next guests have arrived."

"Hello, welcome to Amelia's." I beam as I walk towards my desk. A homosexual couple! This should go over well with my narrow-minded husband. I look at my book. "Marcus and Gerry?"

14

"Yes, doll. I'm Gerry." He grins. "This is my main squeeze, Marcus."

I smile. "I'm Amelia and it is a pleasure to have you two visiting for a few days."

"What is that wonderful smell?" Marcus sniffs the air.

"Oh, that's tonight's complimentary appetizers. I just pulled goat cheese asparagus tartlets out of the oven."

"Oh that sounds divine! They smell absolutely delicious," Marcus says as I take their credit card to finalize their payment.

"Would you two care for a tour of the grounds, since this is your first time visiting?" I ask, handing over their credit card.

"Of course we would." Marcus loops his arm through Gerry's as I walk around my desk.

"Well, why don't we start with showing you two to your room—follow me." We walk up the curving staircase to the second level and follow the oversized hallway to the end. "This is what we call the French quarter room. I trust you will find everything you need." The walls are covered in an elegant country Labrador blue shade, with bright white trimming. A massive four poster bed dominates the room, the rich mahogany fireplace screams romance, and the large box bay window sitting area flows with natural light. "You also have a private bath; complimentary toiletries and fresh towels are provided daily. Just ask when you need more."

Gerry looks pleased, touching the luxurious bedding. "Look Marcus, isn't this just the most charming room? I wish we had brought our handcuffs, if you know what I mean." They giggle affectionately.

I bite my bottom lip so I don't stand there with a gaping mouth, and, feeling the heat of my cheeks, I pull myself together rather quickly and clear my throat. "Well okay then ... I don't supply those," I tease, giving them a playful smile as I turn. "Shall we continue the tour?"

"We shall, you feisty hostess," Gerry teases. "I already like her, Marcus."

Continuing with our tour, I point to another set of stairs that leads to the third level. "Our private quarters are on the third floor. There is an elevator across the hall, it's original to the house so bear that in mind with its small size and age. But you two look healthy, we will take the stairs." I grin, trotting down ahead of them.

Off the foyer I show them the formal living room and parlor. "This is the parlor for sitting ... chatting ... whatever." I point to the console. "There are games as well." We walk down the large hall admiring the craftsmanship of the late 1800s and early 1900s; at the back of the house is the dining room and kitchen with a vestibule located between them leading to the outdoor porch and courtyard area. "Breakfast is served between eight and ten in the dining room or if you prefer alfresco dining, you may eat outside on the side porch or poolside. Evening hors d'oeuvres are served between six and eight." As we walk and talk, I point to additional guest quarters and the library.

16

"This is stunning," Marcus boasts as he walks off the porch admiring the courtyard, gardens, and double Roman style in-ground pool. "Is the pool saltwater?"

"Yes, it is." I nod as I continue to walk. "Feel free to stroll the gardens; we have a variety of flowers blooming. There are some great little private nooks and crannies." Sighing I stare at the garden … it's peaceful. I spend a lot of time here.

"I'm going to tell my boss about this place." Gerry beams. "This is Amelia's best kept secret." His words make me smile.

"Please do. We do a lot of business with repeat guests. Okay, well my husband's name is Eric. He will be here later this evening. Please make yourselves at home and let me know if you have any questions or need anything. You two enjoy yourselves." I leave them venturing into the gardens as I finish my evening preparations.

It's almost seven. The dread is pooling with the anticipation of Eric's return. Although, he's usually pleasant when we have guest staying at the inn. Grabbing the novel I've been reading, I get comfy on the sofa and lost in the pages, lost into the dream of love and romance. After all, it's my only escape.

"I see you're reading … you're always reading." Eric smirks.

Startled by his voice, I jump, and ignore his comment. I was so engrossed I didn't even hear him close the door. He starts unbuttoning his shirt, tossing it aside. He never reads; just another thing we don't have in common. He throws his socks on the floor, plopping his overly pale ass in his chair. I

17

look up, pursing my lips. It would be nice to look at something sexy once in a while. I continue to read my book.

"Why aren't you talking?"

"I am reading." I'm clearly still annoyed with him from this morning's behavior. It drives me insane, why does he think he can act like a complete lunatic? Eight hours later he's supposed to be forgiven and I'm to keep my emotions intact. It's been a long ten years of marriage, living like this.

"How many guests are here?"

"Two couples, both are on the second floor."

"Hmm, that's weird with the festival this weekend, we're usually booked up."

"Yeah!" I don't know what he expects me to say.

"Come rub my back, it's killing me."

"No, I don't want to."

"You never want to touch me. I am your husband. I should buy you some wine." He cuts his eyes down my body. "You know a little bubbly makes you feel frisky."

I roll my eyes. "I don't want any wine and I don't want to touch you," I hiss.

He bites his tongue as he flips the television on. *That's a first*. It's only temporary though, I have figured his game out at this point. He acts like a complete asshole, then he tries to be on good behavior. If he really acts like a super-colossal ass, I always get a gift. I laugh now on the inside when I get one, because it means he's only to do it again!

Chapter 2: Quinton

God she's beautiful. I can't believe she said yes and here we're standing in front of our friends and family, saying our vows. "Quinton repeat after me," I hear the officiant say. "I, Quinton Starks, take thee to have and to hold, for better or worse, in sickness and health all the days of my life." She cries as I slip her platinum diamond wedding band on her petite finger. I massage her finger just a few seconds. She has the most beautiful sapphire eyes I've seen; almost magical in the way they sparkle. Her lips are perfectly kissable, not too full but not flat. I've kissed a lot of women in my day, but her lips are perfect. They melt into mine as if we're one. I grin like a silly schoolboy as I watch her slip my titanium wedding band on my wedded finger. Finally, we've sealed the deal. She's mine to love and hold for the rest of our lives.

I grunt awake, feeling her hands rubbing over my six pack and up my chest; she moans her satisfaction. With my eyes still closed, I grab her hand, rubbing my fingers across her knuckles. There's no ring on that wedded finger, but I don't let my dissatisfaction show. My morning wood is throbbing from my dream; I peek out from heavy eyelids at the mound of blond hair kissing around on my stomach. Hmm, I do have a problem that needs attention … I gently guide her head south. The blonde bombshell is more than happy to oblige as she takes me into her mouth. I close my eyes and imagine the woman in my dreams.

Blondie collapses next to me after giving me head, grinning like a Cheshire cat, still touching my killer body. I really need to be more selective in the ladies I pick up in bars. This one has the potential to be a hanger. I look at my clock, seven a.m. *Fuck,* I've missed my morning run. Exhaling, I sit up, tossing my covers aside, standing with no regard of my nakedness or the wanton woman in my bed.

"I've got to hit the gym before work," I hear my egotistical self saying. Man, I can sound like a douche.

"You're kidding." She giggles trying to play, yet knowing the implied message is 'get the fuck out of my bed.'

"Nope." I walk into my bath, looking at the captivating male staring back at me. I run my hands through my tangled hair and down over my mustache. I'm quite alluring, not to mention I would be one hell of a catch, I think, remembering my dream. "That's never going to happen," I whisper to myself as I see my bathroom door open.

Rolling my eyes, I turn around to see blondie all pouting, arms crossed. "What?" I hiss.

"You're fucking kidding right?" She's starting to squeak. "I just let you blow your load in my mouth."

"And you loved it," I remind her because of course she did. Why else would a woman suck a man's cock if not for the taste of his essence? I carry on, jerking up my workout shorts and put on a fitted tank.

"You're an asshole, Quinton Starks!" she huffs as she's tugging up her red nylon dress. "I can't believe I blew you this morning." She snatches her sandals over her heels. I can't deny it, I am an asshole.

"Ouch, why you going to say such things? You enjoyed yourself last night," I taunt following her towards the door. "I seem to recall you screaming I was the best you've had."

"Shut up." She yanks my door open as she shoves past my buddy, who was about to knock. He smirks as he watches the hot bombshell stalk toward the elevators.

"Well, I see you took the blonde home last night," he says, walking into my apartment. "Damn man, I wish I had your life."

"No, Andy you don't." I blow his admiration off immediately. "You have a wife." He rolls his eyes, which I'll never understand why—his wife is smoking hot. She's actually way too hot for him.

"You missed our run this morning." Which answers my question about what Andy is doing here.

"Yeah, I was getting head." I walk to my fridge, get a water and chug it. I grab my protein powder and make my power shake for breakfast.

Andy laughs. "Well, are you hitting the gym before you head into the office?"

"Really, is that a question?" I ask, annoyed, flexing my pecs at him. "Do you honestly think I keep this killer sex bod by slacking off? I have to work out every day."

Andy rolls his eyes. "You're one arrogant son of a bitch, but you have rights." *Damn right I do*, I nod as we both walk out of my apartment.

"I'll catch you at the office." I punch the button for my private gym on the elevator. One of the perks of being me: the luxury to own a private gym in the building. I love my life.

An hour later, I return to my penthouse to shower and dress for the office. I walk in as Lucinda is stripping my bed. She smirks at the smell of the cheap perfume. I feel somewhat guilty about not picking up my own condom wrappers, but only somewhat. After all, she's very well compensated for her services. I wouldn't survive without Lucinda.

She looks at me, suspicious, as I notice her emptying the trash from the bedroom. "What?" I grin. I know what she's wondering. "Yeah I am that good Lucinda." I am that good ... extended sexual pleasure is my forte. I'm also going to make sure I blow my load every time.

I walk out of the shower, wrapping my towel around my chiseled midsection and towel dry my dark hair. I run my fingers through my hair, causing it to part naturally down the middle; I brush the sides first then the back. I grab some Aveda pomade to style my hair. I groom my mustache and beard to keep a controlled scruff look; women seem to go crazy over it.

Walking into my closet, I look at the array of white dress shirts, plenty of navy or gray suits. *Hmmm, it's Monday, I will go navy.* Thirty minutes later I'm walking out of the building. The valet has pulled up my pride and joy—my red Mercedes AMG GTC Roadster. I toss the valet a hefty tip.

I whip into the parking garage of another building I own, Stark's Industries. I would have made my dad proud, had he lived to see my success. My heart feels heavy remembering him; it's the only weight that ever makes me feel anything. I hop out, tossing my keys to another valet, as well as another hefty tip. I saunter into the lobby, through the metal detectors and straight to the twenty-eighth-floor.

As I exit the elevator, the glass doors open for me to smiling, welcoming faces. I wonder if they really like me for me, or if they see me as the pompous ass who pays them. Regardless, I do appreciate the smiles. I turn the corner heading to my glass office, and there he is, my second righthand man, Gerry! There are two people in this entire world I know I positively cannot live without: Lucinda and Gerry.

"Gerry." I beam. "How was your weekend getaway?" I grab the coffee he has waiting for me and hit the button opening my office door.

I unfasten my blazer before sitting behind my desk, overlooking the little people rushing to their jobs below. From my view, they look like ants in a colony, scrambling.

"It was fabulous," Gerry sings as he walks his runway walk with a file in hand. He knows he doesn't have to wait for me to offer him a seat, he graces his flaming purple suit on my stark white modern chair. Gerry and I met clubbing one night; he was as queer as a two-dollar bill, but I didn't care. I liked him. He has style and pizzazz. Exactly what some stiff backs need to lighten the mood of the corporate world. When he entered one of my establishments a couple of ignorant ingrates thought they would work on building up their male testosterone by beating him down.

I was all too happy to show them how a real, six foot five, two hundred and thirty pound man acts. That night the ingrates were liberated, and I found the best assistant I've ever had. That was ten years ago, and we're still going strong. He adds the color and flare to my gray and navy world; and I compensate him immensely for it. He knows what I'm thinking, sometimes before I do, which is freakishly weird.

"That's great," I chime. "What do you think of the area?"

"Such a lovely quaint town." He crosses his legs, flipping through the file. "I don't see a nightclub taking off there." He poses, looking up.

"Oh," I say, leaning back, "and why is that?"

"It's a small island, the historic sector definitely won't host a club such as your establishments here. It's full of character and charm."

"What about a beach front establishment?"

"I took the liberty of taking some pictures of local bars." He laughs. "Or what they call bars on the beach. I also took pictures of empty plots of land, on the ocean front."

I lean forward, taking the pictures and looking at them. I have some ideas immediately.

24

"There is not really much to do in the way of ocean front dining, dancing, or nightlife for that matter," Gerry says.

"What about the tourist sector?" I ask giving his pictures back. "I mean are there hotels on the strip; resorts and such? I just wonder if, say we come in, open up an establishment, will it have enough revenue to thrive?" I've been to Amelia Island before, but it was years ago. I was in my twenties and it offered nothing to a philandering trust fund brat.

"Hell yes!" He smirks. "That place needs some energy; it's only forty minutes from here, and I found out the locals travel to Jacksonville for clubbing. I say we paint that town." I laugh as he snaps and flips his head like he does when he gets excited about a project.

I lean back looking at the ants below. "Maybe I should take a business trip to the location; check it out for myself. Kind of get a feel for the atmosphere."

"Maybe you should honey." He grins as he flips his file closed. "You have appointments in the conference room the rest of the today."

"Shit." I look at my watch. "Okay, well, we will figure out a time for me travel down to check it out." I smirk as I follow his purple suit out the door. "Great suit by the way!" I flash my bright whites at him.

"Don't I know it, I make it look fabulous!"

"Oh, if a lady calls looking for me, Camelia or something like that, I left the country." I can't remember her name, just that it sounded like Camelia or Cammy.

25

"Oh shit, when are you going to find yourself a nice lady and stop chasing skirts? I'll take care of it like I always do." I nod as I know he will.

I walk into the conference room and take my seat at the head of the table. Damn I feel good. I think I'm going to take a business trip to Amelia Island and check out some of these bars; I may bring it up with the board this week. I stand as my first appointment arrives.

"Ester Miller." I grin as I shake her hand. She's an old prude of a woman, but she holds the company my firm is trying to buy. "If you don't mind waiting for my business associate to arrive," I say, and grin as I see him through the glass. "And here he is."

"I actually have someone coming as well." Well, that's a surprise. I nod, smiling on the outside, pissed off on the inside. I don't care for surprises. "I thought I should bring my lawyer, you know in case you fancy suits try to slip something by an old senile woman."

I laugh as she talks. "Now Ester, you know I wouldn't slip you one." I totally would have. Damn it. I just hope this attorney isn't too sharp. "Anyone I know?"

"Doubtful, it's my granddaughter." My ears perk up, *granddaughter*. "Here she comes." I turn as she pushes through the door. I laugh on the inside, this won't be hard.

Andy and I both stand, dropping our sexiest smiles. Mine has been known to make women drop their panties. She's pretty attractive, I might be able to work my magic. "Quinton

Starks," I introduce myself, taking her hand. Andy introduces himself.

"Jessica Miller." She's cold. She sits next to her grandmother, flipping open the contract. "Let us cut to the chase, your firm is interested in buying my grandmother's shares. This offer is bogus."

She has looked at it. My legal department ensured it would not be noticed: what our true intentions are to do with the company once we acquire it. "Whatever do you mean? We have agreed to the terms of your grandmother, and I think quite liberally." I glance at Andy.

"I'm talking about the money; this company is worth more than the measly one point five million you're offering."

Andy laughs and tosses his pen down. "Do you not realize that your family's company is going under? It's not worth what we have offered. We're being generous already."

I stare quietly at them both; Ester looks at her granddaughter and whispers something. Andy continues to bring the margins out: laying it all out on the table. *That's right Andy, overwhelm our little greedy lawyer.* I lean back in my chair thinking about what her tits look like; I'd like to fuck her, my cock is already getting hard.

"Grandmother you can't." I hear Jessica's authoritative voice faltering. That tone brings me back to the conference room.

"I'm happy to take you out for drinks, Jessica, if you would like to review the contract in greater detail. Maybe it would give you some peace of mind." She looks at me; I can see the desire in her eyes. She may be rolling them, but she still wants me.

"Do you have a pen Mr. Starks?" Ester oversteps her young granddaughter's warnings. I grin as I lean over, pushing my pen to her.

"Sign where the flags are." I grin as I catch Andy smirking. I cut my eyes at Jessica, who is clearly against this. Maybe she knows more is in the contract. I sign my name. The deal is done! It doesn't matter what little Ms. Jessica Miller thinks now.

I shake Ester's hand. Andy handles the remaining legal documents. After all, he's head of my legal department. Ester relaxes, and a look of relief seems to pass over her face. "Jessica, dear, why don't you take Mr. Starks up on his offer? He's such a nice man."

I grin. "Yes Jessica, would you care to join me for drinks?" I look at my watch. "Andy can handle my next appointment."

"Fine!" She smiles as we all stand. I shake her grandmother's hand once more, leaving her with Andy to get the contract copies and money exchanged.

I open the door for her. "Shall we?" She sashays letting me get a lovely view of her round ass.

"We have to make this quick." She looks at her watch. "Unlike you I don't have the luxury of throwing my responsibilities off on a partner. You have two hours."

I smirk, *that's all I need baby*. "Well, how about a quick drink in my office then? Maybe that makes it easier for you. More sensible?"

"Fine," she says, following me to my office. I give Gerry a knowing look as I press the button for the door to open. "You have got to be kidding me," she smarts as she struts inside. Oh I'm going to fuck her like a true asshole.

"Gerry hold my calls; no interruptions until Ms. Miller leaves."

"Ah, shit," Gerry mumbles. I wink as I close the door and hit the privacy button. The glass wall turns dark.

"That's a nice touch, I wondered how you got any work done; seeing everything outside your office." She smiles as she takes a seat on my sofa.

"It becomes a mirror on the other side. I can see out, at all times, but they cannot see inside." I walk to my wet bar. "What are you having?"

"Do you have gin?"

I grin, *a gin girl*. "Bombay Sapphire."

She smiles in appreciation as I fix us both a gin on the rocks with a wedge of lime. "Thank you." I unfasten my coat, before sitting down on the other end of the sofa. She sips her drink, skeptical of my intentions. "Why did you want have drinks?"

I have found that honesty always works best where women are concerned. "Because I want to fuck you." I sip my drink. The shock of my dispassionate sexual demeanor is evident.

29

"Really," she breathes as she took another sip, failing to hide the grin tugging at her lips. "What makes you think I would sleep with you?"

I move closer toying with her hair. "I did not say anything about sleeping." I relax my arm on the back of the sofa as I wait for her response. She's thinking about it, I can see it in her eyes. She looks toward the windows. "No one can see inside, I assure you." I bring my glass back to my lips, emptying my drink. She watches me as I walk to the bar. "Do you want another?"

"No." She stands next to me downing her remaining gin. Her empty glass clinks on the bar. I look down at her, she's so close to me I can smell her body wash.

"You smell like lavender," I whisper noticing her closeness.

"Vanilla lavender to be exact." She's all breathy looking up at me, with those 'fuck me now' eyes. I watch her as she moves her unsure hand across my shoulders. That's all I need.

I turn swooping her up in my arms, bringing her mouth to mine. I can feel her breath on my lips. She opens her mouth and closes her eyes, begging to be kissed. I bend, dipping my tongue deep in her mouth, exploring this new vessel. She tastes like gin and honey. She's so sweet; her mouth feels like silk. She whimpers into my mouth, as I deepen our kiss casually wandering my hands over her ass, squeezing her against me, letting her feel my erection. I want her to understand my intentions.

She pulls back, breathy—her lips parted and red from kisses. With desire-filled, unsure eyes, she rips her blazer off. I rip mine off, tossing it somewhere. I have no idea where it landed. She grabs my face, kissing me with as much urgency as before, tasting me, as I work her blouse out of her skirt, unfastening the buttons, two at a time.

Damn she's fucking hot. I didn't even notice her unfasten my shirt. I grin as she smirks. I unfasten my cuffs. She shoves my shirt off my shoulders, revealing my chiseled midriff; I can see her appreciation of my rock-hard body. *That's right baby, look at me.* I grin as I shove her blouse off, revealing her lace bra. In one flick of my fingers I have her bra undone.

I break her kisses, kissing down her jaw line, her neck, traveling down to her clavicle. Her fingers lace through my hair as she pulls closer, wrapping her leg around my hips. I rub my hand over her swollen tit, my thumb brushing the hardened bud before sucking hard. She gasps. I squeeze and pull her other nipple—it elongates immediately. She's hot for me, flexing her hips against me. I caress her thigh, sliding my hand down the front of her skirt before slipping under it. She whimpers as my fingers stroke her lace covered heat. "You want this?" I growl.

"Don't you dare fucking stop," she hisses. I grab a condom out of the bar drawer and lift her in my arms, hiking her pencil skirt over her hips. She leans back on my couch. I run my hands up, pulling those lace panties off, tossing them aside. I grin as she pulls me down into another kiss. I dip my tongue deeper into her mouth, teasing and sucking her bottom lip. She's melting under my touch. I keep kissing her, traveling

31

down her jaw, her neck, sucking her nipples as she arches back, lacing her fingers in my hair.

I unfasten my pants, pushing them down enough to release my erection. I rip the condom open with my fingers, never releasing her nipple from my mouth. I cover my cock, rubbing my head at her opening. She's lost in lust; I continue to kiss her as I shove into her ... hard.

She gasps, tensing and clutching my biceps. I don't give her time to adjust, she wanted this. I start pounding into her. She's whimpering, biting and sucking on my shoulders.

"Fuck," I growl leaning back, grabbing her legs and wrapping them around me. She's moaning, enjoying the sensation. I thrust harder into her, watching her tits bounce. *Fuck she's loud.* I lean over taking her jaw in my hand, and her eyes open as I cover her mouth with mine. I feel her insides clutching tighter around my cock. Her nails dig into my back as she finds her release; she's shaking and contracting. I'm chasing my own climax—fast and hard—when my mind drifts to my damn dream. *What the fuck?* I shake my head, getting back in the game. I look at her; her sapphire eyes captivate me. I lock my gaze on them—she suddenly feels like heaven. She's all silk; all heat. I caress her face, kissing her lips sweetly, as I feel my release explode. Only it doesn't go anywhere, but hits the end of the condom, flooding back over myself. I growl, dropping down on her chest; her heart is pounding in my ear.

She's breathing hard. I know I can't lay on her small frame long without crushing her. I kiss across her chest, tasting her vanilla lavender scent. I travel kissing up her neck, her jaw,

32

and take her face in my hands. I kiss her swollen lips, looking at her eyes. *Fuck, they're green.* I jerk myself back suddenly, alarming her.

"What?" She's still breathy.

"Nothing ... sorry." I grin as I stand, removing the condom and tossing it in the trash. She closes her legs and slowly adjusts her cloths. I know that look, she's coming down from that sex high she was on. The reality of what we've done is about to hit her.

I slip my shirt on, fastening the cuffs. The silence is deadening as I tuck myself back, and adjust my pants, before zipping and fastening them. I grab my blazer from the floor and shake out the wrinkles before I slip it on. I look at her, holding her blazer in my hands. She can't look at me. Great, she's embarrassed because now she's doing the walk of shame in daylight out of my office. I actually feel bad for her.

"You are welcome to use my bathroom," I offer, gesturing to the closed door. "If you need to freshen up or anything." I make light of it, running my fingers through my hair, calming my sex head.

"Thank you," she mumbles as she grabs her blazer. I watch her walk into the bathroom. I fix another drink and gulp it down while I wait, looking out the windows. What the fuck is wrong with me? Why are those sapphire eyes haunting me? The lady in my dreams is something that I manifested at a subconscious level.

I turn around when she walks out. Her shame filled eyes don't match her confident body language. "Thanks for the

33

drink … and …" She doesn't finish her statement. "I have a meeting to attend," she says motioning towards the door.

"Yes … I quite enjoyed your company." I smile as I clasp her hands, walking her towards the door. She wanted to say more, but I suspect she didn't know what to say. Normally I would tell her my true intentions to eradicate her family's company, but she looks pretty damn shamed. I hit the privacy screen to release and kiss her once more. Gerry looks up as the well fucked attorney meekly walk past his desk.

"Ah honey, you're going to hell," Gerry snaps as he prances in my office as soon as she gets on the elevator. I grin, rubbing my hand down my mustache. He shakes his head, pursing his lips. "One day you're going to get royally fucked by a woman. The shoe is going to be on the other foot."

I sit back in my chair, smirking. "Well I'm thirty-five and I've yet to meet a woman who captures my attention longer than a good fuck." We both laugh about it as Andy walks in.

"I see you sealed two deals already." He sits in the chair next to Gerry.

I grin. "What can I say?"

Andy shakes his head as he drops the original contract on my desk. "Did you let the sweet granddaughter know what they agreed to by selling the company?"

I gave him a knowing look. "I couldn't break her spirit anymore. Once she was well fucked, the reality was hitting her. It's in the contract; they can read it, but it's not going to matter at this point."

"Yeah, that poor girl couldn't get out of here fast enough."
Gerry purses his lips.

"Start the process."

"And that's why you're the man ... the fucking man!"
Andy points as he all but skips out of my office.

"You make that crazy fool a ton of money." Gerry smirks
as he swaggers to his desk.

"I pay you a mad amount of money too," I remind him.

"And I'm worth every damn cent." He blows me a kiss,
laughing.

Chapter 3: Amelia

I dread even bringing the estate sale up, but I really would like to go check it out. I knock on his office door. "Hey Eric, do you want to go check out this estate sale? I don't have any guests coming for the next few days." I walk over to see what he's working on. "We could stay overnight."

"God," he blurts out, clearly irritated. "I don't know … I can't think about it right now. This shit isn't fucking working!" He slams his hand down, making me jump. Then his cell phone rings. Inhaling deeply, he balls his fist at the device cussing the poor ass who made it ring. "I wish everyone would stop fucking calling me," he yells, "fuck it." *Yep, there it goes* … his phone sails through the air.

I turn, leaving him to it. It is so annoying … one simple question escalates into a string of obscenities. There's no con-versation … not even the ability to have one!

"Amelia … Amelia," he yells. I don't answer … there is no reason … he's already pissed off. I sit down on the couch with my laptop to look at the estate sale.

"What did you want?"

"Nothing … I was just going to see if you wanted to go to this estate sale."

"When?"

"Tomorrow." I look up from the computer; his face is distorted like a snarled-up bulldog.

"I'd really love to shake that money tree you seem to think we have." I look at him. "You have no concept of money or the fact that people actually have to fucking work for it," he yells. *Great, now he's taking whatever pissed him off out on me—the doormat he married.*

"Just forget it." I recoil and toss my laptop aside to leave the room. I don't want him to see he wins again … the tears are getting harder and harder to fight.

"Where are you fucking going?" He's so unattractive when he acts like an adolescent.

"Downstairs, I don't feel like listening to you rant and rave."

"Fuck it," he hisses as he slaps the wall, storming back into his office. I jump at his actions. *Yep, and there it is.* This is my life … my husband. I walk out on the side porch, letting the screen door slap. The garden is my secret oasis; I pull the single wooden swing that dangles from the sea oaks covered in Spanish moss. The swing was hung by the previous owner for their little girl. I sit on the wooden seat, rocking back and forth with my eyes closed, listening to the birds singing. It's so peaceful here. Bright lush greenness everywhere, with rich pops of color from the flowering plants; you can't see anyone, it's like a wall of life. I close my eyes: listening to the town's traffic, faint pedestrian voices, and Clydesdale-drawn buggies click and creak over the cobblestone streets. I smell the restaurants cooking the evening orders and birds squawk at the marina.

Sometimes I like to imagine I have a different life: married to the love of my life, a husband who adores, respects, and gushes over me. And of course our sexual desire would be through the freaking roof. Sometimes I wonder if he's out there, somewhere thinking if there is someone meant for him.

I twirl my fingers around the rope as I twist my seat until I cannot twist anymore. I bend my knees under the seat and spin out. I laugh, remembering doing the same thing as a child. Only as a child I didn't feel nauseous afterwards. I do it again, begging for punishment I reckon. I rock back and forth staring at the plush green carpet dreaming of something ... someone. A tear slips down my cheek remembering the feel of a first kiss; the heat, the passion.

I exhale, even more depressed than before. I'm pathetic, standing in the courtyard looking at the door. I really don't want to go inside ... it's going to be miserable.

Taking a deep breath I walk inside. Eric's walking aimlessly around, talking about a deal. *How annoying!* He acts so nice to a client. I wonder what they would think of him if they heard the way he really speaks ... the way he truly acts. He hangs up as I walk into the kitchen.

"Let's go to dinner. I don't feel like waiting for you to cook." He doesn't look at me as he speaks. He's too preoccupied with the text he's sending.

"Okay, let me get my bag." He's on the phone again when I return. I whisper, "I'm ready." He swings his arms at the phone, frowning like I made a huge interruption. I roll my eyes. He leaves me to sit and wait on him for another thirty minutes. He really has no regard for me.

Finally we get into the car to go to dinner. "Where do you want to eat?"

"I don't know, what do you want?" He ignores my question for another call. He's friendly and polite to them. Now we're just riding around at this point ... and I'm waiting for a response.

Eric disconnects his call, impatiently flapping his hands again. "Where are we going?" he yells. "You never told me where you wanted to eat." There is no talking or conversation, just his sudden animated outburst.

I look at him ... *is he for fucking real?* "You've been on your phone since we left the house and ignored my question. What do you want?"

"I don't know; I'm hungry as shit. I'm about to just say fuck it and go to McDonald's." He gasses the car down the road.

"Whatever." I roll my eyes. I'm not even hungry at this point. My stomach is in knots. This has to be what anxiety feels like. I cross my arms across my body, shifting in my seat to look out the window.

"What's wrong with you?" *Really,* I think to myself, *he really doesn't have a clue.*

I shake my head. "Nothing."

39

"What time do we need to leave for the estate sale?"

I look at him. "I don't know ... I didn't think we were going."

"Well, I'm busy, but I figure we could go check it out; we're not staying the night because I have a meeting the following morning." I plaster on a fake smile as I look back out the window. "You sure you don't want anything?" he asks as he pulls up to McDonald's.

"Yes."

* * *

"Oh ... my ... God," I scream as I lace my fingers through his long dark hair; I tug his face deeper into my sex. His lips are strong and soft, brushing over my sex before he sucks my clitoris. Moaning, I throw my head back. He presses my thighs open. I gasp as his tongue swirls and sucks my clitoris. He growls, kissing his way up my body, sucking and nibbling across my stomach. I clutch the sheets, arching my back as he sucks my nipple into his mouth. With his other hand he dips his fingers inside my folds. Gasping, I start to shake and tighten around him as he finger fucks me. My silk covers his fingers as I find my release.

I wake up hunched in the fetal position, my thighs are squeezing tight around my hand. I jump. "What the ..." I gasp, pulling my fingers away from my sex. Breathing hard, I drop back into the pillows. Eric is snoring beside me, and I just had the best organism I've had in years. My toes are still tingling.

Damn, why can't that be my real life? I roll over, fluffing my pillow.

40

Chapter 4: Quinton

Fucking hell, I wake up to a wet dream in the middle of the night. All I can see are those damn sapphire eyes; I can still taste her essence on my lips. I grab my sheet, wiping my cock, tossing it aside. I roll over, fluffing my pillow. That would be her side of the bed, if she existed. I'm going out after work and finding me a blue-eyed companion for the night.

At least I didn't miss my morning run. Andy is getting on my nerves as we run through the park. He's huffing already, and it's only been four miles. "If you want a body like mine, you're going to have to do better than this, friend," I tease, yet I'm fucking serious.

Winded he agrees, "I'm building up my stamina." *Yeah? But at what cost? Bringing me down from mine?* I don't say anything.

After we finish our run, I head back to my apartment and hit the gym. An hour later, I run into Lucinda stripping my sheets to wash them. I hope she doesn't see my dried wad. I don't say anything as I hit the shower. I grab my Aveda shampoo and lather my sweat-glazed hair. It smells nice. The conditioner isn't bad either. I grab my body wash lathering my killer body. I like my forty-six-inch chest—correction I love it. *I do have a sexy body*, I think, flexing my biceps.

I stand naked in front of my floor-to-ceiling mirror, drying my body and admiring my six pack, hell admiring all of my dips and ripples. Thank god for good genetics. Looking at my dark hair and dark eyes, I see both my parents, which reminds me I need to call my mother.

I run my fingers through my hair, causing it to naturally part in the center; I brush the sides first and then the back. I apply some Aveda pomade, *perfect*. I groom my scruff, *perfect*. I walk into my oversized walk-in closet, *Hmmm what to wear? Guess I will go gray today.* I have the same morning routine: workout, shower, and head into the office.

I grin when I see Gerry holding my coffee. "Thanks, love the suit." Today he has donned a chartreuse suit. I might need to put my shades on when he graces my white chair. I laugh on the inside.

"Thanks, it's new." He swaggers into my office. "Marcus surprised me with it last night."

"I do love a new suit, which reminds me, I need to pick one up."

"Are you going to get something other than navy or gray?" Gerry smirks.

"Probably not." I grin. "Why mess with perfection? This is my signature style." Sometimes I dress it up with a fancy tie; on a casual day I don't wear a tie.

"You need some color in your wardrobe." He smirks, looking deadpan.

"That's why I keep you around, you add plenty of color to my life." I grin as I look out of my window at the little ants scattering like their trail was trampled. Lost and now trying to find their way. "What's my schedule like for the rest of the week?" I'm itching to start this new project.

"You're wide open after Thursday. Should I book you some accommodations?"

I nod. "Yeah, something with room service. What are you and Marcus doing tonight? Want to color the town?" I grin.

"Prowling?"

"Something like that." I take my seat behind my desk, thinking about those damn eyes. It really is starting to piss me off, I've never been consumed with a woman in the flesh, but this is borderline crazy—she's a figment of my imagination. My day passes rather quickly, with meeting after meeting. It's almost five when I remember I haven't called my mother.

"Shit." I grab my cell, scroll down, and press her name. "Hey Mom." I stretch my arm out as she screams in my ear. She can't help it, we're Italian. I smirk when she asks me when I'm going to meet a nice Italian girl and settle down. "You're the last nice Italian woman, Mom," I tease her. "Seriously, these women aren't like you." That's the truth: she loves fiercer than any woman I've ever met, fights for what she believes in, can out cook any Italian restaurant in the Jacksonville area, nothing comes before her family, and she's ridiculously passionate. I guess that's what made her a great mother. I grin as I listen to her talk about my sister.

"How is that new brother-in-law of mine doing?" I'm actually curious if he's keeping my sister safe and happy. She's as beautiful as my mother; men flock to her. I remember beating a few asses before she met her husband. I wasn't too keen on the idea of her marrying a military general, but like my mother, when she sets her mind to having someone, that's it. I laugh, I guess we're all like that.

I disconnect my call as I see Andy rounding the corner. He looks pissed. I motion for him to come in as he hits my button. "What has you heated?"

"It's nothing work related," he hisses as he helps himself to my bar. "It's Tierra. Sometimes she just fucking drives me insane." He gulps his drink.

"I told you when you started dating her she was going to be high maintenance," I tease as I make myself a drink. "What happened?"

He shakes his head as he looks at me. "It's not that. It's that damn manager! I knew her modeling was going to take off ... hell we all did."

"Point?" I don't see what the fucking big deal is. He married a lingerie and swimsuit model. "This isn't anything new ... comes with the territory."

"She calls me just now telling me she has a photo shoot in Hawaii." I still don't see the issue; he looks at me. "With that slime-ball manager and photographer."

I sit down. "Look don't take this the wrong way; you married a hot piece of ass. Who happens to be a model ... of skimpy things." I take a swig of my drink. "Don't tell me you're insecure in your marriage." I roll my eyes. "Dude we're way too old to have adolescent behavior; she married you. You've got to trust her."

"I trust her completely; I don't trust that sleaze-ball manager or photographer."

I don't know what to tell him. "Did you two argue about her going?"

"I told her I forbid her to go with them." I laugh without any regard. *Idiot.* "You sound like her now."

"You can't control someone. You can't forbid her to do anything. Look, Gerry, Marcus, and I are going out tonight. Call Tierra, you two come with us. You need to chill and have some fun. Stop taking it all so seriously."

"Maybe you're right. I've been wound up tight with the deals we've got moving forward. We going to your club, Libation?"

"Of course." I grin as I see Marcus arrive. "Go call that sexy piece of ass you call a wife," I tease walking over to Marcus and Gerry.

* * *

45

I love my life. We're having dinner at the VIP table—the best seat in the house. Perfect for scouting single ladies with an unlimited view of all the dance floors and bars. I grin when I see Andy's wife. She's flaunting her catwalk towards our table; his drink misses his mouth as he gawks at her. She's dressed to party; I can practically see her nipples through the thin silver club dress. At least her ass is covered ... well, when she's standing. She's five foot ten, but those heels make her legs appear longer. Her lips are pink and pouty; her bleach blond piecey hairstyle screams she spends a lot of time in the salon. Her eyes are a seductive, horny green heavily accented by smokey eye shadow. *Andy's an idiot.* She's practically drooling over him as she gets closer, oblivious to the heads that turn as she passes. His insecurities are unfounded.

"Here comes your sexy piece of ass." I laugh, hitting him on the shoulder. I don't give a fuck, we're all best friends; she's worth admiring, with the way she moves her body. I wouldn't ever cross him nor any married man for that matter. Married women are like the apple in the Garden of Eden.

"Hmm, work it girlfriend." Gerry stands, kissing her on each cheek. "Love the dress!" She's all model ... touch ... kissy ... fucking flirtatious. She slides in next to Andy, kissing him on the cheek.

"Let me touch them biceps Quinton." She purrs my name. She loves to feed into my ego, and I remove my blazer.

Leaning closer, I say, "Feel me baby!" Andy shakes his head. I laugh at him.

46

She pouts at him. "You still got a ways to go to get those babe." I manage to smother my laugh, which is fucking hard. I understand now why he's taken a sudden interest in working out with me. He's building his body for his wife.

Marcus leans in grabbing my bicep and shoulders. "Honey, this is all man." I laugh. "It takes years to get this body."

I nod as I eat my dinner; I feel sort of bad for Andy. He's years from being anywhere even close to me, if he's trying to achieve my biceps. Andy sips his drink.

"Well, it's more than just working out every day," I tease trying to playoff my efforts to them. "Genetics play a role. Not everyone can get these eighteen-inch biceps." I flex, acting all cheesy. I do sound rather arrogant.

Tierra orders a drink and kale salad. "Yeah and special juice," she teases. She rubs down Andy's shoulders, making kissy faces at him.

"No way." Andy frowns. "Babe, you know Quinton is all natural. He doesn't put that shit in his body." The conversation of my body has bored me. I start prowling, listening to the dance music.

"Ah shit, he's got that look." Gerry laughs as he sips his martini. "He's on the prowl for some ass."

I laugh. "Ass you say," smirking I tease him, "I wouldn't call it ass in my case. But yes, I am looking for some ..." I pause, looking at Tierra, "something."

"Pussy," Tierra screams over the music, "call it what it is." I flinch at the sound of that word. It's pretty vulgar sounding, but some women get turned on using it during dirty talk. "What's that face about? You don't call it pussy?"

"No." I smirk. "Well, maybe in the right setting." I take a sip of my gin looking at Marcus and Gerry. "Andy, why don't you take that sexy wife of yours to dance?"

"Come on sexy." Tierra pulls Andy with her. She can dance circles around him, but he's a good sport and attempts to show her a good time.

"That's one odd relationship." Marcus smirks as he watches the two of them on the dance floor.

"She's bat ass crazy wild and our dear ole boy Andy is about as uptight and straight arrow as they come," Gerry chimes in.

"Crazy and sane works," I surmise. "They met before she went all model brain crazy. That's why I don't date models."

"Honey, you don't date anyone," Gerry corrects me.

I toast my drink at him. "Well noted. That's why I don't fuck models. Plus I like real tits and some curves."

"Like that one." I follow Marcus's direction. "She's all kinds of fine. And I am gay."

I laugh as I watch her wiggle and move with her girl-friends. That purple fitted dress shows her curves and glimpses of her tits. "I need to see her face," I comment as I wait for her to turn toward our direction.

"Why does that matter? Not like you're going to see her in the light of day." Gerry laughs as he watches her dance. "She's got some moves."

"Don't worry about telling this one I'm out of town in the morning." I grin as I down my drink, standing.

"Why, you thinking she might be worth a second hit?" Gerry looks surprised.

"Nope, I have no intentions of giving her my contact information; I can be a royal ass the morning after. Catch you two later." I stride off to claim my companion for the evening.

I move my hips in rhythm to the music, gently touching her hips with my fingertips. Cautious, yet deliberately letting her know she's caught my attention. She turns around. *Her eyes are blue, perfect.* Her grin widens, showing me her perfect white teeth. It's on. I pull her tighter against my body. We grind to the rhythm that fills my bar; she doesn't have a clue she's dancing with the owner.

Her fine, tight-ass body flexes beneath my big hands. I drop my face down to her neck. Her scent is erotic, shooting desire straight to my cock. She turns in my arms when a slow song blares across the speakers.

"What's your name?"

"Quinton. Yours?" I press her hips tighter against me as we move.

"Holly." She lays her head on my chest. Damn her hair smells good.

"You here with anyone?" I ask, leaning back to look at her face. She nods towards a table of girls. I laugh showing her my perfect teeth. "Well, let me buy you all a drink." She nods as she grabs my hands, leading me to their table. "Hello ladies."

I get hit with sexy smiles from all of them. "This is Quinton," she announces me like she's the leader of their pack. She scoots in the booth, pulling me with her. *Shit*, I'm not use to that much directness. I play along. The waitress comes to the table immediately when I throw up my hand. "A round of whatever the ladies would like." She smiles as she takes their orders. I look back at Holly, my next conquest.

"Where's your wingman?" a feisty redhead blurts out. Holly rolls her eyes.

"I don't need one." I laugh. It's the truth. I catch a glimpse of Marcus and Gerry dancing and keeping their eyes on me. "What brings you ladies out tonight?"

"What brings you out?" The feisty redhead is sort of annoying.

"I asked you first," I growl.

Holly crosses her legs, moving closer to me. "Sabrina drop the shit; leave him alone." Her friend rolls her eyes, grabbing her drink stomping off. "Sorry," she says, looking down, "she's just being protective." Great one of those … I don't let on, just sip my drink, giving her my undivided attention.

"Ignore her, we do," her other friend chimes in. "You are some kind of fine!" I laugh. Holly grins, somewhat embarrassed.

"Thanks." I drop my sexiest smile as I flag the waitress for another round of drinks. "I must say this table has the hottest ladies of the night," I say, looking back at Holly. God that has to be the cheesiest pickup line ever. *Not my best moment.* I hate small talk. I need to get the deal rolling before I get bored. "Shots?"

"Hell yeah," the girls shout. I flag the waitress to bring several rounds of shots. That's more like it, they seem to be losing up. Holly is getting all touchy feely, *perfect.*

"You want to dance?" I ask.

She grins, urging me out of the booth. The music is blaring, she's dropping and grinding against my cock. My hand grazes her ass and tits as we move to the music; my body is being mauled by hands reaching around my chest from behind. I feel like a beef sandwich, the girls are all rubbing and grinding. I steal a quick glance at my VIP table, Gerry and Marcus are shaking their heads as I toss them a grin. I turn, grabbing one of the girls, copping a feel. I could probably score an orgy with this group, but that would defeat tonight's purpose.

Holly clasps my face, staring those lust filled blues into mine, before she covers my lips with a soft, inviting kiss. Her eyes open like she's asking for permission. That's all I need, I yank her tight against me, bending and covering her mouth

51

with mine, tasting her, claiming her. She whimpers and pulls back before I'm done.

She's breathy. "You want to get out of here?"

I grin, grabbing her hand leading her away. But not before she's rushed by her friends. I can't hear what they're telling her, but I'm sure they don't want her to leave with a complete stranger. I give Gerry my 'I'm about to get laid' nod. He rolls his eyes and secretly cheers me from our seat. She grabs my hand. "Ready?"

"Absolutely." I grin as I lead her out. I give the valet a look, he rushes to get my car. I love it when they gasp seeing the red Mercedes AMG GCT.

"This is your car?" She's grinning like a chessy cat.

"Get in." I open the door for her. I can't wait to be inside this one. It takes us no time to shoot to my penthouse. I swipe my card once we get on the elevator. As the doors close, I push her against the wall. She moans in my mouth as I deepen our kiss. The doors open on the penthouse level. I lift her under the ass, and she wraps her legs around my waist. We kiss while I carry her. I slide my key card and shove the door open. It slams shut.

I slide her ass across my concrete bar. She's panting as she watches me toss my blazer. I clasp her face with my hands, kissing her lips, demanding her mouth. She whimpers as the kiss intensifies. Her fingers are fumbling, unbuttoning my shirt. I get the feeling she doesn't do this often.

I don't say anything as I slow my pace for her to catch up. Her hands are soft, touching my killer body. "You're so sexy," she whispers, kissing across my chest.

"Damn," I growl. That feels nice, her lips sucking on my nipples turns me the fuck on ... big time! I shuffle my hips deeper between her legs, reaching around her back. Her breath catches in her throat as I kiss down her neck, unzipping her dress.

"You want this?" God, I hope she says yes and doesn't chicken out. I continue to kiss her neck, her clavicle. I pause holding the straps to her plum dress in my hands, waiting for her response.

"Yes," she whispers. Thank fucking god. I pull her straps off her shoulders and down those slender arms. *Damn she's beautiful*. Our eyes are locked, as she watches me unfasten my cuffs. I toss my shirt to the floor. She bites her bottom lip in appreciation of my body and trails her fingers across my midsection. I scoot her quickly into my arms, causing her to gasp. She holds my shoulders, wrapping her legs around my waist. I carry her—kissing, sucking, and biting her bottom lip—to my bedroom.

I toss her on my bed. Grinning I pull her dress the rest of the way off, tossing it to the floor. "Damn you're fucking hot," I growl, looking at her laying in nothing but her bra and panties. I slide my shoes off. She must have lost her shoes along the way.

I unfasten my pants and drop them with my boxers. I kick my socks off and crawl up her body kissing her, starting at her knee. She gasps as she drops her head back. She's extremely

53

sensitive to my lips. I kiss her inner thigh, noticing she's quivering. "Relax," I whisper running my fingers up her hips, kissing her stomach, traveling up her body, and kissing across her lace. I reach behind her and in one flip of my fingers, I pop her bra clasp. I pull it off, tossing it to the floor. Her breasts are beautiful. She gasps when I lean down, kissing her nipple, sucking and swirling my tongue around it. I squeeze and pull her other hardened nipple.

She's flexing her hips into mine. I kiss down her stomach, this time looping her panties with my fingers, pulling them down her legs. I toss them from her ankles. I grin, looking at her naked body laying in my bed. Her eyes are trusting as she sucks the tip of her pinky fingernail.

I part her thighs, feeling her nerves again. I grin as lean down to kiss her inner thigh. She trembles beneath my tongue as I lick and kiss, getting closer to her sex. I want to taste her.

"What are you doing?" she whispers.

"What do you think I'm about to do?" I tease, looking up at her.

"I've never had that done," she admits. *Oh fucking hell. Poor girl.*

"Let me rectify that." I move over her like a flash of lighting. I'm going to claim this: the first time she's had oral. I sniff her, god she fucking smells sweet. I kiss her sex and she gasps. I look up as I watch her fist my sheets. This is going to be fun. I grin as I lick up her slit, feeling her quivering beneath my tongue. She's so sweet and innocently clean tasting. I continue my sucking and kissing until I reach my destination. I suck and swirl my tongue around her clitoris. She screams out,

54

bucking beneath me. I grin as I hold her thighs open for more. She's moaning and shaking as I feel her come. Man that was quick. She's going to be easy to please.

I crawl up her body, kissing her, and I lean over to grab a condom from my bedside table. I start kissing her lips as I tear the condom open, sliding it over my cock. I can't wait to bury myself inside her.

"Look at me," I command her. I want to see those damn blue eyes. Maybe actually fucking someone with blue eyes will get my sapphire-obsession out of my system.

She opens her eyes as I guide my massive cock through her wet folds. She's so hot, wet, and tight. Damn, really fucking tight. She screams and flinches around me. *What the fuck?* I stop, looking at her. "You haven't had this either I take it?"

"No," she whispers, "please don't stop." She cradles my face, kissing me. I'm so fucking confused … a first timer … ah hell. She doesn't want me to stop, so I thrust hard. She screams, falling back.

"Relax, you're tightening up." I can't believe I'm taking this girl's virginity. I feel her relax as I flick my tongue down her neck … kissing … nibbling. I'm going to be one hell of a first time. I pity the poor guy who follows me. I caress her tits sucking her nipple while pulling and squeezing the other, thrusting into her tight ass vessel. *Holy fucking hell she's tight.* I put her ankles over my shoulders as I sit up, pumping hard into her. *This is what she wanted after all.* She whimpers beneath me, fisting my sheets. I toss my head back as I slam into

55

her over and over. Her toes curl. "That's right Holly feel it. Fucking feel my cock," I growl. She screams, tightening even more around my cock—*impossible*—coming and quivering beneath me.

Shit, I feel my release explode into the condom. "Fuck," I growl as I toss my head back, stroking all my cum out into the damn condom. Her legs fall down beside me. I move slowly, kissing her before pulling out. I notice the crimson stain. *Shit, my damn sheets*. I go to my bathroom to dispose of the condom. I don't want to touch her blood.

I walk back into the bedroom, and she's covered her body with the sheet. I smirk as I look at her, tossing the sheet aside as I climb in my bed with her. How the fuck do I throw her out now? I scoot next to her and start kissing her again. She moans into me, rubbing over my arms.

"How old are you, Holly?" She covers her face with her hands, embarrassed. I pull them down. "Hey don't cover your face." I can be charming. I prefer to be an asshole after sex.

"Thirty."

"How in the hell was tonight your first time?"

"It's not like I haven't had offers." She shrugs as she toys with the sheet. "I just haven't wanted them."

I lean back, rubbing my hands over my face. Shit, she's going to be a clinger because I took her virginity.

"Don't worry, I don't expect anything more than what this was." *Great she's a mentalist*. "I can see it in your face."

"Good!" Shit, that came out cold.

"I think I'll go now." Hell this may be easier than I thought.

"Do you need money for a taxi?" Damn I just made her sound like a whore. Yep, she thought that too, I see it all over her face. "I didn't mean for it to sound …" I shut up.

"I can manage." She scoots off my bed, grabbing her clothing.

"Feel free to use the bathroom to freshen up." I watch her close the door. I actually feel relieved she's leaving. This virginal shit isn't for me. I walk her to my door. She's got her head down and I don't want to know what she's thinking.

I grab her and pull her into my arms; she's wanting me to kiss her, I can see it. I run my hand up the back of her head, fisting her hair as I turn her head how I want her to explore that sweet vessel all over again. I pull back and she's all breathy. "You don't have to leave," I whisper. *Where the hell did that come from?* Please fucking don't take me up on staying.

She grins as she opens her purse. She takes her pen out and writes her number on my palm. "If you want to hook-up again, I'm game." I grin as I look at her. "Just sex, no strings," she confirms.

I grab her hand as she turns to leave. "You don't want attachments?"

"No." She leans up on her tip toes and kisses me softly on the lips. "I don't really do relationships." I stand grinning like a fool as I watch her sashay that sweet ass into the elevator.

I close my door, looking at my hand. "A number I may actually keep." I snap a pic with my phone. I don't typically have seconds with the ladies I bed, but I may make an exception for Holly. I'll sleep on it.

Gerry is beaming with my coffee as I arrive. "Do tell." He purses his lips as he swaggers behind me. As usual I unfasten my jacket before sitting behind my desk; Gerry takes his daily spot on my stark white chair.

"Mustard yellow today." I quirk my eyebrow at him. Definitely not one of my favorite suits.

"This isn't about me." He leans forward. "Details? Marcus was quite impressed with your skills last night, but of course you already know this." *Yeah I do.*

"But you know my ego likes the boost of hearing these things." I wink at him.

"Why are you sporting that grin?" He sighs as he looks at his nails. "Who do I have to tell you left the country today?"

"No one, I didn't even have to throw her out. Once we were done she was ready to leave. I think she didn't really know how to handle everything ..."

"Why ... I don't like that look."

"She was a thirty-year-old virgin." I laugh at his expression. "Was!"

"Ah shit you hole-punched the v-card ... you're in trouble now." Gerry laughs. "Please, that woman is going to be like one of those damn wall cling ons. Please tell me your crazy loving ass didn't give her your number. Women always love their first."

I laugh at his response to me popping some woman's cherry. "Hell no! She gave me hers if I wanted to fuck again."

He points his finger at me laughing. "Now that's messed up!" I nod in agreement.

"Let's get on with our day." The sooner we finish work, the sooner the night comes. I need some hard wild sex. At least the blue-eyed virgin took care of my sapphire-eyed obsession.

Chapter 5: Amelia

Mmmm, I can feel him touching my nipples, sucking them, running his fingers over my body. God he's sexy. I wish I could see his eyes. His face. All I can see is his dark hair and sexy shoulders. I feel the bed dip oddly enough to stir me; I can't see him at all now. I just have sensations—his breath over my nipples—this is so weird. Wait! This isn't a dream ... I open my drowsy eyes. Eric's on me. No! No ... no. I squirm, rolling out of his grasp.

"Eric stop it." I roll over shoving him off me. "I am sleeping." *God this shit gets old.* Every time I have a sleepless night, this is my morning fate. "I couldn't sleep last night."

He playfully growls at me, almost a bark sound, which is weird to me. I ignore him. How many times do I have to tell him not to bark at me? It's not that sexy growl you read about in romance novels.

He bites and kisses my shoulder; I wiggle in annoyance, attempting to sleep. Of course I can't now. He keeps reaching around—manhandling my breasts. I keep removing his hands.

"You turn me on so much," he says wrapping his leg around me to roll me over. He pulls my night shirt up.

It always happens like this. "Stop it. God!" Exasperated, I yank my sleep shirt back down. Only he stretches the v-neck further so he can slip his tongue on my tit.

"Let me suck your nipples. You know it will turn you on." I roll my eyes as he continues to pressure me. "I want some attention." Does he not realize how unattractive this behavior is?

He's now rolling on top of me, kissing down my neck, pulling at my night shirt again. I just might as well give up. Maybe I can just pretend my husband's the mystery man of my dreams. I close my eyes as I let him pull my night shirt up. He kisses up my stomach traveling to my breasts; Eric sucks my nipple in his mouth as he palms my other breast, squeezing.

I cringe on the inside with every intimate touch. My whimpers aren't pleasure seeking—it's my internal cry for help. Only I'm the only one who can hear them. I gasp to hold it together, which Eric mistakes for desire. Naturally he would, after all he's Mr. Wonderful.

I clasp his head—watching him suck my nipples—trying to get myself in the mood. Squeezing my nipples between his forefinger and thumb, he kisses down my stomach to my sex. He pulls my panties off. His licks are hard; it's not pleasurable at all. I shift my bottom, trying to get away from his tongue. He doesn't get the hint; it feels like he's trying to lick the inside of a pudding cup. His nose pressing uncomfortably on my clitoris. I can't even pretend he's the mystery man.

I roll my hips away from his assault, which he misunderstands as me being ready for him. I watch him walk across the room to his top dresser drawer to pull out a condom.

61

Eric covers himself as he walks back to the bed and slides into me, holding his breath. "God, you feel good," he whispers as he starts to move. "You're so damn tight." He starts pumping his hips into me, maybe three, four strokes. He stops!

"What?" I already know the damn answer. I flex my hips. "You're already going soft," I hiss.

"It's your damn fault; you're so fucking tight," he tells me as I shove him the rest of the way off. I look down, my breasts exposed and I'm naked from the waist down. Only I'm not satisfied. I glance at him. He's laying on his back wearing nothing but a smile and his stupid ass condom. Disgusted and disappointed, I pull my night shirt down. He doesn't speak as he walks into the bathroom to remove his condom and flush it down the toilet. He plops down in bed with his phone to read his emails.

"What are you doing?" I ask rolling over in his direction, trying to curb my annoyance.

"Responding to these emails." I sigh just laying there watching him. "What is it?"

I'm trying really hard to bury my annoyance. But I'm sick of biting my tongue. "I'm glad you're satisfied! You always finish … one minute man," I snap and storm into the bathroom.

He doesn't knock, bursting into the bathroom. "What the hell is your problem?"

"Don't touch me again. I'm sick of you always getting off and then I'm left high and dry." I pull on my cute sundress and grab the hamper to take to the laundry. "There has to be more to sex than this," I scream as I storm past him.

I hear him slam the front door as he storms out of the house. Well, I guess I'm to blame for that fight. Irritated, I let the inn phone ring a few times, collecting my bearings. "Good morning; thank you for calling Amelia's." My mood lightens as I recognize the voice on the other end ... Gerry. "Yes, I remember you. How have you and Marcus been?" I smile as he talks. "Oh, you need a room for this weekend?" I grab my calendar. "Let me check, yes, I have a vacancy. Is it for two?" I have to admit I am little disappointed when I find he's calling to reserve a room on behalf of his boss. "Great Gerry, and what is your boss's name? Quinton Starks. Okay, got it. I look forward to meeting him Friday."

* * *

Eric didn't bother touching me this morning nor did he bother me last night for that matter. In fact, we're living in solitude since our little rumpled sheet session. I wipe the foggy mirror, looking at my reflection. I look old as shit. I don't even recognize myself. I used to be full of color and life.

"God Amelia, you need to do something with yourself." I sigh, grabbing a navy spaghetti strap dress. I'm not a fan of navy, but the color is obviously a fan of me. I turn, looking at my body. The dress accents my boobs and it's not too short. I have enough makeup to emphasize my sapphire eyes. Normally I wear my hair in a ponytail, but today, I feel like something different. I get my beach wave curler.

Eric is waiting for me downstairs. "Don't you look sexy this morning." He carefully touches my hair. "I like this."

"Thanks. I used to wear it like this all the time." There is an awkwardness. We can't continue tiptoeing around each other. I kiss him on the cheek to make a silent amends. "It looks like we got three on the books."

The afternoon passes rather quickly. I'm preparing my flower arrangements when I hear the door chime. I leave the fresh cut flowers and sheers on the counter. I smile at the couple standing at my desk.

"Good afternoon. What are your names?" I grin as I look at the couple obviously in love.

"Andrew and Kristin Anderson." I smile as I take their card to complete their payment.

"Do you two have big plans for the weekend? I know there are several local events around the island," I ramble.

"Well, we're actually getting married," Kristin squeals. I have no idea why I squeal with her.

"We're having an intimate ceremony on one of the sailboats tomorrow afternoon."

I grasp my heart. "Awe that sounds so romantic. Congratulations! So you will be staying here as your honeymoon?" I'm sort of shocked this wasn't mentioned over the phone.

"Yes, we want 'us time' for a few days."

"Well, if you two love birds will follow me, your romantic room awaits." I beam as I lead them down the main hall towards the dining room, pass the kitchen and walk up a second stairwell. "You're in room ten, I'm sure you will be comfortable." I punch in the key code and hold the door open for them. Kristin is gushing over the accommodations. She loves the private terrace. "The packet on the desk gives you all the information about breakfast and evening appetizers. Let me know if you need anything." I smile as I let myself out of the room. I think I'll make sure to put my other parties away from the couple. I laugh at my dirty thoughts.

I'm writing down another reservation when I hear the door chime. "Give me one minute." I never look up. His cologne tickles my nose … oh my god what is that scent? It is delicious … carnal.

I put my pen down and glance up at my next guest. His broad back is turned to me; his hair is dark, medium length. Damn he's tall. I feel odd gawking. He's looking around at the inn.

I clear my throat. "Hi, welcome to Amelia's." He turns around at the sound of my voice. My breath hitches in my throat. I can't speak. I'm sure I look like a foolish schoolgirl gawking at him. He is positively the most incredibly handsome man I've ever seen.

He looks at me like I have two heads; *shit do have something in my teeth?* Why can't I find my words? After all, this is my establishment and I'm a damn professional. Oh and yes married for god's sake. I break our eye contact—he's kind of freaking me out. I look down. "You must be ..."

"Quinton Starks." He holds out his hand to shake mine. His voice is deep and alluring. I certainly don't make him forget his words, but why would I? I am just average. His eyes pull at mine like magnets. I cannot help but look into his eyes. I smile as I slip my hand into his. I feel an electrical charge: like a zap or something. I try to pull my hand back, but he doesn't let go. His eyes are locked on mine. He gasps. "It's you ... your eyes!" His grip tightens. At this point I'm trying to free my hand, but he doesn't let go.

"I'm sorry ..." I jerk my hand free from his. "I am who?" I'm totally baffled by him. He can't be a psycho—Gerry works for him.

He shakes his head, almost like he was in some weird trance. "I am sorry ... what?" *Now he's talking weird.*

I laugh brushing off the weird encounter. "I must remind you of someone." He smirks as he mumbles something. "Okay so your assistant Gerry already paid for your reservation in full. Would like me to show you to your room?"

"Absolutely," he breathes, all seductive sounding.

"Right this way, Mr. Starks," I purr his name. My hips sway as I pass in front of him. My body is freaking me out now. I don't sway, this is uncontrollable. I walk to the first set of stairs. He walks behind me. I feel like he's checking my ass out. Obliviously I'm creating a fake illusion in my head be-

66

cause I'm undeniably attracted to him. If I was Catholic, I would have to say a lifetime's worth of Hail Marys.

I take him to the second room at the top of the stairs. "You're in room four," I tell him. I punch in his key code. "All the rooms have private key codes, for security." I look at him as I enter his room. This is the most masculine room I have in the entire inn. The walls are painted in Benjamin Moore Hush complimented by a stark white trim; the wood floors are stained in espresso. They're beautiful but a total pain to keep clean. The soapstone mantel is original to the house. The over-size, dark platform style king bed dominates the room. There is also a desk and a small sitting area with a very comfortable loveseat. I watch him walk in, looking around. I can't tell if he likes it or thinks he's in a doll house. "It's a king size bed; your ensuite has both a jetted tub and walk in shower, depending on your preference ..." I let my voice trial off. "Breakfast is served in the dining room between eight and ten; evening hors d'oeuvres are served between six and eight." He doesn't say anything, just walks around looking and touching the furnishings. He's actually making me nervous that the room isn't up to par.

"Fresh linens are provided daily." This is where I typically offer to show him the grounds. I hesitate. Maybe he can sense it.

"What's your name?" he asks me as I watch him take his luggage and lay it across the bed.

"Oh! Sorry, Amelia."

"Amelia from Amelia." He smiles. God his teeth are perfect. He knows he's sexy. You can tell it in the way he saunters around the room; the way he's smiling at me.

"Would you like a tour?" He rakes his fingers through his hair. I watch him take his blazer off and gently lay it across the bed. My mouth goes dry, his tailored shirt fits beautifully against his body. I laugh on the inside, we're both in navy. Navy likes him too.

"Sure." He turns smiling at me, probably catching me eyeing him like he's a piece of juicy candy.

"Okay." I quickly turn. "There are three more guest rooms on this floor." I point toward the elevator. "There is an elevator, it's original to the house so bear that in mind with its small size." I turn to go down the stairs.

"Where do these stairs go?" he asks, pointing to another set heading to the third floor.

"Oh, that's my private quarters." I grin as I continue down the stairs.

"So you live here on-site then?" he questions as he follows me.

"Yes, every room has a call button. So I'm literally a call away if you need anything." I point into the living room. "I'm sure I don't need to give you a description of this room; every place is a common area except private rooms and the third floor." He nods as we walk, looking at the house.

"How long have you owned the establishment?"

"Oh … going on four years or so. This is the dining room, and the kitchen is there." I hear my buzzer as we approach. "Excuse me, I need to get the tartlets." I walk in and grab my oven mitten. The cranberry brie tartlets smell divine. I place them on the counter to cool.

"You do all the cooking yourself?" He smiles as he walks in, looking at the modern kitchen. "I like this space." He runs his fingers across the white granite.

"I do." I smile as I pull another tray out of another oven.

"They smell delicious. Savory." He walks behind me, looking over my shoulder. I look at him suspiciously because he's just too comfortable.

"Cranberry brie tarts," I breathe. I sound breathy and he smells amazing. Even over the aromas in the kitchen, I can smell him. "I like the modern kitchen too." I remember his comment. "I know it doesn't fit the historical aspect of the house, but I like clean, white modern lines." I scoot between him and the counter. He's not blind to his closeness; we move as if we have been doing this dance for years.

Our eyes are locked again. He's practically pinning me against the counter without touching me. I feel a natural pull to him … comfortable. Not to mention my libido is screaming! "Um … okay. Ready to continue?" He steps back gesturing for me to the lead the way. "There are more private quarters here." I point toward another stairway. "And on the second floor three more. We also have a library with a computer and print-er. Of course you look like a businessman, so you probably

69

have your own laptop. If so, the wifi password is in your room." I catch him looking out the windows. "You're welcome to eat outside on the porch or poolside." I open the double doors and we walk down the steps into the courtyard. "Guests are also free to enjoy the double Roman style saltwater pool." I look at his face, which is totally following my eyes. Then I look down his body. He grins. Shit, he noticed me checking him out. I clear my throat and continue forward. "Feel free to walk the gardens." I look back at him. "I doubt that would be of much interest to you, but they are beautiful. Peaceful."

"Your establishment is very nice; I like the character in the details of the woodwork." He grins as he watches me. "Do you have a gym? Is my car fine parked in the front? I wasn't sure if you offered valet."

"Yes, your car is fine there. No valet. No, we don't have a gym. Although not a bad thought to maybe add at some point. The beach isn't too far of a drive; it's lovely to run. If you like to run," I add, looking at him.

"I run every morning." He grins as he looks at the pool. "I didn't bring my suit."

"There's plenty of shopping just a street over. I'm sure you could find one."

He grins as he rubs his hand down his mustache. God he's hot!

"What is there to do around here?"

"It's pretty quiet. We have shopping and restaurants." I look at him, he probably hits the nightlife in Jacksonville. I

70

remember his assistant telling me he's from that area. "We don't have clubs like in Jacksonville. There are a lot of events around the island this weekend. I put the information in your room. Of course there are a couple of golf courses, if you golf."

"Golfing is not really my thing," he tells me. I can see that.

"Will anyone join you later?" Why the hell did I just blurt that out?

He's laughing at me. "No." I feel somewhat annoyed he thought it was a joke.

I shrug to make myself not seem weird. "I was just wondering. We usually have couples for romantic getaways."

"We?" I see his eyes immediately look to my left hand. He's sorely mistaken if he thought he would be able to determine my marital status by my ring finger. I stopped wearing my rings long ago.

I really hate being married at this moment in my life. I smile at him as I start walking back inside. "Yes, my husband and I." I can see the confusion on his face. "Well, I actually run the B and B."

He looks back at my wedding hand. "I didn't realize you were married." What do I sense in his voice? It's different … almost regretful. I don't say anything more about it.

"Please, call me Amelia and ask if you need anything. Make yourself comfortable. I need to get back inside and start setting up for the evening appetizers."

"Yes, of course. It's been a pleasure meeting you, Amelia of Amelia." He drops his sexiest smile.

Chapter 6: Quinton

I toss her across the bed, climbing her body, kissing every square inch of this naked goddess. Her nipples are perfect; her stomach beautifully flat and tone; every inch of her is heaven. I wrap her legs over my shoulders, tasting her. She moans, tossing her head back in the pillows. She laces her fingers through my hair, tugging my head deeper into her sex. She taste like honey, vanilla, strawberries—everything that is sweet in this world combined into one. I lick up her slit, sucking and swirling my tongue over that beautiful clitoris. I pump her swollen clit between my lips until I feel her silk release over my tongue. I've died and gone to heaven. She's panting, pulling at my body. She tells me she wants to feel me deep inside of her. I take her mouth into my hands, and I cover those beautiful lips with mine as my tongue dives deep into that beautiful vessel. Exploring every magical inch of her mouth. Our eyes are glued on one another. Those sapphires sparkle like they are encrusted with diamonds when I enter her. Holy fuck she's tight. I am lost.

"What the fuck?" I lurch up to a sitting position. I look around the room. My sapphire-eyed vixen is very much real. Only she's already someone else's. What woke me up? I can hear mumbling tones. I strain my ears listening for a moment, can I hear another couple fucking? No! These aren't voices of pleasure. I can clearly hear a man's voice yelling. It makes me flinch as I manage to make out a few words ... "bitch ... fuck up ... you're so fucking stupid." Something hits the floor.

"Shit." I look up at the ceiling and jump out of bed, pulling on my lounge pants. I rush towards the door. And I don't know why. Why should I get involved? Yet here I am standing quietly. I can hear the small padder of her feet fleeing down the curved stairs. She's gasping as she reaches the first landing. I run to my window as I hear the screen door slap against its frame. She takes my breath, as I watch her disappear into the garden.

"Fuck!" I hiss to myself. I step back from the window. Yet I find myself standing in front of the door, again. This time my beating heart is the only thud I hear. Do I stay out of it? I know it's not my business. All I can see is that white robe flowing in the moonlight by the force of her legs. "Fuck it!"

I slip out of my room. And softly down the stairs and out the side porch—only I don't let the door slap against the frame. I run swiftly on tip toes into the garden, following her cries. Great, I am now officially a creeper. She wasn't kidding about the gardens being lovely—I look around noticing the ambiance and duck into the shadows. I have no idea what to say to comfort her.

Amelia is sitting on the wooden swing. She's twirled her fingers so tightly around the ropes her knuckles are white, while the insides of her fingers are red. Her head is hung low and she's crying. "I can't do this anymore," Amelia gasps. "Why is this my life?"

I'm frozen listening to her ... watching her. She's the most beautiful woman I've ever seen. I dreamed of her before I knew she even existed. That has to mean something. I look down at the ground, listening to her words. She's slowly rocking back and forth in the swing. I watch as her crying eases up. And then it's like a waterfall, she just releases it all again.

"I hate this life." She stands and gently touches the edge of the garden wall. Tears rolling out of those beautiful eyes. What is she doing?

I watch as she takes her robe off, spreading it out on the ground. She lays on top of it, and gazes at the stars. I catch myself looking up, noticing the night sky. I never take the time to look at the sky. She should be in silk and lace. Although, she's lovely in her white nighty. The night breeze catches her scent. She smells of jasmine mixed with lavender and something fruity and deliciously sweet. I remember my dream.

I feel a natural pull to go to her, but I don't want to scare her. Then she starts humming the sweetest sound I've ever heard. I'm frozen in time as I watch her; listening to her singing softly. She's twirling her beautiful brown hair around her fingers; she's now calmed.

I look back towards the house; that damn bastard! He's not coming for her. He doesn't deserve the angel she is. I need to

75

leave. I can't get caught snooping on her. I pull myself quietly out of the shadows and tip toe back inside.

* * *

"What is that delicious smell?" I ask myself sitting up in the bed ... remembering my nightly interruption. I look at my clock, it's still early. She said breakfast is served between eight and ten. I pull on my running shorts and tank top. I run my fingers through my hair. I practically run down the stairs.

I hear music coming from the kitchen. It's the same dance tunes that I have in my club. I smile as I follow it, as well as the aroma of her kitchen. I lean against the door jamb grinning as I watch her, unbeknown to her. She's swinging her hips, dancing against nothing to the beat of the music. She's cooking and singing the words quietly. She's beautiful.

I can only imagine what she would look like in a tight club dress, grinding against me. I start to get hard. I hear footsteps stomping in our direction. I move rather quickly into the kitchen, startling her. She gasps, as our eyes meet. She knows I was watching, my smile is a clear give away. The moment is cut short as a man storms in.

"I've told you a hundred times to turn this shit off. It is annoying," he cuts her music off and barks at her before he realizes I was standing in the kitchen. "Sorry about that music." He looks at his wife. "I hope it didn't wake you." He's sickeningly polite to me.

"Nope, not at all." I look at Amelia. Her eyes aren't bright and sparkling anymore as she looks at her husband. She's miserable. "I was about to go for a run and wanted to see what you had on the menu this morning."

"Oh." She looks at her husband before giving me a smile. There's that sparkle in those beautiful eyes. "An oven-baked vegetable omelet, homemade cheese Danish, bacon, sausage, fresh strawberries with cream, coffee, and juice."

"Make me a cheese omelet without the vegetables," he squawks at her. I cut him a disapproving look. And I don't give a shit if it is noticed.

"That all sounds delicious." She smiles shyly as she turns around and starts preparing that fucktard's special request. "Quinton Starks," I introduce myself, purposely squeezing his hand hard. I will have the firmest handshake in the room.

I can see it didn't go unnoticed in his face as he introduces himself. "Eric Johansson." He breaks his hand away and continues to mosey around the kitchen. "What brings you to Amelia?" he asks, calmly popping a soda. *Soda for breakfast ... really?*

"I'm looking at buying some commercial space, ocean front." I notice Amelia look up, but she doesn't speak.

"Oh!" He's interested now. "I'm an architect." He reaches in his pocket and pulls his card out, handing it to me. "What are you looking into doing?"

"Thanks." I look at it before I stick it in my pocket. "Oh maybe an ocean front bar, food and dancing." I look back at Amelia who is grinning as she's focusing on what she's making. She's listening though. "My assistant visited your establishment and mentioned the area could use a little something more. So I thought I would check out the location."

"Yeah, Amelia doesn't offer much of anything as far as a nightlife. I mean there are some bars, but they're small. I don't know of anything other than a biker joint, ocean front. Well, that's not tied in with the resorts." Eric likes the idea of a bar, surprisingly.

"Eric likes waterfront dining," Amelia chimes in. "You probably had him interested as soon as you said ocean front and food." She can read my mind as well.

"Right, well, let me get on with my run." I watch as Amelia slides his plate across the bar. He doesn't show any appreciation to her, just grabs it and plops down on the bar stool.

"Yeah let me know if I can help with anything, if you find something." He starts eating his food.

"Yeah, thanks." I watch her watch me. Her eyes are looking at my body. She's subtle to not be noticed. Not that she has to really worry about that, because he doesn't notice her at all. He takes her completely for granted. I smile as I turn to leave. I hate him.

Chapter 7: Amelia

I love the Saturday mornings at the farmers' market. I stroll down the street looking at all the vendors. I pick up some fresh veggies. I can come up with some sort of dish. I need to pick up something special for the lucky couple. I smile as I grab some fresh cut flowers—they smell beautiful. My eyes are closed as I appreciate the memories that flood over me. My grandmother was more of a mom to me than my actual mother; she always loved her flowers. I can almost feel her presence as I run my fingertips over the irises.

"Amelia?"

I turn towards my name. Quinton Starks is here. I smile as he walks towards me.

"I thought that was you." He grins at me. *God he's so sexy.*

"Mr. Starks, how did your property searching go this morning?" I ask as I pay the lady for the flowers.

"Call me Quinton. I think I've found a place." He smiles as he walks casually with me. "Eric around?" *Oh I should have figured he wanted to talk business with him.* I hope my disappointment isn't apparent.

I look up at him as he's casually looking at the vendor tables. "No. Sorry he's gone … somewhere."

"It's quite all right." He grins, looking back at me.

"You see anything of interest?"

"Yes, very much!" He's watching me. Am I reading something into his words? *God, Amelia you have to get out of your own fucked up, romanced starved head.* "Only it's not available for me." I don't say anything, just continue looking at the ground walking. "Do you mind if I walk with you?" he asks me.

"No, not at all." I stop at a vendor selling homemade wedding cookies. I pick up a package of cookies, handing the lady the money.

"Here, let me help carry something." He takes the veggies and flowers. I don't have time to argue.

"Oh, thank you." I bite my bottom lip as we continue our stroll. I see women looking at him. "I think you have admirers."

"It does appear so."

"Do you have a girlfriend?" I pinch my lips closed. "I mean … I … never mind it's none of my business … I shouldn't have blurted that out." I'm so embarrassed.

"No, I don't." He laughs.

"Why?" *Why can I not stop blurting words?* I need to bite my tongue next time.

"Why what?" He grins as we turn the corner. He's toying with me. I look at him, he knows exactly what I asked why to. "Maybe I just haven't found the right one." He looks down. "I don't know; I work a lot of hours." He's staring out in front of us.

"Well, this is the end of the vendors. I have a few more errands." I smile as I reach for the items he's carrying.

"Are you taking these back first?"

"Well, yes."

"Fine, I'll walk with you." I shrug as we walk towards the inn. Inside the kitchen, I grab a vase for the flowers and put the fresh veggies away. He's hanging out in the kitchen with me. I feel his eyes watching me.

"Do you want to come with me?" I ask him. I'm sure he doesn't.

"Sure, where are you going?" He smirks as he follows me out of the kitchen.

"I want to pick up a little gift for the couple staying here." I look at my watch noticing the lunch hour. "They are getting married today."

"Married, huh?" He doesn't look too interested in the word marriage.

"Yes, they are getting married out on the water. It actually sounds romantic to me." I look up at him. "But of course it would, right? Because I'm female." I laugh it off as I have no idea what he's thinking. I can't read him at all.

"I wasn't thinking that. They're marrying on a boat?"

We walk towards the marina. "Yes, one of the sailboats."

"Is this restaurant any good?" he asks as we walk past The Waterway.

"Yes, The Waterway is one of the best in town. Delicious seafood, the only waterfront dining option downtown. Great view of the marina and boats, if you like that." He smirks at me. "What?"

"I doubt it compares to your breakfast." I laugh at him rolling my eyes, *oh whatever*. "What? I'm serious. It was delicious. You want to have lunch with me?" he asks. My breath hitches in my throat, I guess he thinks he should reword his invite because I didn't answer immediately. "I mean, will you have lunch with me?" God he's dropping the sexiest smile I've ever seen in real life.

I look around, *it's just lunch*. "You sure? I don't want to impose on you."

"I wouldn't have asked you if you were imposing."

* * *

The hostess seats us at an intimate table for two overlooking the bay. He pulls a chair out for me. I smile at him, guilt pulling at my insides. Eric would be furious! *Is this a date? No ... no it's lunch*, I tell myself.

"You want a drink?" he asks me. I shake my head no. "Seriously loosen up, I asked you for lunch." I must look uncomfortable.

"I'm not use to guests being so—so friendly I guess." I smile as I look at the menu. He doesn't comment as he looks over the specials. The waitress arrives to take our drink orders.

"Yes, an order of the Rockefellers, water with lime, and a gin on the rocks with lime. Amelia what would like to drink?" he asks looking at me.

"Oh, um water with lime."

"That's all you want," he whispers, "you don't drink?"

"No, I do … I just …"

He stops the waitress before she leaves and looks back at me. "You look like a fruity kind of lady, bring a moscato." The waitress leaves and he smiles back at me. "You like moscato?"

"Yes, it's my favorite actually … how do you know that?" I start to relax as I watch him.

"I'm good at reading people." He winks as he drops another smile at me. He looks out over the harbor. I turn, looking at the water. The wind brings the salty air to our seats. A seagull squawks as it flies over head. This is nice. "Do you and Eric ever go out on the boats here?"

I smile as the waitress brings our drinks. "No." I take a sip of my wine. It's delicious. "We've lived on the island for four years and we've never been."

He sips his gin, processing what I told him. "That's too bad. Sailing is fun." He notices me watching him. "I sail. Well, I have a boat … I sail when I have time." He thanks the waitress as she places his oysters in the center of the table. "You eat oysters?"

"No." He looks at me, surprised. "I've never tried them."

He laughs softly as he grabs one and tops it with some hot sauce. "Here, open your mouth and tilt your head back."

I laugh suspiciously at him, watching him bring his hand closer to me like he wants to feed it to me. "What?"

He leans closer, staring deep into my eyes. "Open your mouth," he breathes. His mannerisms are seductive. I look at his hand as he's bringing the morsel towards my lips. His lips part, like he's subconsciously parting mine. My mouth opens as I touch his hand with my fingertips. I close my eyes as I tilt my head back. Holy shit he just fed me my first oyster. I open my eyes as I feel his thumb brush across my bottom lip. He's grinning. *Damn he's hot.* "Good?"

My sex is tingling. *What the hell is going on?* He repeats his question. "Yes ... very," I whisper totally confused and totally aroused. This isn't my life; I must be dreaming. That's it, he's the sex god of my dreams and I'm sleeping. Well, I don't want to wake up.

He grins watching me. I am completely and utterly under his spell. I see and hear nothing but him. "Shall I feed you another one?" he whispers. I just nod in a daze watching him, as he tops it with hot sauce. "Open your mouth." I do what he wants, I close my eyes again as I tilt my head back. I swallow, slowly opening my eyes as his thumb brushes across my lip again. He's intently gazing at my mouth. "Sorry you had some —something on your lip." He sits back in his seat, breaking my trance.

I smile as I blot my mouth with my napkin. I sip my moscato as he pops an oyster in his mouth. I can't speak, he's smiling at me and all I can do is smile at him. It's like he's in my head. Oh shit, he said he was good at reading people. "Are you trying to read my thoughts?"

He smirks as he looks at the waitress returning to take our lunch orders. "You two look so sweet," she gushes as she gets her pad and pen, "it makes me jealous." Quinton laughs deep as he relaxes back, opening his menu.

I smile as I look back down at the menu. "Please order whatever you would like Amelia." My name rolls off his tongue. I look up and he's grinning, watching me.

"I'll have the grilled shrimp salad. No dressings; lime wedges on the side please."

"Sounds good. And what about you?" She grins turning her attention to Quinton. I watch her eyes roll over his body. He's extremely sexy. His blazer fits perfectly over his broad shoulders. You can tell he works out and takes great pride in his body. He raises his eyes and smiles at me, he doesn't even seem to notice the blonde waitress drooling over him. Or he's so used to it, it doesn't affect him anymore.

"I'll take the grilled special," he tells her. She jots our order down as she tells us it shouldn't be too long. "That's fine. Thank you." He flashes her his sexiest smile.

He leans back, relaxed. "So are you going to make an offer on the property you looked at this morning?" I hope I'll get another opportunity to see him. He checks out in the morning.

"I may bring my attorney down here first. I've got to run some numbers when I get back to the office," he says as he sips his gin. It's intense, the way he's staring in my eyes.

"So Gerry works for you?" I ask smiling. "He was a hoot to have visiting, and his partner Marcus."

"Yes, Gerry is my assistant. He's been with Marcus for years. He colors my world." He leans forward picks up his gin and sips. "I can't live without him or Lucinda, my housekeeper."

I laugh at his admission. "You have a housekeeper?"

"Yes." He smiles and shrugs, "What can I say? I don't clean nor have the time for it." I chuckle softly. *Must be nice*, I think to myself. "What are you getting the happy couple?" He asks. *Changing the subject ... obviously he doesn't want to share much about his life.*

"I picked up the wedding cookies from the farmers' market for them. The lady makes them from scratch." I smile looking up at him. "After lunch, I'm going to the Christmas Shoppe across the street. I think I'll get them a wedding ornament with today's date inscribed on it."

Quinton leans back in his seat. "You're very thoughtful, aren't you? They're just guests at your inn."

"Well, yes, this is a special day for them," I remind him.

"Tell me, how long have you and Eric been married?"

"Too long," I blurt out without thinking. I immediately look up as he laughs. No doubt because I surprised him. I smirk. "I mean ..." I pause as I gather my thoughts. I can't believe I answered his question like that.

"I see." He smiles at the waitress as she brings our lunch.

"Thank you," I tell the waitress. She places our food on the table. "Ten years." He doesn't acknowledge it. And I don't want to talk about Eric anyway. I watch him close his eyes in appreciation of his first bite. He actually hums a little in satisfaction. "Good?" I ask, smiling at him. Damn he's sexy. No one has ever sparked desire in me just by eating.

He nods in appreciation, and taking his fork with a small amount, leaning towards me. "Here. Taste." Again he opens his lips, willing my mouth to open. Which it does, to my surprise. His eyes are glued on mine as I close my lips over his fork. He grins watching my mouth and then my eyes as he slowly pulls back. "Well?"

I smile as I slowly chew. "Wow that's good." Almost as good as being fed by him. He grins as he continues to consume his lunch, watching me. Should I be having lunch with practically a stranger, another man? I don't feel guilty eating from his hand. It doesn't even feel remotely wrong.

I finish my second glass of wine as the waitress brings the check. He pulls out his wallet. I naturally grab my bag, to fish out my half of the bill. He touches my hand. "I've got it." He doesn't remove his hand as the waitress grabs his card to

87

process it. I look down at his hand that's still covering mine. I gasp softly in my throat from his touch. He runs small circles over the top of my hand.

I look up, speechless, it's as if he's trying to get inside my soul through his heated eyes. "It's my treat. I asked you to join me."

"Thank you, it has been lovely," I whisper all breathy, staring at him.

"I assure you, the pleasure has been all mine." He removes his hand as the waitress brings his card back. I quickly slide my purse on my shoulder; I notice he's a gracious tipper. "Ready?" he asks me as we both stand at the same time. I nod and smile as he steps aside for me to lead the way.

We're walking in silence towards the Christmas shop when my phone rings. I look down and see Eric's name. I roll my eyes on the inside. "I need to grab this," I tell him, holding my phone.

"By all means." We stop in front of the jewelry store. I flinch as Eric is screaming at the top of his lungs. He's pissed about something, which doesn't concern me, yet I'm his punching bag. I look up at Quinton who is watching intently. I'm pretty sure he can hear the other end of my conversation. He turns and starts looking in the window, to give me some privacy no doubt.

"Eric, I'm out running errands." I sound irritated, I know. "Well, that doesn't really concern me." I scrunch up my face and hold my arm out away from ear because he's cussing so loud. I pinch the bridge of my nose with my fingers. "Look if you don't have anything conducive to tell me, I've got to go." He hangs up on me. "Well, goodbye to you too," I mumble as I drop my phone in my bag.

"Everything okay?" Quinton questions ... he heard plenty.

I nod, taking a deep breath, to avoid the tears in front of him. "Yeah, you ready?" I'm so embarrassed. Leave it to Eric to find a way to ruin everything that ever happens in my life.

Quinton opens the door of the Christmas Shoppe. "Ladies first." I bashfully smile at him as I walk in.

"Well, hello Amelia, who are you with?" Great! I didn't think about any of the shopkeepers.

"Oh, this is Mr. Quinton Starks. He's staying at the inn; looking to maybe invest in some commercial space on the island." I watch her as she comes from around the counter.

She's close to my age and single. It really doesn't surprise me that she becomes all toothy and smiling as she looks him up and down like he's lunch. "Well, hello ... Mr. Starks, I'm Lori." She holds out her perfectly red manicured hand. She squeezes his as she smiles.

"Right, like Amelia said, I'm Mr. Starks." Quinton looks at Amelia. This woman clearly has no interest in my shopping at the moment. She's definitely single and easy.

"Tell me, Mr. Starks, what type of space are you looking for?" She runs her fingers up and down his forearm. Quinton looks at me, and my eyebrow hitches watching her. Jealousy surges through my veins.

"A bar," he blurts. He moves away from her touch. Quinton doesn't want her touching him.

"You should come by the marina tonight. They are having live music, drinks and dancing," she invites him. "I will be there." She smirks as she walks toward me. "I doubt you will come, right Amelia? You never come to these things."

I roll my eyes at her. "Right." I grab a wedding Christmas ornament. "Lori, can you inscribe today's date on this please? It shouldn't take you too long to figure it out … right?" I hiss. I turn my head to the side. "I mean I know you spend a god-awful amount of time intoxicated and at the salons getting that perfectly bleach blonde hair."

She gasps at my curtness. I just purse my lips. I don't care; she's being a snot to me in front of Quinton and practically drooling over his amazing as hell body. She sashays to the back. "It may take like fifteen minutes for the date to dry."

"We'll wait," Quinton casually comments as he walks up to me. "Well … well, Ms. Amelia has a little sassiness." He grins his approval.

Red faced I shrug, her touching him unexplainably pissed me off. "She's a bitch," I whisper. I look at him to gauge his response to my comment. "We've not been especially close since we bought the inn. Plus she's single and prays on every unmarried man that comes to this area." I look at him before looking back towards the back of her store. "I'm surprised she didn't give you her number," I quip.

"She's not my type," Quinton assures as she returns with my ornament.

"Should I gift wrap this?"

"Yes, thank you Lori." Living with Eric I've learned to fake niceness.

"You having a wedding at the inn?"

"No, two of my guests are marrying today ... actually on one of the boats."

"Well, here you go." She hands me the gift box and I pay her. "Mr. Starks here's my number." She holds out her business card to him. I roll my eyes, adjusting my purse and fiddling with the ornament bag.

"That won't be necessary," Quinton says. I bite my bottom lip. I can't hide my laugh as I start walking away. "I would never call you. I'm not interested." I feel him put his hand on the small of my back as he leans around the front of me to open the door. I hear her gasp as we walk out.

I'm laughing hysterically. "That was priceless. I don't think I've ever heard her turned down." I subconsciously grab his bicep with my hand as we both laugh, crossing the street heading back to the inn. I notice his eyes immediately go to my touch.

"Sorry," I whisper all breathy, still touching his bicep. Flashes of my dreams flood me. My sex is tingling. I pull my hand back immediately, looking up at him.

"Don't be. I'm not." He smiles looking to make eye contact with me. "Seriously, you didn't cross any lines." I just nod as we turn the corner and the inn comes into sight.

I see Eric's car is in the yard. The dread is pooling; I really don't want to go inside—inside to my life. "Thank you," I quickly tell him as we near the porch.

"For what?"

"Today! I haven't enjoyed a Saturday in a long time. Or anyone's company in a long time. Possibly ever as much as I did today." I smile as I look at him. "So thank you for lunch and the conversation." I exhale I as I grab the front porch door.

"Anytime Amelia. I have never had such a relaxing day. Not one I can remember in the company of a female, anyway." He laughs as he follows me in.

I walk into my private quarters to find Eric. "Where the hell have you been?"

Chapter 8: Quinton

My morning run started on Centre Street and I ran straight, all the way to Atlantic Ave. I know I've only run maybe two miles. I look at my shoes, Amelia said the beaches were nice for running. "Lovely" was her exact word, which makes me grin. She's *lovely*. I can always buy new shoes. I run past the vacant lot that I'm interested in buying. It would make a great location for an outside bar, feet in the sand type of atmosphere. I continue to run to clear my head. Amelia is a married woman. No doubt married to an ass. I heard plenty of their conversation to know he was acting like a son of bitch. I wonder *if Eric's physically abusive, he definitely is verbally.* Regardless, nothing can happen between us. I don't cross that line. However, I did enjoy our lunch yesterday. She's quite possibly the most beautiful woman I've ever met. She's attentive and giving. I wouldn't have thought of buying a wedding gift for complete strangers. How did I dream of her before I met her? What the hell does that mean?

I want to see Amelia before breakfast. We won't have any alone time once the breakfast hour starts. I turn around and head back to the inn. I need to see her before I leave. I stand outside the courtyard, watching as the kitchen window lights are on. The sky is purplish pink from the morning sun waking up. I drop down and do some pushups on the lush ground of the garden, thinking about what I'm going to say to her. I need some reason to talk to her.

I roll on my back and start doing ab crunches. Shit, I have amazing body strength, my muscles are going to be bulging with exhaustion when I see her. I do twenty burpees. I wonder what she's cooking for breakfast this morning. She's so beautiful. I do forty pushups to make my morning wood disappear.

Walking inside through the side porch I hear her in the kitchen. The aroma coming from the kitchen makes my mouth water. I slow my walking as I hear Amelia's voice.

"Stop it," she hisses, "stop. I am trying to start breakfast." She's not laughing. She sounds annoyed.

"I want some attention." His desire makes my stomach want to convulse. He's obviously putting the moves on his wife. *That's right Quinton, his wife*, I think to myself as I stand outside the kitchen listening.

"Go away." I steal a glance in the kitchen and she's quickly running around the island. "I am busy. I mean it. I'm not in the mood for you to bother me, Eric. We have guests in the house."

He grabs at her, pulling at her dress. She doesn't like his attention at all. She's pulling her dress out of his hand. Only he's a fucktard and not getting the hint. He's practically man handling her. I jerk back so they don't see me. She's whimpering as she shoves him hard.

"What the fuck Amelia?" He laughs. "You going to hit me with that pan?"

"If you don't stop." I steal another look, she's literally holding a pan at him. Her dress strap is broken. Her lips red from unwanted kisses. Her neck has splotches from being groped. I duck back behind the wall, *shit*. That fucktard needs his ass beat.

"I didn't marry a fucking nun." *Dude, she doesn't want you.*

"Don't you dare talk to me about what we married," I hear her hiss as the pan hit the gas grates. A moment later I hear shuffling and her fussing at him to get off her. She sounds like she's whimpering, almost panicked sounding. *Shit!*

I quickly open the screen door and let it slap against the wood. I casually walk by the door and turn like I didn't expect to see anyone. He's standing with his back towards the door. His hands are on the end of the island and he's watching her. She's wiping her eyes really quick as she looks up and softly smiles at me. Her eyes run over my body. *That's right, I know you like what you see.* I quickly cut my eyes to her fucktard husband in an effort to remind her he can see her checking me out. He turns around.

"Oh good morning, Quinton." *He has to be bipolar.*

"Good morning." I look at Amelia fiddling with her ruin dress strap. "Do you already have coffee, by chance?"

"Yes." She smiles as she quickly grabs me a mug and pours my coffee. "How do you take it?" she asks. I'm imagining breaking every bone in Eric's body.

"Black is fine. Thank you." I sip it watching them, both are quiet. Amelia is working on breakfast. "What's the menu?"

"Baked egg cheese pesto cups, oven-baked apple caramel pancake, bacon, sausage, fresh peaches and strawberries. Coffee and juice."

"Sounds delicious." I watch as fucktard turns his nose up at her menu. "Check out is eleven?"

"Yes." Her eyes are pleading. I can see she wants to talk with me, but he has ruined it. I wasn't expecting him to actually be awake. I cut my eyes towards her husband, with almost a growl on my face. She looks down.

"Is it okay to take my coffee to my room?"

"Yes," Eric responds as he grabs his Coke. "Amelia will clean the room when you leave." He talks about her as if she's a maid.

"Right." I watch him walk out. I look at her, she looks upset. She needs to be with a real man. Her eyes are glassy as she looks at me. I nod and turn to leave as if she understands my thoughts.

"Oh, Mr. Starks ..." I turn around. "You should check the gardens out before you leave." She smiles with a slight shrug. "I'm not sure if you had an opportunity. It's especially nice in the mornings."

We share a smile. "Maybe I will take my breakfast in the courtyard."

"Very well." She nods and grins as she turns her music on. I laugh on the inside. She knows it's going to piss him off and she really doesn't care.

* * *

I stand naked in the hot shower letting the suds wash away my sweat—thinking about her. She's beautiful. He's a fucktard. I hate to leave because no one is going to be around to interrupt his unwanted advances. I guess she can handle herself; she's managed for the last ten years.

"God, years of fucking unwanted advances," I moan quietly as I let the water run over my face. I look down at my fat cock, growing with desire, thinking of her ... my cock responded to her touch yesterday ... I wouldn't be too opposed to the idea ... Nope! I won't allow myself to even consider these thoughts. I cut the shower and towel dry my body, wrapping the towel around my waist and look at myself in the mirror. I'm a good-looking son of a bitch. I run my fingers through my hair, causing it to fall naturally down the center, brushing the sides first and then back. I grab my Aveda pomade and rub it through my hair. I trim my stubble and shape my mustache. I put on my gray suit with my white dress shirt, leaving the first few buttons opened.

I pull the bedding over the bed, smoothing out the wrinkles. I take the small jewelry box out of the bag. After I had left Amelia at the inn, I hit the few bars Amelia Island had to offer. And after a couple of gins I found myself at the jewelry

97

store looking in. The storekeeper decided I must have looked hopeless to fix something or maybe she thought I had forgotten an important date. I don't know what she thought, but the storekeeper unlocked the front door, an offered me entrance. I open the box looking at the blue sapphire dangle earrings, accented with a small diamond. They're easy enough to dress up with a cocktail dress or wear every day. I hope she will wear them. I flip the lid and set them on the bedside table, with the note I stayed up writing last night.

I wipe down the bathroom counter and toss my towels in the shower. I don't want to appear to be a complete slob, but she knows I have a housekeeper. I grab my bags and carry them down before I head for breakfast. Our eyes meet on the landing.

She looks at my bag as she carries plates of food into the dining room. She quickly rushes back towards the door as I am setting my bags down. "Are you leaving … before breakfast?" Her eyes are sparkling, dancing between mine.

"No." I smile. "Of course not. I was just putting my bags in the car. I'll have to head back once I'm finished with breakfast, however."

"Right." She smiles. "Do you want me to fix you a plate and take it to the courtyard?"

"Sounds perfect." I grin as I watch her head back towards her kitchen. I'm sitting alone in the courtyard; it is peaceful out here. I smile as I see her bringing a tray of food. "Wow, you went all out this morning." I grin as she takes the plates and places them in front of me on the table.

"I didn't know what kind of juice you liked, so I brought you a glass of each." She smiles as I pull her a chair.

"Sit with me." She looks around and tucks her hair behind her ears as she sits down for a minute. I noticed she has a mark on her shoulder that wasn't there this morning. "What's this?" I frown as I move her hair to the side a little. She reaches up but I intercept her hand.

"It's nothing." She covers her shoulder with her hair.

"He has no right to touch you like that." I don't give a shit if I overstep my bounds. "Just because he's your husband, he's not entitled."

She nods but doesn't argue with me. "Please don't," she whispers, "I don't want you to leave on this kind of note." She looks up and our eyes meet. Oddly I don't want to leave her at all. I've never met anyone who makes me feel anything more than lust. "You are quite possibly the most captivating man I've ever met." *I know she's the most enchanting woman I've ever met.*

I was about to touch her skin, stroke her cheek, just once I was going to allow myself that little taboo pleasure.

"There you two are," her husband says. I close my eyes to gain my composure, so I can be civil. Her body tenses as he walks closer. She plasters on a fake smile, but I can tell it's fake. Her eyes aren't sparkling now.

"Yes, Mr. Starks wanted his breakfast courtyard."

"I was hoping to talk with you before you left." Eric grabs a chair and drags it over. "I was curious if you found any location you were interested in."

"I did. I've got to run some numbers when I get back to the office and discuss business projections for the area." I can tell he's interested. "I've got your card. I have a project manager that handles the ins and outs of everything. I'll pass it along to him." Amelia sits quietly, watching me eat. Eric continues rambling on about inconsequential bullshit. I don't even know what he's talking about. Amelia has flooded my thoughts, just being this close.

* * *

I see her watching from an upstairs window as I pull out of the driveway. I stare for a moment. We can't ever share anything more than what we've already shared. I need to get back to my life.

Damn I am one sexy son of a bitch. I look at my reflection in the glass windows of my office building tossing my keys to the valet. I slept great in my bed, ran ten miles, and worked out for an hour. I feel fabulous this morning. I intend to hit the club scene tonight after work, I've been in a three-day dry spell. Three days too damn long.

I smile as my office doors are opened for me. My presence is greeted with smiling faces. I've missed the swooning over me. I was just under a sapphire vixen's spell. I still loath Eric Johansson. I'd love to fuck his wife and tell him. If she didn't deserve so much more, I would break my cardinal rule and do just that!

"Gerry the man!" I praise when I walk by his desk. He stands up, giving me my coffee. "Love the suit … my friend." Gerry is gracing my navy and gray world with maroon today.

I walk into my office and unfasten my coat as I sit behind my desk. I turn my chair, glaring at the colony below.

"Someone had a good weekend?" Gerry smirks as he graces his maroon-colored suit on my stark white furniture. "How many ladies do you want me to avoid today?"

"None!" I lean back looking at him. Grinning, I say, "I haven't been laid since I went out of town."

"Shit … please." Gerry doesn't believe me.

"I am serious." I grin as I look at my trusted and well-paid assistant. "You sent me to a bed and breakfast." I give him a knowing look. "What did you think was going to happen?"

"What did you think of the area?" I look at him suspicious-ly, does that question have a double meaning? He's smirking at me.

"I found a location," I say as I sip my coffee.

"If that's all you found, should I book a meeting to discuss the new club?" He's pursing his lips, crossing his legs.

"Yes! I need Andy and Michael." I click my computer on and pull up my email. "Just tell me when they can meet. I do want to make this sooner than later."

101

"I'll do it now. I put some contracts for you to review on your desk that require the top dog's signature." He swaggers out of my office. I grin watching him.

I pull the first contract. My mind drifts to Amelia. I wonder if she found the earrings. I look at my clock, it's already after ten. She should be cleaning up after her breakfast. I wonder if she had any guests this morning. Damn her cooking was delicious.

I sigh, turning looking out my window at my amazing view of this city. I can see my club, Libation. I watch some boats pull into the port. She hasn't been sailing, yet she lives on an island. I'd like to take her sailing on my boat. Sighing, I rub my hand down and over my scruff, this is exactly why I haven't allowed myself to think of her. I turn looking at my desk, the same contract still opened, and I haven't a clue what I've read. Could Gerry read me like he normally does? I find myself watching him through the glass. He's on the phone, probably scheduling my conference.

I sit down to reread the first paragraph, when Gerry opens my door. "Amelia Johansson is on the line for you."

I look up, Gerry is grinning ridiculously at me. "Why are you looking at me like that?"

He's smirking like I'm playing with fire. "Are you interested in this call?" He throws his hip out as he waits.

Grinning I say, "Put her through." I watch him close the door and dispatch her call. When my phone rings, I let it ring twice. I don't want to sound too eager.

I click the speaker on and lean back in my chair. "Quinton Starks." I can hear her breathing, not sure what to say. "Hello, are you there?" I know she is.

"Yes." Her voice is like heaven ringing in my ears. I have bubbles in my stomach. "I wanted to thank you for the beautiful earrings," she says.

"I saw them and they reminded me of your eyes. I do hope you will wear them." I lean forward waiting for her to say more. I hear her nerves. "Amelia, are you still on the line?"

"Yes, sorry ... I ..." she pauses for a moment. "I love them. I haven't taken them off since I found them." I'm grinning like a fool. "They're too much," she blurts out.

I shoot back in my chair. "Too much?" I've never purchased jewelry for any woman in my life, does she not realize this? *Of course she doesn't Quinton,* I tell myself. "Amelia, it's not too much. Please don't overthink things."

"Oh," she says. Her voice has changed completely.

"No," I find myself blubbering. "That didn't come out right." I take a deep breath. "I wanted you to have them. They weren't over the top pricey if that's your concern. It made me feel good to buy them. Please enjoy them, you deserve something beautiful."

I can hear her sniffle. "I don't want to jump to any sort of conclusion of your intentions. It's just ... this sort of thing, just

103

doesn't really happen to me." I'm grinning at her unspoken confession.

"Let your mind run away, sweet Amelia." I grin, she's clearly disturbed by me. "I know my place; where I stand." But I wasn't expecting her question ... her bluntness.

"Will I see you again?" Those five words have so much possibility. She wants to see me again. I grin like a high school boy, something that I haven't done in twenty plus years, easily.

"Yes, I do hope so." I grin, standing. Looking out my window at the water. I can hear the relief in her breathing. "Conversation is easier face to face."

"Yes."

"I can hear your smile." She laughs finally relaxing. "Did you have guests this morning?"

"No, everyone left yesterday."

"I missed your delicious breakfast this morning," I confess, "I wondered if you cooked, but now I know."

"What did you have?" she asks me, shuffling around.

"What are you doing?" I ask her. She giggles. She literally giggles like a high school girl chatting with her boyfriend on the line.

"Relaxing in the garden." I smile remembering her that night, but she doesn't know.

"A protein shake. I had a protein shake for breakfast."

"You poor poor man," she teases, "doesn't Lucinda feed you breakfast?" She remembers my housekeeper's name.

I hear myself chuckle out loud. "No. Not breakfast. She comes in the mornings, cleans, and occasionally leaves a meal." She laughs at my honesty. "Sometimes she doesn't feed me at all," I admit. She laughs again.

"You must live a very fascinating lifestyle, Mr. Starks." She's breathy and beautiful sounding.

"It has some perks, I must admit." I grin as I see Gerry eyeing me. He's never seen me laughing or talking to a woman on the phone. "I've been spotted, by Gerry. He's eyeing me suspiciously talking to you."

"What color has he graced you with today?" *She forgets nothing.*

"Maroon." I smile.

"I didn't let on my reason for calling, so I don't know what you want to tell him." She tells me. "I know you have your own life in Jacksonville." She's turning all nervous again.

"Leave my color wheel to me." She laughs. *Good.* "What are you doing today?" What does an innkeeper do during the week when she has no guests to tend to?

She laughs. "My scullery maid duties. What does a businessman such as yourself have on his agenda?" She doesn't know what I do. She has no idea she's talking to Jacksonville's richest bachelor.

"Oh the usual, corporate world run of the mill things," I tease. But I really do have a lot of business dealings this week. "Nothing that would be of interest to a scullery maid." I hope I didn't offend her. She laughs, making me laugh. She knows I'm teasing.

"Well, I'm sure your random scullery maid would be bored out of her mind; but you're talking to a scullery maid with a master's in business administration."

"Really?" My shock is evident. She laughs.

"Yes, I didn't know what to major in when I went into college. I followed in my daddy's footsteps and got a degree in business administration with a focus in hospitality." *Fuck,* I just found out something real about her.

I grin as I notice we have been chatting for almost thirty minutes. "Intelligence, beauty and she can cook." Eric Johansson snagged up one hell of a bride. I hate him even more.

"You're quite the charmer, aren't you Mr. Starks?" she purrs into the phone. I'm melting.

"Am I now ... charming Ms. Amelia of Amelia?" I see Andy rounding the corner heading towards my office. *Shit.* Gerry stops him. Andy hates to wait. He can see me on the phone. I hold my finger up to give me a minute. "Damn."

"What?" Her voice is serious again.

"My attorney just arrived. He's waiting outside my office," I sigh.

"Well, you are at work." She laughs softly. "You can't spend all morning engaging in coquetry banter with me."

"You're much more interesting," I tell her. It's the truth, she has completely enthralled me, again. I laugh. "I could listen to you for hours. Even if it's just jabberwocky."

She laughs. "I think I could too." She sighs quietly into the phone. Andy is tapping his watch at me. I roll my eyes and hit my privacy screen, just to piss him off.

"I really need to go, dear Amelia from Amelia." I stand, fastening my coat.

"It was great speaking with you Mr. Starks. Thank you again." I smile.

"Again, the pleasure has been all mine." *It really has.*

She laughs. "Go dominate the corporate world. Bye." I smile as I tell her bye. She disconnects our call. I grin, looking at my phone like a kid. I see Andy flapping his hands and pacing. Obviously questioning Gerry about who I've been so engrossed with.

I hide the privacy screen and open my door. Andy sails through, and Gerry looks at me. "Not laid my ass." He snaps his head. Then grins as he turns to his work. I grin, shaking my head as I close my door to give Andy my attention.

"I'll ride out and check the location." Andy agrees it could be a good move. We could both go. I could see Amelia. "What are you thinking?" he asks me.

"Just wondering if I should go with you." I really want to see her.

"We need to meet with Michael and his development team, and the marketing team for the area as well."

"Yes, I've asked Gerry to have Michael join us," I comment as I rub my finger across my lip.

"We going out tonight? Tierra leaves Wednesday for that damn photo shoot." He walks to the bar and pours a drink. "She's modeling swimsuits."

"Hot," I tease as I make me a drink. "I did tell chef not to leave me dinner. You two meet me at my VIP table." I had totally planned to go pick up a chick. That desire has been put on the back burner since her voice melted me. *Fuck!*

"I'll gather everyone within the hour." Andy walks out. I go back to my desk and start the same paragraph for the third time.

Chapter 9: Amelia

My music is loud, and I'm dancing around the kitchen. I dip and wiggle against the cabinet doors as I wipe down my island. All I can do is think about our conversation. For the first time in ten years, I feel alive. Alive!

My music suddenly stops. I look to see what the issue is.

"I could hear it in the driveway," Eric yammers. "What has you in such a good mood?" He's smiling as he walks towards me, reaching for me. "Hug me. My beautiful wife!"

I lean into him, not really hugging him in return. I rest my head against his shoulder. I wish he was Quinton Starks. My admission freaks me out. I've never thought of myself as the cheating kind. As miserable as I have been, I've never entertained the notion of another. Ever! Until ... now.

"What are you doing home?"

"I thought we would go to lunch. How about the marina?" *Does he know something?* I look at him askance.

"Sure," I chime. *I didn't do anything.*

He wraps his arm around me as we walk toward the marina. He asks the hostess for a table for two outside. I look out over the water. It's quiet without the weekend crowd.

"I've got to go out of town next week for a few days."

"Why?" I smile as the waitress appears to take our order. Oh hell of everything that is holy. The same damn waitress. *You've got to be kidding me.*

She beams. "What would you folks like to drink?"

"Two waters," Eric orders for both of us. He never asks me what I want to drink. I just smile and keep my head down. Maybe she won't remember me. She doesn't say anything. I open my menu.

"You think the special is good?" he asks looking at me.

I shrug and look at it. Oh thank god it's a different special. "Maybe." I don't eat Mai Mai so it's of no interest to me. I keep looking over the menu.

She returns with our waters. "Are you two ready to order?" Eric grabs my menu and closes his.

"Yes, two of the Mai Mai specials. Fries with both."

"I want the vegetables with mine, please," I say as he looks at me. I wait for her to leave. "Eric, I don't eat Mai Mai. You should know this by now."

"You can try it," he snaps. He leans back looking at me. "Where did you get those earrings?"

I reach up and touch them. I should tell him they were a gift from Mr. Starks, but he may take them away. "The farmers' market last Saturday," I lie.

"Really?" *He sounds skeptical.* "Since when did they start carrying gemstones? They look real."

I shrug sipping my water. "I doubt they're real Eric. Really ... come on. How real of a gem could they be if it only cost me thirty bucks? Surely you don't think cubic zirconia is a real diamond either." I look over the water. *Of course they're real, dumbass.* He would have a stroke if he knew where I got them.

"I'm surprised you bought them, with your sensitivity to metals. They're not bothering your ears?"

"Well, the lady assured me they were real sterling silver. So far so good."

"Anyway ... back to my trip. The firm is sending me to Alabama for one of our big clients ... some condominium project in downtown Birmingham. Do you want to go?"

"No."

"Well, there's another reason I asked you to lunch."

"I knew it ... what?"

He grins rubbing his finger across my arm. "I was thinking maybe we should try again ... I know it's been awhile and we've not discussed having children ... but ... I don't know."

I gasp, shrugging out of his reach. I squint at him. "Are you insane Eric? There is no way I'm getting pregnant."

"You never know. Condoms aren't a hundred percent." *Yes, he's right, but with my IUD in place it increases the chance of not getting pregnant.* "Well, maybe we should try. It's been six years, Amelia." I am not having this conversation. I cross my arms over my midsection, staring out at the boats. *I wish I*

111

could sail away from all of this! Our waitress returns with our lunches.

The Mai Mai looks absolutely vile. I eat the veggies around it.

"Try the Mai Mai, it's delicious." Eric eats his with no regard for my disgusted face.

"I have no desire to eat dolphin." I roll my eyes. "And don't try to justify it by telling me it's not Flipper."

"I want to try again," Eric blurts, "for a baby."

"Well, I don't!" My appetite is completely depleted. I just met the most amazing man of my life, and this idiot wants me pregnant and bound. "It was a blessing what happened six years ago. A damn blessing," I hiss pushing my chair away.

"Just calm your ass down." He looks around for the waitress. "Check," he tells her as she approaches. I feel my anxiety building. Why is he bringing up this subject? Why is he wanting the check when he hasn't finished his meal?

"Why are you asking for the check? You haven't finished eating," I ask, about to freak out.

"I have had enough." His eyes are on me. "We need to head back to the inn."

"Why?" He gives me a knowing look. "No, I don't want to go back to the inn. I'm not ready to go back there." He's going to try to fuck me. I know that look.

He pays the bill and grabs my hand. "Let's go." I try to pull my hand out of his grasp, but he doesn't release me.

"You're hurting my arm, Eric," I whisper as he practically pulls me down the street back to the inn. "Let go of me." I'm jerking at his hands on me. He's completely ignoring me.

He shoves me through the back door of the house kissing me on my neck, pushing me back against the wall. His mouth is harsh, covering my lips, demanding I kiss him. His breathing is ragged as he starts pulling at my dress. His hands claw up my body, squeezing my boobs. "You're the sexiest woman on the face of this earth."

I ignore his compliment, and he hastily unbuttons my dress. He kisses down my neck. "I want you naked." This could be really hot if it wasn't him. I close my eyes, trying to work up some sort of mood.

"Stop." I pretend to be all breathy and turned on. "Wait. You don't have anything down here." He laughs as he kisses me.

"We don't need to worry about that Amelia. If something comes from it, it does." He reaches up under my dress, rubbing his hand around my ass. "I want you here and now ... raw."

"No." I shove him back. "We can't."

He looks at me. "We can do whatever we like."

"Stop it. Stop it," I scream at him and shove him hard. He falls back, landing on his ass. He looks pissed.

"I don't want to have a baby now or ever, Eric." I can't tell what he's thinking. He pulls at my legs, behind my knees, making me fall to the floor with him.

113

He rolls over on me. "Why not?" He's looking seriously into my eyes.

"Look around. I run this inn. You're an architect. We don't need kids." He leans off me before our conversation can go any farther to answer his phone.

"Hello, yeah this is he." He smirks as he looks at me. "Yeah we can do that."

"What?" I whisper, my curiosity peeking.

He points his index finger up for me to wait. "Tomorrow evening at seven. Club Libation. No, we will manage directions." He grins. "Yes, thank you." He disconnects the call.

"Who was that? What is going on?" I find myself genuinely interested. Eric pulls me up, totally uninterested in having sex now. *Thank god for small favors.*

"Go get yourself a sexy club dress." He hands me his credit card.

"What?" I gasp. We've never gone dancing. He doesn't care for dancing, clubs, or nightlife.

"That call was Mr. Starks's assistant. He has requested us to come for a business dinner and dancing at his club Libation tomorrow evening. He's having his team meet with me and go over my portfolio. He's considering me for designing his new club here."

"What? That's great. Congratulations honey." I hug him. I'm so excited to see him tomorrow. Mr. Starks killed two birds with one stone, one of which he doesn't even realize. I clut-

114

ch his card in my hand as I adjust my dress. "I'll be back later. I'm going dress shopping."

Chapter 10: Quinton

The day has dragged by. Two hours until Amelia is going to be walking into my world. I look at my naked body as I dress for the meeting. My hair is perfect. My scruff, perfect. I walk into my closet, *Hmm, think I will go navy.* I leave it casual with no tie. I hit my cologne. I'm one sexy looking son of a bitch. I can't believe I turned down the brunette last night. It's going on five nights of abstinence. Tonight, at least I get to see Amelia.

I arrive a little early to make sure the private room is ready; I've already chosen a catered menu. I think she will be pleased, remembering how she loved the oysters. I grin when I see Gerry and Marcus. "Love the suit."

Gerry smirks. "It's devil red," he remarks as he swaggers over to the table, "since I'm working for the devil himself."

I grin, shaking my head. "I told you, I didn't get laid."

Marcus hitches his eyebrow as he follows Gerry, wearing a black and red pin stripe suit with a matching fedora. "Let the man be. Lord knows he has no problem catching women. I'm intrigued to learn more about Ms. Amelia if she's caught the attention of our Casanova."

"Gerry." I sound sterner than intended. He shrugs and smiles. I smile at Marcus. "Your beloved seems to believe I have fallen for Ms. Amelia from the B and B he sent me to over the weekend."

"Well ... well, she was quite lovely from what I recall." He smiles at Gerry.

"You two need to behave," I tease as I look up, seeing Andy and Michael with their respective others walking towards us. Thank god, Gerry and Marcus kept their jokes to themselves about me being attracted to Amelia.

We're standing around the private room, shooting the shit, drinking our drinks, and when I look up, my breath is gone. She's fucking stunning in that tight fitting sapphire club dress. *Holy fuck*. She would fit perfectly in my world.

"You sure there's nothing between the two of you?" Gerry whispers in my ear, noticing my distraction. I look at him deadpan. I look back but don't say anything, my tongue is stuck to my mouth. I only watch her cross my dance floor, heading in this direction to my private dinner room. Maria announces them.

"Thank you for the opportunity." Eric immediately shakes my hand as I walk to them. I glance quickly down Amelia's attire. She smiles shyly and looks away.

"Of course," I reply. I lean over and let my lips grace her delicate cheek. "You look absolutely ravishing." I hear her breath hitch. She smells wonderful. I step back immediately, not wanting to appear infatuated with Eric's wife.

117

"I'm glad you two could come with this short of notice. But I'm not a patient man, when I get something in mind." I grin, looking at Amelia. Eric is completely clueless, he only sees the big picture of his new potential client. I can only see his beautiful wife.

"Please, let's take a seat." I gesture towards the table. "This is Andy my attorney and his wife, Tierra." I pull a chair out. "Please sit Amelia." I place her beside Tierra. Then Eric sits automatically beside his wife. "Eric, this is Michael, the project manager." I touch the back of Michael's chair who Eric sits beside. "And his wife Tina." I take my seat at the head of the table. Gerry is already seated to my right with Marcus. "And I'm sure you remember Gerry and Marcus."

I've got a perfect view of Amelia. I'm glad I chose to use the round table. She exhales as I catch her watching me. She looks right sitting in my world. My attention goes to Gerry when I see him walk towards her.

"Amelia from Amelia." Gerry beams. He takes her hand, pulling her up, giving me a knowing look. "The audacious hostess has some curves." And twirls her around … fussing over her body.

Marcus swoons in. "You are one curvaceous creature aren't you, you little vixen?" She laughs, noticing Eric watching her. He's not smiling. He doesn't like them swooning over her.

I could do some damage control, but I am enjoying the view my loyal assistant provided. I need to give him a bonus in his next check. I grin at Eric. "They're harmless." He laughs at my comment, still watching.

Calmly he grabs her hand. "Amelia." I've never seen him touch her with gentleness. I can only imagine his roughness in the sack.

"I've had this dinner meeting catered," I announce as I see the servers walking in with trays of oysters. Within a few minutes Maria returns to take drink orders. I hear Eric order for both of them, without so much as asking Amelia what she would like.

I know she likes sweet drinks. Toni makes a killer cosmo. "Maria, bring Ms. Amelia one of Toni's cosmos." I dare that fucktard to question me in my establishment.

She smiles as she ignores Eric glaring at her. She's looking at the oysters. "Oysters Rockefeller," I tell her with a nod, "please help yourselves."

I watch as she grabs one and looks up at me. She looks around the table, as everyone is helping themselves. I notice Eric isn't. "Sprinkle some hot sauce on it." I grab one and show her. "Now just toss it back like a shot." I know she knows, after all I already introduced her to them.

"You're really going to try those things." Eric looks like he's going to gag. "So you refuse to eat Mai Mai, but you're going to eat those slimy bugs?" I watch her eyes as she smirks at him, tosses it back, and hums. I laugh.

"Good?" I smirk. *She's hot as fuck.* I wish I could feed those to her. I know my grin is touching my ears. I see Gerry smirking his knowing look in my peripheral vision.

119

"Very." She cuts a smirk at Eric and takes another. He shakes his head with disbelief. She's grins at me when she sees her cosmo. I watch her close her eyes and savor the taste.

"Mmmm." She licks her lips. "Eric, this is delicious." Is she rubbing it in his face that she got a drink? I tell Maria to make sure her glass stays full.

I watch Maria bring her another drink. She looks up and smiles. Eric looks at her and whispers something in her ear as dinner is being served. They sit her plate in front of her. She gasps and looks up in my direction. *That's right baby, I know what you like.* She grins as she looks at the exact special I had ordered when we went out for lunch. Of course, I had them dress it up a bit for dinner.

"All right, I would like to thank Eric and Amelia for traveling to Jacksonville this evening to discuss my new club. I'm going to open the floor to Eric once everyone finishes their dinner and we can look over his portfolio; discuss some ideas. Ladies feel free to hit the dance floor." I smile at everyone as we begin. "All drinks are on me; so order whatever you like," I add. "Is something wrong with this one?" I ask pointing to her barely touched cosmo.

"No, it's delicious as the first." She smiles.

"I told her to take it easy on the drinks; my wife doesn't drink much." Eric drops his hand under the table, I'm sure on her leg by her jump. She looks at him, without smiling.

I listen as Andy and Michael joke about women and their drinking abilities. Tierra notices and starts laughing. Andy looks at her. "Really, do you monitor your wife's drinks?" She rolls her eyes. "I don't think so, honey pie." I hear Andy tell her it's none of her business, he knows she's about to say something. "Amelia doll, toss that drink back. When you're finished eating, we're going to hit that dance floor." I watch Amelia laugh.

I grin and lean forward. "Tierra is a model; she doesn't eat much, but she does love a good drink." Andy cheers my drink, laughing and returning his focus to his meal. Tierra rolls her eyes.

I watch as Amelia savors each bite. Damn she's beautiful. I wish she was mine instead of this fucktard I'm actually considering to design my newest club. This may be a bad idea, he's not a party guy. I don't have high hopes he will be able to achieve my depth of partying and club scene. I look around at this establishment, I'll have Michael contact the architect tomorrow who designed it, for comparison purposes.

"Are you done eating?" Tierra asks.

"Well, yes." Amelia wipes her mouth. I like Tierra for bringing the life to any party.

I look at Eric and laugh. "Tierra is tenacious. You wife will be fine." I can read what he's thinking: Tierra is hot and going to get his wife into trouble.

Amelia looks at Tierra and back at Eric. "Really, Eric, loosen up," she tells him. "I don't have a drinking problem." She grabs her cosmo as Tierra grabs her other hand.

"That a girl!" Tierra croons. "I like her. Come on, we're going to go shake our money makers." I laugh out loud as Andy stands for his wife. Michael stands as Tina does.

"Catch ya later tiger," Tina purrs in his ear, as she runs her fingers across his shoulders.

"There goes a bunch a damn trouble." Gerry sips his cosmo. Marcus agrees. "Boss, I'll catch you later, these girls are going to be too much." He kisses the air, pulling Marcus by the finger, shaking his hips as he walks while carrying his cosmo in his free hand.

I laugh at them all. I tell Eric to start whenever he's ready. I semi-listen to what Eric is telling my team. I'm too distracted by Amelia dancing in that tight ass dress: a sapphire ruched mesh bodycon mini dress with thin ass straps. I like the dresses with the built-in bra, less to take off. God, her tits look lovely. If she wasn't married, I would take her to my place and ravish her.

I'm lost watching her wiggle and sway those hips. She throws her head back laughing, I see she's wearing the sapphire earrings. Damn Gerry and Marcus getting to touch that amazing body, as they groove to the beat.

"You're hating this man, aren't you?" Andy asks me.

"What?" I grin, bringing my attention back to the meeting.

Andy looks at Eric. "Quinton loves to party. He'd rather be out there with the ladies dancing, instead of talking business. We typically cut him loose at this point. Michael and I usually handle it from here." Thank god for Andy.

Eric actually laughs, as he orders a beer when Maria walks by. "I don't dance. I'd rather talk business. Amelia dances. She's been quite a pain in the ass to tame." He glances in her direction and laughs. Michael and Andy laugh at his lame ass comment. I want to punch him the fucking face. I'm going to need more than two drinks. I tell Maria to bring me another gin on the rocks stat. "Quite frankly, if you open one of these places on the island, I don't know how I'm going to keep my wife out of it." He laughs as he watches her move.

I down my gin in one gulp. "I suggest you don't. It's good business." I look at Andy and give him a look. He sits back and studies me for a minute. He knows that look, and he shakes his head. I want him to entertain Eric.

"Why don't you go dance with the ladies?" Andy offers. He looks at Eric. "We got this don't we?"

Eric looks at me. "Yeah." He sips his beer. "Amelia is one of those good girls. I don't have to worry." *I hear you loud and clear.*

"Well, Quinton is one of those men, he doesn't mess around with married women. Period! He will make sure no one messes with her," Michael barks. I guess Michael read between the lines. *Thanks buddy.* "Let's gets back to the matter at hand." That's my cue, I'm outta here.

I stop by the bar and tell Maria to bring a tray of shooters. I talk to a couple of people as I make my way to the girls. I smirk as I watch her swaying those sexy hips. She's fucking sandwiched between Gerry and Marcus. I am jealous.

I sway up behind Tierra and Tina who are dancing on one another. Tierra grins, throwing her hips into mine as we start to sway. I close my eyes, moving to the music. When I open them, Amelia is watching me. I feel her. She wants to dance with me.

I grin as I stretch my arm out pointing at her, I bend my finger telling her to come to me. Gerry takes her hand and pulls her out of their sandwich. I move towards her, looking up and down at her body. I can't stop my appreciation of her body. She shyly laughs.

She takes my hand, and I swirl her into me. Her back pressed against my chest. I sprawl my other hand across her flat stomach. We start to sway to the music. God, she's heaven in my arms.

We fit perfectly. Like my well-tailored suits, designed for my body. She's made for me. I know it. I close my eyes as I drop my face down her neck, inhaling her scent. I'm melting into putty. She naturally tilts her face towards mine. I open my eyes, and she's watching me. I grin as I grind into her, taking her arms and pulling them up. She follows my lead, lacing her fingers into my hair. We dip lower.

Tierra and Tina start dipping in front of us. I open my eyes again as we move back up. Maria is on her way the tray of shooters. Bodies are moving all around us. I don't want to break her trance. She's lost in my hair, twirling those wonderful fingers in it and swaying against me.

Tierra sees Maria and hoots, breaking Amelia away. I grin as she grabs my hand. "Take a purple one," I yell in her ear over the music. She grins as she grabs it. Then I laugh as she

124

grabs another one, double fisting it. Tina and Tierra totally approve of her choice. On the count of three we all toss our shooters. Gerry wraps his hands around Amelia's tight waist. "Go ahead shoot it." Marcus grabs two more shooters and I tell Maria to bring another tray. Amelia needs some drinks.

She laughs as she licks her finger. She lost a little over the rim on the last shot. God she's beautiful. We all start dancing as a group, moving to the music. Marcus goes down her front as Gerry goes down mine. Tina wraps her arms around Marcus from behind as he comes back up. Amelia works it down. Tierra turns and shakes her ass against my back, moving up and down.

I turn around as I see some prick rocking his hips against Amelia from behind. She's not paying attention; her eyes are closed. His hands pull at her hips and she freezes when she opens her eyes, realizing a complete douche is trying to dance with her. I walk over and give him a look and pull her against me. She grins, relaxing in my arms. Maria appears with another tray of shooters.

We all shoot again on three. The music slows for a song. I wrap her in my arms, pulling her against my chest. Tierra wraps around her, Tina around me. We're all swaying, and Tierra and Amelia are laughing. This is what it would be like if she was mine. She feels amazing in my arms. I'm lost.

Tierra pulls her away from me breaking my trance. "We're going to the ladies' room."

"Right, meet me back at my VIP booth. I'll check on the guys." I make my way through the crowd. Andy and Michael have already moved Eric to the VIP booth. He's nursing his beer. "The girls are in the ladies'," I tell them as I sit down.

Maria brings me another gin. Marcus and Gerry join me. Maria returns again, this time with a round of drinks. My eyes stroll over Amelia's body as I see her moving through the crowd. I grab my drink and casually start listening to Eric and Michael talk about the club plans.

"What're your thoughts?" I ask Michael. I see Eric grin as the ladies approach. He reaches out for Amelia to sit next to him. Our eyes meet as she slides beside him. I let my eyes troll the crowd, tapping my fingers on the table to the music. I can see him in my peripheral vision trying to cuddle her.

"Don't get too cozy," Tierra warns as she grins at Amelia. "We still got more dancing."

"And drinks," I add, sliding her cosmo over to her. She downs it fast. We're grinning at each other. Maria returns with another one. I need to give her a bonus on her next check.

"Ah hell girl." Gerry smirks. "You have a lioness inside you." He playfully growls at her. I laugh, watching her smirk as she sips her cosmo. She's having a blast. Eric seems to be relaxing.

Gerry leans in and whispers, "You got it bad." I look at him. He grins with a nod. I don't deny shit. I sip my drink as I troll the floor. She's by far the sexiest woman here. Tierra catches my attention with the mention of body shots.

Tierra orders a round, "Hey Maria, a round of tequila shots." I watch Amelia, she's not going to care for tequila. I can't hear what Eric is telling her. She's nodding. Damn, I hope they're not about to leave. I want more time.

Tierra grabs the tequila shots, passing them around. I grab mine with a lime. "Here, Amelia." She gives her a shot. "Take this lime." Amelia is sitting there holding her tequila and lime.

"Body tequila." Amelia laughs as she looks at her.

"Girl, you never done a lover's body shot?"

Amelia shakes her head. "I've never had a shot of tequila period," she yells over the music. She's going to hate it. I laugh on the inside; I can't wait to see her face.

"Watch baby girl, this is how it's done." Tierra stands up and grabs Andy. She licks his neck, he licks her neck, they take the shot together, they bite their limes, and then she plants one on him. "That's all there is to it. Who's next?"

Michael grabs his and Tina. I watch Amelia as she's amazed by this game. I can see it in her face. She's talking to Eric. He's shaking his head. She purses her lips as she looks at her shot. Marcus and Gerry goes next. Eric looks away. It pisses me the fuck off.

"Amelia, Eric" I say. "You guys doing it?"

"Eric doesn't drink tequila," Amelia yells over the music.

"What about you?" I yell back. All eyes are on us now at the table. She shrugs. Tina and Tierra are totally wanting her to do the shot. She looks at Eric, he tells her go ahead. She looks confused, I watch her ask him. He nods as he grabs his beer.

She stands up and grabs her tequila. "Get up," she tells me. The table starts cheering and laughing. I'm fucking floored, does that fucktard think I'm not going in for the kiss? He's sadly mistaken, but he's watching. I smirk and grab my tequila.

"You ready?" I ask her. I don't know if everyone got quiet to see if she does it or if I was in the zone with her. Our eyes are pinned, she wraps her fingers around the back of my head and I follow suit. I think she's going to chicken out. I can feel her breath on my neck; my heart is pounding. Then she licks me. Her fucking smooth ass tongue slides softly and delicately across my neck. I'm instantly hard. I growl deep in my throat and suck her neck. We lean back at the same time and toss the shot.

My eyes are glued on her. She just turned me the fuck on, big time. I laugh as her face scrunches up. "Lime," I remind her. She quickly bites it. The table hoots and cheers her for doing it. Eric snatches her back before the kiss, and plants his mouth on hers. Damn!

I lean back in my seat. Gerry looks at me, smirking. Amelia pushes Eric back, just as fast as he planted the kiss. I don't think she was expecting it. She shakes her head and wiggles. Tierra laughs and hugs her. I grin as I watch her put her arms up in the air and she's dancing in the booth. Tierra is laughing and moving with her.

"Yeah girl. I just love her," she tells me.

Amelia starts pushing her. "Move. I need to get up." Tierra jumps rather quickly. I stand, not sure if she's about to be sick.

"You okay?" I ask her. She's grinning as she pulls me with her. I look back at Marcus and Gerry, grinning and motioning for them to come. "Dance!"

"You're getting drunk Amelia," I yell over the music. She's looking at me with seductive eyes. I know those eyes, she's horny. I'm dancing to the rhythm of the music, watching her rubbing around on me before she comes to the front. Our eyes meet as I grab her hand, spinning her around. She fits perfect; we start to move and sway to the beat of the music. We're one. She's running her fingers through my hair, pulling me down closer to her. I can feel my breath on her neck. I've tasted her skin, her scent. I want more. We're lost in the music; swaying in perfect harmony. Bodies are dancing around us, but she's the most seductive woman on the floor. I see no one else.

"I would have totally kissed you, you know," she whispers in my ear. I look into her eyes. She's watching me and looking at my lips. She's wanting me to kiss her now. I want to kiss her.

"You're drunk Amelia," I whisper in her ear, "you would regret it tomorrow. I don't want that."

She shimmies out of my grasp. "You're wrong Mr. Starks. I wouldn't regret it." She smirks as she turns and starts dancing with Gerry and Marcus. She fucking left me on the dance floor.

Tina and Tierra move on me. We're swaying, but my eyes are on Amelia. "She likes you," Tierra whispers in my ear. I look at her. She nods, grinning.

"Do another body shot, Tierra." Amelia wants a kiss, then I'm going to give her one. She grins as she disappears. I grab Amelia and pull her to me. She lays her head on my chest. "You want to do another body shot with me?"

"Yes." She's all breathy, looking at my mouth. I look up as Maria is following Tierra. As well as Michael and Andy. We're all standing on the dance floor. "Where's Eric?" she asks Andy and Michael. They tell her he's in the men's.

I grab two tequilas, giving one to her; I take two limes. "Here." I hand her a lime. I look around, we all got our shots and limes. "We all doing it on three?"

Tierra holds hers up. "One."

Michael bellows, "Two."

I grab Amelia close. "Three." She licks me again in the same spot. I suck her neck gently. Our eyes are locked as we take the shot. She scrunches up her face and shoves her lime in. I bite mine, and I caress her cheek when Eric walks up.

"I think you've had enough." He pulls her back. She stumbles out of my embrace. We all put our shot glasses back on the tray. Damn fucktard ruined my kiss twice. He pulls her back to the VIP table. Andy looks at me as he walks back to the booth. I pull Tierra next to me. We close our eyes and sway to the music.

"What do you think of his work?" I ask Michael as he's swaying next to me with Tina.

"May have some potential." He shrugs. "He maybe a hot head to deal with personally." I nod as we dance the song.

"Gerry, dance with Tierra. I'm going to the VIP booth." I walk back watching them. He looks pissed. She looks wasted. I slide in, looking at her. "Amelia, you okay?" I yell over the music.

"She's had too much," Eric says as he looks at her. I feel sort of bad for her now. She's going to feel like shit in the morning.

She starts laughing. "My husband thinks he'll get lucky because I'm inebriated." I look at him. He rolls his eyes. She sees him rolling his eyes. "You're making buddies, tell them how you really are with me."

"All right Amelia, you're starting to talk crazy. I think we're about to head back."

"No!" She shrugs out of his touch. "I don't want to go back with you. I like it here." She walks away, dancing. I watch her as she makes her way back to my gang. I look at him, but don't say much. I look at Andy. This is weird.

"Don't worry about it man," I hear Andy trying to make him feel better. "Tierra gets a little too drunk and says crazy shit too. Women, right?" Andy laughs as he's watching her.

"You going to dance with her?" I ask Eric. "She wants to dance."

"Like I said, I don't dance. This has been good for her. Thanks for having us." I nod as I look back at her. There's a slow song starting. "Excuse me."

I can't stay away from her. She's slow dancing with some guy. I touch her hips. She turns, grinning, and wraps her body into me. I let her lean on me, supporting her.

"You okay Amelia?" I whisper in her ear. She feels so good against me.

"Yes." She's all breathy. Her eyes are closed. "You're sexy," she purrs. I laugh at her drunk talking.

"I find you sexy too Amelia," I whisper in her ear. My lips brush soft kisses on her neck. She's perfect for me. "I love this dress on you."

"Good, I admit I bought it with you in mind," she whispers against my ear.

I can feel her breath on my skin. "Well you succeeded in pleasing me, very much." I pull her tighter as we dance to another song.

She feels really lax against me, and I look down. She's about to be completely out. "Amelia," I call her name.

"Yes." She's breathy. Okay, she hasn't passed out on me. I look at Gerry. He goes to get Eric.

"Give the valet your ticket. I think Amelia is on the way out," I tell him. He looks at her. He nods. "I'll help get her out of the club."

"Amelia." She looks up at me. "You're about to leave. Thanks for coming." She nods as she presses her body into mine. "Amelia," I say her name again, "can you walk sweetheart?" I wrap my arm around her as she starts to walk.

She looks up and stops. "Tierra. Tina. I need to tell the girls bye." I laugh as I turn her back. She tells them thanks for a great time. They all gush and talk for a minute.

She turns to me and grins. "You ready?" I ask her as we start walking off the dance floor.

"Yeah, take me home."

I look at her and she falls into me. Fuck, she's out. I scoop her up and carry her outside.

Eric opens the door as I put her in the front seat. He tells her not to vomit in his car as he fastens her seatbelt. I shake his hand. I watch them drive away. Well at least I got her so drunk, neither of us are fucking her tonight.

Chapter 11: Amelia

I roll over, squinting. The sunlight is piercing my eyes. "Shut the curtains," I croak, pulling the covers over my head. I curl deeper into my darkness, drifting back to sleep. *Quinton kisses me on the dance floor as we're swaying to a song. He's so incredibly sexy. I want more. I need more. I tell him to make love to me. He grins as he lifts me up and carries me off. We're in his private dining room on the table. He's yanked my dress up around my hips and my straps are pulled down. I lace my fingers through his hair, tugging him deeper into my breast. I feel him rip my panties off just before he enters in me. Shit, he's fucking me hard. He's good. Really, really good. He pushes me flat on the table. His big hands are sprawled out over my stomach, grinning down at me as he watches me heave against the table from his thrusts. He grabs my ankles, pulling my legs straight up and over his shoulders. He's thrusting harder into me, growling, and tossing his head back. I feel my release all around him. He's amazing. I roll my head and open my eyes. Eric is watching. Shit!*

I jump awake and the covers fall from my face. I cover my eyes with my hands to shield them against the brightness. *A dream!* I look down at my dressed hitched up. Eric left me in my dance clothes. I fall back thinking about that dream. Smiling, I remember the feel of his hands and his body thrusting against mine on the dance floor last night. I roll over, grabbing my phone off the bedside table. Shit, it's after noon. I've never slept this late in my life. Eric has obviously gone into the office. I lay, just listening to the quietness of the house. Remembering everything from last night. He does live a fascinating life. Tierra and Tina were great.

I want to talk to him again. Should I call him? I only have his work number. Eric is at the office. Why would I be calling? I had a reason the other day. I reach up fingering the earrings he gifted me. *If he wanted to talk to me, he would call,* I tell myself. He knows the name of the inn. He may not call because of Eric. Shit, should I call him? Oh for Pete's sake. I grab my phone and find Starks Industries' number. I press it.

Gerry answers. I chicken out and hang up. "Damn I'm an idiot." I toss my phone on top of the comforter, shifting my pillows around. My damn phone is ringing. I look at it, Starks Industries is calling. "Oh fudge!"

I hit the speaker. "Hello?" I answer calmly. My heart is pounding in my ears.

"Amelia, is that your voice?" Gerry questions. "Hello? Honey you best answer me."

"Yes," I breathe out. "Sorry I accidentally dropped my phone when we got disconnected before." I slap my hand over my eyes. That sounds so stupid.

"Sure you did." He laughs at me. "What's the Lioness up to this afternoon?" I grin, looking at my sorry ass laying in bed.

"Not a thing!" Literally.

"Well, what can your Gerry help you with, baby lion?" he teases. "Do you wish to speak with Mr. Starks again?"

"Yes, I do. Thank you. Is he available?" I ask, holding my breath.

"Hold on a sec, let me see what that fine-ass boss of mine is doing at the moment." He laughs and I hear the music flood the phone.

"Amelia, to what do I owe the pleasure?" I hear his voice come over the line. He's so professional sounding during the day.

"Hi," I whisper, feeling stupid for calling.

"How do you feel today?" I can hear the grin in his voice. "I've been wondering how you were doing."

"I wasn't sure if I should call you. I know you're busy at work." I smile as he confesses he's been thinking of me. "Fine. Well, I actually just woke up."

He's laughing. "Really, just now?" I laugh with him. I roll over on my stomach, looking down at my phone. My feet are swinging back and forth. He makes me feel like I'm in high school.

"Yes, I know how crazy and ridiculous is that?" I bite my lip, shaking my head. "Thanks for having us at your club last night."

"I'm glad you came. Tell me, did you make it home all right? No sickness?"

I smirk. "No. I was fine. I slept all the way, until now." I smirk, looking down at my boobs bulging out of the dress.

"Good! You partied hard. Eric said you weren't a drinker."

"Eric doesn't like the club scene," I correct him. "It's been a good ten years since I've been in a club." I laugh, running my fingers over the bedding. I don't want to think about Eric or talk about him.

"You looked beautiful last night." I smile at his confession. "You literally took my breath away when I saw you walk in." I hear him moving something. He's speaking to someone in the room with him, his voice is muffled.

I'm grinning as he finishes talking. "I didn't mean to interrupt you."

"You're never an interruption. Think of yourself as a beautiful distraction in my gray and navy world." He laughs. "I was just signing some documents. Tell me, Ms. Amelia from Amelia, what are you doing?"

"Well, at this exact moment, laying in my bed." I smile. "I do have guests arriving later this evening."

"Really! So when you said you just woke up, you meant you literally just woke up." He's grinning in his voice again.

"Yes, I literally rolled over and called you." *Well, after I had an incredibly hot sex dream, but I'm not sharing that detail.*

"The girls really enjoyed meeting you, Amelia. They hope that you will visit the club again."

137

"Oh, please tell them I enjoyed their company immensely."

"Just theirs?" *Oh did he really just go there?* I smirk down at my phone.

"And Gerry and Marcus," I tease. He laughs loud.

"Well, Ms. Amelia from Amelia, I'll be sure to pass that little tidbit along."

"And of course you, Mr. Starks," I breathe as I roll over holding my phone now.

"I do hope so. I would love to dance with you again, sometime."

"I think I would too," I whisper. Why, I don't know. I'm alone in the house. The line goes quiet for a moment. I don't know what to say. I can hear him on the other end.

"What are you going to do while Eric is out of town next week?"

I grin. "I don't know. I guess be here. I really don't have any plans."

"What days will he be gone, do you know yet?"

"He hasn't mentioned it. He'll probably find out today or tomorrow." Why does he want to know? I'm so curious.

"Would you want to maybe do something?" I freeze. Is he asking me out? "Are you still there, Amelia?"

"Yes, I am here," I breathe. "Are you asking me out or as friends?" I really want to be more than friends with this man, but I'm married. He laughs at my question. I guess it is silly. "I guess that is a silly question," I confirm.

"Amelia, you're a married woman." His admission is like a knife to the heart. "That is a line I've never crossed."

"I know, you're right. This is so crazy." I start to talk fast and babble. I can't hear him laughing anymore. But I know he's on the line, I can hear him breathing.

"I'll take you anyway I can have you, Amelia." I freeze. "Take that statement however you want to take it. You're the most enchanting woman I've ever met. I cannot get you out of my head. I don't want to stay away from you, your life. So if we're to be just friends, then so be it. If ..." He goes quiet.

"Okay then, yes I want to see you." I grin, feeling all sorts of emotions.

"Great! I'll get some ideas. I'll leave it to you to let me know the dates. Probably best to call me, I don't want to risk calling and Eric receiving that call."

"Okay." I grin looking at Eric's side of the bed. What the fuck have I just agreed to doing? "I have guests all weekend, starting today."

"Well, until I hear from you again Amelia from Amelia." He breathes those words with such promise. I feel tingling all over my body.

"Yes, until then Mr. Starks." I smile as I hear him softly chuckle. "Have a good day."

"You have a lovely rest of your day. You will undoubtedly be on my mind, Amelia. Just know that." I grin as I hear him disconnect our call.

Chapter 12: Quinton

"Gerry," I call, "please come in here." I can't believe the conversation I just had with Amelia. I'm reeling in lust and craziness. I know I've lost all sense. *Fuck!* She's a married fucking woman. "Don't smirk at me like that," I warn as Gerry swaggers into my office. He graces my white chair with canary yellow.

I walk over to my window and look at the piss ants below. Why am I fucking angry? I can feel him watching me. "Say something."

"You're in trouble." Gerry laughs as he sighs. "Damn. You should have just hit it like you normally do." I turn and glare at him.

"I don't want to just hit it." I rake my hands through my hair. "Fuck! Fuck!" I hear myself repeating the F bomb. I look at Gerry sitting in my chair, waiting for me to say something felicitous. "Sorry." I yank my chair out and unfasten my coat before I sit.

I'm staring at him, biting my bottom lip, tapping my fingers across my desk. He's grinning at me. He knows me better than I know myself. I laugh. Then we both are laughing.

"Well, well … it's finally happened. My Casanova has found something he cannot conquer."

"I've dreamed of her," I confess, looking at him.

"I'm sure you did after last night." He crosses his legs pursing his lips.

I shake my head. "No. Before I ever met her. I dreamed of this mysterious woman."

"Do tell." He grins, leaning towards my desk. I laugh looking at him.

"I don't know what you want me to say. She's the woman from my dreams. Before you sent me to that damn B and B, I had only thought she was a figment of my imagination. I would never settle down because she was my perfect woman, and she couldn't possibly be real. Then she looked up and knocked the damn air out of my lungs."

"Look, you've fallen for her like I did Marcus." I stare at him. "Hard and fast."

I lurch up out of my chair. "Well this is just fucking great!" I walk to my bar and fix a gin on the rocks. I toss it back, holding it in my mouth, tasting it, before I swallow.

"What are you going to do about it?" He swaggers around my desk, looking at the people below. "They look like ants from up here."

I nod in agreement as I watch him. "Nothing!" He looks back at me. "I'm going to do nothing. It's a line I don't cross. Amelia will be my first platonic female friend." I can't believe

I'm saying it. Gerry is laughing like I'm stand-up comedian. "What?"

"You with a platonic female friend?" He smirks and laughs at the same time. "I can't wait to see how this plays out."

"I have platonic females in my life: Tierra and Tina." I walk to my desk. "This conversation stays between us."

"And Marcus," he chimes. I look at him, cautious. "Marcus already knows ... he saw it in both of your eyes last night. Hell, we probably all did."

I nod, looking out the window. "Pull my schedule. What is my schedule like next week? I want it open." Gerry walks to his desk and grabs his iPad. I watch him glide back into my office and take his seat.

"You have a few things at the beginning of the week." I nod. I'll leave it as-is for now.

"Don't schedule anything else unless I say otherwise." I look at him, grinning.

"Ah, shit I know that look."

"Call my captain. I want them on standby to be ready to leave. We're taking the yacht for a few days: you and Marcus, Andy and Tierra, and Michael and Tina." I look at my phone. "And Amelia."

"Ah shit. I told you I worked for the devil!" He laughs as he gets up. "I'm going to buy me a flaming speedo." He laughs even harder. "Get it? A 'flaming' speedo."

I grin. "Yeah I got it." I watch him shut the door. That's exactly what I'm going to do. We going to party on my yacht a few days. Since we won't be alone, we will be forced to keep it in the friend zone.

* * *

I'm sitting at my VIP table, people watching. Waiting for Andy and Michael to come join me for drinks. Tierra is gone for that damn swimsuit shoot. I need to find a lady for the night, fuck Amelia out of my mind for a while. I hear myself and I sound terrible. I see the guys coming.

I watch them order a drink.

"You trolling tonight?" Andy asks as he looks out over the floor.

"Yep," I hear my despicable self. "It's been too fucking long. After last night's dancing and drinking, I'm due for it." I laugh as they laugh.

"Eric's wife is fucking hot," Michael confirms. "How did such a douche get her?" I shake my head, it's truly unbeknown to me.

"Yeah she is." Andy laughs. "Tierra really likes her. I had to hear about her all fucking night." I laugh. *Good because she's all I think about.*

"So you think Eric's a douche?" I ask Michael. I know he is; not to mention a fucktard in my book.

"Yep! I called the company we used to design this place today. They're working on their proposal. I'll meet with them probably next week or in two."

144

"Good." I toss my drink back. Maria comes immediately. "Tequila shots and keep them coming." I look at Michael and Andy, who are grinning. "What?"

"She fucking licked you in front of her husband." Andy laughs. I laugh about it too. "I really didn't think she was going to do it."

"If she was a male, I'd call her ballsy." Michael laughs.

"If she was a male, she wouldn't have fucking licked me twice." I grin, reminding them that we did the shot twice. "Yeah, I was stunned she did too." I looked at them. "I was going to lay one on those damn lips too, if that prick ass didn't kiss her."

"Twice," Andy reminds me. "The prick ass husband interrupted, twice." I roll my eyes.

"I bet he handled her when they got home."

I look at Michael. "Why you say that?"

"He was keeping his shit together here." Michael looks at me. "Trust me, growing up with an abusive father, you just see little things. She felt safe here, she actually let herself enjoy life for a bit. You heard her drunk admission—she didn't want to leave with him." I nod, remembering her comments. I haven't forgotten anything that came out of her beautiful mouth, nor the little things I've seen while visiting the inn.

"Yeah, Tierra doesn't like her husband."

"Tierra spent zero time around the douche." Michael laughs.

"Women go to the bathroom in flocks," Andy reminds him. "Women talk to each other." I remember them going to the bathroom. I don't want to hear anything about this. I can't worry about her alone with her husband.

"So bottom line is ... everyone is in agreement Amelia is awesome and her husband is a douche," I say looking at them. They're grinning in agreement. "So he's a no-go on the club design." There's another grinning agreement. "We're all going out on the Fortuna next week for a few days?" I question.

"Wait ... what?" Andy and Michael look at each other.

"When did you decide this?" They sound like damn parrots. I toss back another shot of tequila.

"Today! After I talked with Amelia." I looked at them. I take another shot. "And before you two lecture me about her being married, I'm quite aware of it. She doesn't know anything yet. He's going out of town, and she wants to hang out with everyone again."

"I wasn't going to say anything." Michael holds his hands up. "You two are both consenting adults." *That's right, we are.* That's one way to look at it.

"Friends," I confirm.

"That's all." Andy smirks. "You honestly think that's all she wants to be with you? Quinton, you're Jacksonville's richest bachelor."

"She doesn't know that." I shoot my last shot. "She just thinks I'm a businessman who owns a club. She doesn't know the depth of my wealth. I've never let on. Our conversations have been," I pause, grinning, "real."

"Real ... yet she doesn't know that you own practically all of Jacksonville, are the city's mogul of business, or a trust fund baby slash millionaire." I look at Michael.

"Correction, he just hit billionaire status." Andy laughs.

I roll my eyes. "As in real, we just talk, nothing personal. She likes me for me."

"What's not to like?" *Touché*. I grin as Maria brings us another round of shots.

Chapter 13: Amelia

"Amelia wake up," Eric says, kissing my neck. "I want some attention this morning." I roll deeper onto my stomach. *Please just leave me alone.* "Amelia, you awake?" I keep my eyes closed. *Wouldn't I be responding if so, dumb ass?* I really just want to sleep.

I feel him rub his hand up my thigh, kissing the back of my neck. He pulls my hair aside as he kisses deeper around. I'm hoping he stops if I don't respond. He's breathing in my ear and grinding against my hip. *Shit*, he's running his hands around my stomach ... pulling me toward him. I force my upper body not to roll, hoping he assumes I'm in a deep sleep.

He flips me over hard and crawls over me. He's kissing my neck and brushing his lips against my mouth. I whimper not out of satisfaction, but out of frustration. I flap my hands at his face as he's working down my neck, pulling my gown.

"No ... I am sleeping," I moan trying to roll, but he pins my wrist beside my face on the bed.

My eyes flutter open. "Eric what are you doing? Let go of me." He grins, grinding his hips into me. "Get off me," I whisper. We have a full house, and I don't want anyone to hear us.

"Oh god you make me horny," he growls. *Shit!*

"Get off me, Eric."

He looks at me dead in the face. "You're my wife, Amelia. Why don't you ever want me?" I roll my eyes.

"I've had sex with you for ten years. I think I'm entitled to having an opinion about when I feel like it or not. I'm tired. It's still early. Besides, it's not like it's going to last long enough to amount to anything." I can see that hurt his feelings.

"Then we should only do it more. It will build up my stamina." He proceeds to pull my panties down.

"No, I don't want you," I blurt out. He stops and his face looks angry.

"Who the fuck do you want then?" He pins my hands back down. "Say it. Who do want to do it with Amelia? That Quinton Starks guy?" I smirk before I realize it. "You do ... you want him."

I laugh. "No. I just think it's funny you brought him up."

"You said you don't want me, not that you don't want to do it. Which means you want someone." I roll my eyes. "I saw the way you threw yourself at him. The way you made a fool of yourself—he doesn't want you. He's a womanizer—you can see it a mile away."

"I wasn't thinking of anyone," I lie. I totally want to do it with Quinton Starks. I want to do it all with him. Obviously, Eric's jealous of him, belittling him.

"Pretend I'm whoever you want me to be. I don't care. I just want to have sex." With my hands pinned, he continues kissing me, down my neck, working down the front of my nighty. This is fucked up.

"Let me go." I struggle to get him to free my hands, but he doesn't. He only pulls them further above my head, clasping both wrists with one hand. Now his other hand is free for his assault. He pulls my gown up, sucking my nipples. "Stop it." I try to wiggle out of his mouth. It doesn't work.

He works his hand down between my legs. His touch is rough. Hard. I pinch my eyes shut as I feel his finger inside of me. I hate that. He knows this. It doesn't turn me on at all.

"Stop it, Eric. You know I don't like that." My body tenses. Unless I want another lesson—on what his hands can do down there—it's best I stop resisting and give-in, once again. I'm scared he's going to hurt me. I feel him pull his finger out and grab his cock. It's not covered.

"No ... No!" I scream, flipping my hips. "You put something on that damn thing."

He sighs as he gets off me to grab a condom. "Don't you move or I'll put it in without a raincoat. You're my wife," he tells me as he enters me. "I shouldn't have to wear these damn things." I close my eyes, trying to get through this. I hate this with him. *I hate this. I hate this.* Lucky for me it doesn't take him long to reach his goal. He flops next to me, breathing hard. How is he even out of breath? I look at him, he just ravaged me. *Again!* I've lost count the number of times over the years of marriage to him.

Inwardly, I huff sarcastically, *the only sexual consent I have, is marital consent.* That in reality translates to no choice in the matter! I sit up, my gown falls back into place as I get out of bed. There's no romance. Nothing! I feel like a vessel to be poked. "I am showering. Alone!" I add as I walk into the bathroom, locking the door.

I stand in the shower, letting the hot water spray over my body. I want my skin red. I close my eyes, washing my face with my cleanser—I see Quinton. I grab my body wash, lathering the suds over my body. Scrubbing my nipples until they're tender and my sex stings. I am clean. I grab my shampoo and lather, still thinking about Quinton. I wonder what he's going to come up with for us to do next week. The thought makes me absolutely giddy with excitement. I remember Eric laying naked in bed as I finish up. I can't wait for him to leave. In fact, I need that information.

I wipe the frosted-over mirror with my hand—depression is staring back at me. I brush my hair straight back and blow-dry it; I put just enough makeup to accent my features. I walk into the closet and grab a pair of capris and a tank top. "Ugh … who are you kidding Amelia. Eric is right! Mr. Gorgeous GQ worthy model isn't going to really want me," I whisper contemplating my body and features as I move about in front of the full-length mirror.

"Hey, Eric." I walk out of the bathroom. "When are you leaving for your trip?" He's already dressed, gathering his drawings and plans.

"Wednesday through Sunday." He smiles as he walks over and kisses me on the cheek. "You should really start wearing your wedding rings again."

"What?" I look down at my naked finger. In the past ten years, I have rarely worn my wedding bands.

He grabs my hand. "You don't even have a tan line of a ring." He slips his ring down a bit. "I do. I never take my ring off."

I roll my eyes. "Anyway, the ring is not what makes you married."

"No, but it symbolizes to other men you're unavailable."

"What are you even talking about? No one is confused about my availability." He can drop this ring crap, because I'm not wearing it. He's right, it signifies everything that I despise.

"I want you to close the inn for a few days, and come with me on my business trip. It will be good for us."

"What?" I gasp. "No. I don't want to go to Birmingham. I have no desire to go sit in a hotel in the middle of summer while you're doing business stuff."

"There are things you can do. You don't have to stay in the hotel. I really want you there. I don't like the idea of you having guests here, alone."

"Fine, I will close the inn for a few days to guests, but I'm not going to Birmingham."

"What are you going to do?"

I shrug. "I have no idea." That's the god-honest truth at this point. "I may go to the beach, relax and work on my tan." I look at my white arms. "It has actually been a while since I've done that. Or I may work on some projects around the house. I'll be fine here. This is our home. Everyone knows everyone here anyway."

"Fine. Just be sure the inn is closed."

"Don't worry, it'll be closed." He need not dare worry. I have no interest in being tied to the inn. I wish he would hurry up and leave. I need to call Quinton with the dates. After all, I won't hear from him all weekend.

Chapter 14: Quinton

I look at my clock again, when is she going to call? It's Friday and almost four. She will have no way to contact me over the weekend. I look at Gerry, he's sitting on his desk talking with the ladies in the front. At least he can hear his phone should it ring. I'm fucking starving, I skipped lunch because I didn't want to miss her.

I'm going to be suitable for a monastery if I can't shake her. I couldn't take home anyone last night. Andy and Michael thinks this shit is hilarious. I'm glad they're receptive of us all sailing together. I hope she will be.

I take that business call I've put off all day. I hate fucking suck ups. I see Gerry answer a call, he's looking at my office. He knows I've been expecting her call. I see him grin as I look. *It's her.* Within a few moments, my other line lights up. I end my current call immediately, I don't even know where we left the conversation.

I click my other line, speaker phone on. I sit back. "Quinton Starks."

"Amelia," she breathes into the phone. I grin as I hear the sweetest voice I've been waiting for all day.

154

"Amelia," I repeat, smiling. "I've been waiting all day."

"I'm sorry. I have a full house this weekend." I hear the side door slap against the frame.

"You going to your favorite place?" And for privacy, no doubt.

She laughs. "Yes. I have those dates you asked me about."

"All business. Surely, you're not trying to cut our time short," I tease, loving her laugh on the other end.

"I wish it was today," she admits. *She wants to see me.*

"Give it to me," I say grabbing my pen.

"Wednesday through Sunday ... sooo ..." I grin. "I'll have the inn closed during that timeframe. So you can just let me know what day works for you."

I lean back in my chair, looking at Gerry talking again. I turn my chair at an angle so I see the city and a hint of the water. "You're only going to give me one day with you?"

She laughs. "What do you have in mind, Mr. Starks?" *How about the rest of your life ladylove?* I can't say that though.

"I want it all." *Shit!* I even surprise myself with that. I shrug, it's true though. How is she going to respond? "Amelia, you there?"

"Yes." I think I hear her smiling ...

"Yes to?"

"Yes to it all."

"Good!" I grin. "I went to the club last night. Definitely wasn't the same without you and that dress."

She laughs. "Oh really? I'm sure you had plenty of dance partners. I can't imagine anyone not being interested."

"I didn't dance. I drank." It's the truth. I totally went with the intention of picking up a companion, but I couldn't even fake an interest.

"Really! That makes me grin, I admit." I grin at her honesty. "I may have been jealous Mr. Starks, someone getting to rub against perfection," she teases.

I guffaw at her. "I'm glad you appreciate my perfection. Although I guess I can say the same."

"How so? You know I didn't go dancing with anyone." *She's cute.*

"Jealous your husband got to spend time with you." She goes quiet. Shit, did I just bring up the realization of her marital status in her mind? "Amelia, you okay? I didn't mean to upset you." Shit, I can hear her sniffling. She's going to back out on giving me the all. Fuck me and my mouth. "I just meant …"

"No, I know what you meant. I'm fine." She sniffles a little, inhaling. "I wish it was you here too," she says, pausing for a moment, "more than you know."

"Oh!" Damn that just went deep. I hate that fucktard. "Well, I'll be there next week—Wednesday through Sunday. I promise you a good time."

"What do you have in mind?" *She's curious.* "I need some clue in case I need to go shopping."

"Pack a bag of your toiletries, swimsuits—lots of swimsuits—and dresses. I guess whatever you need for the beach."

She laughs. "Okay, anything dressy or just beachy?"

"Throw in a nice dress or two, you never know where we may end up. Pack a selection of summer things; just make sure you have beach stuff … and a passport." I want to tell her to pack everything you have and stay, but I can't.

"Okay." *She's kind of quiet.* "I'm totally curious now. I can hardly wait."

"You don't sound nervous about me telling you to pack your bag."

"I am not. Oddly, I trust you completely."

"Good, you should." I grin. I would never do anything to her. Should I tell her about the others? I think I'll surprise her.

"What are you doing this weekend, Mr. Starks?" She's all breathy. I love when she talks like that. *I'm going to be stuck thinking about you.*

"I'll probably hit the club with Andy and Michael. Tierra is gone on her photo shoot; I have to check in daily, handle business things."

"That's right, Tierra mentioned doing a swimsuit shoot in Hawaii. That has to be exciting for her." I laugh. "What?"

"Her manager and the photographer are pigs. Andy hates that she's there."

"I couldn't imagine modeling swimsuits. I would be way too nervous." I laugh at her comment.

"She started with lingerie."

"Oh! Really? Skimpy or tasteful?"

"The less the better when it comes to lingerie," I admit. She laughs at me. I'm serious though. "I'm not talking leather, bondage shit. Just sexy lace or silk."

"You've seen her shots?"

I laugh. "Of course." One division of Stark Industries is a magazine of fine lingerie and swimwear. "She's my best friend's wife. We were all friends before she hit it big." I look at the time and grin.

"What?" she asks me.

"How do you do that?"

"Do what?"

"How do you know I was thinking something and grinning?"

"The same way you do when I am, I guess, Mr. Starks." *Touché Ms. Amelia.* "It's just a feeling, I don't know."

"I was just thinking, it has been exactly a week now, since we met." I smile as I look at Gerry tapping his foot. "And I do believe we've spoken every day."

I can hear breathing in the phone. "I know." She's smiling. Like she said, I can feel it. "Believe me I've not thought of much else since." *Damn.*

"Me either," I whisper. "I've got to go sweet Amelia. Gerry is tapping his foot at me." I laugh as she does.

"What color is he today?" I grin, *she's beautiful.*

"Tuscan gold or something near that. Oh with a fedora that matches." We both laugh. "Quite frankly, I can't believe they make suits in that particular shade."

"Like you said, he's your color wheel." She sounds like she's purring.

"Yes, I did." *I'd like to hear her purr differently.*

"Well, you go Mr. Starks and have a good weekend." Yet she doesn't hang up.

"You keep yourself safe, sweet Amelia." I hope she reads all of my meaning into that statement. I won't be around this weekend.

"I will ... until we speak again." I grin as I hear her dis-connect her call.

Damn. "Until then," I whisper into the dead phone.

Gerry sees my phone is no longer flashing. I watch him make his way into my office. He's hard to miss in that color. "Well, what did your lioness say about sailing?"

"I didn't tell her what I was planning." I grin, leaning back. "Element of surprise!"

"Romance is on the horizon." He snaps his hand at me as he grins. I'm not going to deny it. Nor admit it to *myself.*

159

"Friends, remember? We leave Wednesday and return Sunday." I look at him. "All of us. What you think about leaving Wednesday morning, sailing to the Bahamas, beaching some?"

"Marcus will be ecstatic."

"Good." I grin. "You two coming to the club later? I've got business matters to attend to."

"Please honey, we're going to have our bodies waxed." I laugh watching him rub over his face. "This beauty isn't god given love. Hell no, it takes money and pain."

"Did you get the captain on standby?"

"Don't I do everything you tell me?" He rolls his eyes as we both stand. I nod in agreement as we leave.

Chapter 15: Amelia

"Shit," I whine as I drop my damn casserole dish. I grasp the burn and bend at my waist squeezing my hand between my thighs. I haven't quite figured out why, that move certainly doesn't ease the pain. I guess makes it more bearable.

I look at my well-worn oven mitt. "It's time for new ones." At least I didn't spill the orange marmalade breakfast bake. I walk over to the sink and run cold water over my hand. My grandmother always used fresh aloe.

I slip on plastic gloves, and work my homemade apple sage sausage mixture into patties. I should have made these for Quinton. I grin, dreaming about him; I hope I'm on his mind.

I close my eyes when I hear Eric walk into the kitchen. He wraps his arms around my waist and kisses me on the neck. "Good morning!"

"Morning." I smile, moving out of his grasp to my skillet. It's hot and ready for the sausage.

"What are you cooking this morning?" He grabs a soda and pops it open. I hate when he gulps.

"Orange marmalade breakfast bake, apple sage sausage, fresh fruit, coffee, and juice." I answer frying the sausage.

"What are your plans today? Do you have to get stuff ready for your trip?"

"I talked to the office, they said to bring you along. They're buying you a plane ticket."

I can't even hide my shocked face. "What?" I feel my eyebrow hitch out of annoyance as I flip the sausages. "I told you I wasn't going," I snap. I am so not going. *I've already made plans.*

"And I told you I wanted you to come with me." He gets up and grabs a piece of cooked sausage. "It's pretty good. I like just plain sausage." *Of course he does.* He doesn't like any sort of seasoning nor trying anything new. I always have rave reviews on my apple sage sausage from our guests. I don't say anything about the sausage or the trip. I'm not going with him, simple!

"I'm going to run some errands after breakfast." I need to get a few swimsuits. After all, Quinton's used to seeing a freaking lingerie swimsuit model. I sort of dread that part. He's going to be sorely disappointed. Maybe I should go to the beach and get a few rays today.

"Good! Have you thought anymore about what I mentioned the other day?" What the hell is he referring to?

I finish the sausage and put it in the warmer. "I don't know what you're talking about." He hasn't asked me about anything but that stupid business trip.

"About us trying …" I watch him dumbfounded as he crosses the kitchen. He wraps his arms around my waist. "I was serious." He kisses me on the neck.

"No, I haven't given it a second thought." I grab his hands and push him back. "Eric, you need to listen to what I am saying. I am not having a child. Period! I have no desire to have children." I'm done with this conversation.

"And that's it? Just because you said so."

I cross my arms across my midsection. "Well um yeah, Eric. It's my body."

"It's my body too. When you said I do, you promised to belong to me as much as I belong to you." I roll my eyes.

"It's my body that carries and delivers a child, not yours," I scream. Shit. My throat burns from the rage. "I'm going to have a say in what happens to my body." This really is a fucking moot point, because that IUD is in place and has been for six years. "You may take your pleasure on this body, but that's where the line ends. If you really want children that bad, Eric, then maybe we need to discuss other things."

"Discuss other things?" *Shit,* he looks pissed as he closes the gap between us. "What the fuck does that mean?" I look down, crossing my arms. "You're talking about divorce?" His spit hits my face as he lashes out. My ears ring. Divorce does sound wonderful. He pinches my face, making me look at him. "You're mine Amelia. You took vows with me … until death do us part."

163

I jerk my face out of his grasp. I don't look at him. "I am not having a child."

"And I am not going to let you go. Ever!" I watch him as he looks at his phone, brooding over the text that just dinged. "You're mine Amelia! So you just get the idea of a fucking divorce out of that goddamn head of yours. Do you understand?" I don't say anything. He grabs my jaw, squeezing. "Do you understand?" I push his hands away from my face.

"I've got to get breakfast served."

* * *

I walk down Centre Street to the Island Boutique. "Hi Gail." I smile as I walk in. She's lived on the island all of her life. Gail and Greg have a wonderful marriage. They swoon over one another all the time.

"Amelia, what brings you in this morning?" Gail beams.

"I need a couple of new swimsuits," I admit, digging through the racks. I pick up a bright yellow string bikini. Quinton likes to keep his human color wheel to add color to his life. I smile, holding it up against my body. *I'll try it on.* The black bikini is sexy. I snatch a sapphire colored one. *Damn it would have a Brazilian cut ass.* "Gail does this blue one come with a different bottom?"

"No dear, that line is my new Brazilian cuts." Gail frowns. "I don't know anyone who would wear such skimpy things, but they're supposed to be hot selling pieces this year." I smile and don't put it back.

164

I slip into the dressing room. I try on the blue first. Shit, my tits look huge in this. *My tits are my best feature.* I turn and gasp. I don't know if I can pull this Brazilian ass off. I mean, I'm a perfectly toned size two. I could get a cover up with it … I am getting it.

Next the yellow string. At least the yellow bottoms cover and still look sexy with the strings. My full bust dominates the string top. It fits good. I've never had a bandeau swimsuit before. I try the black one, it's cute. It does have a removable neck strap. The top is twisted and ruched, but at least it has built in support. The bottoms are cute, ruched with decorative strings on side.

Gail's smile reaches her ears when I hand over my credit card. "You must have something planned to tease that husband of yours. He's not going to be able to keep his hands off you." I smile—that's the idea, but only it's not for him. If I'm honest with myself, I felt a small pang of guilt … but then I see Quinton's heated smile. I tell myself to *shut up* as Gail proceeds. I can't believe I just spent four hundred and fifty dollars on three swimsuits.

I continue my beachy shopping expedition. Are we going as friends or more? He left the more open. Do I want more? *Yes!* Shit, I'm married. I really can't believe I'm considering this. Can I keep it platonic with him? I want him in my life, like he said, anyway I can. Eric will never give me a divorce.

I find myself standing in front of the inn. Eric's car is gone. *Good!* I slip into my new black bandeau bikini and hit the beach. I can't look like a ghost in front Quinton. Somewhere between dancing with Quinton and buying skimpy swimsuits today, I decided against doing the moral thing, and for once follow what I physically I want. And after this little trip, we might discover we weren't ever meant to be together ... and well then, I can deal with the aftermath.

Chapter 16: Quinton

I pull up at the docks. I love this place. There she is, my first toy I bought when I hit millionaire status. Fortuna. I picked her name to signify the start of my fortune building empire. She's a two hundred eighty-foot, luxury motorized sailing yacht. Party deck, plenty of lounges and bars; similar to my club but on water. Private crew cabin. She even has a pool, toys, and swim deck. I hope Amelia loves her like I do. She will be the first woman I brought aboard with a romantic interest and overnight. Sure, we've had plenty of day parties and women. But hell, I've never met a woman I've developed a romantic interest in. My companions have always been strictly for sex.

I smile as I see Captain Pete waxing her rich sparkling navy finish. "Mr. Starks." He immediately straightens, giving me his full attention. I grin as I walk up, checking out his work.

"Captain." I grin, walking aboard my vessel. "How is the Fortuna?"

"She's fully stocked and ready for her voyage on Wednesday sir. Chef will bring perishable items Tuesday night."

"Good ... good! We will have the usual group here. I do have a special guest coming, her name is Amelia."

"Very good sir. I'll make the crew aware." I nod as I walk through the upper deck, checking the alcohol choices. "She likes sweet drinks. Make sure there are plenty of fruity flavors available. Toni knows she likes his cosmos. He's to have an unlimited supply."

I continue my walkthrough with Captain Pete in tow. "I want some of the high-end French line of toiletries with lavender and jasmine scents ... maybe some coconut."

"Yes, sir. Chef is here, would you like to review the menu?"

"Yes." I head towards the galley. "Chef."

"Mr. Starks." He stands as I walk in.

"I would like to see the planned menu. I told Captain the usual gang is coming. I also have a special guest: her name is Amelia. I want the best moscato."

"I understand sir." I sit down with him, looking at his menu choices. I'm pleased. "Ms. Amelia loves oysters Rockefellers. Make sure we have plenty for the voyage. I also want a selection of finger foods available throughout the day; plan for several courses. We're sailing, drinking, and dancing. We will dock some. You and Captain will work that out," I confirm, looking between the two of them.

"Captain, I don't want to be presumptuous," I tell him as I walk towards the sleeping quarters. "Put Marcus and Gerry, Andy and Tierra, and Michael and Tina in their usual quarters. Please have the fourth bedroom prepared for Ms. Amelia."

"I understand sir. It will be fully stocked for her every desire."

"Excellent." I walk into my master quarters. I don't have any condoms on board, she may be offended if I bring condoms because that screams expectations or she may look at it as prepared. *Shit!* I've never thought twice about this, I always have condoms.

"Have you taken her out?" I ask.

"Yes, sir! Running perfectly," the captain confirms. *Good!*

"We're leaving Wednesday morning as soon as Amelia arrives. So have the crew here no later than eight and ready to depart immediately upon our arrival." I walk back out on the sundeck. I can't wait to see her lounging on the white sofa. My cock is getting hard just imagining her. *Friends, remember Quinton*, I tell myself. I shake Captain Pete's hand as I leave the Fortuna.

This has been the longest damn weekend of my life. Sundays are so boring. I wonder what sweet Amelia is doing. I sit down in my empty penthouse. The solitude has never bothered me. I'm glad the gang is all on board for the trip.

I guess this day was somewhat productive. After all, I did head to the docks. The captain, crew, and chef are all prepared for the trip.

Chapter 17: Amelia

"Why?" Eric screams. I look at the clock, it's not even eight in the morning. "I told you Friday they were getting you a ticket."

"I told you I had no desire to go to Birmingham, before you had them purchase one." He yanks the covers off me. I really just want to relax. I wish I could wake up to the sound of nothing.

"You're really fucking pissing me off about this!" I look at him like he's an idiot. "You're fucking going. Start packing your shit." I grab the cover and pull it over my head. "Get the fuck out of the damn bed." Eric grabs my foot, dragging me to the foot of the bed.

"Shit! Eric stop." I'm kicking my captured ankle at him. "Let me go." He doesn't until he successfully busts my lip on the foot of the bed. *Thanks for the morning face plant.* I hold my lip, tasting blood. "Well guess you're satisfied. My lip is going to be swollen."

"Shit Amelia, I didn't mean for you to hit your face." Eric bends, trying to check my lip. Yeah right, he just doesn't want his anger shown to the public.

"Don't touch me," I hiss pushing him aside. I slam the bathroom door shut. Not even eight in the morning, and I have a busted lip. I cry into my hands, listening to Eric begging for me to open the door. He's all apologetic.

"I'm not going Wednesday with you. You can get mad and throw shit. I don't care," I scream through the door. I'm crying as I pace back and forth. "I told you already I didn't want to go. I thought it was settled." He is too quiet. It's creeping me out. I walk to the door and place my ear against it. I don't know if he's still here or not.

Whack!

I jump back from the door and scream. He just slapped the door with his hand, possibly punched it. I don't know. I do know I'm not unlocking it.

"Fuck it. I'm sick of this fucking shit Amelia," Eric screams. "Fuck! I'm out of here. You can get your goddamn shit and leave." I hear his stomping fade. He slams the front door so hard, the bathroom door pops in the jam.

My heart is still pounding when I open the door. I look at the comforter yanked to the floor. "Asshole," I whisper wiping my nose. I don't understand his sudden bursts of anger—his tantrums. I walk downstairs. He's gone.

I walk into my kitchen and grab a mug to make a latte. He wants me to get my shit and leave, *I should*. The realty is I have nowhere to go, nor the means to make that happen. I'm stuck in hell! He's crazy. I wipe my eyes, sniffling. Quinton

171

floods my thoughts. I don't know if he's in the office this early. I don't really know his work schedule. I dial his number.

"Good morning, Gerry." I touch my lip. It stings to smile. "Is Mr. Starks in yet?" I laugh as he calls me Amelia from Amelia. I hold as the music floods the phone. I walk to the living room and get comfy on the sofa. I can keep an eye out if Tantrum returns for some reason. I take a sip as I hear his voice. My stomach knots with uncertainty.

"Quinton Starks." His voice is stern.

"Is this a bad time?" I'm timid.

"Amelia." I hear a change in his voice. "Gerry didn't tell me it was you. You're calling early." I look out the window.

"I can call later if I interrupted something." I'm all nerves sitting on the edge of my seat.

"No, I'm glad you called." I can hear him smiling. "I've missed your voice."

Now I'm grinning like a fool. "Really? I've missed yours too." His voice eases my pain. I lean back on the sofa, pulling my knees to my chest as I sip my latte. "Did you have a good weekend Mr. Starks?"

He laughs. "It was long. Time has stood still since you agreed to seeing me this week."

"Glad to know it's not just on this end." I smile as he laughs. "I went shopping."

"What did you buy?" Quinton is grinning.

"A few new swimsuits." I really want him to find me attractive in them.

"Now I really can't wait to see you." I hear him laugh. It makes me laugh.

"Well, I'm no model, but …" He laughs, cutting me off.

"Amelia, you forget I've seen you in a bodycon dress, shaking it on my dance floor. I can't wait to see you in a swimsuit." I think I'm blushing. "What time is Eric leaving Wednesday?" he asks. I really don't want to talk about Eric.

"Early morning flight … before eight."

"Well, what time are you going to meet me? I want you here as soon as possible." I can hear him grinning.

"What time can you leave?" He laughs at my question.

"I can leave whenever you get here. My schedule is cleared."

"Well, I'll confirm his flight time tonight and call you tomorrow to let you know exactly my arrival. Does that work?"

"Yes, and Amelia, I really hope you will come as soon as possible. Are you nervous about going with me this week?"

I laugh. "Nervous? No, I mean I've never done anything like this before, but I'm not nervous. Excited is a better word."

"I meant what I said before Amelia, I'll take you in my life anyway I can have you." My stomach flutters. "I'm really glad you've accepted my invitation."

"There's no place I'd rather be Mr. Starks." I turn when I hear a car pull up. "Shit."

"What is it, Amelia?" I can hear his concern. I don't want to alarm him.

"I've got to go. Eric's home." I jump up, running through the foyer to the back of the house. Quinton hears the door slap against the frame.

"Amelia, are you running?"

"Yes," I whisper. I'm a mix of emotion: excitement, fear, nervousness, and happiness. "I'm so excited about Wednesday. I cannot wait to see you again. I've waited all weekend to hear your voice. I'm sorry I have to rush off." Adrenaline rushes through my body. My hands are shaking, and I disconnect the call before he can respond. Quickly I delete my call log. My mouth is dry, my heart is in my ears. I toss my phone under the blooming azalea bush and sit on the swing, rocking back and forth.

He's near, and my body is tensing up. "Amelia, I'm sorry I lost my shit." Eric's voice is guarded as he walks towards me. I stop swinging.

"If you want me to get my goddamn shit and leave, I will Eric," I hiss. "I do believe that's what you told me this morning. I have no problem doing so. I am tired of this shit anyway." In the words of Gerry, hear my lioness roar. A spark of my destroyed strength is starting to flicker. Maybe Quinton Starks has ignited something more than desire.

174

Eric stoops in front of me. "I was mad. I shouldn't have said that to you." I really don't care what he says. He reaches up to touch my lip, but I jerk my head away.

"Amelia, stop being like that," Eric warns. I just turn my cheek to him.

"How do you expect me to act Eric?" I look at him. "You busted my lip acting like a complete idiot this morning."

He drops his head. "I didn't think you would hit your face."

"What did you think would happen when you pulled someone feet first off a bed?"

"Look, I said I was sorry. You're just going to have to accept my apology." He reaches in his pocket. "I got you this ring. I hope you will wear it."

I looked at the diamond and sapphire band and then at him. *Sapphires—really*! He does this every time he knows he royally fucked up and crossed some imaginary line in his head.

"Why diamond and sapphires?"

"You've worn those earrings since you got them. I thought you must like them, figured you would wear a ring that matches." He takes the ring out and slips it on my ring finger. "You refuse to wear a wedding ring. This works." I sit staring at the ring as he walks off. It's just another shackle to suck any remaining life or hope way—*kill me now!*

We don't speak the rest of the day. I'm just waiting for Tuesday to come and go. I get to talk to Quinton. Then Eric will be flying out and I'll be going to my unknown destination.

Chapter 18: Quinton

"Tierra wanted to hit the dance scene." Andy grins as we're sitting at my VIP table. "She has a friend she's bringing." I roll my eyes.

"I don't fuck models, Andy." I troll the floor as I tap my fingers across the table to the music. "However, I don't know if I should go on a four-night voyage with Amelia with a loaded cock. It might make me a horn dog."

"I don't think you need to fuck anyone." Michael sips his beer. I look at him. "You're about to go away with Amelia. Do you really want to have that tainted shit on your conscience, if something does happen?"

I look across the floor. "I know you're right … but my fucking balls are going to be blue, if I don't get some action on this trip." I sound like a horn dog.

They laugh at me as I see Tierra and her friend walking our way. She's a model, all legs, and blonde kinky curls. They practically could be twins in the face. "Shit," I growl as I look at Michael. I down my drink. Maria brings me another gin on the rocks.

"Ladies." I grin, looking at her friend's tits. I hate fake tits.

"Meet Tara." Tierra grins, sliding in next to Andy.

"Tara, what would you like to drink?" I'm totally not fucking her. Michael's right. Shit, I feel guilty just having drinks.

"Shots," Tierra answers. "We met on the swimsuit shoot." I start looking out over the floor as she's grinning.

"Andy tell you what we're doing Wednesday?" I yell over the music. Maria brings our shots. I grab a tequila.

"No, what?" She's already dancing in her seat. I pass Andy and Michael a shot. Tara grabs the last one.

"Shoot." We all toss the shots and bite the lime. I start dancing my shoulders. "We're cruising on my party yacht, heading towards the Bahamas. Coming back Sunday."

"That sounds absolutely fabulous." Tara grins, throwing her tequila shot. I look at her, shaking my head.

Tierra is dancing in the seat. "That sounds good."

"Amelia's coming with me." I toss another drink that Maria brought. Tierra starts grinning, looking at Andy. Andy nods, confirming.

"Fuck me! What happened while I was in Hawaii?"

I laugh, grabbing her by the hand. "Come on doll, dance with me." I take Tierra and we start to dance; rubbing and grinding to the beat of the music. "Get rid of your friend, not interested," I yell over the music.

She grins, turning her back into my chest. We start to sway and I close my eyes. "Help me get Amelia to open up."

"I got you covered babe; she's totally into you anyway." I grin as I wrap my arms around Tierra tighter.

177

***

Her dress is pooled on the floor. My clothes are haphazard around the room. God, she feels good beneath me, kissing me. Her legs wrapped around my hips, pulling me deeper. I can't breath as I'm pumping harder and harder into her. "I love you," she screams as I feel her release around me. God, she's like silk around my cock. I explode in her. I keep grinding all of me out. I never want to pull out of her. This is it. She's it.

I wake up calm. My heart is pounding in my chest as I look down. Shit, I don't have to worry about a loaded cock anymore. I wipe my cock with the sheet and toss it to the floor. I've got to taste her. I can't wait to get to the office. She will be calling.

Gerry has donned a fuchsia suit, chatting it up with some-one on the phone. He sees me grinning. I grab my coffee as I walk into my office. I leave my door open for him to join. I look out the window at the ants below, drinking my coffee. Tomorrow she will be coming here. I need to make arrange-ments for her to get into the building.

I grin when Gerry swaggers into my office. "Sharp suit! New?" He grins in confirmation. "Tomorrow we set sail. Everything in order for you and Marcus to leave?"

"Yes, he will come here. How do you think Amelia is going to swallow the truth of your wealth?" He purses his lips as he flips his hand around.

I laugh. "It's who I am. Make sure security is expecting her tomorrow morning. She needs a visitor pass, and I want her personally escorted up here. Make sure valet is expecting her as well. Tell them to park her car on my private level. Call my driver, the limo will take us all to the docks. Captain and crew are ready to leave port at eight. I told them to be ready to move as soon as we get there. I don't want to be docked and waiting." I look back out the window. "I don't want Eric to possibly get wind of something and interfere."

"You think he's going to cancel his flight?" Gerry stands as he sees his phone flashing.

"I have no idea what that fucktard may try to pull at the last minute." I watch him grab his phone. He's grinning as he looks back at me and fires his index finger at me. I close my door and unfasten my blazer as I sit. My phone flashes, I hit the speaker.

"Quinton Starks." I grin hearing her breath on the other end.

"Good morning," she breathes into the phone. She sounds cozy.

"Good morning, Amelia." I lean back thinking about sharing breakfast with her. "You okay? I was concerned with how abruptly you disconnected yesterday."

"Yes," she whispers. I can hear her sniffling. She's not okay. What has that fucktard done?

"Why are you sniffling? Amelia, are you okay?" I can hear something off in her voice.

"Eric's company purchased me a plane ticket as well. To accompany him to Birmingham tomorrow," she tells me. *Fuck him!* I turn my chair and stare out the window. I am Quinton fucking Starks. I could crush him and his little firm. "Are you there?" Her voice pulls me back to our phone call.

"Yes, sorry, I was processing what you said. So, I take it you're not available this week." I snatch my tie from my neck and toss it against the glass wall. Gerry looks up. I see him stand, but I shake my head not to disturb me.

She laughs. "No, I'm going with you." I don't believe what I just heard. Did she really say she's still coming? She chose to spend the week with me instead of her husband! I'm grinning like a fool. Gerry is relaxing back in his seat. I give him a thumbs up.

"Really ... I'm happy to hear this. Do tell me how you managed to pull this off."

She titters. "Let's just say I battled it out with him yesterday morning, through a locked bathroom door." *I don't like the way this sounds.* "Team Starks one—Johansson zero."

"Yesterday?" I question. She goes quiet. "You didn't mention this yesterday."

"It's fine. It's worked out. I told him I wasn't going with him. Period! He didn't like it, but he's dealing with it."

"Did he put his hands on you?" I hiss. *I have to know if that fucktard touched her.*

"Mr. Starks, you sound concerned." She's teasing me with her safety. "Don't worry, he has no clue what my plans are. I told him I was going to relax at the beach; maybe work on some projects around the house."

180

"Amelia, I don't want you getting hurt to see me." *I will bury his ass.*

"Are you having second thoughts about seeing me tomorrow?" She sounds nervous.

"Hell no! I want you here now." She laughs. "I love your laugh."

"I love your voice," she purrs in the phone. *Fuck, she loves my voice.* I grin at her confession.

"I don't think anyone has ever said that to me before."

"Well, that's a shame, it's as deep and powerful as you are handsome Mr. Starks."

"Is it now?" I growl. She just spoke straight to my cock.

"What time should I come tomorrow? Wait, where am I meeting you?" She giggles.

"Come to my office, Starks Industries. I'll leave you a visitor pass at the front desk. It's all valet parking, so let them park your car."

"Okay." She smiles. "You sure it's okay to leave my car there?" I laugh. She's adorable "What? I'm serious, I don't want you to get into trouble with having my car there or god forbid it gets towed." *How is she going to react seeing my world?*

"It will be fine, Amelia. I promise. What time should I expect you?"

"Is ten good?" I grin. "I have to wait for him to leave, to pack."

181

"Perfect. And Amelia, bring your luggage inside with you, because once they park your car it's parked."

"Okay, I'm so excited." I can hear her practically jumping.

"Oh me too, Ms. Amelia. You have no idea." I flag Gerry into my office. "Amelia give me a sec." I mute my phone while I inform Gerry of our plans.

I turn my chair back to the window. "Amelia," I breathe her name.

"Mr. Starks," she teases. "I can't believe it's really here. I've been waiting for tomorrow it seems like forever." *I love that.*

"I know, me too. I went to my club last night. Tierra was back and wanting to dance." I'm going to tell her about that Tara chick. I don't want any secrets.

"Tierra's back? I'm sure you two had a lot of fun." I smile, it would have been better with her there.

"She hadn't heard about you and I planning a trip." I pause for a minute. "She brought a friend."

"Oh, I see." Amelia goes quiet. "Was she nice?"

"I sent her packing."

"Really?" I can hear her smile.

"I danced with Tierra, only her."

"You don't owe me any sort of explanation Mr. Starks," she tells me. "I am not naive. You're a very attractive bachelor. I've seen the way women look at you."

I laugh. "You don't seem to understand. I don't care what any of them think, only you. It's only you in my mind. I just wanted you to know about it. I have no secrets with you." I'm going to make sure she understands how deep my desire is for her. It's way more than a few nights in the sack.

She's quiet. "Amelia?"

"Yes, I'm here. I'm just thinking about what you said. I have no right to ask you to refrain from your desires."

"My desire starts and ends with one person Amelia."

"Damn," she whispers, "sounds like we have quite the predicament."

I smirk. "Why?"

"Mr. Starks, you're a smart man. I'll let you figure this one out. I'm sure you have some corporate relations that need your attention. I don't want to be kept waiting tomorrow," she teases.

"Well, played Ms. Amelia from Amelia. I cannot wait to see you. I'll leave you to your scullery maid duties, so you're not late leaving." She laughs. "Ten tomorrow," I confirm.

"Yes, ten." She's all breathy. I hear her disconnect the call.

Chapter 19: Amelia

I pull in front of Starks Industries. He works in the tallest building in Jacksonville. "Wow!" I whisper to myself. The valet rushes to collect my car.

I open my door as the valet is reaching for the handle. "Amelia Johansson, Mr. Starks told me to give you my name." Everyone is rushing about.

"Certainly, Ms. Johansson." I watch as the valet snaps his finger and another guy rushes to get my luggage. They act like bellhops. "Please follow me. Mr. Starks is expecting you."

"Oh ... okay." I smile as he holds the glass doors open. "Thank you."

Security greets me, "Ms. Johansson?"

"Yes," I confirm, looking around. White marble or granite everywhere. It's modern and sleek. Everyone is in suits. Even the security look like secret service men: black suits, white crisp shirts, and black ties. He attaches a visitor pass to my dress.

I feel so underdressed, looking down at my short mini strapless white sundress and wedge heels. Thank god I had a pedi and mani done. I wore my hair beach waved, and my makeup is like it was the day I met him. *I'm so nervous.*

"Please follow me." I smile as security takes my luggage. I grab my purse and toiletry bag. He scans his clearance card and presses number twenty-eight.

The elevator sweeps up twenty-eight floors. Another set of glass doors open. I hear security tell them I'm there to see Mr. Starks, which they already knew. I walk around the bend and see Gerry, relaxing and hanging out at his desk. "Marcus, Gerry." I smile as I get closer.

"Oh hell ... Lioness is a vision." Gerry grins as he looks into Quinton's office. I can feel his pull, I follow his eyes and there is Quinton, standing on the other side of the glass wall—all domineering. His office is huge. "Go on in Lioness."

I smile as I walk pass him. Quinton meets me at his door, beaming.

"My god you look beautiful." He's smiling, looking at me. He's as handsome as I remember. My dreams of him haven't diluted what he really looks like at all. I don't know if it's nerves or excitement causing my stomach to tingle but I'm tingling—everywhere!

"To be honest I feel a little underdressed." I look around. "This is your building?"

"Yes." He's grinning. God his teeth are perfect. His smile just pulls me.

"You don't work for anyone?" I smirk as he pulls me into his office. No wonder he laughed about my concern yesterday.

"No, people work for me," he confirms. I just nod as I walk to his windows.

I laugh, looking at the street below. "They look like ants from up here." I turn, smiling at him.

He is watching … I have no idea what he's thinking. "That's exactly what I say. Amelia, would you like a drink?"

He walks to his wet bar and fixes a gin on the rocks. "I'm good. So what is your big surprise?"

Quinton sips his gin looking at me. "Let me see your cell phone."

"What? Why?" I'm perplexed but hand it over anyway. "What are you doing?"

"I'm cutting your location off. You wouldn't want Eric tracking you."

"No, I don't." I toss my phone back in my bag. I can't believe I'm really doing this.

"Shall we go?" He grabs my luggage. I follow him out of his office to the elevator.

"I was going to tell Marcus and Gerry bye, but I didn't see them," I tell him as we shoot down the elevator. He's just smiling at me.

"May I hold your hand, Amelia?" I laugh; he wants to hold my hand.

"You may." I slip my hand in his. He grins, looking down at our hands. I let him lead me out of his office building, everyone knows him. *Damn, he must be important here.* He leads me towards a black limo.

"Mr. Starks." I hear the driver open his door.

"This is yours?" I ask him and he nods.

"Get in." I crawl in and see familiar faces smiling.

"What the hell is going on?" I gasp, grinning. Gerry, Marcus, Andy, Tierra, Michael, and Tina are all here. His gang!

"Amelia, I believe you already know everyone." Quinton gets in and grabs my hand, lacing our fingers. I have an emotion growing inside me. I don't know what it is: anxiety, excitement—perhaps a mixture of both. It's deep and fills my entire chest.

"There's a bar in your limo?" I gasp. "I've never seen anything like this." It's true, I've never seen anything like what I've seen in the last ten minutes; from the swooning service of my car being parked to this party limo.

"Here man." Andy hands Quinton his gin on the rocks with lime. I notice they all have cocktails.

"How can you drink and ride?" They laugh at me. "I'm serious."

"Relax, you're in a limo." Quinton grins as he leans forward. "Andy pour Amelia some moscato."

I take it. Mmm, the fruity sweetness makes my taste buds tingle. "Oh wow it's delicious." He grins, relaxing back. "Where are we going?"

"You'll see." He's tapping his thumb on his knee to the beat of the music Tierra turned has on. It's loud. I laugh, watching Tierra dancing from the waist up. This is their lifestyle—they seem completely relaxed.

"They all know, don't they?" I ask. He smugly nods.

"You look beautiful, really beautiful Amelia." I still cannot believe I'm doing this. It feels like a dream. Our eyes are pulled together like magnets. He strokes my cheek. I melt under his touch. *Shit!*

"What's this?" he asks looking at the small spot on my bottom lip. He softly brushed his thumb over it. He looks back to my eyes, I think he already knows the answer.

"It's fine." I touch his hand. He cuts his eyes to Michael and Andy. No one says anything.

"You don't have to ask to hold my hand," I whisper, all breathy. I don't think I can do this … keep a platonic friendship. I want more with him.

He drops that sexy ass smile. "Good." He brushes his lips across my knuckles. My breath hitches in my throat. I drop my eyes to our hands. His lips are soft and warm.

"You're out of moscato," he says, taking my glass. "Andy my man, Amelia needs topping." He's dancing his shoulders and playfully grinning as he hands my glass back. "I told you, I promised you a good time. You ready?"

"Yes," I breathe, sounding more seductive than I intended. I watch his eyes travel to my mouth.

"Good." I feel the limo stop. I look up as everyone is grabbing their drinks. The door opens and I follow Tierra.

"Thank you," I tell the driver who held my hand. I brush my hair out of my eyes, looking at the marina. I grin, spinning back towards Quinton. "We're going out on your boat?"

"Yeah." He naturally puts his hands on my hips, pulling me closer. "Come on." I follow him. His gang prances and struts down the dock, knowing exactly where they're heading—not admiring any of the boats.

My face is in awe as I walk, looking at the different sailboats. I can't believe he's taking me out on his boat. We're going sailing. "Mr. Starks," I hear as I look up. I gasp; we're standing in front the largest boat in the port.

"You okay Amelia?" Quinton turns at hearing my gasp. He turns back to the man without waiting for my response. "Captain," I hear him say as he starts walking me aboard.

"This must be Ms. Amelia." The captain knows my name. He smiles as he greets me. "Welcome to the Fortuna."

"Thank you." I smile as I follow Quinton. He's still lacing our fingers. I watch Tierra and Andy make themselves comfortable; Michael and Tina disappear down below. I have no idea where Gerry and Marcus ran off to. Everything is a blur as I take in my surroundings, looking at his boat. I laugh on the inside, *a boat my ass.* This is a yacht. I don't even hear what he's discussing with the captain.

I feel like I'm in a daze, walking around the upper deck, the outer deck has wrap around seating, tables, bars, a sun bed … a freaking pool! I look up and notice a shade. I walk into the first cabin, consisting of wrap around seating and dining table, bars, counters, and there are stairs that go down and turn. Which I'm being led down. I'm still amazed as I follow him. Another luxurious L-shaped sofa and sofa table with additional seating. It's a living room, there is a flatscreen and cabinets. "You okay?" He's grinning. "You haven't said anything."

I continue to follow him down another set of stairs, into the lower deck. This is a huge party space, with a full media center, another L-shaped sofa, more seating but extra large. His yacht screams sexy and lavishness. Nothing is lacking in anything, from what I've seen. It's abundant in rich woods and whites. Luxurious and modern collide into the perfect space. "Those doors." He points at the back wall. "That's the crew area." I nod and smile as he pulls me the opposite direction, up another set of stairs. He looks back at me. "Sleeping quarters."

I inhale as I follow him. I haven't really given that aspect much thought, which I know is absolutely insane. That should have been the first thought. I hear my angel side, reminding me I am married, while my sexy devil side is saying just go with it.

He opens the first closed door to the right. "This is your cabin. I hope you'll be comfortable. All the bedrooms have their own ensuite." I smile as I see my luggage already sitting in the bedroom.

"It's beautiful." The color scheme keeps with the rest of the boat. I touch the bedding.

"It's queen size." He's watching me. "You want me to show you the rest?"

"Yes," I whisper. Well, at least I know he's not expecting us to have sex. He put me in my own room. I haven't slept alone in forever. He holds out his hand for me. I naturally go to him.

190

"Andy and Tierra are in the room next to yours; Marcus and Gerry are across the hall. Michael and Tina are beside them." I follow him up another set of stairs at the end of the hall. "This is my quarters." I walk in with him. It's massive, and easily accommodates two with more than ample space. "Say something, you haven't said anything since you walked aboard."

He's watching me, waiting. I walk around, looking at his space. "I hardly think I would call this a sailboat." I smile as he smiles, almost looking like he's relieved. "You own a yacht!"

"Yes, she's mine." He smiles, looking around, pleased.

"You have a full crew." He's watching me. "I've never been on anything like this. Not even in my wildest dreams."

"Do you like it?" He grabs my hands, rubbing circles over my knuckles with his thumbs.

I laugh. "Seriously! What is not to love? It's absolutely gorgeous ... stunning." I watch him laugh. "How does someone afford such a lavish vessel? I mean you don't have to tell me, I'm just saying." I shut up.

"She was the first toy I bought when I hit millionaire status." He said that way too casually.

"Millionaire!" My shock is apparent.

"Hence why I named her the Fortuna." I squeak instead of speaking. He laughs, grabbing my hands. "Come, sweet Amelia let's join the others on deck. We're about to set sail."

I'm still speechless as I walk back up the stairs to the outside deck. Tina and Tierra have already changed into their swimsuits. I look around, everyone has changed into their desired boating attire. Thank god I bought some new beachy clothing.

"Toni, I think Amelia could use a cosmo," Quinton tells the bartender.

"I'd say." Tierra grins. "A lot to take in, isn't it?"

Quinton rolls his eyes. "She's fine. Aren't you Amelia?" He grins, sitting next to me, and handing me my drink. I lace our fingers, looking at him. *Sweet baby Jesus!*

"So where are we sailing to Mr. Starks?" I breathe. I cannot believe I'm actually on a yacht, going on a secret rendezvous, with a man ... that's not my husband!

"The Bahamas."

I titter, looking around, and feeling the yacht moving out into the water. "Really, we're going to the Bahamas?" He laughs as he watches me. I could kiss him ... but I can't.

"Pleased I take it, sweet Amelia."

"Okay you two, stop the googling eyes. Amelia, get your ass in your swimsuit." Tierra pulls me up. "Come on. Time to get this party going." She grabs my cosmo. *Oh wow, she's very demanding.* "Here lover boy." I laugh as she hands my drink to Quinton. "Tina, come."

"There goes some major mother fucking trouble." Gerry laughs, drinking his cosmo.

Chapter 20: Quinton

I hear the girls giggling and going up the stairs, while I change into my boating shorts. I grin as "I'm Yours" by Jason Mraz flood the stereo system. I look at my body, damn I'm sexy. I can't wait to see what she looks like in a bikini.

Andy and Michael are grinning when I hit the upper deck. I follow their eyes, *fuck me!* There she is: laying on the sundeck with Tierra and Tina. They're all on their stomachs, with their asses up. Hers is by far the hottest ass out there.

"Platonic friends," Michael reminds me, grinning as we stand admiring the women on the Fortuna. I scowl at him. "You're going to need a lot of these this week, my friend." I take my gin. *He has no fucking idea.*

I look at Gerry in his flaming speedo and laugh. "You really found a flaming speedo."

He swaggers over. "Man, there is all kind of fineness up on this yacht." He runs his hand down his chest, sipping his cosmo.

"I concur my friend." I toss my gin back looking at her: appreciating her body. "Her husband is a complete fucktard." I cut them a look.

"Her husband is the last thing on her mind." I look at Marcus as he walks up. We're all standing, watching over them, like prey.

"You're Quinton Starks. The ultimate playboy. I've never known you not to go after something you want." I look at Andy. They're all looking at me ... watching me ... admiring her.

"I've never crossed that line." I look at them. "She's married to another man."

"A douche. I think we determined that last night," Andy reminds me.

"A hot-headed douche," Michael adds.

"Like I said, hard and fast." I look at Gerry. Marcus is nodding ... grinning.

"I think that's both ways," Marcus adds. I just listen to them, watching her laugh. God she's beautiful.

"You're married. How would you feel if someone made the moves on your significant other?" I hear myself rationalizing his feelings. *His fucking feelings*!

"That would never happen. We're not hot-tempered douche bags. We don't treat our significant other like that. If she wasn't at least a little interested in you, she wouldn't be here right now." Andy makes a good point. Michael seems to agree. Marcus and
Gerry totally think I should just go all in.

"Her heart is out of that marriage. And was long before you walked into her life."

194

"God, Marcus you sound like a marriage therapist," I tease. "Don't bring your job on my yacht. You're supposed to be on vacation." I laugh remembering when Gerry told me he was dating a therapist. I teased him about finally seeking therapy. Marcus is a great marriage therapist—with good insight.

"It's my professional opinion, just go with it." Marcus grins. I look at my guys nodding in agreement. I can't believe I'm even having this internal battle. Her laughter brings me from my thoughts. That's the most beautiful sound I've ever heard.

She's looking around for me. I grin as her shades find me. She smiles and waves. "Go to her." Michael gently shoves me.

I walk over to Toni. "Another gin on the rocks and cosmo." My eyes are glued to her fantastic ass in that black bikini. I can't wait to see her tits. I'm not going to be able to keep my hands to myself. "Thanks Toni." I saunter towards her with our drinks. My body naturally moves and responds to music.

"Amelia from Amelia," I whisper holding her cosmo. She leans up about to speak when she sees me. Her mouth drops open in a crooked smile while her eyes dance with excitement. I know that look ... she appreciates my body probably as much as I do. I grin shaking her drink and bringing attention to my hand. "Something wrong?"

She clears her throat. "No." She rolls over into a sitting position taking her drink and sips it. Ah fucking hell her tits look fabulous in this damn black bikini. I let my eyes stroll down her body. I don't care if she notices. She's beautiful.

195

"You look sexy Amelia," I growl in a low voice. "I don't know how I'm going to keep my hands off you."

She smirks. "Well, then don't."

I smugly curl my lips into a smile. "What?"

She rolls back to her stomach. "Will you put some lotion on me?" She looks over her shoulder, smiling at me.

"Hell yes!" I grab her lotion. Her humming to my touch makes my cock hard. I'm going to die this week. I let my hands linger a little longer than necessary as I rub the back and inside of her thighs. I hear her breath catch. I grin, I know she's attracted to me. I can feel it in her body. She feels incredible beneath my fingers.

"Do you want me to put some on your shoulders?" she asks, leaning up. "I don't mind." She's grinning.

I hold out my hand, for her to take, after all we're on the open water—she could get a little off balance. I grin as I watch her lean up on her knees. I turn around, handing her the lotion. She scoots closer, I close my eyes as she rubs her hands over my shoulders. I can feel the fabric of her bikini top barely tracing my skin as she responds to Tierra while rubbing me down.

"All your muscles take a lot of lotion." She laughs as she squirts more. "All done!"

"With my back and shoulders." I grin looking at her. "You want to do my chest?" I hope she does, I want to feel her fingers on me. I stand up as she motions for me to turn around. She's still perched on her knees.

196

Her tight ass stomach flexed as she balances herself. She rubs her hands together as she grins, looking over me. I hear her breath catch in her throat as her fingers rub over my clavicle and pectorals. I watch her mouth open as she's intently stroking her fingers, massaging. She smiles looking up at me as she focuses on not missing a single inch. She feels every ripple and dip of my chest and six pack. *That's right baby, I have a V and you can feel it anytime.* "I'll do your arms." She grabs her lotion and rubs her hands up and down, watching it absorb into my biceps and my forearms. Thank god I worked out this morning. They're extra pumped. I look up, watching us being watched. I just smirk.

"You're very, um, built." I laugh at her. "You must take great pride in your body. I don't think you have any fat on you." She runs her fingers across my shoulders, and down my chest. We hit a small wave, and she shifts forward. I quickly grab her as she balances herself against me. She grins looking up, pushing herself steady. I just got a good feel of her body against mine.

"I do take great pride in it. Thirteen percent body fat to be exact," I admit. I look back at her readjusting herself on her stomach. I lean back relaxing, drinking my gin and listening to the music. I watch as Andy sneaks up on Tierra. He pours cold water over her ass.

She screams jumping up. "You ass!"

Amelia jumps like a scared kitten. She's not laughing. She looks at me and then back at them. She starts to smile as she takes in the scene.

Tierra springs off her mat chasing Andy. He's laughing as he pulls her into him and starts kissing her. I roll my eyes as she wraps her legs around him. Amelia is watching it all.

I lay down in her spot, turning on my side so I can look at her.

"What?" She's grinning at me.

"I can't believe you're really here." It's the truth.

She shyly grins at me. "Me either." She looks across the water. "It's beautiful … peaceful."

"I am glad you came."

"Me too!" She looks around. "Where are Michael and Tina?"

I give her a knowing smirk. "You're a grown woman, I'll give you one guess where they're gone to." I wiggle my eyebrows at her.

"Oh." She laughs, looking at me. "I guess that's where Andy carried Tierra off to then."

"Yep!" She's watching me. "What?" I'm grinning at her as my eyes troll her body.

"Why are you looking at me like that?" She laughs looking back out at the water.

"Like what … I'm just admiring." She doesn't say anything.

"How do you want me Mr. Starks? You can obviously have anyone you want. You would be quite a catch." She looks at me. "You have more than enough to offer anyone."

198

"I told you, I want you in my life any way I can have you."

"The way Tierra and Andy or Michael and Tina are right now?" She's looking at me, deadpan.

I sip my gin looking at her. Should I be honest like I typically am? "I didn't bring any condoms with me. I didn't expect that from you."

She nods looking across the water. She rolls over on her back. "You want to put more lotion on me?"

I grin. "I'd love to." She watches me as I take my time rubbing her legs, until the lotion absorbs. She bends her legs as I work up her thighs, watching her glasses. I get close to that little black bikini. She closes her eyes behind the lenses. I can see her heart pulsing in her neck. *Fuck, she wants me.* She opens her eyes watching me as I get more lotion. I rub my hands together before I cover her stomach. She flexes and giggles.

"Stop." She giggles, shifting as I run my fingers over her hips and ribs.

"That tickle Ms. Amelia?" I dig in a little more, tickling her —laughing with her. She's squirming and laughing beneath my fingers. *God she's beautiful.* She grabs my hands, lacing our fingers giggling a little as she watches me. That's the most beautiful sound. "I won't tickle you anymore." She looks suspicious as I grab the lotion. I rub my hands together and lotion her beautiful arms. I wish I could see those eyes without the shades. I massage lotion over her clavicle and down over the top of her cleavage. She sucks in from the surprise of my hands. I see her toes flex out of my peripheral vision. Her

199

breath hitches in her throat. "This okay Amelia?" I ask as I continue. I really want to dip my fingers under the black material, but I don't.

"Yes," she whispers, practically purring looking at me. I pull her shades off, so I can see her eyes. She's biting her lip as she grabs my hand, lacing our fingers. She's looking at my eyes and my mouth. She wants me to kiss her. I can feel her pulling me. I feel myself leaning and she's not stopping me. Her eyes are about to close. I can smell the coconut on her skin. I'm about to die.

"Amelia ... Amelia." I stop, leaning back. Gerry is walking towards us. I could kill him right now. He looks apologetic. She smiles up at him, seeing her bag in his hands. "Sorry, your phone has been going off constantly."

"Oh, thanks." She sits up.

Gerry mouths "sorry" as I scowl at him.

"Everything okay?" I ask as she holds her phone. It's not ringing now.

"I need to call Eric. He's called over ten times." She frowns, looking at her phone.

"Call him." I look at her. "Hey Gerry, cut the music. Make sure Tierra and Andy are quiet if they come back up." I nod at her.

She hits the missed call button and lays on her stomach with her phone on speaker in front of her.

"About fucking time," he barks when it stops ringing. I flinch at his tone. I see Andy and Tierra returning. "What is the fucking point of you having a damn phone if you're not going to answer it?"

"Eric, stop yelling at me. I didn't hear it ring." Amelia's body is tensing in front of me. She looks out over the water, closing her eyes. She's searching for strength, maybe some sort of patience to listen to his garbage. I want to break every fucking bone in his body.

"I need you to go into the study and look on my desk. I forgot a document. It's on top, scan and send it to me." Asshole needs something and totally expects her to do it after speaking like that.

She drops her head. "I'm not home right now." I look as we're all just listening, waiting to hear his response.

"Where are you?" She looks back at me, and jumps noticing everyone is listening. She grabs her phone and walks over to the cabin. I watch her as she hits the music back on. I laugh on the inside because she knows he hates this kind of music. "Amelia where the fuck are you?"

"I'm at the beach, working on my tan. I'll look for that document when I get home."

"You need to go now. Take your fucking ass to the house. You've got a pool you can tan in."

"Goodbye Eric!" She cuts the call. She looks at her phone for a minute. Then shuts it completely off. "Asshole," she

201

whispers. She grabs her bag and tosses it back inside. I watch her swish that cute ass by us going downstairs.

"What a fucking douche bag." Michael grabs another beer. "I told you he's a hot head."

"Tell the chef we're ready for lunch." I walk off in her direction.

"Where you going?" Gerry grins. "I told you she was a lioness." He curls his fingers at me.

"I'm going to grab me some fine ass, that's where; platonic off the table." I run down the stairs, and find her door is open. "You okay?"

"Yes, I'm sorry about that." She looks down. "I didn't realize we were going to be the entertainment for you all."

"Amelia," I sigh walking towards her. *Shit*. I don't want her to think that. "It's not like that. Tierra, Andy, Tina, Michael, Marcus, and Gerry, we're all so close knit, we don't keep secrets. We're like family here. They're accepting you into the family."

She sniffles looking up holding tears back. "Well I don't want them to pity me." I grab her, pulling her into my arms.

"That's one thing you won't get. They think he's a douche!" I love her body against mine. She wraps her fingers around my back, her face is pressed into my chest.

"You're hot," she breathes into me. I laugh, I know I am. "No, I mean hot from the sun." She sniffles a laugh.

"Oh." I laugh. "Well, damn, guess I need to up my work-outs then. Here all this time I felt pretty confident in my body."

She laughs hard. *There's that beautiful laugh.* She's relaxing back into me, *good.*

"Well, you definitely have a hot bod, but you know this." *Yeah I do.*

I lace our fingers. She looks at them, before looking up at me. "Come on let's have some lunch. Don't let him ruin your time." I refuse to let him ruin my time with her. She nods.

Chapter 21: Amelia

I'm completely embarrassed as we walk out. They're all looking at me with questions, but not saying anything. The sideboard is covered with trays of food.

Tierra sashays over to me. "Here, take this shot."

"What is it?" I grin and ask her.

"Does it matter?"

I shrug. "I guess not." I take the pretty blue glass and toss it back.

She laughs. "It's a Chuck Norris—you badass little lioness. Gerry's right: you're a lioness." She hugs me. "Forget him. No man should talk to any woman that way." I nod. She grabs my hand, whooping as she shakes her derriere walking to the sun deck. "We're here to have fun." I laugh watching her breaking it down to the music.

I turn around. Gerry is pumping his hips out in a fucking motion, he's bringing another shot. "Shoot it." He wraps his arms around my shoulders as he puts the shot to my lips. I toss it back ... shaking my head.

"That's disgusting!" I gasp patting my chest. "What was that?"

Quinton laughs wrapping his arm around my waist. "It called liquid cocaine. Come on, let's eat some lunch before you start shooting anymore shots." He leads me back to the covered deck, his hands sliding around my stomach and back as he walks. The shots are already warming my tummy.

Andy calls for his wife, "Tierra, bring your beautiful body in here to eat." Andy grins as he watches her and Gerry grinding on one another—they're flirtatiously playful.

"Amelia, relax and have fun!" Quinton tells me as he gives me a plate, "Come on. I had the chef prepare you some oysters."

"Really?" I grin as he smiles at me. There's surf and turf selections; all sorts of veggie sides and fruits. "This is a crazy amount of food, Mr. Starks."

He laughs. "When are you going to start calling me Quinton?"

I shrug as I let my fingers run across his lower back. "I don't know ... I will think about it." I'm being flirtatious, I know it. I know Eric is boiling mad. I know he can't come home because of work and he has no way of finding me on a yacht headed to the Bahamas.

I follow Quinton to the dining table, scooting all the way down the bench seat. Toni brings me a fresh cosmo. I've never drank this much in a day. I hope they don't suffer from liver disease one day.

"Open your mouth." Quinton's holding an oyster Rockefeller with hot sauce. I open my mouth as his eyes study my lips. He places the oyster on the tip of my mouth and I tilt my head back. "I wanted to feed you at my club that night." I grin at his confession.

"I wanted you to," I whisper. Shit, I have no idea where that acknowledgement came from. He grins looking at me. I watch everyone else sit down.

"You two are cute together," Tina blurts out. I grin at her. I don't say anything. We're not really together. The reality is, we can't be. I'm living a dangerous fantasy. Eric will never let me go.

"Tina," Michael warns.

"What? They are."

"Oh wow!" I grin, turning and hanging over the side rail … a pair of dolphins are soaring along the side of the boat. "Look at them. They're beautiful." They're not overly interested …

I jump and gasp, looking over my shoulder at Quinton resting his big hands on my derriere. I hear them laughing.

"You can't shake this in my face." He laughs as he pops it softly. "It's practically naked." I turn red as I scoot back to a sitting position. "You can ask Andy, if Tierra shakes it in my face, I will smack it."

"It's true." Tierra rolls her eyes as she bites her lobster tail. "Quinton has never had a girlfriend, so he's always been a terrible flirt. We feed off each other."

"Yeah they do." Tina laughs. "You'll see Amelia, we all flirt and play. But we all know where our boundaries lie. That's

206

something you never have to worry will be crossed by any of us."

"I'm envious of you all having such a close relationship." I look down at my plate. "I don't have anything like this with anyone."

"Yeah you do." I look up as Tierra reaches her hand out touching mine. "You got us. We all like you." I laugh as I sip my cosmo. "I'm serious girl, we're here for you. You got a group in your corner now."

"Tierra you're getting too deep for lunch," Tina teases. "She gets it. We like her and we hope she likes hanging with us." I laugh as Tina rolls her eyes. "We have no secrets, so you're going to have to open up about this marriage disaster."

"Oh wow!" I exhale as I grin taking a bite of lobster. "Well, no secrets, huh? This is my first time on a group trip, yacht, or eating lobster." They laugh at me. "I'll keep the deep shit for when we're not eating, how about that?" I tease looking at Quinton. His friends have accepted me! I'm going to spill it and get it off my chest. This will be the first time in my life.

Quinton laughs. "Oysters were a first for her too. That weekend I went down to check out the new club location I took her to lunch."

I smile looking at his eyes. "Yes, another first with you!" God he really is quite sexy. I wish this could be permanent. Him! His gang! I exhale as I grab my cosmo.

"Can you let me out?"

207

He grins, shaking his head as he stands. "You okay?"

"Yeah I just need some air." I walk to the outer deck and relax on one of the lush sofas. He's watching me. *I need some air, what the hell?* I'm on a damn yacht. That's all I have ... air! I smile as Toni brings a fresh cosmo. "Oh thanks!"

Well, I succeeded in holding his attention with this bikini, it was good choice. I've never pranced around uncovered in a swimsuit before today. My mind is reeling with everything.

I walk downstairs and grab my bag. *Shit* twenty miss calls. His texts are as ugly as his words. I don't delete them, I've got ten years of it saved: text messages, voicemails. Our marriage is a disaster, Tina hit the nail on the head. If it wasn't broken all ready, I wouldn't be here. I've already emotionally checked out. It's an empty shell of people walking through the emotions, about like the shell that I exist in, when I am with him.

I grin thinking about Quinton rubbing me with lotion, tickling me, and laughing together. I look at my fingers, they've been intertwined with his all day—another man's! A man I am not married to. I wanted him to kiss me today and would've been powerless to stop it. My body wants him; my lips want to explore him. Holy sweet baby Jesus, I'm truly turned on. I cannot remember the last time I felt desire. I'm really falling for him and cannot act on these emotions. We cannot do anything other than flirtatious banter. I hate being married.

I need to call Eric before it gets too late. I lay a towel on top of the bedding before I plop down on my stomach. Inhaling I press Eric's name. I hate his face right now. His phone rings and I get his voicemail. I hang up.

"Knock. Knock," Quinton says. "You sure you're okay?" He's so careful how he studies me.

"Yeah." I look up, laying across the towel.

He laughs tugging it. "What's this?"

"A towel," I tease. He rolls his eyes. "I didn't want to get sunscreen on your bedding."

"You're funny Amelia. Trust me, I'm not worried about it." He plops down on the foot of the bed. "Calling Eric?"

"Yeah." I show him the missed calls. "I wanted to clear it up with him before I get to many drinks in my system." He just nods as he rubs his palms together. "What are you thinking?"

"About you." He laughs. "I like you, Amelia. Really like you." I turn on my side so I can see him. "I want so much with you and I've never wanted it before. Tina wasn't joking up there; I don't have girlfriends. I don't even date." He's looking at me, strolling his eyes over my body. "I don't want to be just your friend." There it is, his affirmation of what he really wants.

"You can have anyone you want. Why are you interested in some married scullery maid?" I tease.

"Scullery maid; you're funny Amelia." He chuckles, looking up at the ceiling.

"I am serious. Why are you interested in some married lady? Is it because I'm off the market; the thought of conquering forbidden fruit?"

"What? No!" I watch him spring off the bed. I stand too. He's looking at me. "I dreamt of you. I can't explain it, but I dreamt of you … before we ever met. You were mine. We were perfect. Then when I met you …" he pauses, shaking his head, "you knocked the wind out of me. Every day since has started and ended with you! Then I dream about you." He closes the gap between us—sliding his hands around my waist —pulling me towards him. "I don't know what to do about it."

"I've dreamt of you too." Even I can hear my seductive tone. "You were in my dreams for weeks before you walked into my inn." I look up at him. "I don't know what we can do about this. I am married."

"Do you still love him?"

Now there's a simple question. "No."

"Leave him." I stare at him. I wish it was that easy.

"He won't give me a divorce. That was one of our fights recently." I touch my lip thinking about it all.

"He can't stop you from leaving him. He can't force you to stay." He's now sitting me down on the bed. "I know I can't tell you what to do."

I lace our fingers, rubbing his hand. "Can we please just have a good time? I've had the best day of my life with you. I don't want to stress over this."

"I'm just letting you know, I'm not promising I'm going to play nice. I see you. I want you. Bottom line."

"I've never cheated on anyone in my life. But I …" I jump when my phone rings. "It's Eric."

"Do you want me to leave?"

"No, you don't have to. Just be quiet." I eye him as he pretends to zip his smug mouth. He lays back on my bed lacing his fingers behind his head. He has no shirt and he looks hot. I click the speaker.

"Hello." He's watching me and I'm watching him. Can I have an affair? I certainly want to see what happens with him.

"Amelia I've been calling you," I hear Eric's pukeage voice.

"I turned my phone off."

"You hung up on me."

"You were yelling at me. I wasn't going to listen to it."

"Are you home?" I look at Quinton.

"Why?" I shake my head. "Where do you think I would be?"

"I need you to go look on my desk for that paper. It should be on top."

"Ok." I sit right where I'm at looking at Quinton. I mute my phone and crawl towards him. He releases his hands. I rub my hand down his chest as I feel him wrap his arm around me cuddling into his body. He feels good. I unmute my phone and lay it on his chest.

"I don't see it."

211

"Well, it should be there. I don't have it."

"I don't know, there's nothing on your desk." I troll my fingers across his stomach. He's grinning, biting his bottom lip. I shrug and smile.

"Fuck. I don't know where it would be then." I'm not really listening, Quinton is lacing our fingers again. I'm tingling in my bikini bottoms. "Well, what are you doing tonight?" he asks me.

"Turning my music up loud and dancing since you're not in the house. You hate it when I do. So it's the perfect time." Quinton rolls his eyes as our fingers are laced. I hold my breath as he kisses the back of my hand softly. I shift, resting my leg on his.

"Yeah I do." Eric laughs. "I'll be late Sunday."

"That's fine. Don't rush back."

"You don't even care I'm not there." I roll my eyes.

"Let's just say I'm using this time to put things into perspective." Quinton is nibbling my fingers.

"Perspective? Don't try to get any fucking ideas Amelia." Quinton stops kissing my fingers. "I already told you, divorce isn't an option. You can get that out of your damn head. You're mine."

I grin watching Quinton. He really isn't playing, nice nibbling the back of my hand and fingers like I'm an ice cream.

"I've got another call," Eric tells me. "I love you. I'll talk with you later." Quinton stops his teasing.

"Okay, bye." I hang up. I look at my phone, shutting it completely off.

"Perspective?" Quinton growls. "How's this for perspective Amelia?" He's on me in a flash digging and tickling across my hips, ribs, and stomach. "I love to hear you laugh." We're laughing as I'm wiggling away. "It's the most beautiful sound I've ever heard."

"Stop," I scream laughing. "Stop. I can't breathe." He's laughing and not stopping.

"How's this for perspective? I want to make you laugh for the rest of your life!"

"Oh ... my ... God, Quinton Starks is smitten." Tierra laughs. We stop laughing and look towards her voice. Quinton grins as he pushes off me, pulling me up with him.

"We want some water time, it's hot as Hades out there." Tierra smirks as she watches us. "You two are too cute. Tina might have melted if she walked in on that."

"Well, let's go play." Quinton kisses Tierra on the cheek as he pops my butt before he runs out. I laugh at him.

"I told you, he's a big flirt and a big kid. Boys and their toys." Tierra wraps her arm through mine. "Come on, let's get another drink."

Chapter 22: Quinton

Amelia is watching the crew set up the floating trampoline. Her ass felt amazing against my hand. Fucktard is out the door. I'm going to make that my personal mission.

"Tierra said she found you two pretty cozy." I looked at Andy. "You going to hit it tonight?"

"You going to hit that fine piece of ass you're married to?" I grin looking at him. He smirks as we're watching them. "I didn't bring anything. I didn't want to have something and her assume I was expecting it."

Andy laughs. "Well, I certainly don't have anything. Tierra has one of those IUDs. No babies. No weight gain like the pill or shot."

"I wasn't asking, I think I'm just going to see how it plays out." I smile looking at him. "She called his ass."

"Oh, was he a shit?"

"Somewhat, he would have been livid if he knew I was laying beside her." He laughs. "I dig her."

"About damn time, we all 'dig her' as you put it." I turn as Michael joins. "Here ... thought you might need a gin on the rocks." I nod and drink it.

"Look at Gerry in his speedo with her, he's a terrible flirt. Thank god he swings the other way."

I walk over to the sound system. "We need music and booze." I turn it up loud. She looks up and I point my finger for her to come to me. "Look at the way she moves." I grin looking at Andy and Michael. I see the appreciation on their faces.

"Dance with me." I pull her into me. I've got my gin in one hand and she's in my other. We're swaying to "Slow Dance" by AJ Mitchell. My eyes are closed, and she's lost in my arms. I'm never letting her go. I can't go back to the way it was.

When I open my eyes, we're all dancing to this song. Marcus and Gerry are a hoot to watch. Gerry in his speedo and Marcus in speedo shorts. Marcus is definitely more conservative. The captain comes up and tells me the swim deck and trampoline are ready.

Another song comes on, and she's pulling me back to her. She's not ready to stop. I grin as I watch her turn out of my hands. She's slinging her hair, arms in the air, hips moving. Tierra and Tina join in, sandwiching her. Damn her seductive eyes are looking at me. I motion for Toni to get us a round of shots.

"That's hot." Michael grins watching.

"Yeah it is." Andy snaps a picture with his phone.

"Send it to me," I tell him as I watch. "They don't even need us to dance." I look at Gerry and Marcus with them. The song ends and another starts. "Shots," I yell.

"Here." I give Amelia a tequila and lime. I wait for everyone else to get theirs. "On three: one ... two ... three." We toss it. She's cute with her face scrunched up. "Lime," I remind her. She's laughing as she sucks the lime. I grab her and suck her neck gently. She gasps, looking at me. I just grin.

She grabs my hand. I watch her ass swish as she heads to the bar. "Toni, two more shots please. Well, make it three."

"Here." She gives me a shot and lime. "Go." I grin as we toss the shot and bite the lime together. She grabs and sucks my neck, just below my ear.

"Fuck," I growl as I pull her hair aside and suck her neck, kissing down towards her clavicle. "Who gets the last shot?" I whisper against her skin.

She laughs and tosses the shot, then bites the lime. She strums her fingers up and down my chest. She moans as she softly licks and sucks my neck, near my clavicle.

"If you don't want me to take you downstairs and do really naughty things to you, I suggest you stop," I growl as I watch her. My cock is rock hard.

"You wouldn't dare, Mr. Starks." Is she teasing me?

"Oh yes I would, sweet Amelia."

"You've got a crowd watching."

"That won't fucking stop me. They know how I am. How I can be."

Her seductive eyes looks up at me. "Really?" She's grinning.

I swoop her off her feet and carry her to the lounge sofa. She's laughing and scooting back. She's a playful vixen. I crawl on her, tickling her hips and ribs. "You want to tease me?"

I'm lost in her teasing me. I kiss her neck, traveling up towards her ear. I hear her moan. Her fingers lace in my hair. Damn she's got the perfect body.

She's beautiful. I'm leaning over her; her lips are so close. I don't want to kiss her for the first time with a production crew. I feel them watching and grinning. "Y'all can go to the water," I yell. My eyes are pinned on her.

"This is much hotter," Gerry purrs. "Y'all don't mind us. We'll just watch and drink."

She laughs. "I like your lips Mr. Starks." She wiggles out of my grasp. I think she's drunk. I watch her walk to the captain. I don't know what she's asking. He's showing her the sonar.

"Hard and Fast," Gerry gushes. I don't even try to deny it. "That Lioness is a feisty little thing, isn't she? I didn't see her teasing you like that."

"I think she's a little inebriated." Michael laughs. "Good, maybe she'll relax and have a good time."

I laugh as she walks by with Tierra and Tina. "Where you going sweet Amelia?"

"They're going to the swim deck." Andy follows with a drink in hand.

217

"Toni, a round of drinks," I tell him as I follow.

She's jumping on the trampoline. "Have you ever done this before Amelia?" I yell watching from the swim deck.

"No." She laughs. "Well, not in the water." She does a back flip off.

"What the fuck?" I laugh as I look at the guys.

"Yeah girl," Tierra screams. She jumps off.

I hold my hand out as Amelia climbs up on the swim deck. She adjusts her swimsuit. I watch her as she wipes her face. She's like a kid.

"Having fun?"

"Yes, I feel silly. I haven't done anything like this in years."

I run and jump onto the trampoline. I do a backflip.

"You going to wait for me?" she screams. I nod. *She better believe it.*

I watch her get into a gymnast stance, she starts doing a walk-over, over and over until she walks off. *Damn she's bendy.* She's laughing when I pull her up to me. "You're hot!"

"You're not too bad yourself, Mr. Starks." We're treading water together as one. She's perfect for me. We see Andy and Michael doing double flips. "Showoffs," she yells.

She's laughing when she sees Gerry and Marcus floating on a pink flamingo. "Gerry are you not going to get wet?" she asks.

"Y'all white folks are crazy. You're asking to be a meal for a shark." Gerry looks around the water for fins.

218

"The captain has a sonar," she tells him. I laugh, that's what she was asking him about.

"You want a drink? I see Toni bringing you one." Andy helps her up, while I get a nice view of her ass.

She takes her cosmo and goes back to the sun lounge she started off on this morning. I follow her like a little puppy. Her hair is as dark as mine sleek and wet. She's completely relaxed, drink in hand, tapping her foot to the music. Her sapphire eyes sparkling against my boat. I am lost.

"You having a good time so far?"

"Yes." She looks at me, smiling. "My face actually hurts. I haven't smiled this much in a long time."

I relax back, bending one arm behind my head. "You wanna lay here and watch the sun set together?"

"Yes," she purrs softly. I feel her hand reach for my forearm—strolling her fingers up and down. She has no idea how sexy she is. "Thank you," she whispers.

"For what?" Our eyes meet.

"For waking me up … making me feel something again." She softly smiles before she looks out at the horizon.

Chapter 23: Amelia

I took a lukewarm shower this evening. I don't want to replace his touch with heat. His confession make me grin—he wants more—he wants more with me! I slip a black mini strapless dress on.

Knock! Knock!

"It's open."

"Don't you look ravishing!" His voice melts me.

"Oh my," I whisper, "you're very sexy." I drool over his nautical printed navy button down short sleeve shirt and distressed khaki shorts. The shirt hangs loose around his six pack but is fitted around his biceps. He smells amazing.

"You ready for dinner? I hope you're hungry. Chef is serving in the closed dining cabin. It can get a little chilly in the evening on the water."

"Yes."

"Looking good." Andy grins as he kisses me on my cheek when we walk in. They really are all terrible flirts. Marcus and Gerry are standing by the bar talking. Tierra and Tina are lounging on the white L-shaped sofa, sipping their cocktails, wearing really skimpy dresses. Tierra has a beautiful body and knows it. Michael greets him with his gin and lime in hand as soon as we walked in. They know him so well.

I walk to the bar and Toni immediately slides me a cosmo. "Thank you!" He nods making quick eye contact before he returns to wiping the bar.

Gerry wraps his arm around my waist and kisses me on each cheek. "You really are a vision, Lioness."

"I love your style," I admit looking at him. "You're one snappy dresser."

"Yes, he likes to dress … expressively." Marcus walks up running his fingers up and down Gerry's back. Marcus is dressed more conservatively. "How are you doing Amelia?" he asks as he leans over kissing my cheeks; his tone reminds me of a shrink.

"I'm having a great time." I sip my cosmo. I really am, I can't believe this is real. I skim the room, seeing the table prepared for a sit-down meal. Quinton is across the room, smiling at me. He's really handsome. His smile makes me tingle under my dress.

"I bet you didn't think you would be partying with us on a yacht when we met." Gerry grins as he wraps his arm around me. "I told you my boss was great. I just didn't tell you what a fine-ass man he is."

"He's a good man," Marcus confirms.

"Marcus what do you do? I know Gerry is Quinton's assistant and a dear friend." I smile at him. He toasts his cosmo to mine before he drinks.

"I'm a marriage therapist." He smirks at me. *Oh fudge*!

I gasp. "You've got to be kidding me." My shock is evident. "Really? A marriage therapist?" He's the devil's advocate. Is this a sign I should be 'working' on my marriage? I really feel deflated.

He laughs. "I know, I don't fit the norm for a marriage therapist: a gay man."

"No, that's not it at all." I feel horrible now. "It's not your sexuality at all. I'm sure you're a wonderful therapist. You don't lack the sensitivity that most males do. I'm sure you can see both sides of a marriage with issues, very clearly." I take a sip. "Here I'm married to someone and I'm on a yacht with all of you. While my husband isn't." Shit, I feel like he's going to be in my head. Maybe he's already been in my head.

"I'm not working this week." He winks. "I'm not going to pick your words apart and come up with an opinion on your marital status."

"Oh." I feel sort of disappointed. "You don't have any thoughts, generally speaking, from your years of experience?" I grin. I definitely don't want to get into a counseling session.

"Thoughts?" He's smirking at me. "About why you're here?" I nod carefully, not sure if I really want to know his thoughts. Does he think I'm bad person? I am a bad person. I shouldn't be flirting with Quinton, he's not my husband.

"Quite frankly, Amelia, you're here because you're in a toxic marriage. You're physically married to this man, but your heart and mind left it years ago. I suspect something happened, something big that changed the way you saw him. Sometimes women find it easier to stay in toxic marriages for different reasons, especially if emotional abuse is present. I definitely see the signs of verbal abuse, which turns emotional and eventually emotional will turn physical."

"Oh," I whisper as I listen. Does he think I'm a bad person? He probably thinks I'm the reason our marriage is toxic.

"It's a cycle. Some days are good. Fine perhaps, but at some point in the day, a fight happens. Now I'm not saying couples don't fight or shouldn't, but it shouldn't be every day and over every single topic." I drop my head, looking at my drink, boy he's insightful. I look up when I hear Quinton's voice.

"You okay?" he questions with his hand on the small of my back. His eyes are looking at all of us.

"Yes, Amelia and I were discussing her marriage. She just realized I was a marriage therapist." Quinton looks at me, curiosity brewing. I can see it in his face. I smile between the two of them. "Do you want me to continue?" I hear Marcus ask.

"Maybe we should hold these deep conversations, until after dinner," Quinton suggests. "Chef is ready to serve dinner. Let's eat." I nod as he walks us to our seat. "I could feel your tension." I look at him. "Are you okay?"

"Yes, although I'm curious what Marcus thinks of me being here ... now that I know he's a marriage therapist. Aren't they usually advocates for keeping a marriage together?"

"He's in the practice of making happy marriages. Not keeping two miserable souls confined to one another for the sake of their vows. He's good at pointing out incapability and helping find a solution." He sits once I take my seat. "You look beautiful." He leans over and softly brushes his lips on my cheek. "Relax, enjoy your dinner."

The steward places a small caprese salad in front of all our seats. It looks delicious. I do love balsamic reductions.

"Everyone enjoy their day?" Quinton asks the table as he grins. He knows we all have. "We will be at sea all day tomorrow, and should port at Nassau Friday morning. We'll explore during the day, maybe hit a club before leaving. Saturday morning we'll port at Freeport and play. Then we will arrive back at Jacksonville Sunday."

"Hell yeah." Tierra holds her drink up. They all do. I'm the last to join the toast. I watch the steward take my empty plate away. Once the table is cleared, the stewards bring our main course: herb crusted lamb on couscous with spring vegetables and a drizzle of the same balsamic reduction.

I don't eat lamb, but don't want to be rude. I nibble around the lamb, tasting the couscous and vegetables. Delicious! I feel Quintin's eyes as I look up. "Is something wrong?" He's grinning, watching me.

"No." I smile as I pick around the lamb.

"You're picking at your dinner. You don't like lamb?"

"I don't eat lamb." I shyly smile. "The vegetables and couscous are tasty though."

"Your face looks at that piece of lamb as if it's vile." I titter looking at him. "This won't do." He immediately throws his hand up and the steward rushes to his aid.

"Sir?"

"Yes, have Chef prepare Ms. Amelia something else. She doesn't eat lamb. My apologies to him."

"No, no." I touch his forearm. "It's fine. I can eat around it. It's no trouble. I don't want a fuss made about it."

"Amelia you will eat. And it will be something you enjoy." He smiles, and looks at me. "Filet mignon?"

"You don't have to have your chef prepare me something different." He smirks at my comment and turns to the steward.

"Have chef prepare the herb crusted filet mignon. She was pleased with the sides, fresh plate." I watch as the steward rushed away. "It will only be a few minutes."

"Quinton aims to please, Amelia. So you might as well get use it, if you're going to stick with our boy!" Michael laughs as he takes a bite of lamb. "I don't understand why you don't like lamb. Quinton's chef prepares the most delectable lamb."

I want to gag, but I manage to smile. "You like having a personal chef?" I ask Quinton.

He grins. "Of course. I don't cook Amelia, nor do I pretend to want to be good at it. I like my food prepared for me. I'd rather enjoy being with you, like today, while our food is being handled by a professional. Someone who enjoys doing such things." I laugh at him. "This was my oversight, Amelia. So no Mai Mai or lamb."

My voice hitches a little, "How do you know I don't eat Mai Mai?"

"The night at my club, I overheard Eric's remark at the table while you were eating the oysters." He grins. "I filed that useful tidbit of information away."

"Chef would like you to taste it, to make sure it is cooked to your liking," the steward tells me as he places my new dinner in front of me. He stands so formal, waiting.

"Oh," I whisper as I cut it. It slices beautifully. I smile at Quinton as I take a bite. It's like velvet on my tongue. I literally have died and went to heaven. It's better than any orgasm I've had in ten years. I close my eyes, and do a little dance in my seat, humming to the taste.

"I take it you like it," Quinton whispers in my ear.

I look at him, grinning and watching me. The steward is still waiting for confirmation. "Oh yes. It's absolutely delicious. I haven't had an orgasm in ten years this good." I take another bite as everyone bursts into laughter. I pinched my lips into a firm line—as the steward had hard time keeping a straight face. *Maybe I should have kept that to myself.*

"Should I tell him that ma'am?" He's serious.

Everyone is watching me. I shrug, *Might as well. Once again I blurted something out.* "Yes."

"Add it's only because she hasn't been with me," Quinton quips. I look at him, he's grinning, eating his dinner.

"Lioness," Gerry growls.

"So my chef pleased you more than any orgasm in the last ten years," he teases looking into my eyes. I blush, even more embarrassed. "I do love sex talk."

I gasp looking at him. "Mr. Starks!" He's incorrigible. He's not even quiet about it.

"We should totally share sex stories," Tina pipes up.

"Yeah we should, it will get us in the mood." Michael starts nibbling on her neck.

"You two are always in the mood," Andy smarts.

"And you two aren't?" Michael questions. Lord have mercy, what have I started?

"Sweet Jesus this yacht is going to be rocking and it won't be from the waves," Gerry gushes as he sips his cosmo.

Marcus and I just look at each other. He's laughing on the inside, hidden behind that smirk.

"We told you Amelia, no secrets between any of us," Tierra confirms as she trolls her fingertips over Andy's forearm.

"Okay." I grin looking down. "I'm just going to eat my orgasmic piece of beef." I put another bite in my mouth.

"She has no idea of the pun," Michael remarks. I hear them laughing.

"I'm not even going to bite," I remark keeping my face down.

"Oh damn, I wouldn't mind those beautiful teeth sinking into my shoulders," Quinton quips. I gasp a squeak looking up at him.

Our entrée part of dinner passed rather quickly with constant sex banter. I smile as the steward smirked at me grabbing my plate. "Chef said he's glad he could oblige."

"Oh hell." I laugh sitting back. Quinton laughs at the comment. I smile as I watch the stewards strategically place dishes of chocolate covered strawberries. Four to be exact, one dish between each couple. Quinton is grinning as I look at him. A few minutes later, stewards return carrying a dark chocolate lava cake, topped with a raspberry reduction and crème for each of us. "Wow this is a beautiful dessert."

"It's flourless. Tierra doesn't like flour cakes, she worries she will look bloated." I laugh at him roll his eyes.

"I'm excited to try it. I've never had a flourless cake."

He grins holding a strawberry. "Open that beautiful mouth." God, he sounds so sexy—breathy.

I open my mouth and close my eyes as he slowly graces my lips with the fruit. It is the best tasting strawberry. "Mmmm." I open my eyes as I suck my bottom lip. His eyes are intense watching my mouth, like he could devour me.

"More," he whispers. I watch him as he takes another one, and again he feeds me. I close my eyes, savoring the bite. How does he make eating feel seductive?

"Open," I whisper. He grins as he does. I tease his lips with the strawberry, pulling back. He starts to laugh. "You want this Mr. Starks?" I purr, touching his forearm.

"Very much." He groans looking down my body and then back at the strawberry.

"Open then," I whisper as I feed him. I smile watching him chew. Damn he's sexy, kissing my fingertips and never breaking our eye contact.

I'm throbbing between my legs. *Wet!* I've never been wet —my body wants him. I want his breath on my lips. He's looking at my eyes, slowly dropping to my lips.

"Damn it's getting steamy." Gerry breaks my trance. Quinton looks at me, watching my lips as I lean back. I see him shoot Gerry a scowl.

"Dumb ass Gerry," Tierra hisses, "you ruined the moment."

I take a deep breath as I grab my cosmo. What the fuck was that? I've never wanted to kiss another person this badly in my life. I actually hurt between my legs for him. My lace panties are wet. My body is freaking me out, betraying me. The clear line between right and wrong has blurred; there's no more black and white in my life, it's gray. I see a man I'm absolutely smitten with; I want to feel his skin and breath against me. The only thing that's stopping me is a damn piece of legal paper. If it burned in a fire, then there would be nothing. The evidence I'm married would be gone. I've never thought of myself as a cheating woman, as a cheater!

I've got to get out of my own head. I pick up my fork and take a bite. Holy hell, this is delightful. I look up, Quinton is watching me. I lower my eyes back to my lavish dessert. He's quite stimulating. I feel him take my hand and lace our fingers as he smiles while talking to Andy. I sit quietly gazing at our fingers intertwined, his thumb is running circles over the back of my hand. He's completely relaxed. Eric hasn't ever touched me so tenderly in the entire time I've known him.

"Excuse me." I release my hand from his. *I need air*. I want to cross that line and when we do, what's next? I walk outside on the deck. It's not too chilly. I inhale the crisp salty smell of the ocean. The stars look like a bazillion shattered diamonds— not a cloud in the sight. I lean over the railing looking at the dark sea illuminated only by the moon.

"Beautiful, isn't it?" Quinton asks.

"Yes, lovely," I whisper looking into the night sky.

I close my eyes as I feel his hand graze the small of my back and turn into him. He wraps both arms around me. He doesn't ask me what's wrong or if I'm okay. He starts swaying like he's got a song in his head. We walk, holding hands, to the deck, where we've been dancing and drinking all day. He clicks on the song he wants.

He curls me into his chest as the music fills the quiet, "Not Ready" by Kensington Moore. He holds me tight and we dance, without speaking. I close my eyes, with my head on his chest. I can hear his heart beating behind his wall of solid perfection. His body is beyond anything I've ever imagined I would get to touch.

The deck is illuminated by few tinkling boat lights. The song ends, yet we're still dancing. "Quinton, I lose my mind around you," I whisper looking up.

"You're beautiful," he whispers as he kisses the top of my head.

I shake my head pulling away. "This is what I mean. I can't think clearly. I want nothing more than to fall ..."

"Fall ... I'll catch you!"

"... But it doesn't change the fact I'm married. And I've loved these little touches. You need someone not already attached."

"I need you." I shake my head, about to speak. "Amelia, you're just scared."

Terrified actually. "And what if I am right ... that you decide that I'm not ..."

"Shhhh." Quinton shakes his head pulling me back against his chest. "Amelia, don't say that. I've been searching for you ... subconsciously that's probably why I've never wanted to settle down. I knew no one else was the one."

"I'm not this person ... one who steps out on someone." I slide my hands up his chest, wrapping them around his neck. "But when you look at me like this ... and your touches ... I want you."

He smiles looking at my lips. "You know I want you ... anyway I can I have you. So if you're married for now, so be it!"

God what am I doing? is all I'm thinking as our desire is pulling us closer. We're about to kiss ... he's leaning in. *I do want to taste his lips.* I lace my fingers through the back of his hair—coaching him towards me—or maybe he's doing the coaching. The gap between our lips has dissipated. I feel the heat from his breath. My lips part, and my chest is about to explode with an energy of excitement, nerves, desire.

"Quinton!" *You have got to be joking,* I tell myself as I hear Gerry's voice. "Tierra said come on …" he stops talking as he sees the situation, that he once again messed up. "The game and shots are ready."

"I'm going to kill him," Quinton whispers. I can feel the vibrations of his words on my lips. His breath warmed my lips, *Thanks to Gerry that is all that warmed them.*

I step back. "No, you can't live without him. Remember."

"I might be reevaluating that theory," he growls looking at Gerry. "Really, Gerry, your timing is impeccable." His words drip with sarcasm. I giggle under my breath as I lace our fingers.

Gerry smirks as he eyes me. "Lioness."

We walk down the steps and take our seats around the table. I see about twenty shots in the center and a quarter. "Okay, so we all know each other, but the newbie." Tierra beams as she's prancing around. I roll my eyes, *the newbie.*

"We're going to play a little game to get to know Amelia. So basically Amelia, we each flip the coin, you call it. If you're right no question, you get to take a shot—or sip your drink because you can get drunk really fast doing this. If you're wrong, we take the shot or sip and ask you a personal question. We'll move right around the table. When it's your turn to flip, same thing applies, and you can choose who you want to ask a question. If the question is too personal to answer then you have to take a shot."

"Let's do it." I grin as I get comfortable in my seat.

"Good!" She hits the music on.

"Amelia, you don't have to share anything you don't wish to." I look at Quinton. "They can be a little intrusive."

"Curious." Tierra smirks. "We can be a little curious of this new lioness. I'll go first." She flips the coin. "Call it."

"Heads."

She grins and grabs a shot. I roll my eyes shaking my head. "Tales. Okay so, tell me about your first time."

"Oh Lord! Okay ... um, well I was working on my master's."

"A master's ... huh," Michael cracks in.

"Yes," Quinton confirms. "Continue." He's grinning about hearing about my first time. They're so weird.

I shake my head. "Anyway, we had just finished our last week of finals. So we all went out to celebrate. I had way too much wine and ended up losing it to my best friend."

"Details please, like was it good ... where it happened?"

I laugh at Tierra. "That's two more flips, you didn't specify detailed answers."

"I don't know, details are needed for a full flip," Quinton teases.

"Fine." I roll my eyes. "Um, well, let's see, we went back to his place and got interrupted by this new girl in his life." I look up at interested faces. "You all are crazy nosey, she didn't get pissed but got naked. I got jumped my first time by two people."

"That's fucking hot," Michael chimes in. "Did you let her go down on you?"

"That's definitely another coin question."

Andy grabs the coin. "Call it Amelia."

"Tales."

"Damn it." I see tales on his hand. Thank god, I need a drink. I grab a shot.

Quinton flips the coin. "Call it."

"Tales."

He grins grabbing a shot. "Heads. How many partners have you had?"

"Two guys ... I don't really count that chick thing." My turn to flip it. "Mr. Starks," I tease, "call it?"

"Tales." I flip it over. He laughs. "Tales it is." He passes me a shot.

Gerry grabs the quarter. "Call it?"

"Heads." He grins as he pulls a shot.

"Tell me, did the girl go down on you?" Michael high-fives him.

"This is not my best hour." I say, rolling my eyes.

"Fuck, she did?" Michael high-fives Andy. I roll my eyes.

Marcus takes the quarter and flips it. "Call it."

"Heads." He grabs a shot. "Damn it!"

He laughs. "Here's an easy one ... I'll piggyback on our earlier conversation. What happened that ended your marriage in your eyes?"

"Oh ... um ... okay, well, for starters we never had anything remotely like what I see between you guys." I look up at them all. "I knew it was a mistake from the start. Can I take a shot anyway?" They laugh as Quinton slides one to me. I toss it back. "Okay. Like I said, it was a huge mistake. I wanted an annulment. He persuaded me to give it a try. So I did. It was always work." I roll my eyes. "Anyway the turning point that you're interested in, happened six years ago."

I bite my bottom lip and sigh. "Six years ago I found out I was pregnant." I don't look up at Tierra and Tina's gasps. I stare at my drink. "My dad was sick and in the hospital. I was staying late nights with him because he had a poor prognosis. Well, I didn't want to bring a child into that environment. So I decided I could raise the child alone better than as a couple. I came in late from the hospital. He was ragging me about being so late and pregnant. I told him I was leaving him. He got really pissed and—well, let's just say I ended up at the bottom of two flights of stairs. It all happened so quickly." Quinton cusses under his breath. I digress, "Anyway apparently, I had been unconscious for almost a week in the hospital. Bottom line, he died to me that night on the stairs—the day my daddy died alone in the hospital—and I lost the baby, which I was relieved for that blessing. The details of the event never did come back to me. I went behind his back and had one of those IUDs inserted while I was still there because I had no intention of ending up in that condition again." I look up and grab a shot.

"I think we can all use a shot after this horrific insight," Marcus says as they all toss a shot.

"He still doesn't know I have an IUD; and when he does force his marital right, he fusses about wearing a raincoat." I take another shot. My head is starting feel fuzzy and warm. "He's a true asshole." I pull another shot towards me, fingering the glass.

Quinton slides the shot back and wraps his arm around me. "I'm sorry. I hate him even more now."

"Sorry, that part of my life just puts me in a vile mood," I whisper. I shake my head and inhale. "Pass the coin."

Michael grabs it. "You still want to play? That was deep."

"Flip it."

He grins and flips. "Call it."

"Tales." He takes a shot.

"Tell us about the chick going down on you. Did you like it? What was the guy doing? Basically details of that."

"No, I didn't care for it. She was all over the place. He was all over me. I couldn't focus and was bored. I started drinking more wine in bed next to them while they ended up having sex. He had a little vibrator thingy, he used on me while she rode him. Hell, that was better than her tongue or his cock."

"That's hot." Michael grins. "I'm officially turned on." I roll my eyes. He passes the coin to Tina.

She flips it. "Call it?"

"Tales." She takes a shot.

"I'm truly terrible at this game. I seem to call all the wrong faces." I laugh as I wait for her question.

"What's the best sex you ever had?"

"I'll let you know when it happens." She dies laughing. "I'm serious, it has to be better than one-minute guys or vibrators or female tongues." I start giggling.

"She's drunk and cute." Tierra laughs. "Shall we continue?"

"Yes," I breathe, sounding sexier than I intended. I see Quinton grinning and watching me out of my peripheral vision.

She flips it. "Call it."

"Tales." She grins as she pushes a shot to me. "Finally I got one."

Quinton slides it back. "Maybe you should take a sip. You're getting pretty inebriated."

"You're right I am." I start dancing in my chair as I take a sip. "You're so sexy," I blurt looking at him.

Tierra starts to laugh. "Yeah he is. Here babe." She passes the coin to Andy.

Andy flips it. "Call it."

"Tales." I watch him toss a shot.

"Do you give head?" Quinton chokes on his gin. I laugh looking at him. Tierra slaps his arm for being nosey. "What? Y'all asked deep questions."

"Not in my current situation." They all laugh at my response.

He passes the quarter to Quinton. I watch him flip it. "Call it."

"Tales." He grins taking a shot. "Ah, fudge." I toss my head back laughing.

"Have you ever fantasized about fucking another man?"

Embarrassed, I cover my face. "Not until recently." He laughs … they all snicker.

"Are you getting bored with this game?"

"Yes!" I laugh. "I really don't have that interesting of a life and nothing to hide. Hell the most secretive part of my life, I've shared."

"Me too!" Quinton stands pulling me. "I want to dance."

Tierra grins. "Yeah let's shake our money makers."

"Why don't you come shake it on my lap?" Andy takes her to the lounge. She's working her body like a stripper.

"Come on." Tina grabs my hand and we go outside on the deck. The music is still playing. Toni changes stations. He starts mixing drinks at this bar. The song playing sounds sexy. Tina slides down Michael's front, rocking her hips and ass against him. She grins, pulling me into them, and we all start moving.

Toni is grinning watching us move. "Thanks." I take my cosmo he brought me.

"You are way too damn sexy," Quinton growls as he wraps his arm around my stomach, twirling me into his body. Our bodies bend and move into some dirty dancing tricks. He's kissing down my neck. I am lost.

Chapter 24: Quinton

I knew Tierra was going to play that question answer game, I just didn't expect the questions to be so deep. It got heavy. Now I'm completely turned on kissing down this goddess. She's drunk. I could easily fuck her ... but I'm not. I'm not kissing her beautiful lips until she's sober. God, she feels good, rubbing against my cock. She has no idea how fucking hot she is.

"Mr. Starks, you do love to party." She wraps her arms around my neck. She's pursing those sexy lips as she's wiggling out of my grasp. I watch her sing the lyrics to this club song. Michael is laughing, sipping his drink while watching Tina and Amelia spanking and rubbing on one another. I see him take a pic with his phone.

"I'll send you that one buddy." I nod as I watch her breaking it down. "We should pay Eric an impromptu visit and beat the living fuck out of him. I'd like to shove a dildo up his ass," Michael hisses.

"That would be sodomy. He's not worth jail time." I sip my gin. "Although, I would like to break every bone in his body."

"Why are you grinning like that?" Michael asks me as I watch her.

I look at him. "Because I'm going to fuck his wife and take her from him. That will hurt him more than anything. He's all about control, ownership over her."

"You son of a bitch." He laughs as we walk to the bar. I get another gin on the rocks.

"I'm totally into her. I don't want her to go back to him Sunday." I look at Michael.

"Lay it all out for her. Play your cards. She's into you. Let her know where you stand, before then. I don't want serious talk or you will kill my buzz." Michaels laughs. "I think I'm going to retire with my wife."

I laugh. "You do that buddy." I walk over and lace my fingers with Amelia's. She follows me.

We sit back on the L-shaped sofa. She falls in beside me, laying her head back on the cushions. "I can't believe I'm here."

I take her drink and set it down on the table. I nod to Toni she's done. I wrap my arm around her, she cuddles into me. That's it, she's out. I look down at her, her face is pressed against my chest. Damn she's beautiful.

"Toni, we're done for the night."

"Yes, sir." He grabs our glasses. "Is the bar to remain open?"

I look at my watch, it's after midnight. Michael and Tina are retired for the evening, as well as Marcus and Gerry. "I think close it down. Mimosas in the morning with breakfast."

"Yes, sir." I watch him walk off.

That fucktard has royally pissed me off. I should buy the architecture firm he works for and break it apart. Fire his ass. I'll have to look into the market and cost. I don't want to make a bad business purchase thinking with my heart.

I look down as she moves her face against my chest. She's the most beautiful woman I've ever seen. I need to know if she plans to return to the way things were before today. I want her to stay with me. I cannot believe I'm even fathoming that. My penthouse is big enough for us both. She could get a job with her degree or not. She doesn't have to work, she could be like Tina.

We can afford the best divorce attorney and rectify this situation immediately. "Mmmm, Quinton ..." I look down as I hear my name. She's never calls me Quinton. Damn it sounds sexy rolling off her lips. She's dreaming of me.

I lay my head back on the pillows staring at the stars with heavy eyes. I just want to hold her for a few more minutes.

* * *

I jerk awake, startled by her movements. She's whimpering, "Eric no, stop. I hate this."

"Shhh I got you," I whisper kissing her temple. Her words sent chills across my skin. I look at my watch. "Damn it's after two."

I scoop her up in my arms and carry her inside to her room. She doesn't weigh anything. I rip the covers back and lay her down. She moans and rolls over. "Sleep my beautiful sapphire-eyed vixen." I cover her, killing the light before closing the door.

I rip my clothes off, crawling naked into my bed. It's big and empty. I fluff my pillow, looking at an empty side.

* * *

She looks fabulous laying on the white lounge in her little black bikini. She pulls me down on top of her. She wants me. I can see it in her eyes. She laces her fingers through my hair, pulling my mouth to her nipples. She tastes like a tropical paradise: coconut, pineapple, and rum. I get drunk on her. I leisurely stroll my tongue down her stomach dipping in her belly button. Her head arches deeper into the cushions, as her hands guide me further down. "You want this?"

"Yes, please," she begs as I kiss her inner thigh. I watch her bite that beautiful bottom lip. She likes it. I lick and nibble her inner thigh working up to her sex. Her hips are flexing up, begging for more. I grin as I pull her bottoms off, tossing them aside. I swoop her legs over my shoulders spreading her open so I can see all her perfection. I start kissing her folds. She gasps as I tickle her with my tongue, gently flicking it up her slit. I look up, her eyes are closed and she's biting that damn lip. I French kiss her clitoris. She screams, "Mr. Starks ... Mr. Starks!" I look up to see what is making that knocking sound. It's totally ruining my moment.

"Huh." I grunt awake. I realize the knocking sound is real. I roll over, covering my head with a pillow.

"Mr. Starks." I raise my chest off the bed, bending and looking at the door.

"Amelia?" I ask. I'm so fucking confused.

243

"Yes!" What the hell? I flip over and realize I was dreaming. Now she's really at my bedroom door.

"Hold on." I know I sound grumpy. I sit up, looking at my hard on. "Shit." I grab a pair of gray lounge pants and fling open the door. She just knock the wind out of me. There she is standing, with bed hair, wearing white lace hipster panties and a blue sleep tank ... shifting uncomfortably on her feet.

"Are you mad?" she asks while biting her lip.

"What? Mad ... no." I move aside for her to come into my bedroom. I close the door, turning to look at her, as I run my hand through my hair. Damn her ass looks sexy. "Everything okay Amelia?"

"I woke up alone. I haven't slept alone in over ten years." She laughs as she looks around. "I couldn't go back to sleep."

I laugh. "Well by all means Amelia from Amelia, join me." I get in my bed and pull the covers back.

She grins crawling towards the center. I stretch my arm out, watching her as she cuddles down into me. *Fuck* she feels good. I hit the light off, noticing it's five in the morning.

I feel her shift and scoot her body next to mine, laying her head on my chest. She laces our fingers. "I like this," she whispers.

"I do too." I tickle her shoulder with my free fingers that are holding her. "You don't have to stay in your cabin. You can stay in here with me."

She's quiet. "Amelia?"

"Yes," she sighs as she's holding me.

"Do you want to stay with me?"

"Yes," she finally responds. "You're going to spoil me with all of this." I laugh at her confession. "I don't mean your lifestyle, yachts, dancing, private chefs. I mean you."

"That's all I want," I confess as I stroke her hair until she drifts back to sleep.

Chapter 25: Amelia

I roll over, moaning and stretching my fingers out over his sheet. I sit up, his spot is empty. I stretch and then curl into a ball, rolling back in his bedding. It smells like his cologne.

His quarters are clean and masculine. A warm honey gold light is shining through the large windows, setting a romantic glow about the room. I can hear talking outside the door.

Then I hear him, telling them to keep it down, I'm still sleeping. His remark is followed by hoots and whistles of approval. I roll my eyes, his friends are sex crazed.

He opens the door and quietly closes it. I roll over, looking at him. "You're awake." He sounds shocked. "I have your morning coffee."

"What?" I grin as I scoot my butt back to a sitting position. He sits beside me. He's already dressed in his boating clothes.

"Here." He hands me the coffee. "It's hot."

I smile, taking it and warming my hands around the mug. "Thank you." I sip it. "Yum, it's kind of sweet. I like it."

"Good."

"What? Why are you looking at me like that?"

"No reason, you're just crazy beautiful in the mornings."

"Ha, I'm sure I'm just glorious to look at." I rake my fingers through my bed hair. "You've showered?"

"Yes." He steals a peek under the sheets at my panties. I roll my eyes as he smirks.

"You're a terrible flirt, Mr. Starks." I sip my coffee, watching him.

"You like my crass behavior." He drops a soft kiss on my cheek. I watch him as he dances around my coffee, and drops another kiss on my jaw. He's watching my eyes, as he drops open-mouth kisses down my neck, tickling me with his tongue. He moans deep in his throat as he tickles his fingers across my clavicle, dropping an innocent kiss. My sex is starting to throb. "Don't you?"

"Yes," I whisper. He takes my coffee and sits on the bedside table. He scoots next to me, we naturally shift so I can lay back. He's leaning over me, stroking my hair. I close my eyes as he softly glides his finger down the side of my face, over my jaw, running his thumb over my lip.

"I really want to kiss and nibble this beautiful mouth," he breathes as he leans closer, taking my ear lobe and nipping it with his lips. I giggle as he does it again. I really want him to kiss me too, but not without brushing my teeth.

Knock!

He sighs. "I swear to god if this is Gerry again I'm going to make him shark food."

I giggle as the door opens. I gasp pulling behind him. "Hey, you best have a damn good reason …," he growls as he

247

turns his attention to the door. Damn his voice just got deeper and oh so sexy. He's intimidating.

"Oh sir … sorry sir." A woman turns around immediately. I lean up, looking over his shoulder at who just burst through his door. Her head is down. "I knocked. I was coming to make your bed and clean."

"Well, I'm still in my bed," he snaps.

"Yes, sir. Sorry sir."

"She didn't mean to," I whisper touching him gently across his shoulders.

"Please collect Ms. Amelia's things from her room and bring them in here. She will be sharing my quarters."

"Yes, sir. Is it okay to do that now?"

"Yes, bring her belongings now. Then clean her room. Thank you."

"She doesn't have to move my stuff, I can do that." I shift to get up.

"No, that's what she's paid to do. She would get offended."

"Oh." I run my fingers over his arms. "You got very intimidating Mr. Starks."

"Did I now?" He rolls, pulling me back into his embrace. "I don't like to be disturbed with you in my arms. Gerry has done so wonderfully twice already." I laugh. "The staff know their roles; that was a rookie mistake."

"Do you like having staff? You like having someone to make your bed for you, something that simple?" I ask him, smirking. I watch him lace our fingers. He starts kissing my fingertips.

"Show me one person who wouldn't want someone to do the daunting tasks of bed making or any scullery maid duties. This is what they choose to do. So without my employment, they wouldn't have an income. Plus I pay members of my staff very, very well. Yes, I like staff." He continues to kiss my fingertips, watching my eyes.

"What about me?"

"What do you mean?"

"These scullery tasks ... I did them at the inn. Do you see me in the same light as your staff?"

"Yeah ... you would have never done such things had we run the inn together. There would have been a hired maid service." I laugh at him shaking my head. "What? Did you actually enjoy doing all the cleaning and cooking? It brought you happiness?"

"Well, no ... not happiness. But it had to be done."

"Exactly! My wife would never be a maid. Period!"

I laugh shaking my head. "I've just been in their shoes ... I guess. They probably don't look at it as mundane tasks. But their job, it doesn't define them." He shrugs kissing my fingers clearly uninterested in discussing this matter. "I find you very sexy," I whisper.

"Excuse me sir, I'm bringing in Ms. Amelia's items."

"Thank you." He doesn't turn towards her. He's grinning at me. "You hungry? I haven't eaten breakfast."

"Thank you," I tell her. "Yes, I just need to find something to wear."

"You're welcome ma'am." I watch her take my toiletries to his bathroom. Then she unpacks my bag.

He laughs and whispers, "Staff," as he hops off the bed.

I slip on a pair of shorts. He's grinning and watching me. I walk into his bathroom, flip the light switch, and close the door. She even unpacked my toothbrush. I bet she would offer to put my toothpaste on it. I laugh as I do it myself.

"You ready?" he asks as I walk out of the bathroom. I nod, grabbing my mug. She is already stripping my sheets when we walk by.

"Has everyone already eaten?" I ask as we reach the deck.

"Yes, it's after ten." He grins as we sit at the table. Toni brings us mimosas. Within a few minutes the steward from last night appears. "What would you like for breakfast?" Quinton asks me.

I look at him. "I don't know. What are my options?"

"Ma'am, we have anything you would like," the steward says. I look at Quinton wearing a smug expression.

"Really … so, if I wanted a Belgian waffle with fresh strawberries, blue berries, whip cream, bacon, and fresh ambrosia, you have all that available?"

"Is that what you would like?" I look at Quinton who is grinning.

"Yes."

"Very well ma'am. Sir?" he asks Quinton.

"Make it two, sounds delicious."

"This is crazy." I laugh looking out over the water.

"What?" Quinton grabs my fingers lacing them with his. "I like kissing your fingers." He's nibbling the back of my hand.

"I like it too," I whisper scooting into him as he wraps his arm around me. "Your life is like a dream. I'm almost scared to pinch myself because I don't want to wake up." He laughs as strolls his free fingers across my shoulder, toying with my strap.

"You look sexy in this, especially those lace panties." He wiggles his eyebrows at me when the gang comes up to the table.

"So do you two have anything to share with the group?" Tierra asks grinning.

"Yeah, you said you would let me know when you had the best sex of your life," Tina teases.

"Oh lord." I laugh. "I will if that happens." I sip my coffee.

"We just slept." Quinton rolls his eyes. "I see your faces. I know, it was a novelty for me too." He drinks some of his mimosa.

"Shit." Michael laughs. "Well, someone was screaming last night. I heard it."

Tierra raised her hand. "Guilty. Andy was all up in my junk."

"You gave me a lap dance, what did you think I was going to do?" He looks around. "Right, Quinton?"

"Sweet baby Jesus," I whisper dropping my face into Quinton's body. He laughs about it.

"Tierra doll, turn some music on," Quinton tells her.

"I didn't hear anything, I don't even remember going into my room." I admit, sipping my coffee and looking at them.

"That's because I carried you." Quinton smirked. "We fell asleep until two up here." He pointed to the sofa. "Then you came crawling into my bed this morning. And I'm not complaining." He teases looking at them, "So we didn't hear anyone doing anything."

I see the steward bringing our breakfast. Tierra grins. "Okay, guys why don't we leave these two to have breakfast." I watch them leave as our breakfast is placed in front of us.

"It looks delicious." He knows it does. Damn he's handsome in his mannerisms. I do believe I could sit and look at him for the rest of my life. *No, you can't* I hear that little voice in my head say. This fantasy all ends Sunday. I look down at my breakfast.

"Are you pleased?" I don't even have to look at him to know he's grinning.

"Yes, it's delicious. It's lovely in the morning." He looks at me. "Out here on the water. Away from the world … troubles … everything really." He leans back wrapping his arm around me while he chews. "You always have this relaxing of a life?"

"Unless I'm in the boardroom or handling corporate matters that are taking longer than I would like. Then things get a little heated at times." He sips his mimosa. "But yes, in my leisure time, it's very relaxing."

I lay my head on his shoulder. "I like being here with you," I admit.

"Good! I like you here, with me." He's looking at me, tickling my shoulder with his fingers.

"Your touch is very tender," I whisper. He doesn't respond, but I know he heard me. I feel his touch all over my body. How can I throb down there for him? When he's not touching anywhere near it. I've never craved a man, ever!

I look up at him, his bare neck is right here; my mind can taste him. I've wanted to kiss him so many times, yet we've been interrupted every sweet moment. I close my eyes and press my lips to his neck. His touch changes, he's holding my shoulder as I open my lips and kiss his neck softly. I taste his cologne on my tongue.

I dare to look at his eyes. I kiss him again, this time a little higher, just below his jaw. His fork clinks on the plate as his hand laces his fingers through my hair. He's coaching my face up towards his. My body naturally responds, he's a magnetic force.

My sex is going to explode. I tickle my fingers through his scruff, stroking his face. "I like this," I purr against his lips.

"I like the way your fingers feel." I feel the heat of his words on my lips. His breath surrounds me. The heat. The

253

desire. I can't breathe. My breath is literally trapped in my lungs; the music is replaced by my pulse; it's the only beat I hear. I look at his eyes, he's watching me intently. He leans in and I feel like I'm about to suffer a panic attack, when I feel his warm, soft lips. His lips are barely parted, testing the waters. My chest is tightening, but my libido is on fire.

He hovers a minute, just feeling our lips touch. I nudge the tip of my nose on his, smiling as I welcome him. This newness. This energy. He catches my eyes once more before closing his dark lashes and consuming my lips.

His mouth covers mine, slipping his tongue inside to explore this new forbidden vessel. A moan escapes my throat as I accept him, dancing our tongues together, exploring his mouth. God, he's absolutely delicious. I feel his tongue dip deeper and swirl with mine.

He twists his torso, wrapping me in his arms, deepening his kiss. I think I hear a small growl in his throat. I feel his strong hands, clasping the sides of my face, passionately stroking up and down my neck to my jaw, tilting my mouth to how he wants me. His tongue is like velvet as it glides and caressing me. It's wonderful. He's wonderful.

I lace my fingers through his dark hair, pulling him deeper. He's matching my desire perfectly. I want to feel more of him on me. I need to before I die. Damn this table! I feel my body shifting as he guides me onto his lap. He still hasn't released my lips, shifting beneath me.

He strokes my back; my fingernails tickle his scalp. Our mouths are still consumed with one another, tasting, dipping our tongues deep and melting into one. I can finally hear our

254

breaths. His breathing is ragged. I whimper a small moan deep in my throat. I never want this moment to end. I have finally found what heaven on earth feels like.

Chapter 26: Quinton

Holy fucking hell. She's paradise. She's better than anything I've ever experienced in my entire life. Her mouth is like silk. She is ecstasy. I'm high on her. She's driving me insane with those fingers; my cock is going to explode.

An uncontrollable moan escapes my throat as I continue discovering her beautiful mouth. This gorgeous orifice is mine! Our tongues dance their own tango. She's perfect. I need more, I want more. What a fool I am, to believe I could have ever had a platonic relationship with my queen. She's my soul mate, the missing puzzle to me.

Fuck, she's flexing her hips against me. I know she had to feel my cock. She's whimpering into my mouth. *That's right baby, rub that sexy body on me.* I stroke her back, running my hands up and down her sides. I graze the sides of her breasts with my hands. She doesn't stop me. That's all I need.

I push my hand under her tank top and cup her breast in my hand. She gasps, releasing my lips. *Shit.* I watch her, looking at me. She grins and closes her eyes. I start kissing her jaw, nibbling that bottom lip as I softly squeeze her breast, and her nipple hardens under my hand immediately. She has small nipples. I can't wait to see them. Suck them. I continue to rub circles with my thumb around her areolas, teasing her nipple between my thumb and pointer finger. I'm lost in kissing her again and touching her.

"Shit," I hear her sweet, startled voice; I feel her tense and curl around me. Her face is in my shoulder.

Fuck, someone has interrupted. I slip my hand out from under her shirt. "What is it?" I growl as I look around. That damn steward is really fucking pissing me off.

He looks like a fucking virgin watching a taboo flick. "What is it?" I hiss. This time I sound extremely harsh. Even I feel it.

Great, he's fucking stuttering. "S-sorry sir, I …" Yeah I know he was coming to check if we needed anything. I get it.

"Leave us," I command. I watch as he scurries away like a little rodent. "He's gone," I whisper. I run my hands up the side of her face, making her look up. She's grinning.

I laugh as I watch her crawl off my lap, she's adorable looking shy. "Well, that was one hell of a kiss," I tease looking at her. I lean back, moving a strand of hair from her eye.

"I do believe you hit second base, Mr. Starks," she teases. I grin at her, letting my eyes move down to her breasts.

"I do hope to hit another base." She turns red. I watch her lean up and grab her mimosa. She sips it, looking out over the water and the decking.

"I'm sure it can be arranged." She's not looking at me. I laugh at her shyness and her boldness.

"My sapphire-eyed vixen, I look forward to it." I lace our fingers and resume eating my cold breakfast.

257

She grins, stealing glimpses of me while she eats. She's cute. Our serenity is short lived, as we hear laughter coming our way.

"Gerry." I grin. "No devil flames today, I see." He spins in a circle smiling. "What are you wearing over your suit?" It looks like a satin Komodo. Amelia laughs as he struts over, running his fingers down the front trimming.

"It's my wrap." He wiggles his eyebrows.

"What color suit are you gracing us with today, friend?" I tease as I finish my waffle. I notice my drink as well as Amelia's is empty. Where the hell is that pesky steward? I scour the surroundings. There he is hiding behind the bar, with Toni. Looks like Toni is berating him. Good! Toni notices me and I subtly point to my glass. All my staff know I hate for my drink to be empty.

Gerry grabs my attention as he unties his wrap. "Feast your hungry eyes on my leopard print ass." He turns and shakes it. Amelia laughs as she looks at me.

"I wish I could wear leopard like you Gerry," Amelia teases as she reaches for her empty glass. I notice it and looked back towards Toni, but he is already en route. "Thank you." She smiles, accepting her mimosa.

"If you two will excuse me, I need a word with my staff." I'm fuming. Amelia looks up at me as I stand.

"Ah, hell." Gerry sucks in his breath as he talks. "Boss isn't pleased with something," he says as I walk off.

I head to the bar first. "Toni." I see the little steward still present, I look at him. "I don't appreciate interruptions nor to repeat myself when I acknowledge you."

"Yes, sir." He looks nervous. I know I'm being harsh.

"Toni can explain the ropes to you. I realize you're new. Do not stare at my woman, ever. You may see things that will give you wet dreams, but you are to look away, do I make myself clear?"

"Yes, sir. I am truly sorry for the interruption."

"It may be wise for you to peek before making yourself fully present. And never let my glass or any guests of mine be empty." I look back at Amelia and Gerry talking. "I believe she's done. You may go check ... if so, clean off the table." I watch him scurry off.

"Am I really that intimidating, Toni?" I ask laughing with him. Toni works for me at my club Libation as well as my personal bartender whenever we take the yacht out. He's been with me for years and understands how I like things to operate.

"You can be sir." He grins. "Looks like things are progressing well with Ms. Amelia." I grin back at him.

"Yes, yes it appears so. Show the newbie the ropes." I leave him to find the captain to deal with the situation.

When I return to the lounge, I don't see Amelia. Instead everyone else is sitting around. "She's changing into her swimsuit." Tierra smiles. "You get your crew under control," she teases. I roll my eyes.

Toni brings me a gin with lime. "About time to start party-ing." Andy grins as he grabs Tierra's hand. "Let's find some tunes. Toni, I need a drink," I hear him yell. Tierra is excellent at picking mood music playlists.

"Marcus." I grin as he sits down beside me. "Do you two always coordinate your attire?" I notice his leopard swim shorts.

"He loves to match me." Gerry perches next to him. I laugh, he's already drinking his cosmo. "We want to do karaoke when we go inland."

"Good, you know I love to karaoke. I wonder if Amelia does." I grin remembering her sweet voice singing that night. God, she has a magical voice.

"We will get her to sing with us." Tina smiles. "You know a group of drunk dancing, singing chicks, what's hotter?" I laugh.

"Nothing," Michael concedes. "Look at you three groov-ing." He pulls out his phone. I lean over, damn she's hot. "I for sure want to see you three on a stage dancing on one another."

"I think I'll see what's keeping Amelia." As I approach the door I can hear her crying. *Shit*, does she feel like the kiss went too far? Then I hear his voice, that's the reason she's cry-ing.

She turns as I open the door and quickly wipes her tears. I motion to leave, so she can have privacy, but she doesn't want me to go. I swagger quietly to my bed, where she's laying with her phone.

"I expect your fucking ass to be on that flight Friday, Amelia. Saturday we're attending a formal dinner, so find something appropriate. Nothing like what you wore to Libation."

She's watching me. "Eric why can't you accept I'm not coming to Birmingham?" She rolls her eyes.

"You're acting like a fucking bitch!" I come off the bed at his words. I'm about to tell that fucktard a thing or two. Amelia grabs my arm. She's shaking her head. "You've made your point—you're pissed about the other morning. Get over it. I told you, you had to accept my apology. This is the end of it," he yells. He has no idea how correct he is—*this is the end of it!* "Look they were able to issue a flight credit, not a full refund. I'll have a car pick you up Friday to bring you to the airport. That way we don't have to drive back separately on Sunday." Amelia is shaking her head.

"I wish you could hear how you sound," Amelia pleads. "You can't make me get on a flight, Eric. I wouldn't waste your time sending a car Friday because I won't be here."

He laughs. "What do you mean you won't be there? Where the fuck do you plan on being?" She rolls her eyes.

"The Bahamas," she sighs. I cover my face, muffling my laughter. "I just won't be here, don't worry your small brain about it." I laugh quietly at her smartness. I crawl next to her, running my fingers up and down her back. I can feel her swimsuit straps under the sheer coverup. A small moan escapes her throat as she closes her eyes; she likes my touches. I lean down, pulling her hair away from her face and kiss her cheek. I taste the salt of her tears. Fucktards' voice is irritating me as he continues hounding her.

"You feeling brave? Let's see how brave you are face to face." I flinch at his enjoyment of scaring her, but I keep touching his wife's lovely body. He doesn't appreciate her at all, but I do. I can literally feel the tension leaving her body under my touch. "Don't be stupid Amelia. You will be sorry if you miss that flight."

No, she won't be sorry. I start sucking her neck as I gently caressed her back.

"Do you understand?" he asks her.

"Yes," she purrs but it's not in response to him. My lips smile against the sheer fabric as I continue my kissing. I stroll my hands down over her back, grasping her ass. I really want to run my hand under her coverup.

"Amelia, what are you doing?"

She giggles and thrashes around, as I start tickling and digging into her sides. "Stop it" she whispers, trying to keep quiet. I don't care if Eric discovers she's found someone new.

"Who is at the house with you?" She freezes at his question and smirks at me.

"No one is at the house, Eric." That's the god's honest truth. "Are you done?" she asks him as she strokes my forearm. I watch her nibble my fingertips. I take a deep breath. She grins before she sucks the tip of my thumb. Clasping her

262

hand to mine, I nibble and kiss the inside of her hand. Damn his wife is sweet. I close my eyes. She just spoke straight to my cock.

I hear him take a deep breath. "I guess I'm just short because I'm tense. I need you here to get rid of my tension." Well, that comment is a cock blocker. She gags with her finger down her throat. I quietly laugh.

"I would be no use to you. I am not touching you." I can hear the disgust in her voice. *No, she certainly won't be touching you, nor you her.*

"You always say that, but I always win." She rolls her eyes. *That's now past tense!*

"Yeah for two minutes. It's not worth my time," she remarks and I cover my face with my pillow.

"I've told you it's your fault, you're so fucking tight." Oh shit, now I'm interested. I remove the pillow. She's turning red.

"I'm not getting into this on the phone Eric. It's not my problem you have zero stamina." *No babe, it's not. It's called erectile dysfunction.*

"Why not talk dirty to me? We've never done that." She rolls her eyes and shakes her head.

"And we're not going to ever do that." *Damn right, if she's talking dirty, it's going to be to me.* "Don't you have work stuff to do?"

"Yeah, I'll check in with you later. Answer this time." She rolls her eyes. I grin looking at her, shaking my head. That's not going to happen. She smiles as she waits for him to say goodbye. She doesn't tell him she loves him or bye. She just disconnects. I watch her put the phone on the bedside table.

"I'm more than happy to handle him for you." She shakes her head like she doesn't understand. "I'm more than happy to put some perspective in his head. I don't like him speaking to you that way." I roll her body to me.

"He was really intense as I soon as I called him back." She looks at me. "I had missed calls."

"Why call him back?" I don't want her to call him any-more. I know I can't tell her not to talk to him; after all, he's legally bound to her. I hate him.

"You don't think I should?"

"Do you want me to be honest?" Shit that just came out.

"Yes, I do." She's cuddling into me as I'm wrapping my arms around her. I feel her fingers go under my shirt, rubbing across my six pack.

I sigh because this could go either way. "I understand why you did. I can't tell you what you should or shouldn't do. Legally, he is your husband, but that does not mean you be-long to him. He doesn't respect or deserve you." I feel her fingers slow. *Shit*, what is she thinking?

"I wasn't lying, I don't love him," she whispers. She starts stroking my six pack again, feeling all my dips and ripples with her fingertips, circling my belly button with her pointer. "I don't want him."

"Well, do you know what you want?" I whisper, running my fingertips up and down her back.

"I don't want to feel like I'm cheating you out of more." *Fuck!* That's not what I wanted her to say. "He will never give me a divorce. If I did move on with someone, he would make their life a living hell. If he ever finds out about me being here, he'll kill me." She continues to rub my six pack. "I don't want to dump shit and drama on your relaxed life."

"Look at me." She leans up. "Do I look like I'm worried about his ass in the least?"

"No." She laughs. "You don't seem concerned at all with him."

"So I ask you, what do want? Do you want things like they've been for the last ten years or do you want to try something else? I don't know, maybe take an adventure with me." I grin as I lace her fingers in mine, kissing them.

"Take an adventure with you," she purrs. *Oh thank fuck!*

"There's your answer, don't talk to him." That came out easy. "Our adventure has already started." I roll her over on her back, looking into those captivating sapphires. Her eyes are smiling while she bites her bottom lip; fuck it is pulling at me. I lean in, kissing her open mouth, dipping my tongue ... discovering this beautiful vessel.

She giggles as I kiss and nibble down her jaw and towards her ear. My hand playfully rests on her hip. She's so beautiful. I love her laugh.

"God!" I turn around to Tierra's voice. "We've been waiting forever for you two. Should have known you two would be hiding so you could make out." I roll my eyes as I sit up.

"Amelia was talking to the soon-to-be ex-husband." I grab her hands as I stand.

"Good, so I guess that means that this is going somewhere." She motions between the two of us. "Somewhere special?"

"Yeah." I grab Amelia's hand and lace it with mine. "Let's celebrate." *God, I hope so,* she's grinning at me.

"Whoo hoo," Tierra shrieks, grabbing Amelia's free hand up in the air. "Let's party! Oh honey you're going to have the most amazing sex life now."

"Oh my." I hear Amelia laugh as she lets her lead her to the sun deck. *Oh, Amelia has no idea what I can do in bed.*

Chapter 27: Amelia

The music is loud and everyone is already drinking. "Damn it's bright." I hold my hand up, shielding my eyes. Toni immediately approaches me with a cosmo and holding my sunglasses. "Oh, thanks!" I grin sliding them on.

"Yes, ma'am, you left them on the lounge last night." I watch Toni walk back to his bar.

"Okay, listen up!" Tierra sings, while fanning her hands to gather everyone around. "Our Casanova is going off the market!" She holds her drink up. "Whoo hoo," she shrieks again, jumping with excitement. I laugh, shaking my head.

"Damn right," he growls kissing my neck, slipping his hand around my waist. He takes his gin from Toni.

Michael and Andy high-five him like he's engaged or something. I guess it's a big deal; their buddy has never been in any sort of relationship.

"Casanova give me some love," Gerry demands. "I knew the Lioness would be the only one for you." He grins, giving me his attention. "Lioness, get ready for your world to be rocked!" He laughs as he drinks his cosmo, wrapping his arm through mine. "You are too covered in this wrap."

Quinton is grinning and watching, like he could devour me. Hell, they all have that look when they're looking at us. Gerry snaps his fingers for Marcus. "Sweets, hold the Lioness 's cosmo." He takes it from my hand as Gerry snatches my coverup over my head.

"Oh god," I breathe, failing to catch my wrap as he tosses it to the ground. "Okay." I laugh. *Shit, I feel exposed.*

Gerry stalks around me. "Girl, this little suit is seriously sizzling. You sultry Lioness."

Marcus circles. "No wonder our Casanova is so smitten. You bring color into his world too." They look like barracudas.

Whistling from Andy and Michael follows. "Don't cover up Amelia," Michael warns.

"We like to see our women," Andy adds.

They're all too much! My abs flex as I adjust my yellow bikini. *Thank god I don't have any fat,* I think standing next to Tierra. I didn't plan my coverup being ripped off. "I've never worn such a bright color."

"It's hot." I turn around to Quinton's voice. "I totally approve." He wraps his arm around my waist, taking my cosmo from Marcus. "Drink. It's time to party."

"Tierra, I like your swimsuit." I'm envious of her ability to wear such glamorous pieces. It's sparkly silver and tiny. The ass is equally as small as the front. It looks expensive.

268

"I've got another one similar if you want it; I get them from designers that I model."

I grimace. "I don't think I can pull that style off."

"She'll take it," Quinton tells Tierra. "You've got a beautiful body ... don't be shy of it!" I simper, watching him circling and nodding; he kisses me. "I didn't think you could look any hotter than yesterday ... WRONG!"

"So do you ... you're, um ... very attractive," I whisper, blushing. Quinton guffaws at my confession as we walk to the sun lounges.

"He likes his body too." Tina laughs. I lay down on my stomach beside her.

"I do," he admits. "I take great pride in keeping it hot and ready to go."

"He seriously works out every day, runs like ten miles in the morning, then at least an hour or two in the gym," Tierra brags. "Andy has started working out with him."

I look at his upper body. "You do have a big chest and arms. I do good to get a yoga or Pilates workout in a couple days a week." He laughs, holding his hand out for my lotion.

I close my eyes feeling his hands on my shoulders. His touch is strong, sensual. An involuntary moan slips from my throat as he works down my back, dipping his fingertips under the yellow material. My breath catches in my throat. "You like this?"

"Yes," I whisper watching him grin. My sex tingles in response as he squeezes and rubs the inside and back of my thighs. He keeps stealing my breath. He grins like he heard me but doesn't say anything.

He rubs all the way to my feet, then sits back, taking my foot in his hand. He starts rubbing small circles on the bottom of my sole and wraps both of his hands around my foot, pulling over my toes towards his chest.

"Are you fucking kidding me?" Tierra whines, "Andy doesn't give me foot massages."

"I would offer Mr. Starks' services to you, but I'm afraid I'm going to be selfish with this." I look over my shoulder at him. "That feels amazing."

"Andy," Quinton yells, "get over here and pleasure your wife. She has unfulfilled needs that I discovered you're missing." I laugh as he switches feet. "You have beautiful little feet."

"You're really good at that." I lean up taking a sip of my drink. "Do you want me to lotion you?" I ask looking over my shoulder. "If you keep doing that, I'm going to fall asleep." He grins standing and holding my hand. Everything about him feels right. I watch him caress his thumb over my knuckles. *Why don't I have any guilt?* I look up as Toni appears with a fresh cosmo. *How does he always know?*

Quinton sits in front of me. I start massaging him with lotion; his muscles bulges are almost too much for me to grip deeply. I don't have masseur hands.

"Mmm." He tilts his head to the side. "Your hands feel like heaven." I hear him suck in, making a deep throaty growl before he reaches up and grabs the back of my head. He's watching me out of the corner of his eye, and we're grinning at each other. His eyes drop to my mouth as he closes the distance. His open-mouth kisses are seductive.

"Mmm," he hums. He looks back at my eyes, his lips still hovering over mine. I smile before he covers my lips again—dipping his tongue in, exploring my mouth. I can taste his gin, he's absolutely tantalizing. Our tongues melt into one, rolling and dancing. My sex feels heavy. He pulls me around into his lap. "I like this," he growls, as he kisses and sucks my bottom lip. I mindlessly drape my arm around the back of his neck, tickling my fingertips across his shoulders, while my other hand strokes his incredible, sexy forearm. My apprehension is gone; I left it behind when I went all in. My senses are overloaded by him, his smell, his taste ... his tenderness.

"Does the sun make you horny too?" Tierra asks. I don't know if it's a combination of the heat, booze, the atmosphere or just him, but something has awoken this desire I never knew existed. I can't fight it. I don't want to fight it.

Quinton continues kissing down my neck, sucking and nibbling. I giggle, turning into his playfulness. He's tickling his fingers across my stomach, making small circles around my belly button. Our eyes meet. He looks like a schoolboy seeing his crush for the first time. He drops that megawatt, sexy smile. I melt all over again.

"You two are so adorable," Tierra breathes as she sits up, looking for Andy. "Andy look at Quinton's stargazed eyes. I've

271

never. This makes me happy, to see him finally feeling something more." She grins at me as she sips her drink.

"I've seen it." Quinton looks at Gerry sporting his leopard print speedo. "He had that doe eyed expression every time they talked at the office." Gerry sits on the lounger with his cosmo.

"If I could live without you Gerry, I'd fire you for giving out classified information," he teases.

"Here let me finish your lotion." I stand maneuvering around his body ... I laugh at Gerry giving me eyes. "Let me get my hands on the chest and abs of perfection."

"Oh lord, she's going to fuel his ego." Gerry laughs, drinking his drink.

"Does he know how sexy he is, Gerry?" I tease as Quinton is grinning at me. I squeeze lotion in my hands, rubbing them together. I lean up, rubbing over his clavicle, his pecs ... down over his six pack, feeling every ripple and dip. I bite my bottom lip as I glide over his body, moving over his forearms and biceps. His eyes are glued to mine. My sex is throbbing.

"Hell, yeah he does!" I keep looking at his eyes.

"I really want to bite that lip when you do that."

"Do you now, Mr. Starks?" I gasp as he snatches my hip tighter against his body, *Damn he's strong.* He impishly grins, fisting my hair, resting his other hand on my lower back, and his seductive kiss covers my lips; our tongues begin to dance and massage each other. We are in perfect harmony.

"Ah shit," Gerry mumbles under his breath, "I know that look." Marcus laughs.

"You want to go inside?"

"Yes," I hear myself whisper. I don't even think about what he's asking. I feel him lift me, and I wrap my legs around him. His hands dip below my ass, supporting me, as I wrap my arms around his neck. He's sucking and nibbling my bottom lip as he walks. *Shit,* he's carrying me across the deck like Andy did Tierra.

"Have fun," Tierra teases.

Chapter 28: Quinton

Mm, damn, she tastes good, like a cosmo and her. She feels amazing; her ass fits perfect in my grip. I knock open my bedroom door, and kick it shut. I could totally fuck her holding her against the wall, that may be too harsh right now. I walk over to the bed and lay her down.

She's grinning at me as I lock the door and hit the music on. "You are one feisty little sapphire-eyed vixen," I tease crawling on the bed. I grab her ankles and pull her down my bed—climbing over her body, nudging her legs apart. I look down, she's laying there beneath me in that little yellow string bikini.

"Now that you have me inside, Mr. Starks, what are you going to do with me?" she teases. If she was like the others, I would fuck her for hours. But no, this time I want more; I desire more. She's too precious to rush and go all in.

I hover over her small body, leaning down I kiss her lips. "I don't want to rush anything with you, my sweet Amelia," I whisper.

"Oh," she whispers, "then don't." She leans up and softly wraps her lips around my neck, kissing and flicking that perfect little tongue … tasting my skin. Her fingers are laced in my hair, tugging on my scalp with her nails. She's humming, kissing around my neck and clavicle. Her touch is soft and sensual. My cock is going to explode.

"Oh god," I groan looking up to the ceiling for strength not to ravish her. "You're going to give me some hellacious blue balls."

She giggles as I roll on my back, wrapping my arm around her she cuddles into me. *Okay, this is nice.* Why is this satisfying me? "You want a drink? I need one."

"Yes." She smiles, rubbing her fingers across my chest. She grazes my nipple. I hold my breath, wanting her beautiful lips to suck it. She runs her fingers down and over my six pack. "I think I'm in love with your body as much as you are," she teases.

I laugh, reaching over to the phone on the bedside table, watching her kiss around on my stomach. Her lips are fucking hot. I can't believe I dreamed her into reality. "Yes, I need a cosmo, gin, strawberries, and a glass of ice brought to my cabin, STAT. Thanks." I hang up.

She runs her hand up my chest, laying her head beside me. "Ice?" Her eyes are curious.

I grin, kissing her fingertips and working my way down her hand. I swirl my tongue on the inside of her wrist, kissing up her arm. She deserves to be savored ... I intend to do just that!

Her giggles make me smile. I can't stop looking at how damn beautiful she is ... her face as she gasps. I continue trailing my tongue, sucking her sun-kissed skin between my lips.

Desire filled eyes watch me, as I troll my pointer finger down her jaw. Pulling her lips towards mine, I close my eyes as I graze my lips across hers. She makes a small whimper.

I grin, looking at her mouth. Her perfect lips have parted into a soft smile. I scoot closer, adjusting so I'm not crushing her. I nudge the tip of her nose with mine. I can feel her breath on my lips. I close the distance with an open-mouth kiss, dipping my tongue deep in her mouth. Her body naturally flexes back, humming as she accepts it. Her tongue is like a beautiful piece of silk, sliding and caressing mine. *Fuck*, she melts into me, perfectly. Our kisses glide and move as if we're one—the perfect grooving bodies in a club: she's my tango, my cha cha, my mambo. I'm her freedom, and she's my adventure. All I know is I've never been kissed the way she's kissing me; I've never felt this brewing nirvana deep inside.

She's wanting more, pulling at my shoulders, wanting my weight on her. I oblige, shifting between her thighs. She naturally adjusts, wrapping her legs around my hips. Our tongues continue their dance as I let my hand wander down her body, across the strings covering those beautiful tits, her flexed tight abs, and another set of strings tying a thin piece of material to shield her apex from me.

Oh fucking hell, I can feel her heat. She's wet. I drop down, kissing and nibbling her neck as she tosses her head back in excitement. I tickle my fingertips over her hips, caressing her leg. I know she feels my hard on. Fuck I can even feel a bead escaping the head.

I start stroking my covered length against her hidden treasure. I want to be inside of her, but I don't want to rush this. I hear her gasp. I kiss down her breast, really wanting to suck those beautiful nipples in my mouth, but all in good time. I continue kissing down, covering her diaphragm. She's touching my shoulders, squeezing those beautiful fingertips against my muscles.

My tongue has found that sexy belly button. I feel her muscles contract as she giggles. I look up, *fuck*, our eyes meet. I'm so fucking lost. I kiss over that thin piece of string, and kiss her trembling thigh.

"Relax," I whisper.

"I'm nervous." She laughs softly.

"You're beautiful." I keep kissing and nibbling. "Is this too much?"

"Yes!" she purrs, "Don't stop." I grin, lifting her leg over my shoulder.

I nudge her sex with my nose, inhaling her. Holy sweet mother of Jesus, that's the best scent I've ever smelled. I want to taste her. I need to taste her. She gasps, grabbing my shoulders, tickling her fingers through my hair. I nip the material with my lips. I kiss over her other thigh, letting my tongue travel awful close to the edge of her bikini. I could easily slip under.

Knock! Knock!

She gasps and jerks. I lean up, her leg slipping from my shoulder. She's looking at the door and giggles as I roll my eyes. I had totally forgotten about our drinks. I watch her laying seductively on my bed, perching up on her elbows. Making those beautiful abs flex. "That's a sexy little string bikini," I add as I open the door.

277

I really hate this steward; he has to be a virgin or I scare the hell out of him. I stand aside for him to enter. His eyes keep flicking to the goddess laying on my bed. *That's right buddy, take a good look at what you will never claim.*

"She's so far out of your league," I tease him, making his hands tremble.

I chuckle as he turns his back to me to put the tray on the sideboard. Amelia shakes her head at what I said. This time he turns the opposite way, keeping his back towards the bed, head down as he excuses himself. I lock the door.

"You like to tease him? You know he's terrified of you?" she comments.

I give her a knowing grin. "I don't know why, but his presence irks me. He's on a trial run this week." I take a sip of my gin. "I don't think he's going to make the cut. I demand certain behavior from staff, with my lifestyle. He's too young, shy, or googly-eyed for my ladylove. I do believe he admires you."

She laughs as she sips her cosmo, watching me intently. "You do seem to have an intimidating edge to you." Her eyes are dancing over my shoulders and chest. "You like things a certain way."

"Yes, I suppose I do." I sip my drink watching her. "A man in my position has a lot of power. With that comes responsibility. There has to be a sense of control or there would be no order to things. Chaos would take over."

"I get the feeling you're a multifaceted person." She sips her cosmo.

"I'm not going to deny it." I take her drink pulling her into my arms. "I'm very passionate ... driven ... accomplished." I drop a small kiss on her forehead. She's cuddling into me.

"I find this intimidating side of you, your power side, extremely alluring." She admits as she strums her fingers up and down my breastbone. Looking down at her, I feel my heart racing in my chest—those damn sapphires. I have no idea what I'm feeling. Love is an emotion I've never felt. Surely it's lust ... even infatuation with her ... I can dote over her every need. But I can't love her! It's impossible to have that kind of raw emotion ... the kind my mother and father shared. The end result is only severe heartbreak.

Her phone rings on the bedside table. Breaking her eyes from mine, she leans over looking at it. She doesn't have to tell me. I already know it's him. I really hate him.

"So are we really doing this?" She looks at me, incredulous.

"Do you want me to answer it or kill it?" I ask taking her phone.

"I don't want him to find out like this." I decline the call and turn her phone off. "I'll tell him it's over in person."

I toss her phone onto my bedside table. She's scooting down in my bed cuddling into me. "Not alone ... you're not doing this alone. Men get crazy when they lose control." I kiss her lips. "We will tell him together."

"You don't think that's going to devastate him even more, seeing us together?"

I snicker. "You're worried about his feelings? He's a huge ass to you. Honestly, his feelings are the least of my concern. I'd love for him to see he lost you to me." Yeah, I know that sounds super arrogant.

"I don't want to discuss him." *This can be arranged.*

Chapter 29: Amelia

"Oh my god!" I gasp at the coldness of the ice cubes. His eyes are full of desire as I watch him hold the ice between his lips, he's dragging it down between my breasts. I whimper as my abs constrict at the coldness; he's swirling it around my belly button.

"Don't move, or it's going to slide off that sexy tummy of yours." I giggle watching him. "Now where was I before we got interrupted?" He looks like a devil, grinning.

I close my eyes savoring his tongue kissing and licking over my bikini strap. "Mmm." I open my eyes; he's nibbling my inner thigh. I watch him as he takes the melting ice with the tip of his finger, pulling it from my naval. He's sucking on the inside of my right thigh, fingering the ice down.

I jerk, feeling the ice on my sex. He grins, looking up at me, and messages the ice gently in a circling motion over my covered clitoris. "Oh shit." I toss my head back. It's cool. I feel my hot wetness on the inside and now he's wetting the outside with cold ass water.

He laughs tossing it aside, running his cold fingertip across my skin. "I really want to touch you." *Is he asking me?*

"I don't know," I whisper. I'm so turned on, but fingers down there really aren't my thing. I feel him kissing around my bikini line, tickling his fingers across my covered clitoris, running his fingertips up and down my slit.

I clasp my hands on each side of his face, tickling his scruff. Grinning, he's closing the distance. I can feel his breath on my lips. He nudges my nose with the tip of his as he covers my mouth. I moan into his mouth, his tongue dipping, dancing, and gliding with mine. My arms wrap around his neck. I'm gone, soaring into him.

He shifts, his weight to the side, as I feel his fingers toying with my bottoms. He's wanting to dive deeper. I flex my hips against him, his hand. My body tenses as I feel his fingers ... on my skin ... under the material.

"Relax," he breathes into our kiss. "I'm not going to hurt you." He lightly rubs little circles around the rim of my clitoris. *Okay, I like that.* I deepen our kiss, relaxing under his touch. *I like that a lot, actually.*

I moan flexing into him; he's still being so gentle. "You like this?" he moans against my lips. He knows I do. I'm practically soaking.

"Yes," I purr as he continues to seductively flick my clitoris with his fingers.

"I'm just sliding my fingers down, I'm not hurting you," he confirms as he takes my mouth again, deepening our kiss, distracting me. I whimper at his touch, he's stroking my slit, running back up to my clitoris, repeating that wonderful circular motion.

"Yes," I whisper, naturally opening my thighs for him. I'm lost in him. I don't care what he does to me. "Fuck," I whimper against his lips. His lips are like heaven. His fingers are the devil's tool.

"You're very beautiful and fucking wet. So damn wet!" he growls, breaking our kiss as he sucks and bites down my jaw. I gasp, closing my eyes and wrapping my arms around his head as he continues to suck and nibble down my neck.

"I want more," I moan pulling his face to mine. I suck his bottom lip—leading our single-lip kisses. I feel his finger separate my folds and gasp when he enters me. I clutch his bedding.

"Breathe baby!" *I am trying.* He coaxes me as he takes my lip, sucking it. "You don't like something, just tell me. I will stop." He groans as he starts moving his finger in a come-hither motion. My insides are tensing around his finger. He grins, looking at my eyes before he covers my lips with another open-mouth kiss.

Oh my god, I've never felt anything like this. It's already lasted longer than any sexual experience I've had in my entire life. I can't breathe, my toes are curling. He's strong and consistent in his movements. Our tongues are one, naturally dancing and twisting their own sexual parade.

"Let it go baby, let me own your come," he breathes into our kiss. He drops down, sucking my ear lobe. Holy hell, he is hot.

"Quinton," I scream hitching my upper body tight around him, whimpering, thrashing my hips against his hand.

Chapter 30: Quinton

Fucking hell, her silk is covering my fingers. I could come in my shorts, but this isn't about me. It's about her and she's coming hard. Damn, she has to be the sexiest woman I've ever seen. I love the way my name sounds across those lips. She claps her hands around my cheeks, pulling me into her lips, whimpering, she sucks and kisses my bottom lip.

She kisses so sweetly. Her husband is right, she's fucking tight. I want to get lost in her. I slide my fingers out, running my hands up her body, rolling her into me. We just naturally fit.

I run my hand down her hip and she slides her leg over mine. She's still coming down from the climatic high. She can grind those hips out on me anytime. Her breathing is settling out. I've never made out with a woman and didn't end up having sex, another novelty for me. I'm going to need to soak my balls in the rest of the ice.

"You're very gentle." She's been quiet. "I've never been touched like that, that way I mean." *I hate that fucktard.*

"You have over eight thousand nerve endings at your clitoris, there is only one way to touch—heavy handed isn't it."

"No, I mean what you did with your fingers inside of me, it wasn't painful. This was the first time I didn't cry, wanting it to end." My stomach clutches as I hear her sniffle softly. I'm going to crush that fucktard. "Feel free to touch me whenever you like, I trust you."

I pull her chin up to me. "No one will ever touch you that way again." She climbs up and presses her lips against mine. I love these small, single-lip kisses with her.

She sighs as she rolls back against me, relaxing. "I am sort of hungry." She laughs.

I look at the clock, it's almost one. "We've been consumed with each other almost all day."

"What?" She looks at the clock. "Oh wow! I didn't realize we've been gone that long. Now I feel bad Mr. Starks; keeping the host from his guests."

"You're the only guest I'm concerned with hosting." I lean over and grab the plate of strawberries. "Here sweetheart."

I watch her bite; she closes her eyes and smiles, savoring the sweetness. "Mmm, these are the best strawberries." She leans over and pops the last bite into my mouth.

"Yes, they are." I grin looking down her body.

"Must be another perk of your lifestyle." She pushes the plate aside, climbing on top of me kissing me seductively, dipping her chocolate laced tongue into my mouth. Humming as she explores, she rocks her hips against me.

"Oh hell," I growl, flipping her hard, causing her to laugh. "If you start that up, we will never get of this room." I growl looking down her body rubbing my shaft against her sex. "I want nothing more than to strip and ravish you."

"I feel bad, you didn't get to ..." She purses her lips as she leaves the statement open. I laugh.

"Oh, trust me, this has been quite satisfying for me. I will get off, all in good time." I watch her get up and start straightening her swimsuit. I've got a boner from hell right now. "You're going to have to give me a minute before I can go up." I stand gulping my warm gin. I like it better cold.

She walks over and wraps her arms around my waist, kissing my chest. "Thank you."

"For what?" I give her, her cosmo. "We'll get you a fresh one." I walk with my hand on the small of her back.

"For being the most unselfish man I've ever met."

"You're worth the extra time, ladylove." I kiss the tip of her nose as we go up to join the others for lunch.

Chapter 31: Amelia

"Well, well they do live in the sun." Tierra beams at me. She's totally trying to decide if we had sex. I laugh as Tierra and Tina are both eyeing me.

"Go ahead, I know what you want to ask me," I tease as we playfully walk towards Toni, who is already holding my cosmo.

"Oh yeah she had an orgasm, I see it in her walk." Tina laughs. "Toni, three red-headed slut shots."

"Toni, can I get Mr. Starks a fresh gin on the rocks, please?" He's already grinning as he slides it across the bar.

"And your shades Ms. Amelia; you left them on the lounges earlier."

"How do I keep forgetting these? Thank you." I slip them on as I walk over to the L-shaped sofa. "Here sexy," I breathe, sounding a bit sexier than I intended.

Quinton grins when I give him the gin. "That's pretty damn hot, you serving me in a bikini." Andy and Michael grins their appreciation.

"I guess my scullery maid attire was a bit overdressed at the inn." He bursts into a deep, throaty laugh as he reaches for me to sit with him. I lean back on the cushions—the sun feels

287

good, warming my skin, my face. I keep my eyes shut, listening to the sound of the yacht cruising through the water, music playing in the background.

They're drilling him about what we did. He sounds like a frat boy bragging about hitting third base. They rag him about not bringing it home. I feel his hand slide around my knee, caressing my thigh. "I've brought it home countless times, this is different."

"Damn right it's different, you smitten kitten." Gerry swaggers up. "Some things that are hard and fast are amazing."

The steward stumbles, tipping the shots over. "Shit," I hiss, jumping up as cold liquid hits my thighs. Quinton, does too, noticing the culprit. He already doesn't like the steward.

"Oh! Ma'am I'm so sorry. Let me get it." He grabs his towel, trying to blot the spill, groping at my legs. But he doesn't register where he's putting his hands, trying to get the liquid before it gets on the cushion.

"Hey ... hey!" I scream swatting his hands away.

"Ah hell." I hear the anger in Quinton's voice as he shoves him back, snatching the towel from his hands. "Toni," he calls. Pointing at the steward he yells, "You don't fucking put your virgin hands between her legs."

Toni snatches him by the shoulder, almost pulling him to the ground. I watch Quinton take the towel, wiping my legs and thighs. "Did he touch you?"

"No." I see Toni reaming him.

288

"Really, what a fucking loser," Tierra comments.

"How the fuck does he not understand his position?" Tina asks. "If that had happened on my daddy's yacht, he would've been thrown overboard."

I roll my eyes and shake my head at her remark. "It's fine … just startled me, that's all."

"I thought we were all about to have lay some pansy out," Andy joked.

I looked at him, sitting my drink down taking the towel from Quinton. "It was an accident."

"Code of brotherhood sweetheart. You're Quinton's woman, you're our responsibility. Same as if I'm not around, Quinton and Michael watch over Tierra."

"Yep, and if I'm out, Andy and Quinton watch over Tina. We help keep safe what matters most to each of us in this entire world—Tina, Tierra, and until now, Quinton never had anyone."

"Oh," I whisper, watching Quinton's features soften.

"You sure you're okay, he didn't grope you?" I watch him standing, towering over me. He's scary when he's pissed. *That poor steward.*

"It's fine." I kiss him on his lips. "You scare him … he's nervous around you."

"He should be." Quinton's not laughing … he's serious. He watches my eyes briefly before kissing me hard. I let him lead our one-lip kisses, sucking my bottom lip; I know he likes this. I feel him wrapping his body around mine, deepening our kiss.

289

I can feel his frustration in his movements. *It's sort of turning me on.* We're lost kissing each other.

"Ladies." I turn from my lips of pleasure to Toni's voice. Quinton is kissing and nibbling my neck. "Let's try this round of red-headed slut shots again."

"Sir, lunch will be served shortly." Quinton leans up at Captain's voice, giving him his attention. "Ma'am, sorry for the mishap. Sir, do you want another steward? I think it's best he not help with bar drinks."

"Fine." Quinton nods. "He can finish this trial run, if he can manage not to drop lunch."

Tierra pulls me out of Quinton's grasp, laughing. "You have hogged her all day. We're going to do this shot, then lay out away from stewards who want to grope her."

I laugh as I grab the shot. "He wasn't trying to deliberately touch me."

Tierra shrugs, dismissing it.

"One, two, three," Tina counts. We all toss it. I do a little dance. Tina and Tierra wrap their arms through mine. "Let's get some music pumping," Tina comments.

We get situated on the cushion sun lounges on the font decking. You can see everything from this position. "This is amazing," I tell them.

"Compliments of the boss." Toni is grinning, handing us fresh cosmos. We all turn looking at the men. They're all relaxing, throwing back drinks, and watching us.

"Do they always watch like this?" I ask.

"Oh yeah." Tina giggles.

"So tell me, how was it?" Tierra grins, never lifting her head.

"Unlike anything I've experienced in my entire life. He's very unselfish." I feel wet thinking about it. The sun warming my sex is intensifying the desire. Is this what Tierra meant by the sun making you horny?

"The best ones are," Tina pants. "Michael is amazing. We can fuck for hours."

"I know you two do, you forget I've heard." Tierra grins, sipping her drink.

"Well, I've heard you and Andy too, need I remind you of last night." Tina laughs.

"I've never had any kind of relationship like you two have with each other."

"You do now, sweetie."

"Do you think I'm a bad person, being here with Quinton and married to Eric?" I haven't even thought about him since his last call. He's like a gas pain that just appears occasionally.

"What are your intentions when we return Sunday?" Tierra asks.

"Telling him it's over. Quinton said he would be happy to tell him now, but I don't think that's the right way to handle this situation."

"Quinton is a very rich man. He can take care of things very easily for you." Tierra looks at me.

"He's a very powerful man as well." Tina smirks.

"I've gathered he's successful." They laugh at my comment. "I don't care about material objects. I like him very much. I don't think he should get in the middle of it, and I'll figure it out when I get back."

"News flash, he's very much in the middle of it." Tierra leans, over grinning. "He's in the middle of all of it." She wiggles her eyebrows, laughing. I roll my eyes. "He's not going to let you fight this battle alone."

"I don't understand why he's even interested in me. I really don't live that interesting of a life, especially compared to you guys."

"Honey, most don't." Tina laughs. "He likes you. We all saw it the night at the club. We've been friends forever, and I have never seen him look at anyone the way he looks at you."

"It's true, you maybe divorcing one man, but you're not alone. You've got Quinton and I don't mean like a temporary fix. I mean he's all in." Tierra is serious. "If you fucking break is heart, I'll fucking break you!"

"What?" I gasp at her threat.

"It's true, we love him. We love you, but if you end up fucking him over for that douche bag you're married to, because you get cold feet about leaving, you will have some crazy mad bitches looking for you. We will find you and fuck you up."

I laugh at their threats. They both drop their shades simultaneously, turning to me, so I can see the seriousness in their eyes. They're like a set of furious Siamese cats. "We're not fucking around, Amelia," Tierra says, deadpan.

"I think I love him," I whisper looking straight out. "I haven't been in love with anyone in I don't know how long. Hell, maybe I've never been in love before. I don't know. I just know I'm not staying with my husband." I hear them awe in appreciation for my words. "And after what we've shared today, I'm scared to death of never feeling the way I do feel when I'm with him."

"Damn right." Tina grins sipping her drink.

"You have no idea what it's like to be married to the wrong man. Hell, I wasn't even sure our marriage was consummated it happened so fast. We waited to have sex until then, big mistake!" My gaze is on the beautiful view as I sip my cosmo. "My voice is never heard. The anxiety is so overwhelming at times, it felt like I was drowning inside of my own body." I bite my lip, thinking about it all. "I lost myself—became an empty shell just to make it through another day of hell." I'm so completely lost in my thoughts I don't realize there's a crowd listening. "I let him alienate my friends, and didn't even realize one day they were just gone. You know my father died. My mom's alive but she's in his corner. We don't talk. In her eyes, he can do no wrong, and I'm a horrible person; she's defended him every time he's belittled me; every piece of smashed furniture, window shattered, wall punched, phone replaced." I laugh. "I cringe at the thought of my husband touching me when I don't want it. It wasn't ever about me. He'd shove his fingers in me, to prove he could. It felt like the worst gyno appointment ever." I finish my drink, and continue, "You ever had someone screaming in your face, waving a gun? What kind of person even does that?" I wipe a tear. "It's pretty traumatizing. I actually faked a break-in, and I buried it in the yard." I laugh. "Ironically, he was worried for my safety. That's when we moved to Amelia. So you see, you don't have to worry, I have zero intentions of returning to him."

"And I have zero intentions of letting that motherfucker near you again!" I whip around, seeing Quinton. They were all listening ... *when did they even walk over?*

Shit! I wasn't ready for him to know all the fucked up details of my marriage to Mr. Wonderful! "How much did you hear?" I can't look at him. Tierra and Tina quietly disappear with their husbands. "Were you all listening?"

"We heard enough to piss us off." I feel him wrap his arms around me. "You're not telling him it's over without me."

I pull away. "I don't want you to see me that way." *Great!* Now he knows too damn much. He's not going to want to get mixed up with me. I've ruined something before it had a chance to blossom.

"Look at me." He's coaxing my face up to see my eyes. "I don't see you any differently than before." He lowers his face to mine, kissing my lips. I let him suck my bottom lip.

"The guys will." I drop my head, toying with the lounge strap. "I was confiding in the girls."

"No secrets in this group, remember? They don't see you differently." He looks back at them. "If anything, they're probably going to be more protective now. Think of them like the big siblings you never wanted." I titter at that thought. "Come on, let's go eat lunch, take some shots." He stands holding out his hand. I bite my bottom lip, slipping my hand into his. He kisses the back of it before lacing our fingers.

Chapter 32: Quinton

"Toni, a round of shots, different types—some fruity flavors," I tell him as we pass the bar to go to the table. Everyone is already seated, drinking their drinks and waiting. I pull Amelia's chair out, as I watch that pesky steward start serving the appetizers. If he drops her oysters Rockefellers, he will be tossed overboard.

"You're going to spoil me to these," she whispers in my ear. I can't help but grin.

"I look forward to it." I see Toni with a tray of shots. I know she can use one, maybe five. I pass her two purple ones immediately.

"Everyone get a shot, shots to new beginnings." I grin looking at her.

"New beginnings," everyone sings. We toss them back.

"Toss it." I point to her second shot. "I'm sure you could use it."

"You have no idea." She grins throwing it back. I laugh as she does a little dance in her seat.

"Your tits look hot in that bikini." I wiggle my eyebrows at her. She gasps at my frankness. Probably too much gin and I'm horny. I laugh playfully.

"Yeah they really do," Michael confirms.

"Y'all are crazy," she tells Michael. She's laughing, *Good, she knows we're messing around in good humor.*

"Open that beautiful mouth." She smiles as I bring an oyster to her lips. "Tilt, swallow." I smirk. She rolls her eyes.

She tickles her fingers through my scruff. "I like this," she purrs. Her tits brush against my forearm. As she leans over, I feel her breath on my lips. She kisses me softly. I love these single-lip kisses ... sucking her bottom lip, as she sucks on my top. She's so sweet.

I grin like a kid, watching her as she relaxes back, sipping her cosmo. I pop an oyster. Damn she's sexy. I want to get lost in her tonight. I watch the pesky steward like a hawk as he approaches our table. He's nervous—*she's right that I scare him.*

"At least you're not wearing it," I whisper in her ear. She giggles, taking a bite of her lobster roll.

"Good?"

"Very delicious. I can see why you like having a personal chef."

"Is that something you could get use to?"

"How so?" she asks me.

"Well, I know you enjoy cooking, but my personal chef is part of my lifestyle." I have no intentions of giving him up. I want her in my life, enjoying my perks.

"Oh." She looks down. "You mean if I could get use to someone being around to make me whatever my heart craves?"

"Well, yes." I grin.

"Well, yes. Like I said you have a very interesting lifestyle Mr. Starks. Many satisfactory perks. Although I do like to dabble in the kitchen," she teases as she takes another bite. God her mouth is beautiful. I could watch the way she eats for the rest of her life.

"Good!" I grin, relaxing and enjoying our lunch. I love having her with me; the gang loves her. I want her to move in with me. I must be insane. I haven't even slept with her, and I already know it's going to be amazing.

"What are you grinning about?" I ask her.

"Do you care if get a few more shots? I really want to get buzzed." I laugh, she's cute, 'do I care?' I throw my hand up for Toni.

"Shots, something good, you know what she likes. Keep them coming." She smirks, watching my eyes. "You can drink as much as you like, Toni will get you whatever you want."

I watched her take a few more bites of lobster and kale salad. She grins as Toni returns with several shots. "Here you go sweet Amelia." She tosses them back to back.

"Damn girl, thought that husband said you didn't drink." Gerry playfully rolls his eyes. I give him a look. It's clear he's joking, but I don't want anything about him breathed around her.

"No, he didn't drink, and since he didn't, he didn't want me to." I watch Toni return with four more shots.

"Drink with me Gerry." She slides one over. "Here Marcus, take one. Ready? Shoot." I laugh as the three of them do their girly shots.

"Yeah that's what we're talking about, let's get boozing." Andy grins as he watches. "Toni, hook us up with shots down here."

"Yes, sir." He grins as he brings Amelia four more shots. "Sir, would you like some shots?" I grin watching her starting to dance in her seat.

"Yeah, a round of shots for us all. Lay off Amelia … she's starting feel it." Toni laughs and nods.

"She had a pretty big emotional release," Marcus whispers to me. "That has to feel better off her chest. She hasn't had anyone to talk to."

"Don't go all therapist on me," I tease. "I do agree though. Now she can relax."

I grin as Toni starts sitting shots out. "Tell Captain to stop, set up the swim deck, and let's get the toys out."

"Yes, sir." He smiles as his eyes dance over Amelia dancing. Toni can enjoy her dancing. He's different from that other pipsqueak.

"Let's all shoot on three," Michael counts. Amelia grabs mine and shoots it. The table laughs. She stands and walks behind me, bending my head back into her chest. She covers my mouth, giving me my shot from sexy ass lips. Damn she's hot. She grins as she sucks and nibbles my lips.

"Damn!" Andy laughs.

"Dance with me Mr. Starks!" She's grinning, shaking her hips. I really want to watch her for minute.

"Ladies go shake it," I tell them as I watch her move. I want to see those tits in that suit bounce. "I want to watch you, sexy vixen," I growl.

She grins as she grabs Tierra, pulling on her arms. I move my seat to other end of the table, by Michael and Andy. I toss my hand up for another shot from Toni. "Let's watch."

"Yeah." Tierra is squealing and dancing. They're breaking it down. Toni is grinning. I laugh, watching Amelia shaking her ass. She moves her hips to the music perfectly. I like it when she shimmies her shoulders, grinning and looking like a fucking sex symbol moving her body.

"She's going to be a great fuck," Michael says, looking at me.

"My cock is about to explode," I admit, laughing. We throw our shots back. "I need to get some condoms when we port tomorrow."

"She has an IUD, don't worry about it," Andy reminds me. Oh, I haven't forgotten. "You know she's clean and you're clean."

"Yeah." I lean back, watching her. "I don't know how she'll feel about that idea." I chuckle, what are they doing now? "Dance with them Toni," I give him permission. "Look at

300

them. Wonder where the little smitten steward is, she would give him a conscious wet dream." We all laugh as she's dropping down the front of Toni. I like Toni, he has a lot of fun with the ladies. He's rubbing and dropping it with them.

Her back is to me, she's dancing, shaking her money maker. I go over to her. Her are eyes closed, running her hands through her hair. Damn, she looks like a temptress. I move my hips, thrusting against her. She grins turning her face to the side, looking at me. She wraps her hands behind my head as she's grinding her hips into me.

Her sexy stomach flexes beneath my fingers with her every move. "You're fucking hot," I growl in her ear. This is how we first danced in my club over a week ago.

I notice Michael is snapping pictures of us together. I'm going have some sexy ass pictures of my vixen.

She turns around, wrapping her arms around my neck, and we start swaying to the beat of another song. She's so bendy in her dancing. "I love your body Mr. Starks." She grinds her hips into mine.

"I love your body Ms. Amelia, I'd love to make you moan again," I tease sucking her neck.

"I think I'd like that too." She grins, looking up at me with seductive eyes.

I laugh, pulling her tighter, swaying her, and feeling her body against mine as we get lost in the music. She's perfect for me. I really hate that she's married. I'd love to see Eric's face tomorrow, when he discovers his wife is gone!

"Come on Amelia." Tina pulls her from embrace, breaking my thoughts. "We're going to lounges, drinking some cosmos, and talking about our men." I laugh as she holds my fingers until she's literally pulled from my grasp.

I relax back on the L-shaped sofa. I've got the perfect view of my ladylove. She's having a blast. Damn she's beautiful. I laugh watching Gerry with the girls, and his girl-like mannerisms.

"Do you want to beat the husband now?" Michael asks as he takes a seat.

"Not to be put in jail, for him free to roam the streets harassing her." I grin, sipping my gin. "It will give me plenty of satisfaction, knowing he knows she's here with me. That she left him for me. I know I sound like an arrogant son of a bitch, but it's the truth."

"How's that supposed to happen?" Andy smirks.

"You are looking at Jacksonville's most eligible bachelor. You know how we're always followed when we hit the island. Shit, the media will have a frenzy seeing me with Amelia. I have Steve meeting us with extra detail." I grin watching her. "She really is the most fascinating woman I've ever met."

"You really are one smitten son of a bitch too!" Andy points out. "You going to warn her about the media? Or tell her who she's partying with?"

I laugh. "Nope." I hold my hand up for another gin. "I'll let her figure it out on her own. I'm still the same guy." And … if Eric's get wind of her being with me, because of it … well, good riddance!

"What are you going to do about the husband?" I look at Michael. "You don't seem to be having an issue crossing that line."

"We're way past that line." I look at him. "I'm going to crush him. When we get back, Andy, I want you to look at the market for architecture firms. I'm going to hit him where it will really hurt. I want to buy the firm he works for, dissolve it, and make it so no one will hire his ass. When he doesn't have that to fall back on, I want him to discover I'm also fucking his wife." I smirk. "I'll definitely be fucking her by that point."

Chapter 33: Amelia

"Do you need me to lotion that beautiful body?" I grin looking up at Quinton.

"Here." I hand him my lotion. "Did you think you would be rubbing lotion on me on your yacht when we were eating lunch at the marina?"

He laughs. "No. I wanted to have you here, but I didn't have any idea how to get you to come out."

I watch him grab more lotion. I hold my breath as he rubs his hands over my cleavage. "Breathe or you'll pass out," he tells me. He continues to massage me and lets his fingertips graze the inner rim of my top.

"Are you hoping to feel something Mr. Starks?" I tease, feeling his fingers linger longer than necessary.

"What straight male wouldn't?"

"I could just take my top off and sunbathe topless for you," I tease looking out at the water.

"Yes! You can, but then I'll have to lotion every part of your tits, I don't want them to burn."

"And is that a problem?" I tease. I really do want to take my top off. "I've never sunbathed topless." I don't know why I find this humorous.

"You're going to flash the crew and the guys? Because I'm sure you'll have many onlookers. I can't even begin to try to stop that from happening."

I strum my fingers lazily up and down his arms. "Your forearms are awful sexy Mr. Starks." I grin looking at them.

"Are they now, Ms. Amelia?" he teases lowering his face towards mine.

"Oh, yes very," I whisper dropping my eyes from his to his lips. God, he has a beautiful smile. I tickle my fingers through his scruff making my way to his beautiful hair. "I love this." He's got that sexy grin now.

I smile when I feel his breath on my lips. His eyes are intense. I nudge his nose with the tip of mine. He opens his mouth as I hover my lips over his, just barely grazing them, dipping my tongue, teasing this new space. He growls, covering my mouth with his. His open-mouth kiss shoots straight to my sex, he has my libido on fire. His tongue glides smoothly and seductively into mine, searching me, studying me. Our tongues dance the perfect waltz. Complete harmony.

He's shifting his weight, getting more comfortable, which I totally welcome! An involuntary moan escapes my throat as he runs his hand down my side, pulling my leg up around his hip. "You feel good beneath me," he breathes into my mouth. Correction, he feels good on top of me, but I just keep kissing him. Threading his hair with my fingers. I'm so lost in him. I think I'm in love.

I gasp into his lips as he cups my breast in his hand. He's grinning when I open my eyes, as he massages my breast. I look around and notice the girls slipped away.

He kisses my jaw, nibbling and sucking down my neck. "I want to kiss you," he mumbles into my neck. He sucks my sun-kissed skin as he kisses lower down my breastbone.

"You are kissing me."

He smirks. "I want to kiss you here." He dips his hand under my bikini, teasing my nipple with his fingers. It elongates instantly. My sex throbs and gets wet. I moan, flexing my hips against his hard on as he circles my areola with his thumb.

"I want that too … but we can't … I can't …"

He grins, massaging me. "Why?" He asks kissing my cleavage, nipping the skin. "Everyone is at the swim deck." Holy mother of Jesus, I'm about to die.

"Because it turns me on big time Mr. Starks." He grins watching me. And he knows this, I can see it in his eyes.

"Did you just share with me what makes you want to get naked, Ms. Amelia?" I cover my eyes with my arm. He's the devil.

"You're a very naughty player," I tease.

"I never said I wasn't naughty." He flicks his tongue across my skin. "You taste tropical."

I smirk at him. "I'm done talking about this. Between your kisses and fingery things, I know you're going to blow my mind once you start kissing my tits." He grins and nods; he knows this is true.

"Fingery things, huh?" He laughs. He strolls his fingertips up and down my outer thigh. "You loved my fingery things. You will love what I can do with my tongue too, Ms. Amelia."

I roll my eyes. "Oh, god! Well, I'm sure I will." I smirk watching him as he pulls me to standing with him. "Where are we going?" I ask grabbing my cosmo.

"To the swim deck. If you're not going to let me kiss your nipples, I at least want to see you wet in this string." I roll my eyes.

"You're a terrible flirt, Mr. Starks." I wrap my arm around his waist as we walk towards the others.

"No, I'm an excellent flirt." He playfully nips my neck. "I'm terrible at waiting."

Chapter 34: Quinton

"There's the man of the hour," Andy yells as he sees us approaching. Amelia laughs as we watch him do a backflip off into the water. Damn, she feels good hanging on my arm. I'm about to die with the desire to get in between her legs.

She grins, taking my gin and setting it down. "You're awful dry, Mr. Starks."

"Don't you even think about it," I tease.

"Okay, I won't think about it." She shoves me off the swim deck. "I'll do it." She laughs as I hit the water. She's laughing the most beautiful sound when I come up.

"Oh, you're going to pay," I tease. "Andy, Michael, toss me that beautiful ass."

"What?" She looks at them as they grab her. "You wouldn't …"

Andy grabs her arms and Michael has her ankles, and they swing her like a hammock. She's laughing and screaming. They toss her over towards me.

I grab her in my arms when she comes up, still laughing. "I got you now," I tease, covering her lips with my mouth, tasting the salt water. I dive my tongue deep, swirling ours together. She wraps her beautiful body around me. She sucks and nibbles at my lips, moving our kiss to a sensual one-lip kiss.

I'm wading us both further into the water. "Now you look awful sexy wet."

"Mmm, I like the way you taste Mr. Starks," she purrs pulling back looking at me. She's grinning as she shoves me under the water, pushing away. She's laughing as I come up swimming after her. I grab her ankle, pulling her back and she goes under a little. Laughing, I grab her, and wrapping her legs back around me, I dip under the water and nip the outside of her swimsuit at her nipple. She gasps as I come up grinning.

"Don't tease me, I'll strip you," I growl. I'm horny as hell!

"Keep it for the bedroom," Andy yells as we look at him. He nods. "This is some clear water my friend."

"I guess my fingery things are off the table then," I whisper in her ear. She laughs, grinning at me. She can't tell if I'm serious or joking.

Michael helps pull her back on the swim deck as I get another nice view of her ass. I'm totally going to try to fuck her tonight. Maybe she just didn't want her husband's shit up in her. I'd love to fill her with my cum. That would be another novelty for me.

"I can see your thoughts buddy," Michael warns as I stand and grab a towel to wipe off the water.

"What?" I tease watching her talking to Toni. He seems to like her. "Do you blame me?" I ask, grinning, as Toni hands me a fresh gin.

"I'd be trying to seal the deal before tonight." He laughs as he gets another drink as well. I look up to the sound of a yacht horn. "Who is that?" Michael asks as we stand. I look, the girls are all out of the water, laying on the swim deck.

"I think that's Trek Powers's yacht." I turn to see the captain coming.

"Quinton Starks," I hear the man yell my name. Yeah, I was right it is him.

"Trek Powers." I wave.

"I thought this was your yacht. You heading down to the islands for a few days?" He asks as he's skimming the ladies.

"Yeah, hitting Nassau tomorrow for the day, then Freeport. I've got to be back Sunday." I see him wondering who the third chick is. He will recognize Tierra and Tina. "You coming from the islands?"

"Yeah, you got the usual with you?"

"Yep." I hate his nosey ass. The only reason I tolerate him is because his family's estate in the Hamptons is beside mine.

"Who's the yellow canary?" I knew it. I grin looking at her fine ass. He can admire her and eat his heart out.

"Amelia," I yell as she waves, sipping her cosmo.

"Beautiful lady."

"Yes, she is." I look at Michael.

"He's waiting for his usual invite aboard," Andy whispers. I roll my eyes.

"We're anchored for a bit. Feel free to join," I call. He grins as he talks to his captain. He gives us the thumbs up. "God, he has a mouth that loves to talk. I'm sure he'll drop my new billionaire stat real quick," I whisper to Andy and Michael as I walk towards Amelia.

"You want to go up top, get fresh cosmo, something to snack on?" I grin watching her stand. She's by far the sexiest lady here.

"Why did you go and invite douche bag?" Tierra whines as she rolls over to sun her back.

"Civilities." I hold my hand out as Amelia takes it. "You look beautiful." I kiss her softly on the cheek.

"Well, you know he always travels with his pig friends." She looks at Amelia. "Trek can't get a girl interested in him; he's a man slut. So be prepared to be gawked at. He knows we're married and off the market."

"She's off the market," I confirm. "Let's not mention marital status as a reason, either." I look at them all. "He'll have a blast spreading the news of Quinton Starks being with a married woman." I watch Amelia drop her eyes as she walks to the upper deck. "Shit."

"Smooth Quinton," Tina barks as she follows her.

"I didn't mean it like that," I hiss as I follow the ladies. Michael and Andy laugh. "I didn't want him running his mouth," I growl at them.

"We know, it's funny; you're finally going to see how it feels when our women get mad at us." Michael laughs. "You've never been on this end with us."

I walk up, looking for her. She's nibbling on finger foods the chef prepared on the sideboard. Tina is with her. The pesky steward is standing in the corner. He sees me and stiffens. I must have a broody look about me.

"Finding anything you like?" I tease as I walk up behind her. Tina cuts me a dirty look. "Don't look at me like that Tina, I meant I wanted him to know Amelia's with me and that's why she's off the market."

Amelia looks at me. "I'm with you Mr. Starks." She kisses me on the cheek as she continues filling her plate. Good she's not mad. "I'm not married. I am very much off the market. We got it." *Shit,* she's mad. Tina smirks.

I sigh, shaking my head. "Amelia you're being harsh."

"I like her," Tierra chimes cutting me a smart look. "She's teasing you," she whispers as she walks by.

"Fine, fine if he comes on to you, tell him you're married." I mosey around the table getting a plate. "I won't interfere with his flirtatious ways. He'll just think you're tagging along with girls."

"Do as you wish Mr. Starks," Amelia teases, "I'm not intending to converse with him. If you don't want him to know we're together, that's your choice." She blows a kiss at me as she sits down. Toni grins, bringing her a fresh cosmo and me a gin.

I fix my plate and sit down on the sofa. Trek and his two goons are grinning when they hit the upper deck. "Quinton, thanks for inviting us aboard." He's looking at Amelia as he talks to me. "Tierra and Tina." They give him the typical 'fuck off we're not interested in you' girl look.

I'm not going to play ... he comes on to her, I'll fix it. "Help yourselves, Toni will make you a drink." I look at Amelia and she smiles. I don't like her being curt with me.

I scoot beside her. "I don't play games," I whisper to her. "I'm madly into you."

"I don't want to play either Mr. Starks," she whispers kissing my cheek. She looks like a damn goddess, sitting on her hip, relaxing into me, her fingers toying with my hair. "Tina said you shouldn't be so cold."

I wrap my arm around her. "I wasn't trying to sound cold." I look down her body. "I didn't want that kind of news to get out—believe me it would." I know she doesn't appreciate the comment in its entirety, but once she discovers my status, she'll get it.

She looks at my eyes. "I didn't think anything of your comment, other than I hate having that title. It's just a legal document. It's not where my heart is." Damn she's beautiful. I know I look like a lovesick dog grinning at her.

I look up as Trek is taking a seat. "You remember Todd and Sean."

"Yep." I nod at them as I take a sip of gin. "You heading back to the Hamptons?"

"Yeah, got some dealings in New York next week." I watch him studying the situation on the couch in front of him. "Have you been to your place in the Hamptons lately?"

"No! My sister and her husband visited a few weeks ago." I smile at Amelia as I rub her knee. She's looking at me, smiling, but I can see she's surprised about my place in the Hamptons.

"I didn't realize you were dating anyone, that kind of news you would expect to hear about." And here it begins. I look at him. He's grinning as he's watching me stroke her leg.

"Yes, we've been keeping it on the down low, so if you don't mind helping us out that would be great!" Amelia interjects. She leans over sucking my bottom lip. "I'm going to tan, lover." Oh, hell my cock is about to burst.

"She's hot," Trek barks craning his neck checking her out as she walks by the bar grabbing her cosmo. "You serious about this one?"

"You have no idea," Andy chimes, taking his seat.

"I see your boy Gerry is laying with the ladies." Todd laughs. I glare at him—I will beat his ass if he smarts about Gerry's status.

"Yes, our ladies love Gerry and Marcus," Michael barks back. I feel like I'm about to get into a pissing contest.

Chapter 35: Amelia

Oh my god I can't believe I pulled sultry off like that. I guess Quinton Starks makes the sexy come out in me. I look up as Gerry is panting. "I wish I could have seen that dick dweeb's face."

I laugh, covering my face. "I don't know what got into me. Sorry Tina I can't play games with Quinton."

Toni walks over. "Boss ordered you all a round of shots."

I grin as I swallow my purple shot and look at Quinton, who is watching and smiling. "They're watching us," I tell them.

"You want to put a little show on for them … give them something to watch?" Tierra smirks.

I'm almost afraid to ask. "What?"

"Toni, bring a tray full of shots; we're going to toy with boss and the boys." Toni laughs as he nods.

"Okay come here, Amelia, you get here." Tierra is placing me in front of her. "Tina you're there. Gerry lay down in front of Amelia. Marcus come here by me. I want lots of rubbing and shot tossing, we can give each the shots or whatever you're feeling. Just don't make direct eye contact with the guys."

I laugh, she's a nut. Toni returns with a tray. "Toni, stick a shot in Amelia's cleavage," Tina orders.

"Hey ... what?" I look around.

"It's fine Amelia," Toni assures me as he sets the cleavage shot up. I titter as I steal a glance at the guys, they can see perfectly. Tierra places her hands on each of my tits and takes the shot out my cleavage. Tina tosses my head back in her chest, pouring my shot from her mouth. Marcus pours a shot in Tina's mouth. I lean over Gerry, pouring him a shot in his mouth. We're all laughing and taking body shots off each other ... I forget the point.

"Gerry, I'm fuzzy brained." I giggle as he strokes my hair.

"Open Amelia." Tierra is standing over me, I open and she pours another shot. Marcus pours a shot into Gerry's mouth. We're both laughing.

"Lioness, I knew when we met, you had to meet boss," Gerry slurs, giggling. He's drunk. "I like your hair, it's soft."

I laugh. "I like your hands, you could be a scalp massager." He chuckles. I hear the music get louder. He starts singing.

"Do you do karaoke?" Gerry asks me.

"I don't sing. This is a sexy song."

"Yeah it is." I open my eyes looking up at Quinton. "About as hot as that shot display." I laugh, grabbing Gerry's hands. "It was Tierra's idea."

317

"Well, I guess the three guys still lounging on my sofa will be jacking off thinking about it." I grin, shrugging at his crudeness. He pulls my hands from Gerry. "Bring that beautiful body with me." I stumble in his hands. "Easy there." He's grinning into my eyes. "I do believe you're buzzed again. I'm sure you weren't keeping up with the shots."

"Nope." Tierra laughs.

"Come on, I got the music loud, let's dance." He looks around at all of us. "All of you." I let him lead me to the dancing deck. His hips are swaying and moving to the beat of the music. His shoulders are dancing with the rhythm. He's so sexy.

He grabs my hand and twirls me into his body, bringing my back against his chest. His movements against me are making me want his body.

Tina is rubbing and grinding on him. Tierra starts rubbing on me. I open my eyes, stealing a glance at the lounge sofa, Andy and Michael are snapping pictures with their phones. I close my eyes, wrapping my arm around his neck as another song starts to play. It's a slower dirty dancing grind. We're lost in the music, swaying together. He's kissing down my neck. I kiss him, tasting his gin. "Mmm." He tastes good. He growls as he deepens the kiss, his tongue is taking charge, dominating my mouth—showing his ownership of this orifice. I feel his hands sliding down my body, grabbing my ass, as we sway and grind to the beat.

318

"Do you mind if I cut in?" I hear a voice. Quinton breaks our kiss, looking at Trek.

"You've got to be kidding," he says. He pulls me back into his embrace as he's nibbling down my neck.

"Come on, Tierra and Tina won't dance with us," Trek says. *Well, why does he think I would want to?*

"Not my problem," Quinton mumbles, kissing my neck. I pull tighter to him. I don't want to dance with anyone else. "I think we're going to start back out again, we've been sitting for a while now."

"Ah, you're not going to party hard tonight?" Trek sounds like he's trying to stir Quinton up. "Your boyfriend is the ultimate partier."

"She knows me well enough Trek," he growls. I open my eyes as he pulls back from my neck. "We've got to keep to the schedule. Be sure to tell your folks I said hello. I'll bring Amelia to meet them next time I'm up that way." I smile friendly enough at Trek as I close my eyes, wrapping my arms back behind Quinton's head as he starts kissing and nibbling my neck again.

"See, civilities," he whispers in my ear. "No way in hell he was touching this body." I grin turning to look at him.

"I think I'm pretty inebriated Mr. Starks. No more shots for me please, sir." I don't want to pass out.

"Understood." He walks me to the sofa. "I don't want you unconscious all night. Here, sit with Marcus, I need to speak with the captain."

"Lioness, you want another shot?" I laugh at Marcus.

"No way! I'm good for the rest of the evening." I close my eyes laying my head back on the cushions. "I'm already so tired."

"The sun, water, and booze does it to you." Marcus laughs.

I look at Marcus. "Can I ask you something? I mean it's on my mind and you are a doctor in this field."

"He's been given orders not to be a therapist this week." Gerry laughs as he plops down beside us.

I laugh looking at Marcus. "Ask me anything dear," he says.

"I've always heard relationships that start as affairs never end well." I don't know how to actually form the question.

"And you're worried about you and Quinton." I nod, laying my head on his shoulder.

"Well, I told you he was going to rock your world. This week is just a glimpse, a savory taste of what your life will be like." Gerry laughs, stroking my hair.

"I like him so much, probably more than anyone or thing in my life," I whisper. "But after the thrill, and he comes down from this high, will I be enough? Is the thought of conquering another man's wife a turn on for him?"

"Oh damn, Lioness is equally smitten." Gerry grins.

320

"If people start a relationship off in an affair, won't that relationship suffer because one of them will miss that rush and feel the need to fulfill it by cheating?" I look down, feeling nervous. My hands are tingling; my cheeks heated. I feel weird. "I've never cheated nor considered myself a cheater. I've always known I couldn't ever do that to someone ... but now I can't say that because I am a cheater. Up until now, I've never betrayed anyone on any level." Shit, who am I becoming? What path am I following? "Whether I like it or not, I am married. Married to man not here." I think I'm going to vomit. My head is spinning.

"It's true a lot of times, once a cheater always a cheater." Marcus is now stroking my hair. I think he can feel my tension. "But those people also have a cheater personality or traits about them. Quinton doesn't have those. I suspect by the fact you've never in the past, you don't either. Bottom line is you've been in a toxic marriage for years. You've finally accepted you want more, and a person's heart wants what it wants."

I pull back, looking at him. "And now?" I feel like I'm about to have a panic attack. *Shit, shit. My chest is tight ... heavy.* "I can't breathe ..."

"Amelia are you alright?" Marcus asks. "Amelia?"

I don't answer, shit my chest is about to explode and I can't breathe. My head is spinning. I think I'm drunk. I hear Gerry leaving to get Quinton. I don't look up, my feet and the deck are spinning.

"Amelia." I hear Toni's voice closing in as he swoops me up. "She's probably just a little dehydrated. Too much sun and booze." I feel him carrying me downstairs to the inside lounge sofa. "You need get out of the heat Ms. Amelia. Get a cool rag."

"Amelia!" Quinton booms flying down the stairs. "What happened to her?"

"She's too hot, maybe a little dehydrated from the sun and booze." I feel him move so Quinton can take his seat. God he's handsome.

"Here." Tierra stretches out a wet cloth.

Quinton is blotting my face; it's cold. "I'm fine." I'm pushing the rag out of my face. "I'm fine." He's not buying it.

"Get her some water stat." He leans me up in his arms. "Here, drink." I listen to them talk as I sip the water.

"You're fussing over nothing," I assure them. "I just started having like a small panic attack. I'm fine."

"Why would you have a panic attack?" He looks at Marcus. "We're you being a therapist again?" He smirks, shaking his head.

"She asked me, I didn't know she was going to get so excited talking about her feelings for you." Quinton looks down at me. I grab the cold rag and cover my face.

Tierra and Tina giggle as they walk off. "See, she said she was fine. Andy, why don't we go to our room for a little bit of nooky before dinner?" Tierra offers.

"Yeah, that may be good idea, why don't we all take a break before dinner?" Quinton looks back down at me. I can see him, even with a rag over my eyes. "Dinner is at seven tonight." I feel him lifting me up. "Come on."

"I can walk," I tell him, but he chuckles as he carries me.

Chapter 36: Quinton

She doesn't weigh anything. I should have been making sure she was at least switching off with water. Tierra is a hard partier, she can toss shots like nothing.

"Mr. Starks you can put me down, I'm not that fragile. You all are fussing over nothing." She's squirming. I like it.

"I will now," I tease as I sit her down in my room. "You sure you're feeling okay, no nausea?" I really don't want her vomiting inside.

She laughs at me. "No. I wasn't feeling drunk sick." She looks at her suit. "I feel dirty. I need to shower."

"Well, by all means, shower." I grin, opening the bathroom door. "Or soak in my tub. I don't care."

"I'll just take a quick shower, get the sea water and lotion off. I don't want our bed to smell like that tonight." I grin as I watch her grabbing some clothes, talking about 'our bed.'

She does have a good point. "I'll shower when you're done." I make myself comfortable on the sofa. I turn some music on as I grab my phone to check messages and emails while I wait. I wonder if douche bag has called her. I killed her phone. I look at my side table, walk over and grab her phone, power it up. Damn, twenty missed calls and several texts. Curiosity gets the best of me; I start reading his texts. Asshole is an understatement. He's going to be beyond pissed tomorrow. He might even come back early. Well, he won't be able to find her.

"What are you doing?" I look up as she walks out of the bathroom. Her hair is towel dried and hanging down over her shoulders. She has on those cute ass boy-short lace panties and a white tank top. I can totally see her through it.

I grin holding her phone up. "Curiosity." I toss it aside. I close the distance between us. "Damn you look sexy." She lays her head on my chest as I wrap my hands around her, tickling my fingertips over her ass.

"You need to shower." She softly nips my chest with her teeth, walking out of my grasp and plopping down on her stomach on my bed. She grabs her phone and starts deleting his texts.

"You're not going to read them?"

"Nope, I don't care what his words are. They're just words. I worry about his actions. And right now his actions can't touch me." I smile as I grab a change of clothes.

"That's right Amelia, his actions will never touch you again, I'll make sure of it."

"I trust you Mr. Starks." She grins looking at me. "Hurry up." I smile as I close the door.

My shower has the remnant smells of her shampoo and body wash. Damn she smells nice. I could get use to her always being around, sharing my space. I close my eyes, welcoming the warm spray. I'm quite besotted with Amelia. We haven't really discussed her plans; I don't want to get ahead of myself with the direction our relationship is going. But I hope we're on the same page.

I lather my hair, washing away the sea water. I let my conditioner sit while I wash my body, paying special attention to my cock and balls. I want to make sure they're nice and clean, if sweet Amelia feels inclined to go down on me. "Fuck," I whisper. I've got a full-on boner, just thinking about her beautiful mouth sucking my cock. I walk out of the shower clean and still hard.

I dry my body, checking out my nice, tanned muscles in the mirror. I'm one sexy son of a bitch. What woman wouldn't want to live with me? I can offer her anything her heart would ever desire. I run my hands through my towel-dried hair, brushing the sides first and then towards the back. I grab some Aveda pomade and style it. I look at my scruff, it still looks fine from this morning's trim. I wipe down everything and toss the dirty towels in the hamper. Her swimsuit is hanging. I smile, tossing it in with my laundry. She's not used to having her clothing laundered. Another perk I hope she will accept.

I slip on my fitted navy tee and a pair of loose dark gray lounge pants. I kill the light as I open the door. I guess I took too long. Amelia has dozed off. She's adorable cuddled under the sheets. I walk over to my side, noticing her phone has two new missed calls. My is heart stuck in my throat, what if she had tried calling him while I showered? *No, that is her right,* I tell myself. I look at her call log, she didn't. I check to see if she texted him, she didn't. I grin at my paranoia. I've never had that emotion before.

I kill her phone before climbing into bed. She's so beautiful. I spoon her while she sleeps, kissing her neck softly.

"No!" She jumps, snatching the sheet up to her neck. Her eyes are like saucers, adjusting to her surroundings. I freeze looking at her. What the fuck has he done to her?

"Easy sweetheart." I'm cautious as I sit up stroking her back. "I wasn't trying to do anything ... just holding you."

"I'm sorry." She looks down. "I must have crashed. I'm not afraid of your touch." She looks at me. "Ghosts."

"Come here." I pull her into the crook of my arm kissing her forehead rubbing her hair. "That's history." *That is what that is, pure fucking history.* She smiles as she scoots in. "Damn you smell good. Feel good too."

She laughs into my chest. "You do too—smell and feel good." She runs her fingers under my shirt, touching my six pack. "I like to feel your skin."

"I like you feeling me." I really do, and so does my ego. I look down at her cuddled into my side tickling my fingers up and down her arm.

"So you've got a place in the Hamptons?" She's making little circles around my belly button.

"I have an estate there, yes. It's quite lovely. I would love to show you sometime."

"Wow, an estate! I seem to think there are so many more perks about knowing you, Mr. Starks, than you let on." She's sporting an inquisitive smile as she continues rubbing me. "Oceanfront?"

"Yes, it is, pool too. Modern." She looks at me. "I hope you're more into dating me instead of just knowing me, Amelia." She lays her head on my chest, *shit* that's not the response to that question. "Amelia, what is going through that beautiful head of yours?"

"A ton of things." I hear her sigh. "I've had the best two days of my life with you."

"Good! It has been two of the best for me as well." I grab her hand, lacing our fingers. "I hope we will have many more days like what we've already shared." Why is she being so quiet?

"What am I going to do Sunday?"

"What do you mean? You said you wanted to go on adventure. You can come back to my place with me. I have more than enough room."

She leans up. "You want me to come to your place and stay with you. Like live with you?" I know how crazy that sounds, I hear it, but yes, I do. I grin, nodding.

I sit up as she shakes her head in disbelief. "You don't even know me. What if you can't stand the way I chew my food?" She titters, hugging her knees to her chest and looking over at me. Damn she's adorable.

I chuckle pulling her back in bed with me. "I love the way you chew your food, I've already been studying your little mannerisms. I know enough to know you're the one. Have you forgotten we dreamt of each other? Living together, we'll learn all kinds of fun things about one another. Like you're going to have to deal with my huge ego, and I do mean it's huge!" I nod excitedly as she laughs.

"And all your 'I am Quinton Starks' perks!" she teases.

"Exactly, now you're getting it. I have many, many perks and I love them. I want to share them with you," I tease nibbling the back of her hand.

"You haven't even slept with me, I may not be up to par for you." She looks down. She really has her doubts. *Oh baby, you have no idea how much I want to sleep with you.*

"Well, I've dreamed about it, and it was amazing." She looks at me and rolls her eyes. I laugh. "I'm not concerned about that department either, just from other intimate moments we've already shared. If you're worried about that being a deal breaker, I'm sure we can rectify that easily enough." I grin, rolling her over, kissing and nibbling her neck.

She laughs softly as I readjust between her legs. She's quiet, stroking my forearms. Her eyes are full of trust. I grin, leaning over and kissing her lips. She moans into my kiss as our tongues start to slide and dance against each other. She feels like silk.

How can she possibly think we wouldn't be great in the sack? Her fingers are in my hair, tugging me tighter against her. *God, I love that.* My cock is rock hard. I'm stroking my length against her lace covered heat. Our tongues are one, moving in perfect harmony. Her breathing is ragged or is it mine? I open my eyes as I feel her fingertips reaching for the end of my shirt. I lean back, she's following biting her lip. She tosses my shirt to the floor.

"This is sexy, Mr. Starks," she purrs pushing me back, climbing on top of me.

"Oh yes, it is," I growl. She leans over, covering my mouth. Her tongue feels like heaven teasing me. My cock is about to fucking explode. I reach around, grabbing that fine ass, stroking her against me harder. I need to get her naked. I slip my hands under her tank, caressing her back. She leans up, staring at me; I know that look.

"What do you want sweetheart?" I know what she wants … she wants to fuck. I've seen that look too many times. I grin, watching her grab the bottom of her tank. "Show me." I move my hands to her hips. I've been waiting to see these beautiful tits.

Knock! Knock!

"Sir."

What the fucking hell? She laughs as she looks up at the door. "Go away," I growl. I pull her back down to my mouth, lord I don't want her to stop now. Damn she's hot, grinding her sweet sex on my length.

The knocking starts again. "I said to go away!" I bark this time. More fucking knocking. "What the hell?" I roll her off, she's laughing. "I swear to god if it's that damn steward, he's shark bait."

I make sure my cock isn't saluting and that she's not showing those sexy undies. I yank open the door.

I stood there with a bamboozled look on my face, rolling my tongue, as I watched Andy and Michael's playful, mischievous grins spread across their faces. "I'm going to fucking kill y'all." I fly out the door. Andy and Michael are running out of the lower deck. I chase them all the way to the dining deck. "Assholes." I laugh. "Really, are we still living in the fraternity?"

"Well, you said dinner was at seven, here it seven thirty and they won't serve us without you." Michael grins, looking at his watch. I look around, noticing everyone seated with drinks.

"Shit, it's after seven already?" I laugh. "Okay, we'll be up in a minute. Keep your fucking asses away from my door from here on out." I see Toni grinning as he rounds the corner with her cosmo and my gin.

"Well, we sent your favorite steward to fetch you, but he came back up here with his tail between his legs," Tierra teases.

I roll my eyes as I head back down to get Amelia and change. I walk in and she's wearing a sapphire lace over mesh strapless mini dress. Her body looks fucking amazing, and her hair dried looking beachy.

"You're stunning," I gasp, looking at her as I close the door. "Dinner won't be served without us. Hence the asshole interruption."

"Well, you better get changed Mr. Starks. Shall I wait?" She kisses me on the cheek before she lays down on her side of the bed, watching me.

"You shall." I walk into my closet. I think I'll wear my white linen button up with distressed navy boat shorts. The shirt fits like the one I wore last night, she found it sexy. Of course, all my clothes fit sexy. I grin at my arrogance.

"Ready sweetheart?" I ask, walking out.

"Yes." She's meeting me at the door. "You look very handsome, but I'm sure you're quite aware of this," she teases. "If it's all right with you, I don't want to spend the evening with everyone; I think I'm at my quota for group activities for the day," she whispers as we walk up the stairs. I grin looking at that short as hell dress.

"It shouldn't be a problem." I slide my hand up her thigh, gracing the edge of a very different pair of panties.

She jumps and turns. "Mr. Starks is that a perk you have, groping?" she teases, walking into the dining cabin. My cock is hard.

Chapter 37: Amelia

"Sorry chickie," Tierra apologizes as I walk past her. "We're hungry."

I nod sitting next to Quinton's seat at head of the table. Apparently head of his universe, as well as his friends. They all seem to love him. I'm crazy about him. I smile looking at him. He's so suave in his movements.

He rests his hand on my knee and starts rubbing small circles with his thumb. My sex is throbbing. I watch as the stewards start bringing our meals out.

"This looks delicious." I smile glancing at him.

Quinton replies, "It's grilled wild salmon on quinoa, roasted carrots, and a cilantro apricot dipping sauce. I hope you like it." He waits for everyone to have their dish.

"I do like salmon, I'm sure it's going to be superb." I rub the top of his hand. This is nice … the way it's supposed to be. "I like this song."

He smiles as he listens. "Yes, it's by John Legend. 'All of Me.' It explains exactly how I feel about you, sweet Amelia."

"Oh." I feel completely giddy with his confession. It's such a beautiful love song. I've heard it a billion times, but it wasn't until this moment that I want to cry at how poetically beautifully it really is: a man loving his woman.

"I'm mad about you."

I tickle my fingers in his scruff, stroking his face. He leans into my lips, kissing me in a sensual, single-lip kiss. "I'm completely smitten by you, Mr. Starks," I purr across his lips.

"After dinner, Amelia, you need to try that swimsuit. You can wear it tomorrow while we're in Nassau." Tierra is beaming.

"Yeah, I will." I smile at Quinton. I really want to get naked with him and let him do sexy things to my body.

"We're turning in after that, we should be in port by the morning. It'll be a full day of touring, shopping, beach, and karaoke that night." Quinton made it perfectly clear we're going to be alone.

"That's probably good idea, because we will be late partying," Andy agrees.

"Amelia doesn't sing in front of people." Gerry says. Quinton grins, looking at me.

"No, I've never been to a karaoke bar either. So this should be fun." I laugh, devouring the salmon.

"Well, we're going to do a song together, just us girls," Tina pipes up.

"I don't think so." I shake my head. "Trust me, singing isn't my forte. I would ruin it. You guys would pretend you didn't even know who I was." Quinton chuckles at me, like he doesn't believe me. "Why are you shaking your head? You've never heard me try to carry a tune."

"That's what makes it so fun, drinking, singing, and dancing on a stage. Just being silly," Tierra chimes. "No one is expecting a top twenty soloist."

I hold my hand up. "Well, you will see when I ruin your song."

"You're going sing with me too." Quinton squeezes my leg. Is he talking sex singing in code or karaoke? I really don't know.

"Quinton is a big karaoke guru." Michael laughs.

I look at him. "Oh, really, why didn't you have karaoke at your club?"

"Friday nights we have karaoke." Andy beams. *Well, okay then. I guess that's that.*

"When I finish this cosmo, I don't need anymore. I could use sparkling water with lime, if you have it. Or regular water is fine." He laughs as he throws his hand.

"Toni, no more cosmos for the evening, S. Pellegrino with lime." He winks at me. "There is nothing you cannot have." *I'm starting to see that.* I just smile.

Once the stewards clear our entrée dishes, they bring dessert, a pomegranate sorbet. "How do you like the sorbet?" Quinton asks.

"It's delicious; refreshing." It has been a long freaking day. Tierra and Tina look like they could still be partying. Hell, they all do as I look across the table. I just want to go to bed, and not to sleep.

My mind is in overdrive from talking about us living together. First, I've got to find a lawyer so I can actually be free. I've been miserable far too long. I'm ready to start my life, and I want to with Quinton Starks. Looks like I'm moving to Jacksonville. Adios bed and breakfast, hello … something.

"Earth to Amelia," Tina teases. "We've been talking …"

"What? Sorry I was a billion miles away."

"A billion ya say." Andy laughs. Quinton shakes his head.

"Come on, let's go try that swimsuit on; decide what to wear tomorrow. The guys are going to stay up here and have a few evening caps. Guy time. Girl time." She laughs as she and Tierra stand.

"See you in our room later." I kiss him on his lips. He grabs my wrist, running circles around in the inside with his thumbs.

"Can't wait. I won't be long." His eyes burn into me.

I follow Tierra to her cabin. It's a lovely room, not as nice as Quinton's master. His has huge windows for amazing views.

"Okay here it is Amelia, I think you will look hot as fuck in it." Tierra and Tina plop down on the bed. "Strip, show us. I might need to help fit you."

I laugh as they're watching me. "Strip right here?" I've never stripped in front of girls. "Tierra it's new. You haven't worn this." I look at it. "Holy shit, it's got a fifteen-hundred-dollar tag."

She laughs at me like that's nothing. "Take it. I have tons of them."

"How do you afford something like that? I mean I know you're a model and get paid very well, obviously very well, but still." I'm just freaking floored.

"Honey, you're going to have to lose the modesty of a dollar. Quinton spends much more than this on a regular basis. Andy and Michael are both very well compensated. None of us are at the same level as Quinton, if that gives you any indication. Okay sweetie. Now get naked and put that on."

I roll my eyes. "Turn around."

"Really sweetie, I'm a model. I see tits and cunts all the time."

"Right, sorry. I don't okay? Well, don't judge me. I don't have a perfect body with perfect boobs." I slip the bottoms on and drop the dress. I put the strings around me. "Tie me."

"Honey we've been looking at this flawless body for two days. Stop downing your bod. It's hot. Quinton hates fake tits. Our tits are real," Tina confirms as she ties the strings.

Tierra walks over, prowling around me, thinking. She adjusts the bottoms some. "How does it feel? It looks amazing."

I walk over to the floor-to-ceiling mirror looking at my body in a sparkling silver sapphire string bikini. "It actually feels like it's a fifteen-hundred-dollar swimsuit." We all laugh. "Seriously, it feels good." *I'm totally out of my league here.*

"These don't shift or anything, it holds you perfectly. Get ready for Quinton to cream himself." I laugh at Tierra's comment. "Here, take this sexy strap dress. It goes with it. You can wear it while we're out exploring tomorrow. Try these shoes, it's all one complete outfit."

I grin, playing dress up. "I can't believe we're the same size even down to the shoes. Quinton asked me to move in with him." I turn staring at myself in the mirror. The reflection staring back is stunning ... happy! *I look like someone else.*

"What?" Tierra grabs me sitting me down on the bed. "Are you shitting us?"

"No, he wants me to when we get back Sunday. I've been trying figure out what I should do, do I go home, pack a bag, end it? Or just don't go back, end it, and buy new clothes? I'm so freaking confused." I look at them. "Tell me what to do."

"Fuck no! You move in with him," they both concur at the same time. "If you have something you need to get, go get it with Quinton. Material shit can be replaced."

"So you two don't think it's a crazy move." I look at them. "We've only known each other a few weeks."

"Have you ever felt the way you feel with him?" Tina asks.
"No."

"The last few weeks, what was the first and last thing on your mind?"

"Him."

"Who did you fantasize you were fucking? Because face it honey, everyone on this yacht knows you weren't wanting your husband," Tierra questions.

"Him."

"Ok and who is responsible for the way you've felt the last few days? Who has been stealing your breath, giving you those amazing butterflies, the gentleness?" Tierra smiles.

"Him."

"Him!" Tierra and Tina both say. "That's right—him—Quinton Starks! He's head over heels for you. You're smitten as shit with him. You need stop overthinking and feel. Life is crazy. So love is crazy. If it feels crazy, then it's right!" Tierra purses her lips. "So we got us an official third chick for our weekly spa visits."

"Well, I don't know if I can afford the spas you two do. I don't have a job or money or clothes but what I have with me." I laugh as I grab my little blue dress. I need to put this on.

"She's cute." Tierra laughs. "Worrying she can't afford the spa. Honey, Quinton is going make sure you're one of the glitterati." I look at Tina nodding and grinning. "Now look, tomorrow when we're out and about, don't be surprised if we get some attention." Tierra smiles as she looks at Tina.

"Right, the model thing. Got it." I grab my new clothes. "Okay I'll see you two in the morning. Thanks for the clothes and the advice."

I lay the swimsuit on the bed next to the dress and shoes. "It's freaking amazing. Well, yes Amelia it would be, it's only fifteen fucking hundred dollars for the suit," I tell myself as I run my fingers over it all.

"I see you like it." I turn around at Quinton's voice. He's grinning.

"Yes," I gasp looking back at it. "Fifteen hundred dollars for a swimsuit," I whisper, "that's insane."

He smirks as he watches me closely. "How did it feel on your body?"

"Amazing! Like fifteen hundred dollars should." I laugh as I grab the items. I hang the dress in his closet. "You don't mind, do you?" He grins shaking his head as he watches me, sipping his gin. I take the suit and put in the drawer and the shoes in the closet.

"Amelia, come sit with me." I turn around, he's patting the sofa. Shit, I feel nervous.

"Have I done something? Are you mad?" I'm about to freak out. He's all serious sounding. "I don't mind if you want to spend time with your gang, I just don't."

He laughs. "No, no. It's not anything like that." He clasps my hand, pulling me down beside him. I shift so I can look at him. But I can't without smiling. "Look you know I want to be with you, like with you." I nod. "I wasn't kidding, I didn't bring any condoms. So if you want me to buy some tomorrow I will." I shake my head no. "Okay, well if you want more time, I'm fine with that too. I don't want you to think you have to do something you're not ready for; or we have to rush into it —we don't. Don't get me wrong, I really want to ... really bad, but you're worth waiting for Amelia."

"Okay." Does he think we can't have sex because he doesn't have any condoms? I'm protected. "Is this why you seem sort of weird now?" I laugh as he's grinning.

"I don't want you to feel pressured or anything."

I straddle his lap and kiss him on his cheek. "Trust me! I don't feel pressured by you at all. You turn me on." I take his drink and set it on the side table. He grins, looking at my mouth as I drop another kiss on the corner of his.

He runs his hands up and down my sides with intense eyes. He lowers his mouth to mine, leading us into a passionate open-mouth kiss. His tongue is perfection ... gliding ... seeking. I'm melting.

Chapter 38: Quinton

Holy hell, her mouth is like heaven. My fucking cock isn't going to survive her. I pull her tighter against me as our tongues become one. Dancing the perfect tango. I really want to tango with her. I hear her moan into my mouth. I keep kissing her as she's falling more, I run my hands down her body, gliding her sex against my hard cock. She naturally flexes against me. That's all I need.

I swoop her up and carry her to the bed. She gasps as she clasps her hands around my face. She doesn't laugh, her eyes are full of desire. They're fucking amazing diamond sapphires. She nudges my nose with the tip of hers as she starts single-lip kissing me, letting me take the lead.

Her breathing and kisses are harsher. She's leaning forward, working my buttons. *Oh fuck yeah baby*, she pushes my shirt off my shoulders. I sling it to the floor. She's grinning, watching me. "You look hot laying beneath me in that dress. I really want to rip it from your body."

"Do it," she purrs. *Baby you don't have to tell me twice*. I look down, her dress is hitched up around the top of her thighs. She's fucking hot. I reach around, unzipping her dress. My hands are actually tingling with excitement. *That's a first*!

"You sure want to go this route, Amelia?"

"I have an IUD, unless you just prefer condoms. The ball's in your court."

"Oh fucking hell," I growl as grab the edge of her dress and start pulling it up. Her stomach flexes as I slowly pull the material over it; her sexy-ass ribs, and next the fucking prize. I've been wanting to see those tits all day. I stop breathing as I pull her dress the rest of the way off and toss it to the floor. She's got the most perfect set of tits I've ever seen. If it wasn't Amelia, I would swear they were manmade. Flawless. Gorgeous. Her nipples are small and perfectly sized to her areolas. Damn they're the perfect shade of pink. Like a delicate rose bud.

"Breathe," she purrs in my ear pulling me back down and sucking my neck. My forearms support most my weight as she kisses and strokes my chest and down my arms. Her tongue is licking and nibbling around my pecs, my nipples. Fucking hell, she's turning me on. She grins as she runs her finger back and forth over my waistband.

I grin ,watching her. "Well, Amelia with beautiful tits, what are you going to do now?" She pops my button, unzipping and pushing my shorts down, pooling them around my shins.

"Oh you are a vixen," I growl as my hand grazes over her hardened nipple, traveling the length of her torso. I kiss and suck the crook of her neck. She bucks beneath me. *She likes her ear and neck sucked*, I make mental note. "You're beautiful." Her fingertips strum across my shoulders.

She wraps her legs around my waist. She's so beautiful, more than I ever dreamt. I've dreamed of tasting her nipples. I caress her jaw, running my thumb over her lips. "You're breathtaking Amelia," I whisper looking into her sapphires. She's not sure, I can see it in her eyes. "If you don't like something or change your mind, just tell me. I will stop. I won't be mad. You're the most beautiful woman I've ever seen, I'm in awe of you." I kiss her lips, as she nods. "I could look at you forever."

I cover her lips with a deep open-mouth kiss. Our tongues are sliding and massaging one another. I feel it in my cock, she's whimpering into my mouth. Oh I'm going to take my sweet time fucking her.

I kiss down her jaw and neck, running my fingers over her mouth and down her neck. She gasps, tossing her head back as my hand passes over her hard nipple. She's going to be very receptive.

Her skin tastes like coconut and jasmine. I'm so fucking excited. I kiss her fleshy boob, working my way to the nipple. She cries out when I suck the bud between my lips. I grin, letting her feel my breath over it. Then I close my lips around the beautiful nipple again: swirling my tongue around the areola and sucking the nipple gently. It feels fucking fabulous on my tongue.

"Mmm." She's grinding her hips against my length. Her fingers are lacing through my hair, tugging me towards her other breast. I grin as I slide my tongue across her chest and suck hard. She screams again, tossing her head back. I squeeze her other tit, making circles around her areole tugging her nipple with my thumb and pointer fingers.

She's lost. Her hips are flexing against me. I can feel her wetness through her lace panties. My cum bead has already wet my underwear. I need to get them off.

I lean back, letting her nipple slip from my lips as I sit.

"Where you going?" she whines, opening her eyes. They're completely full of lust. I pull down her lace panties. Fuck her sex is beautiful, I want to get up all in that shit. I tickle my fingertips over her pubic mound as I reach down, removing my shorts and boxers. There we're both naked. I spread her legs.

"You want this?" I ask, stroking my cock and rubbing my wetness over the head. I can see her appreciation.

"Oh yes." She leans up, grabbing at me. She covers my mouth with an open-mouth kiss; it's demanding. She's horny and wanton. Our tongues start their own sexual battle. She's cradling my head in her arms. I'm fucking lost, rubbing my length against her. She's whimpering. Fucking hell she's hot. Really fucking wet. I run my fingers down between her legs. "Mmm ... fuck!" Amelia whimpers. I keep circling and tugging her clitoris.

She's gasping as she tosses her head back. I suck her nipple, slipping my fingers into her folds. She spreads her legs more. I start fingering her, in that come-hither motion that she loves. Her fingernails are digging into my scalp, pulling me deeper against her tits. Her hips flex harder. "That's right, feel it, Amelia. I'm going to fuck you hard in a few minutes, is that what you want?"

"Yes," she screams. I keep finger fucking her.

"You want my fucking cock in you?"

"Yes," she throws her head back. "I want you." I'm fucking oozing.

I cover her other tit: sucking, swirling, and flicking my tongue. She's starting to shake. "Give it up Amelia," I growl, "you know you want to fucking come. Let me own your come."

She's tightening around my fingers. I lean back watching her writhing beneath me. She's coming hard on my fingers, her hips are pulsing, I press my hand over her clitoris. She screams, tossing her head to the side, she feels like pure silk. I pull my fingers out.

"You ready Amelia?"

"Yes, please," she whimpers.

"Open those fucking eyes Amelia, I want to see you," I demand. She opens her crushed diamond sapphires. I'm so fucking excited I feel it in my toes, it's electric. I take my cock, rubbing the head over her fucking silky, hot opening. She arches her back. "Keep those eyes on mine sweetheart." I slowly enter her. *Holy fucking hell.* I stop. She flinches and screams, hitching her entire torso off the bed, turning into me. Her nails dig into my shoulders; fuck she's tight. Real fucking tight!

346

"You okay?"

"Yes ... don't stop!" *She doesn't have that to worry about.* I thrust the rest of my cock in her. She cries out, tensing around me. If she wasn't married, I'd swear her ass is a virgin. She's tighter than that fucking virgin I had a few weeks ago. I give her a minute to adjust to my massive cock. I lean down, sucking that beautiful bottom lip. She's kissing my top lip, moaning. We're good to go!

I start thrusting into her. She feels like heaven. I kiss her neck, sucking and nibbling as I work my way down, pinching and tugging her other nipple. I swoop her leg over my shoulder, thrusting harder. She's wrapping her other leg around my waist, squeezing.

I'm fucking moaning, making sounds I've never made. "Fuck you're tight," I hiss. She feels better than anyone I've ever been with. I can feel every ridge of her insides. She's smooth, tight, silky, wet, and hot.

"You're fucking huge," she gasps. I grin listening to her moans.

"Damn right I am." That's right, I'm arrogant. "I like your fucking tightness. Your tits are gorgeous."

"I want you to like it." She's flexing her hips in perfect sync with my thrusts. I can't believe the moans and whimpers that are coming out of my mouth.

She's whimpering and tightening even more, *impossible.* She's grabbing at me, pulling me deeper into her. I cover her mouth in an open-mouth kiss, her tongue is going deep and demanding. *That's right baby, claim it.* Our tongues are one having their own fuck battle. She feels amazing on my tongue and her tightness is beyond anything I've felt before.

Amelia cries, "It's too much." *Shit, I don't want to stop.* She feels too fucking good.

"You want me to stop?" I'm slowing my thrusts, whimpering from my own damn pleasure.

"Hell no! The intensity is too much. Amazing," she screams.

"Thank fucking god." I pick up my thrusts again. She's starting to scream again. I can feel her tensing and constricting. Oh fucking hell, she's coming again. I deepen my thrusts, harder. Giving it to her how she obviously likes it. Her hips are matching my thrusts perfectly. I'm going to fucking blow my load in a minute. Her toes are starting to curl, she's holding her breath. She's feeling good. I grin as I keep working it. Fuck she's working it like she does dancing. I'm about to die.

My perfect counterpart is writhing beneath me in throes of passion. I hear her scream, her body constricts and tightens around me. *Fuck*, her silk is covering me, she's sucking me deeper and deeper. My heart is going to explode. I growl as I release all of me into her. The force! This time it doesn't wash back over me. It fills her, our essences become one, we continue to move and groove on one another.

Amelia cradles my face. Her eyes are hot and wild, mystified as she's still reeling from her climaxes. Her breathing is ragged and she's gasping to get air. The sweat glistening down

348

her face, over her brow, only makes her diamond sapphire eyes sparkle more.

Breathing hard, I cover her lips with mine. Her mouth is dry, but I can feel her getting wetter as I start dancing our tongues together. She moans, hugging her body into mine, deeper. She drops her head back in satisfaction.

We're soaked with sweat. Her legs relax beside me. I continue to slowly stroke her insides, supporting my weight with my elbows and my knees; my hands cradling her head. She's beautiful wrapped in the afterglow. Her arms are wrapped around my biceps, kissing them.

Her cheeks are flushed, and her silk feels fabulous. I've never blown my load in anyone. I'm going to stroke her until I can't; the storm has calmed. Our mouths are loving on each other. Amelia's the last woman I ever want to sleep with. This is it. She's my home. My rock. My everything. Damn she's perfect.

Chapter 39: Amelia

Mother of Jesus of all that is perfect. Quinton Starks is a sex god. I can't believe it. I don't ever want anyone else. He gets me.

Damn his face is super-hot right now—stroking deep—moaning in pleasure; his sexy forearms supporting his weight. I roll my face to the side, kissing them. I love him so much I hurt to feel it.

"I'm not ready for you to pull out," I whisper. I close my eyes moaning. "You're an amazing lover."

"I know I am," he whimpers. "Amelia, I don't ever want to pull out. I could stay inside of you forever. Fuck, you feel good."

"You sound incredibly sexy right now." I lean up, kissing him in a single-lip kiss. I like when he sucks on my bottom lip, because it pleases him.

"Wrap your legs around me." I do, holding tight around his neck and shoulders as he rolls us to his side. He adjusts his arm under me the way he does when we cuddle.

He nudges my nose with the tip of his as he closes the distances with an open-mouth kiss. I moan, he tastes so good. His tongue feels like heaven. He's gliding and swaying with me in perfect harmony, still pumping; my hips flex in perfect rhythm. He feels wonderful. I'm in complete awe of him.

"You feel really good, Amelia from Amelia." He grins, caressing my back, nibbling and kissing down my neck.

"So do you Mr. Starks," I purr in his ear. "I never want this to end." He laughs.

"Well, it will end for a brief period, sweetheart. I'll revamp rather quickly and take you again, again, and again."

"I hope you will." I kiss his lips gently as he rolls on his back, rolling me with him into a cuddle. He's finally flaccid.

I look at the clock. "That can't be right … the time."

He's smirks. "And …" *He's so smug.* I exhale, laying my head on his chest, rubbing my hands across his chest, and kissing his nipples.

"I like you doing that, kiss my nipples anytime." He's relaxed. "You're tight, really tight!"

"Just me … nothing special."

He laughs. "Well, you're way wrong there sweetheart, you're extremely special."

I grin, kissing him. "Mmm, I love your lips. I've never been this relaxed before." He chuckles with his eyes closed, stroking my arm. He's going to sleep naked like a real man. That was something I always hated about Eric. He always had to have something on, like a child.

"Hey, are you falling asleep on me Mr. Starks?" He grins as he caresses my arm.

"No, I'm relaxed. You felt amazing. I want more. That was only one round sweetheart, I think you're due another, don't you?"

I laugh; he's watching me. "You're serious?"

"Honey, I can go all night. I probably should have told you, sex is my favorite pastime." I laugh at his comment. "I'm serious, when I'm not busy working, it's working out, sex, and dancing. I enjoy doing those things."

"Oh, well you forgot your gin fixes," I tease.

"It comes with the territory." He's sated, looking at me out of relaxed eyelids. "Now my favorite things are you, making love to you, working out, and dancing."

"Oh." He laces our fingers.

"You're a loud lover." I jump up looking at him. His smile is arrogant.

"What?"

"You're loud. Don't be surprised if comments fly tomorrow." I'm utterly embarrassed. I cover my head with the sheet. "Don't be shy. That makes a guy feel amazing, if we can make a woman scream in pleasure. Huge deal." It doesn't make me feel any less shy. I keep my head covered. "Not to mention you sound incredibly sexy. You look incredible writhing beneath me too. Fuck, I'm getting turned on thinking about it."

I laugh at him, but he's shifting us. "You're serious?"

He smirks. "I like my women loud. Don't be shy with me Lioness." He yanks the sheet from our bodies, and he's rock hard. "Look at me, see what you do to me Amelia."

I let my eyes troll to his massive cock. My mouth goes dry; he truly is huge. He has every right to be arrogant. "I see you're pleased. You can check out my cock anytime you'd like sweetheart. It's only for you!"

"Good!"

His megawatt smile meets his ears, as he gazes down my body. His hands are soft and tender as he wraps them around my waist, rolling me to my back. He's on his side strolling his fingertips in small circles around my belly button. "You want some water? I'm thirsty."

"Yeah, let me grab something to cover myself."

He laughs. "You're cute." He shakes his head giving me a funny look. He presses a button on his phone. "Two S. Pellegrino waters with lime to my room."

"Do you not know what time it is? Does the crew never sleep?"

He snickers, shaking his head. "I know what time it is. I pay them to do their job. They sleep, but their primary responsibility is to be at my beck and call." I bite my lip. "Hey, it's no different if you're at a high-end hotel with room service. They come all hours. Trust me, they know what is expected of them."

"I still need my wrap ... I'm naked."

"Bring that beautiful naked body back to this bed." He's watching me like a lion, waiting to pounce. I knee walk towards him, holding his hand. He coaxes me to straddle him.

He sighs, sitting up and stripping my wrap. "Don't be shy of your nakedness. Not in our bed." He wraps his arms around my back, tangling his fingers in my hair. He pulls my body down. "I love to taste you," he whispers as he softly covers my lips with his. I moan as his tongue slips into my mouth, feeling like pure platinum. Smooth and hard, warm and sensual. He's stroking me, loving my mouth, just like he strokes and loves the inside of me. Our tongues become one.

I'm getting wet. I know he can feel it. His hips are starting to thrust against me, running his length up the front of my slit. I gasp as I look at him. He's full of desire, with his mouth parted, watching his cock stroke me. I start flexing my hips against him, holding his shoulders. I drop my head back, and grin feeling his lips kiss down my neck.

"You feel amazing, your wetness and heat." He shifts his hips, lifting me up. I watch him, guide his cock into my folds, sliding deep into me. "That's better, now I've got your tightness all around me."

"Fuck," I gasp, throwing my head back. His hands are holding my hips tight, controlling my speed, guiding me up and down his shaft.

He's moaning and hissing air through his clenched teeth, looking up at me.

"Oh ... God ... Quinton." I toss my head back pulling him tighter against me. "Just your cock moving feels like the prelude of an orgasm." I squeeze his shoulders, sinking hard and deep on his massive cock.

I gasp, feeling his lips suck my nipple and his tongue swirling around the areola. He licks and sucks across my chest to the other tit, and does the same thing, only he twists and tugs the nipple he'd been sucking.

He grunts, grasping my ass, moving me harder against him. I squeeze my body tighter around him, he's hitting something oh so right. I can't breathe, just suffocating in pure ecstasy. My heart is racing, my breath is short. His breathing is ragged. He's sucking my nipple, pumping my ass harder up and down on him.

I can't open my eyes, I can only feel him. He's whining, whimpering. *Fuck those could be my whines*, I don't know. My toes are curling. "Quinton," I scream as I sink my teeth into his shoulder. "Oh god," I cry, sucking and kissing him, his shoulders and neck. My silk floods over him.

"Fuck, you're sucking my cock deeper. You're so fucking tight," he growls and whimpers as he explodes. I feel his liquid heat rushing through me. It's like a dam breaking. I think he hit my cervix. Our breaths are ragged. He falls back, pulling me with him.

His heart is pounding against my ear—his chest heaving. His cock is still pulsating deep inside me. I giggle at his deep throaty growl, running his hands through my hair bringing my face up to his. He covers my lips with his open mouth, I accept his tongue eagerly: moaning and tasting him. We're lost in each other when our waters arrive.

355

He looks around—pulling the sheet over us—shielding my body with his massive wall of muscle. He doesn't pull out but wraps my leg around him. "Don't worry sweetheart, you're covered." He kisses me on my cheek. "Door's open." The words vibrate against my skin. *What the hell?*

"Yes sir." *Oh god it's the steward he despises.* He rolls his eyes as he continues kissing my lips. I sink deeper under him.

"Just sit it on the bedside table. Thank you." His expression tells me he knows I'm bashful about being naked in bed with someone in the room. He softly tickles across my hips … making me giggle under the sheets. We hear the glasses clink. He looks over his shoulder. "Lock the door as you close it buddy."

"Yes s-sir," he stutters and trips over our clothes. His feet get twisted and he falls on the floor.

"Oh shit," I whisper covering my mouth.

"Ah fucking hell boy," Quinton says. He's become flaccid as he rolls off me, shifting the sheet over me. He sits up, letting the sheet slip from his perfect sculpted body, pooling around his hip. "Babe he's tangled in our clothes."

"Sorry sir." He's shuffling his legs and turning red with embarrassment.

"Do I need to help you, or do you think you can manage to find your footing?" Quinton goads him.

I lean up, tucking the sheet tighter around my body. Quinton turns to see what I'm doing, and grins. "Damn, you looked thoroughly fucked." He grins, leaning over and kissing me.

"I feel thoroughly fucked Mr. Starks," I purr against his lips, overly satisfied and sounding way too sexy.

The red-faced steward shuffles a bit more before finding his footing. Quinton is toying with my hair as we watch him stand up.

"Sorry ... s-sir ... a-again. Ma'am." He exhales but doesn't look at us. He starts to walk towards the door.

"Panties," I whisper. Quinton looks up as the steward stops. "My panties are on his shoe."

He drops his head back and look up to the ceiling. "Oh for the love of god, you are teasing me, please ma'am tell me you're teasing?"

Quinton laughs. "Let me help you out buddy." He stands, completely naked, and even flaccid his cock is impressive. He walks over to the steward's foot, bends down and grabs my panties. "See, they're lace. Lace is delicate and clings very easily to things." He dangles my panties over the steward's shoulder.

"Quinton," I gasp. "Don't taunt him with my panties. Now bring your fine naked ass back to bed. I want more of you."

"With pleasure sweetheart." Quinton tosses the panties to the floor and crawls back in bed. "Now if you can manage this time, lock the door on your way out buddy. Don't be whacking off to those panties in your mind either."

I cover my face up as the steward's embarrassment shines bright. We hear the door close and lock. "I can't believe you said that to him."

He laughs. "He has to be in his twenties, apparently he's never seen women until he arrived on my yacht."

"I think you're overly enjoying torturing him," I tease as he hands me my water. He winks at me as he looks awfully smug drinking his water.

"I could have kept going, I just knew our waters would be arriving." He grins watching me. "That was fucking hot, you on me like that."

"I feel turned on thinking about it," I admit as I shift back down under the sheets, tossing my leg over his hip. I can feel his body heat on my sex.

"Oh, you're a true vixen." He grins setting down his empty glass. "I'm going to take you again Amelia."

Chapter 40: Quinton

I can't wait to bury myself in her tightness again. I knew we would be great together. Her husband was right about one thing, she's fucking tight. Time to have his wife for a third time tonight. I don't know why, but it turns me the fuck on thinking about him knowing I'm fucking her and she's totally loving it.

She's fucking beautiful and she's mine. I put an ice cube in my mouth, tossing the sheet aside, exposing her nakedness. I like her legs spread and knees bent open for me. "You are one fine sight, sweetheart." She giggles as she slides her hands up my biceps. Damn they look good flexed, holding my weight and her fingers rubbing all over my arms.

Holding the ice in my lips, I kiss her, dipping it in her mouth, but not releasing it. She moans as I run it down her lips, over her jaw. It's melting, leaving a trail of water. I drag it down her jaw line, sucking it in my mouth, nibbling at her neck below her ear.

I continue holding the ice between my lips as I glide it down her neck, down her throat. She's gasping, watching me with those beautiful sapphires. I drop a quick smirk, sliding the ice over her breast, and she gasps. I suck the ice in my cheek and suck her nipple.

I swirl my cooled tongue over her nipple, sucking and flicking. "Oh god," she moans, cradling my head. Her legs climb up my sides, her toes pointed.

I grin as I move the ice over her other nipple in a circle, making her moan and flinch before sucking her nipple, teasing it with my tongue. She jerks, whimpering and flexing her hips into me. Her legs are hitched so far up, gliding with my hips, thrusting my shaft against her wet folds.

"Fuck," I growl as I slide down her body, letting the ice cube leave a trial of water down from her breast to her tummy. I look up at her, she's watching me with those damn sapphires full of desire. I grin, holding her legs open where she's spread them for me. I drop the ice cube in her belly button as I kiss my chilled lips on her stomach going south, making her flinch. Her fingertips toy with my hair.

She's like a rare orchid. She's beautiful, her soft pinkness and her folds. She's perfect. How could any fucktard handle this with a heavy hand? I want to kiss away every painful memory she holds. When I kiss the outsides of her folds she jerks. I can feel her tension. She's trusting me but holding her breath. *Oh baby, you have nothing to fear from me.* I close my eyes as I kiss her again, softly with shallow licks up her slit, going for the gold. She's breathing hard; she hasn't felt anything yet. I French kiss her clitoris. She jumps and relaxes back. I suck and swirl my tongue around it. She screams, I look up and grin. Her head is tossed back, game on!

I keep her legs pinned into the position she has them. "You're fucking beautiful Amelia," I hiss as I lick up her slit.

She's gasping and quivering under my touch. I start French kissing her clit again, sucking and tugging it gently with my tongue, swirling it, and repeat. She's tugging my head deeper and grinding her hips into my mouth. *That's right sweetheart, let me fuck you with my mouth.* God she's delicious. She's so sweet, I could just eat her for the rest of my life. I've never tasted anyone like this, just delectable. Pure gold, heaven.

I press her legs down more, increasing my pressure. She's clawing at my shoulders. "Quinton," she gasps. Oh god it sounds so sweet.

I slide my hands under her hips, lifting her more into my mouth. She's starting to quiver. Her legs flex tighter around my face. She's not breathing, her toes are curled. I hear her crying. Fuck she's beautiful. She's pressing my head deeper, hands fully open, holding me where she wants me. I love it. Her silk floods over my lips. I didn't think she could taste any better. Wrong! I suck and lick every liquid drop of her essence.

Her hands release me as I continue grazing on her beautiful sex. I'm in just fucking awe. I lean up on my knees, I need to fucking blow my load. "Turn over!"

She flips immediately. She's eager to satisfy me. "Get on your hands and knees." She does without objection. I grab her around the hips with one hand while I hold my cock with the other. "You ready?"

"Yes," she whispers. She grips the sheets and cries out as I enter those beautiful folds from behind. "Fucking hell," she moans pushing deeper against me.

"Fucking hell right," I growl thrusting deep inside of her. I smack her ass—I can't resist. And yank her hips against me as I fuck her hard.

She's totally taking it too. She looks back at me, those fucking sapphires. I dig deeper. I reach around, scissoring her clitoris with my fingers while grabbing her hip with my other hand.

She's pressing back on me deeper. "Harder!" she's whimpering. I slam harder into her with each thrust. She's lost; moaning and sinking deeper into my pounding. Her silk floods over my fingers and cock again.

"Fucking hell," I gasp through clenched teeth. Her sex is sucking me deeper and tighter. "Shit, you feel like you're milking my cock. What the fuck?" I growl. I feel this shit in my toes, an energy is surging all through my veins. I'm going to fucking explode. This is the best surge of energy I've ever known. I can't stop.

"Quinton," she screams.

I snatch her back against my chest, like when we're dancing. She's dropping deeper down on me, taking me as deep and hard as one possibly can. I'm thrusting all I have, hard into her. She reaches behind her head, grabbing mine, and pulls me down into her neck. I bite and suck. I'm palming and squeezing her perfect tits—pinching and rolling her nipples between my fingers. Her breath is all over my face. I find my release, exploding my liquid heat into her.

"Fuck," I yell as we both crash forward. I can't even try to hold myself off her. I'm pulsating every fucking drop in that beautiful wet tight vessel of heaven. I kiss across her shoulder blades and down her back. She's fucking beautiful. "I'm going to stroke you until I can't." I gasp for words kissing her neck, rolling us into a spooning position.

"Yes," she purrs into the pillow. Her breathing is hard. She's completely relaxed beneath me. I can't help myself ... I keep rubbing my hands all over her. I can't believe she's here with me, naked and ravished in my bed. I want to scream so everyone knows it. I'm soaring high as a motherfucking kite on her. She's a goddamn drug.

"Mr. Starks, I do believe you topped your last two productions with that one," she purrs looking over her shoulder. I laugh a deep throaty satisfied laugh, my cock is finally going flaccid. I roll back, pulling her into my embrace.

Her eyes are closed. I pull her tighter against me. I can't let her go. Ever!

I kiss her cheek. "Amelia?"

"Hmm." She's totally sated.

"Rest sweetheart, close those beautiful eyes." I kill the lamp.

Chapter 41: Amelia

This time I'm not pushing him away or dreading his touch. I very much want him touching me. "Mmm." I stretch against the wall of perfection pressed against me. Damn, my sex hurts. I feel completely ravished.

He's growling, nibbling and kissing down my neck. I clasp my hands over his as he squeezes my breasts, rolling my hardened nipples through his fingers.

His strong leg pushes between mine. "Good morning sweetheart," he breathes in my ear, sucking on my lobe. I can feel his morning wood pushing against me.

I turn towards him, reaching up and lacing my fingers through his hair. "Good morning." He kisses my cheek, then the corner of my mouth. I really want to brush my teeth before we start kissing. He rolls me into him, covering my mouth with his. *Ok!* I moan as our tongues start to wake up together—greeting each other, sliding and caressing, melting into one. I'm lost.

He's adjusting between my legs, taking his cock and rubbing it at my entrance. How am I already wet for him? He slowly slides into me.

"Ahh." I flinch against his chest from the tenderness. The rawness is a reminder of his cock, claiming me as his.

"Sore?" He kisses me on my cheek.

"Yes." I wrap my legs around him, locking my ankles.

"I'll take it slow," he hisses, nibbling my lips, soft morning pecks meeting my eyes. I nod, resting our foreheads together as I watch him tenderly stroke me. He's grinning. My fingers are lazily toying with the back of his hair.

"Ahhh." His eyes are watching me. My toes are curling, I close my eyes, getting lost in what he's doing my body. He drops kisses down my jaw, sucking my neck.

"Amelia, you feel so good." He's whimpering ... wanting to get lost.

"So do you ... you can move harder." He growls, kissing down my clavicle and sucking my nipple.

I scream, arching my back. "Oh god." He's hitting something just right. "What the fuck," I hiss as he keeps this pace. My toes are curling, my hips thrusting into him. He sucks my nipples, squeezing and rolling them between his strong fingers.

I lace my fingers through his hair, tugging him deeper into me. His body is so sexy. "Quinton," I whimper as my silk floods over his cock.

He leans down, covers my mouth with an open-mouth kiss, his tongue hard and demanding, controlling the situation. He's getting close. His forearms are incredibly sexy, his hands cradling my face. I stroke his upper body, kissing and sucking across his chest, thrusting my hips against him, matching his force.

"Amelia," he whimpers against my lips, thrusting deeper and harder.

I gasp. My insides constrict and tense around his cock as I reach another climax, feeling his cum. I scream as I tighten and suck his cock deeper into me.

"Fuck, you're coming again." He keeps pumping into me. My toes are curled and my torso is leaning into him.

"You feel good coming," I moan. "I've never felt it before. It turns me on."

"Oh holy hell, you're hot." He's lost in kissing and making love to me as we're both coming down from climatic highs. I clasp his face in my hands, kissing his lips gently, feeling him stroking deep in my core, until he becomes flaccid.

He rolls, pulling me into his body. I wrap my leg over his hip, he laces our fingers, and tickles my shoulder with his other fingers. This is nice—the cuddling. I could stay like this all day with him.

"So my cum turns you on." He's grinning at me. I purse my lips, shaking my head.

"I'm sure that won't help your arrogance, now that you know this," I tease as he laughs.

"Oh baby you know I like my ego fed, but you're sending me into overdrive." I laugh at him. "We're in Nassau." I lean up, looking out the windows.

"Here, get back next to me, we're docked. Wouldn't want anyone seeing my angel's beautiful tits." He grins, pulling me back. "We'll shower and hit the island."

"Sounds wonderful." I tickle my fingers down his chest. "You going to shower with me?"

"Oh baby, I thought you would never ask." I grin as he rolls me out of bed with him. He hits a button to close the shades as we walk into the bathroom.

Quinton turns the shower to medium heat and pulls me by my hands in with him. I close my eyes as the spray splatters my face from his huge shoulders. "Sorry, I'm not use to showering with someone." He rotates us.

"Me either." He looks at me funny as he runs his fingers through my hair, wetting it. He leans over and gets his hair wet. I laugh; he's dripping over me. He laughs as he grabs his shampoo. "That smells nice." His fragrance fills the shower.

He nods, watching me lather my hair. "So does yours." We both start laughing.

"Shower small talk," I tease, turning him so I can run my fingers through his hair. He closes his eyes, holding my hips in his big hands. "All rinsed." He smiles as he grabs his conditioner and applies it to sit for a few minutes. I watch him as I rinse my hair. He's watching the suds wash down my body.

I look down at his saluting cock and smirk. "That's totally your fault," he teases as he grabs my conditioner, running his fingers through my hair. "Do you let it soak any?"

"Not really." I lean back, rinsing it out. We're just staring at each other, grinning. He's rock hard. My sex is throbbing just looking at him. He moans as I brush against his cock, grabbing my bodywash.

"You're fucking hot lathered in those suds," he growls. I roll my eyes as I rinse out my sponge, letting the water cascade over me.

"I'm done! You're going have to move so I can get out, Mr. Starks." He laughs, shaking his head. "Why are you looking at me like that?"

With lascivious smile, he covers my mouth. His kisses are tantalizing. "Show me what you want," I whisper against his lips, stroking his length and feeling his cum bead.

I hear him groan deep in his throat as he lifts me up against the wall. "Quickie," he growls, thrusting deep inside of me, holding my ass in his hands. I wrap my legs around his butt. My back heaves against the shower wall with his force.

"Quinton, fuck, you're so deep," I moan, biting across his shoulders. "You feel so good."

"Fuck," Quinton hisses, "you're tightening around my cock."

"Yes," I gasp, "you make me cum so easily." I cry out, sucking him deeper. My toes curl and I can't breathe. My silk releases all around him, and he slams hard into me, releasing his liquid heat. My toes curl again; I suck him more.

"Damn your sex is greedy, it wants all of my cum," he hisses, emptying himself, "and I want to give it all to you."

I tighten my grip around his shoulders, kissing and sucking his neck. "I've never wanted anything more in my life," I whisper in his ear.

He slowly slides me down his body, holding one leg still high around him, while he finishes stroking every drop into me. He's breathing hard as he pulls out. "If you don't get dressed, we're never going to get out of my room today." I laugh as he hands me a towel, and wrap it around my body.

I watch him walk over to the mirror and look at his body, admiring himself. I chuckle as I dry off.

"Are you smirking at me sweet ladylove?"

"Yes, you're totally checking out how fine you are." I grin, wrapping my hair. He laughs and nods. I roll my eyes. "You're too sexy for your own good, Mr. Starks."

"Not possible," he yells as I walk to the closet.

"Okay." I slip on my fifteen-hundred-dollar bikini. "Damn it's expensive!" I turn, checking it out on me. I do look good. I grab the matching dress. It just glides and flows down my body. It really is damn sexy and short. Quinton will approve. My tits look really good in it. I slip on the matching heel sandals.

I grab my cute beach bag and throw in a pair of short shorts and a tank. "Flip flops, definitely. A hat. Sunscreen. Oh, my towel." I'm mindlessly talking to myself, digging through my beach cover ups, when I hear Quinton laughing.

"Do you always think out loud?" He saunters inside, with his towel wrapped around his waist. I watch him put on his sexy navy button up and distressed khaki shorts and slip on his loafers. "Ladylove, you got room in your bag for my suit and towel?"

369

"Of course." I move my stuff off my legs and stand up. "Hand it to me."

"Damn, Tierra needs a thank you gift." He's grinning. I laugh, looking down at my ensemble.

"Is it too much?" I ask, grabbing his suit and towel.

"No, perfect. You're very beautiful Amelia. You should be dolled up." I laugh at him as I go into the bathroom to dry my hair. He's the sex symbol. Not me.

I touch my face with a little bronzer and highlighter for my cheeks and eyes, then gloss my lips. I catch my reflection in his floor-to-ceiling mirror. I do look different … sexy.

"Who is admiring themselves now?" I laugh at him gawking in the doorway.

"No, not admiring myself." I sigh as I grab my bag. "Just trying to decide if I look good enough to be next to someone as sexy as you."

"Hey … hey." He grabs my hand, tossing my bag out the way. "Come here, look at us." I laugh, trying to break away. "No, I'm serious. Look at us together in this mirror. We're one sexy couple." I laugh and turn my head, studying us.

"We do look good."

"No, we look fucking awesome! Great! We belong with each other!" He wraps his arms around me, kissing my neck while looking at us. "One of the sexiest things about you is your inability to see how fucking hot you really are. Trust me, I've got enough of that for both of us." I laugh at him, but he's serious. "I like to admire myself and look at my sexiness, I can't be with a chick who is equally arrogant. We'd clash." He laughs, smacking my ass, as he laces our fingers. "Come, let's have breakfast."

Chapter 42: Quinton

Hot damn, she likes to fuck! I knew she was my soulmate. Thank god. Can't wait to see her in that little bikini today at the beach, I may have to sneak a little nookie in somehow.

Her husband is a stupid man, just stupid. I should thank him for being a fucktard and ruining their marriage. If he had been a stand-up guy, she wouldn't have given us a shot.

"You look absolutely ravishing." She smiles at me as I kiss her cheek. I've had her twice this morning and I'm ready to go again.

"Good morning all." I laugh as they start whistling and snickering when we walk to the dining table. I look at Amelia blushing, rolling her eyes.

"Well, someone looks refreshed this morning." Michael is grinning. Tina is smirking and nodding.

"Damn Tierra baby, Amelia could model with you. You look hot." Andy grins as she walks by, leaning back and checking out her ass.

"I told her ass that, she doesn't think so." Tierra grins.

"Hey, keep that sleaze-ball manager away from my vixen," I tease pulling out her chair for her.

"So how was your evening, any interesting things to share with the group? Late night sounds or things," Gerry quips looking out over the water and casually smirking.

"Oh god!" I laugh as Amelia ducks her face behind her hand. Everyone laughs at her. I told her last night she was a loud lover.

"Maybe a celebration of shots," Marcus teases.

"What was it, like six fucking times?" Michael chimes in, sipping his mojito. I watch her turning red as she smiles at Toni for bringing her a mojito.

She's looking at me as I smirk about it. "You're all incorrigible," she teases finally saying something. They laugh at her comment, with waiting faces.

"I am not discussing this." Amelia smirks, she can't keep a straight face.

"You said you would tell me when you had the best sex of your life," Tina reminds her.

I laugh, grinning at Amelia, turning my attention to her. "Well that was a question from the game the other night."

She sighs, chuckling. "Yes, fine, it was fucking amazing last night as well as both times this morning." She grins, leaning over and kissing my lips. "You know you're the best I've ever had."

"Damn right I'm the best and the last," I growl letting them all hear it.

"Yeah, it was," Tierra squeals.

"Yep." Tina smirks. "Oh hell, you just said 'and the last.' What are you saying Quinton?"

"Yeah, what are you saying bro?" Andy grins. *You know what I'm fucking saying.* I see it in all their faces.

"Can we just hush about it please," Amelia pleads, grinning and looking away, "what is for breakfast?"

"Oh yeah the pesky steward said Chef is making lace pancakes." Tierra grins.

I couldn't keep it together, nor anyone else at the table. "Oh fucking hell," Amelia whispers, laughing.

"How the hell do you guys know everything? He tripped in my panties leaving our room." I laugh as he walks up.

She turns, around looking at him, he is equally as red. "Oh shit." She smirks "Thanks for the heads up. I'm done talking."

"It's fine beautiful, it's all in good humor." I laugh, resting my hand on her knee.

"Boss what's the itinerary for the day?" Michael asks leaning back, relaxing.

"I want to take Amelia to the shopping boutiques, check out the stairs, beach scene, then end the evening with dinner and clubs." I smile at Amelia thinking about showing her the sights. I drop my hand to her knee as the steward returns carrying plates of food, continental style.

"Sounds good, should we hit some shops first then finish with beach?" Tierra suggests. "We can come back to clean up before dinner and clubbing. I have another dress Amelia should wear for tonight."

374

"Good." I nod at Amelia as she nibbles her breakfast. "You okay?" I know that look. She's thinking something, overthinking. "They were just teasing about last night. Don't be bothered."

"I'm not upset about them teasing us." She smiles as she sips her mojito. "I'm fine, seriously." She doesn't look fine … something has to be bothering her. "It's just … Eric probably has discovered I'm not at the house or getting on that plane by now."

I laugh. "Good riddance. I wish you would let me tell him about us now." She smirks and rolls her eyes. *I'm going to make you forget that fucktard.* She laces our fingers.

"I like this," she purrs as she leans her head on my shoulder. *So do I sweetheart.* I intend to keep her forever. I've just got to get rid of her husband.

Chapter 43: Amelia

"You ready sweetheart?" Quinton asks, holding out his hand.

"Yes." He looks down and smiles at our intertwined fingers. "You're very sexy in your shades."

"As you are sweetheart." He leans over, grinning as he sucks my bottom lip in a quick one-lip kiss. My heart flutters. "Come."

"Do the captain and crew always stand when you leave and board the yacht?" I whisper. He's grinning, watching the gang walk ahead of us. I can't see his eyes, but I suspect he's scoping the area.

"Yes, of course." Standing on the docks by his yacht are four men in suits. They're dressed similar to the suits in his building. He knows I've noticed them but explains zilch. Two file out in front of the gang. The other two are behind us.

I look over my shoulder, his driver and Toni. "Toni!" I gasp and lean over. "Why is Toni in a suit like that?"

"Because he is. Just smile and look beautiful Amelia." I look straight ahead and notice some onlookers, talking and grinning. Of course, Tierra's smiling and posing for the cameras. *Shit*, why are the cameras on Quinton? He grins, wrapping his arm around me as we walk towards his limo. Andy, Tierra, Michael, Tina, Gerry, and Marcus literally strut off the yacht and down the boardwalk like they own the damn universe. They all have this suave saunter about them; an arrogance that doesn't match their lovely laid-back personalities at all. Tierra and Tina have this air about them like they're some hot socialite hardasses: their perfect bodies, legs, hair, clothes. They both have that model face and walk about them.

Quinton has that 'I'm a sex god master of the universe' presence for sure about him; he screams money and maintenance. He has a natural sexy suave to him. With his hand on my hip, I feel that natural flow of energy to flaunt, that I normally wouldn't have. I feel like I did yesterday, with Trek Powers. You would think he's the world's sexiest man the way people are gawking and looking back at his yacht and snapping pictures of him. Well, he's the sexiest man to me. I smile at him. "Tabloids," he whispers, "what are you thinking Amelia?"

"That they're walking like they're masters of the universe, when the only master of the universe is you. Well, at least mine anyway." He laughs, strolling his fingers across my cheek, kissing my lips.

The walk wasn't even that far but watching it all felt like a green mile; as if we were walking in slow motion. All Tierra needed was the model fan, to blow her hair, working her sexy face.

"I'm sure you remember my driver Steve." He smiles as he opens the door, and we all file into the limo.

Everyone is adjusting themselves. Andy is passing drinks around. I see Toni get in the front passenger seat. Quinton hits the privacy screen. He sips his gin on the rocks. Andy gives me a moscato.

What was that entrance about? No one is talking about anything, but where our first destination should be. I hope we go to the market shops and the tourists traps. I look at Quinton as he rests his hand on my knee, making small circles. He's different than he was at the inn.

"Let's hit the high-end boutiques first." Tierra suggests. "Amelia, you'll love it." I smile as I share a look with Quinton. He's watching me intently.

He leans over, playing with my hair. "I see you're wearing your earrings."

"Yes, I wear them every day." I smile, touching them. "The only jewelry I wear."

"Oh yeah, I noticed you didn't have any other pieces at the club that night," Tina chimes. "Not even a wedding ring?"

"I haven't worn it in nine years. I didn't like it for numerous reasons, but it wasn't really my style."

"What's your style?" Quinton laughs, looking at me.

"I don't know." I shrug. "I've never thought about it. I just didn't care for it."

Tierra takes her ring off. "Here, try it on."

I shake my head. I don't want to touch it, there's no telling how expensive it is.

"Try it!" Sighing, she grabs my hand and slides it on my finger. She doesn't like to be told no. I suspect Andy gives her the world. "That style is gorgeous on your hand."

I laugh, handing it back to her. "It's a gorgeous ring." Quinton smirks.

"It's a halo diamond style." Tierra slides it on her finger. She turns her hand admiring how the light bounces off the facets. "Andy knew exactly what I wanted."

"What does your ring look like Tina?" I have no idea why I ask ... girl talk maybe. I've not had girlfriends in so long. Sadly I missed all this jabberwocky when my old girlfriends got engaged and married.

"Here, try it on." Tina leans over holding it.

I laugh. "No, I don't need to. I was just curious if you two had the same style."

Quinton takes it from Tina and slides it on my finger. "No, Tina's is a single diamond solitaire with diamonds in the band. Both are very classy rings, don't you agree?" My stomach ignites, feeling him slide a ring on me.

"Yes." I slide it off my finger and give it back. He wraps his fingers through mine. He leans in and covers my mouth with his sexy, sweet open-mouth kiss that makes my panties wet.

"Mmm," I moan as our tongues make love to one another: loving and dancing together in perfect harmony. I stroke his face tenderly. He kisses the corner of my mouth, cupping my face, kissing down my jaw and neck, before he leans back, sipping his gin.

Chapter 44: Quinton

Damn it felt right sliding that ring on her finger. She definitely needs the halo. I've got to get those fucked up ideas out of my head. She's married.

The limo stops. "Looks like we've arrived on Bay Street." I grin, taking her wine and setting my gin down.

"Bay Street is *the* street Amelia," Tina sings.

"Oh." Amelia looks out the tinted windows at the onlookers; some look and stop to see who is going to get out of the limo, while others mind their own business.

"I want to take sweet Amelia to the Straw Market for an authentic Bahamian experience." I grin. "It's on a much larger scale than the little market we walked at Amelia."

"Oh." She grins. "That sounds fun."

Tierra rolls her eyes. "It's full of tourist sinkholes, crafts, gifts, and souvenirs. However, it is right in the damn middle of the high-end boutiques." She laughs, looking at me as I roll my eyes, smirking at her.

The door opens; Andy and Tierra file out first, then Michael and Tina. I let Gerry and Marcus go ahead, then I take her beautiful hand as we're the last to exit the limo. The two suits are in front and Toni is behind us.

"Steve, we're going to walk Bay Street. I would like to take Amelia on a carriage ride, please arrange it." I hand him my card. "I trust you can make it happen, to take us to the Queen's Staircase and Fort Fincastle. Reserve a few carriages, I want alone time with Ms. Amelia."

"Yes sir, shouldn't be a problem." Steve grins as he departs.

I take her hand so we can catch up to the others. Tierra waits for no one. I laugh on the inside, kind of like me. Of course, I'd wait for Amelia.

"Do they follow us all day?" she asks me as we causally walk.

I kiss the back of her hand, fingers laced with mine. "Yes. You won't even see them. Well, maybe Toni." I grin. "Stop wherever you would like to look."

"Tierra is high-tailing to the boutiques I believe." *She's so sweet.*

"You look wherever, we have all afternoon with them." I smile, looking at some of the touristy mess. We walk and walk, in and out of stores. Amelia hasn't shown much interest in wanting anything. She didn't even seem to desire anything from Tierra's favorite boutique. I see the carriages ahead. Thank god, I'm tired of shopping this sector. I want to take her in the shops of Baha Mar.

"Nothing striking an interest sweetheart?" I laugh looking at her.

She smiles and shrugs. "I see things, but I wouldn't have any use for it back home." She looks up. "Wherever home is now." I laugh as I loop our arms. She's right, there is no place for this junk in the penthouse. "Aw, look at the carriages."

"You like carriage rides?" I ask her as we keep heading straight.

"Yes, something about the romantic ambiance of it." She grins looking up at me. *Well, good, sweetheart, you should be pleased in a few minutes.* "We have them at Amelia, I can hear their stomps and wheels over the cobblestone streets from my garden." I haven't thought about her missing her gardens.

"Is that something you and Eric partake in?" She looks at me. "Carriage rides."

She's laughing at me. "No. He said they're overpriced for what you get and a waste of time. He's always busy. Another thing we never did living on the island."

What a fucktard. Again, I should thank him for screwing up and pushing her away. "So no sailing or carriages." I chuckle, looking at her. She shakes her head. I don't think they spent any time doing anything together.

"Quinton Starks!" Tierra squeals turning around. "I should have known you would pull something like that." I start laughing, she's spotted the carriages and Steve. I'll give him a huge bonus in his check, securing four private carriages. He even managed to find two with extra seating for himself and the other suits.

Amelia gasps as she looks at me, seeing what Tierra is fussing about. "You knew those carriages were for us?" I nod, grinning, and watch her eyes dance. They've sparkled constantly the last two days. She's all but jumping. She really is adorable.

"Sir, you have them for as long as you wish, they will take you to the requested locations, even wait if you choose to have lunch somewhere," Steve tells me.

"Well done, you will be compensated." I grin as I watch Amelia looking at the carriages. "Choose one," I tell her. She chose the one I would have, a deep navy carriage with bright white interior. The horse is a rich black; it's quite beautiful.

"Mr. Starks," I hear my name as we climb in. "We trust these carriages will meet your approval. Like I told Steve, we're with you until you tell us otherwise."

"Yes, thank you." I grin as I wrap my arm around Amelia.

"This is perfect." She caresses my cheek. I cover her lips with an open-mouth kiss, tasting her, loving her. She's fucking perfect.

She giggles as she leans back, looking around. Our tour guide is rambling about the history of the providence, buildings, etc. I'm just reeling about her being in my arms. I could care less what he's talking about, but she seems happy. I stroke her thigh as we casually ride.

"I really wish I could be inside of you right now," I whisper. "You look sexy and feel amazing."

384

"Mr. Starks," she teases. "You're one naughty man." I laugh at her remark as she shakes her head, looking at the vista. "Although I would like to feel you coming in me right now." I gasp, looking at her.

"Amelia, you dirty talking vixen!" She has me rock hard. She laughs as she lays her head on my shoulder. "I'm beginning to think you like to taunt me. You're like a poisonous apple, dangling in front me." She looks at me, grinning. "I'll totally bite." I stroke my fingers up and down her shoulders. "I would do anything with you Amelia."

"Me too," she purrs laying her head on me.

"What did you think about the girls' rings?" I really want to know her thoughts about ever remarrying.

She doesn't move her head. "Beautiful. I can't even begin to fathom how much Andy and Michael must have spent on them."

I laugh. "More than two months' worth of salaries." She cuts her eye up at me. "Remember, I know what they make." She smiles, looking back down, and toys with my buttons.

"You think you will ever remarry?" There, that was casual enough.

"Have you ever wanted to marry?" *Answering a question with a question.*

"No!" She doesn't say anything. "I've never met anyone that I found interesting enough to even date, Amelia, until you."

"Oh." She's moving her fingertips along my forearm.

"You haven't answered my question, about remarrying." She's obviously processing it.

"I don't know," she breathes. "I mean, I guess one day. You know once I actually get this marriage dissolved." We both laugh at her comment. I'm going to make sure this one is dissolved immediately.

The carriage stops, and she brings her head off my chest. I climb out first and hold my hand for Amelia. "Everyone has to check out the Queen's Staircase."

"Why?" She looks at the stairs. "Where does it go?"

I look up at it. "Nowhere." We start laughing. "It leads the way to another attraction for you to see. Come sweetheart." I grab her hand and we start climbing the steps.

"Amelia, Quinton turn around, strike some sexy poses." Tierra is grinning with her phone. "I'll get pics for you. Amelia, you look fucking fab in the dress by the way."

"Yeah she does," I quip. I wrap my arm around her waist, pulling her tight. She naturally flips her hip out, with her hand resting on my chest while her fingertips dangle up and over my shoulder. This just feels natural. Relaxed.

"Damn that looks sexy, give me a model face." Tierra giggles. Amelia rolls her eyes.

"I have no model face." She laughs, looking at me. Yeah, she has a beautiful face. I lean down and start smooching her seductively with our single-lip kisses, she always lets me lead with sucking her bottom lip, and her my top.

386

"This works too." Tierra is in the background. "Okay I got some shots. You can stop."

"I don't think it was for your benefit," Gerry smarts as he loops his arm with Marcus, and they sashay up the steps. "Easy love birds, drawing attention," he whispers as they pass.

"Shall we continue?" I grin, dropping my hand to just above grazing her fabulous ass. "You're my queen." She laughs at my comment.

"I've been thinking of you as my sex god after last night, but I guess I could call you a sex king." I look at her, grinning.

Chapter 45: Amelia

"I thought the guide said sixty-six steps, I only counted sixty-five." I laugh looking back down the stairway.

"They've covered the first step in concrete," Quinton reminds me.

Tierra huffs, "Really Quinton, you're dragging us up to this old ruin? News flash, we're not dressed for this." I laugh looking at Quinton.

"Amelia hasn't ever been to Nassau," Quinton smarts as he looks back at me. "This is Fort Fincastle. It overlooks Nassau."

"So does a helicopter ride," Gerry quips. I laugh, looking at his gang. They're all miserable. "Haven't we sightseen enough of this place? I'm parched and my veins are going to convulse in cosmo withdrawals shortly."

"Yeah, me too. I need a cosmo and something to eat," Tina whines.

I'm with his gang, but I don't want to be a damper to him. "I could go for a cosmo too." I grin, looking at him.

"You ready to leave this hellhole." I laugh at his comment.

"Thank god Quinton Starks has returned." Andy laughs as he grabs Tierra's hand. "Watch those beautiful heels baby." I laugh as he starts leading her back towards the carriages.

"Yes." I look shyly. "Forts really aren't my thing."

"Oh thank god," Michael chimes, pulling Tina with him.

Quinton laughs. "So you made me endure this shit and heat for myself?" I'm laughing, watching him.

"Pretty much! I thought it was important to you, so I did it for you." I grin grabbing his hand.

"That is a relationship, Quinton," Marcus teases, "Doing something you might not enjoy for the enjoyment of someone else."

"Well, what the hell is it when you're both miserable doing it?"

"Hell," Gerry smarts, sashaying by us.

"Don't do anything you don't enjoy for the benefit of me, sweetheart. If you don't like something, tell me. I'm not a fucktard, I won't make you do anything you don't want to do." I can't help but laugh at him. He couldn't get the hell away from that place fast enough.

"Are we going to the Baha Mar?" Michael asks after we're all seated back in the nice cool limo. "Thank god for air conditioning."

"Andy pass the drinks ASAP." Gerry rolls his eyes, fanning himself.

"Yes." Quinton smirks, sipping his gin and looking at me. "I can't believe you endured that for me."

"Would you like a cosmo, Amelia?" Andy offers instead of wine.

"Yes, please." I smile, sipping. "Mmm ... this is so good." The crispness tingles on my tongue.

"Thank you for the carriage ride." I kiss his cheek.

"Any time sweetheart." He's sipping his gin quietly.

"And hiking sixty-five steps and the sweltering fort tour," I tease, rubbing his arm. Everyone laughs at his face as he rolls his eyes.

"Just keeping the touristy shit real sweetheart." He grins shaking his head. "I'll keep it Quinton Starks real, if that suits everyone."

"Yes!" I laugh as everyone agrees. He really is sweet.

"I like it Quinton Starks's way," I say, stroking his scruff.

"You've only had a sample." Michael laughs grabbing Tina's hand. Quinton smirks, shaking his head.

I lean over and whisper, "I really love Quinton Starks's way in the bedroom and the shower." I flick my tongue at the tip of his ear, sucking his lobe through my lips. I lean back in my seat, innocently.

"Ah fucking hell." I jump as he sets our drinks down. He covers my body with his, rubbing his hands down my hips and legs, sucking my neck.

"Get her boss." Gerry whistles.

"That sounds like a great idea," Andy chimes. "Come baby."

I giggle at his affection. Quinton kisses my neck and clavicle. "Show me your tits," he whispers.

"No!" Is he crazy? "We're in a car full of people."

He leans off me. "We're of no interest to them." I look over his shoulder and Tina and Tierra are practically naked from the top down, sitting on Andy and Michael. Gerry and Marcus are huddled in the corner seat doing their own thing.

He shifts. "Come on, make out with me sweetheart. We got this entire bench seat to ourselves."

I'm grinning. I can't even believe I'm thinking about it. "What do you want to do?"

He's laughs pulling me on top so I'm straddling him. My dress is hitched up at the top of my thighs. "Don't worry, your ass is covered and they're preoccupied anyway. Another known code of ours." I exhale as he reaches around and unzips my dress. I cannot believe I'm letting him undress me from the waist up with his friends in the car. "Fucking hell your tits look amazing in this top." His smile reaches his eyes—he brushes his thumb across my lips, pulling my mouth into his. His kisses are tantalizing; our tongues are dancing and massaging each other, igniting my libido. I can't think anymore. I close my eyes, feeling his lips kissing my neck, my jaw …

"Mmm." I rock my hips against his hard on. He cups my breast as he kisses around my clavicle, dragging his tongue down my breastplate. He looks at me before he slides my swim top aside, freeing my breasts. I bite my lip, watching his thumbs brush over my nipples. *Fuck that feels good.* I gasp as he leans forward and sucks my nipple into his mouth. *Oh holy hell.*

He kisses across my chest and sucks my other nipple.

I whimper, biting my lip. He grins, looking up. I lace my fingers through his hair as he pulls me towards him more, so he can relax back and suck my nipples. My toes are curling while his beautiful tongue is swirling, licking, and sucking my tits. His fingers squeeze and pull at my other nipple.

I open my eyes when I feel him release my nipple and his hand slides down my stomach. He slips his fingers in my bottoms. "Oh god," I whisper, leaning my head deeper on him, kissing and sucking his skin between my lips.

"You're so wet," he whispers.

"Yes." I whisper sucking and nibbling.

"I want to bury myself in you, do you think you can handle that?" I look at him. Is he serious? "No noise." I bite my lip and nod. What the fuck am I doing? He grins as he leans over and hit the volume up for the music.

He unzips his pants and slides my swimsuit to the side. I feel his heat—every single inch of him—rock hard … smooth and oh so wonderful. *Oh hell.* He looks like the devil, grinning at me and flexing into me.

"Shhh," he reminds me, pumping harder and deeper. Yet he's so controlled. I close my eyes as he takes my nipple into his mouth. His hands are digging into my hips. *This is so risqué and hot … having me in the back of his limo with the gang.*

"Fuck you're tightening all around me," he whispers against my mouth as I cover his lips ... demanding him. I can't believe I'm keeping so quiet. He increases his grasp; his kisses become even more heated. Our tongues are doing their own fuck session.

"You feel amazing," I cry into his mouth. *Shit, I'm starting to whimper.* I bite my lip, dropping down against him.

"Shhh ... I love being like this with you sweetheart," Quinton growls in my ear. I can't breathe, my toes curl in my sandals. My fingertips dig into his shoulders, he sucks my nipples hard, digging his fingers into my hips. He's pushing harder into me. I've tightened every muscle in my body, feeling his warmth fill me. I grind slowly against him, sucking more of him into me.

He releases my hips as he cradles me to him, kissing my neck. Our breath is ragged. "I feel your silk all over me," he whispers.

I whimper as he shifts. I wasn't ready for him to leave my body. I readjust my clothing as he tucks himself back. He zips my dress. He's stroking me affectionately as we come down from our climatic high. We're grinning at each other as he covers my lips with another heated open-mouth kiss ... his tongue is controlling and dominating the situation. He can take charge; it turns me on. We're lost in kissing each other when I feel the limo stop. "Everyone needs to adjust whatever needs adjusting." He laughs. "We have arrived."

Chapter 46: Quinton

I'm reeling from my high of getting Amelia in the backseat of my limo. Lunch was perfect, now we're hitting the last high-end stores. I hope she finds something at the jewelry store, I want to cover her in diamonds and sapphires. I hang back with Andy and Michael, while the others are prancing in front of us, hitting all the clothing boutiques and fragrance shops. Tierra and Tina have spent their usual when we hit this sector. Amelia did finally bite her lip about me buying her a piece of lingerie. Tierra insisted she let me. I don't think she could get past the price tag.

"How do you like having a lady on your arm?" Andy asks, grinning, watching me all starry-eyed no doubt.

"Love it." I grin, watching her cute ass switch in that dress. Gerry has his arm wrapped around her hip. "They walk like they own this mall."

"How long do you think it's going to take for the local paper to hit with you out on the town with a lady?" Michael laughs as I shrug. "I really don't know why you haven't told her. She's clearly not a money whore."

I cut my eyes at him. "No Michael she's not." I shake my head. "It may freak her out, she had this weird expression when I mentioned buying the Fortuna with my first million. I decided not to broach the subject."

"She's accepted all the perks so far," Andy reminds. "Even played it up for you with Trek. That was fun. She realizes you're wealthy."

I laugh as we walk. "Tina said they were talking, and she made the comment she knows you're successful and would figure this husband shit out when she got back ... she doesn't want to involve you." I look at Michael. "Tierra and Tina told her you could help her handle it quickly."

"I'm going to handle it quickly ... I can't be shacking up with a married woman." I look at Andy. "When we get back find her the best divorce attorney. She doesn't want to include me in her sorted affair with him, but that's too fucking bad. You heard some of the shit shared when she thought it was just the girls."

"I've already got a name for you, I sent her a message the other night, hope you don't mind me being presumptuous." I grin at Andy.

"Not at all. She's coming back to the penthouse Sunday. We'll figure things out then. He was expecting her ass on a plane this morning to Birmingham to meet him. She was fucking me instead." I laugh.

"She good in bed?" Michael chides, "Normally you've commented something."

"Normally he fucks a different lady a night, sometimes two in a day," Andy smarts.

"We all knew she was going to be great in the sac." I grin, looking at her as I stop in front of the jewelry store. "Tierra, let's go in here," I yell, stopping them. "She's the best I've ever had."

They grin at me as we walk into the fine jewelry store. I casually stroll the counters looking. "There are some beautiful pieces, don't you agree?" I look up to the lady behind counter. She's all teeth and grinning. "Oh my, it's you ... Mr. ..."

"Quinton Starks." I shake her hand.

"Yes, Mr. Starks I was just reading a piece about you the other week in Forbes." I grin as she speaks.

"And you are?"

"Sorry ... Rose. Are you looking for anything specific or just browsing today?" She smiles, looking at the ladies with me. "Are one of the lovely ladies your girlfriend perhaps?"

I grin. "Perhaps." She seems like a nice older lady.

"Well, as you know we only carry the finest gems and diamonds. We have everything out. If you want something custom made, we can always help you with that. Since all of our jewelry are custom pieces, you don't have to worry seeing anyone else wearing it."

"Good!" I like that thought. "Yes, I'm aware of this establishment and the quality." I look around for Amelia, I really want her to see the sapphires. "Amelia sweetheart, come here."

She smiles as I wrap my arm around her waist. "You see anything that strikes that beautiful eye of yours?"

"Everything is beautiful in here Mr. Starks," she purrs in my ear.

"Amelia, I'm Rose." She shakes Amelia's hand. "Like I was telling Mr. Starks, every piece is one of a kind. We're also very confidential here." That remark doesn't go unnoticed. I look at Rose and nod. Amelia is looking over the pieces.

"Do you like anything?"

She's smiling, looking at me. "Of course, but I'm not telling you."

I laugh. "If you don't tell me, I'll ask Tierra. Or I could just buy every piece in the store." I know that sounds smug, but I could. She laughs like I'm kidding.

"Tierra what was Amelia drooling over?" She grabs at my arm as I go to where Tierra is grinning. "Rose, darling, can you please open this cabinet?"

"She loved this pendant." I smile as I look at the diamond. It is quite lovely.

Rose takes it out of the cabinet. "It's in a platinum setting, five carats." I hold it up, admiring the way the light dances in the facets. "Beautiful isn't it?"

"Quite! Amelia, sweetheart, come over here." I'm in awe of her choice. It would look absolutely stunning against her skin. I watch her as she slides up next to me. "Is this the necklace you liked?"

"Yes, it's beautiful." She can't but help grin at it.

"Turn around, let's try it on." She only hesitates for a second. I catch Tierra grinning big time out of the corner of my eye.

"Here dear, look in the mirror. It's absolutely stunning." Rose smiles as she admires how it looks against her skin. Amelia touches it like she's afraid.

"Touch it," I whisper in her ear. "It's only a diamond." She smirks looking at me as she fiddles with it. "How do you like it on?"

"It's gorgeous," she breathes.

"You're absolutely right, it's beautiful against your skin." Our eyes meet in the mirror as she continues to admire it. I'm buying it for her. "I want to make love to you wearing this diamond," I whisper in her ear. She gasps at my words. As well as the engagement ring I was admiring, but I'll leave that little tidbit out. I want her to have both of these pieces.

"Rose, we'll take it." I beam as I unfasten it from her neck. Amelia spins around, grabbing my hands.

"You can't buy this necklace for me Mr. Starks." She looks down at the price and gasps. "Holy shit," she whispers before she looks up, "you really really can't buy this necklace."

I laugh, Tierra laughs, and Rose smiles pleasantly as she waits for me to hand it over for her to proceed. "I most certainly can and will. Rose, please box it up."

"Yes, sir! I'll get this wrapped." Rose quickly goes behind the counter.

"Mr. Starks, you cannot buy this. It's much too … much too expensive." She's holding my hands. She's cute still calling me Mr. Starks. She's only called me Quinton when she's coming hard around my impressive cock.

"I'm glad you're holding my hands, now I don't have to catch you."

"What?" she gasps looking down at our hands.

"Come, I saw something … I want your opinion." I pull her with me. "Walk sweetheart." She smiles as she drags her feet. "You see anything in this cabinet that you like?" I watch her eyes. "Rose, will you unlock this cabinet?" Amelia looks up at me and then Rose.

"What would you like to see Mr. Starks?"

"This ring, the diamond with the halo of sapphires."

Amelia leans over, whispering, "I believe you've lost your mind."

I grin, looking at her. I hold it, admiring it. It's perfect. It's exactly like the wedding set in my dream, when my soulmate first appeared to me. "Tell me sweetheart, what do you think of this ring? The style of it I mean."

"It's everything a girl could ever want." She smiles as she looks at. "Can I touch it?"

"You can try it on if you like." I grin, watching her eyes as she slides it on her right hand. "It looks beautiful on you. Perfect. Do you like it?"

"Yes, of course I do," she whispers. "Don't you dare get any ideas. You've already purchased me a beautiful necklace and I love it." *Oh sweetheart, I'm way ahead of you.*

"Yes, it is absolutely stunning against your finger. The cut is perfect for your hand." Rose is beaming. "Shall I tell you about it?" Amelia shakes her head no as I nod yes.

Rose smiles at me as I nod for her to proceed. "The center stone is a thirteen-carat emerald cut diamond with a double halo; cornflower blue sapphires accent the exterior edge of the halo. Additional diamonds cover the gallery and split shank band." She smiles as Amelia turns her hand admiring the piece. "It really is quite lovely on you. I see you like the cornflower blue sapphires." She noticed Amelia's earrings.

"Yes." Amelia smiles as she touches them. She grins at me.

"This ring is part of our sapphire wedding set, but you could wear it on your right hand." *Shit*, Rose why did you have to say that?

"Oh." Amelia slides it off her finger and gives it back to Rose. "What sort of wedding band would one wear with such an elegant piece?" *What the fuck?* I wasn't expecting her to be interested. I look back at the group. They're grinning. I flag Steve to come inside before I turn back to Amelia.

"It's designed to wear with this band." *It's perfect. I will buy both.* "It definitely makes a statement worn as set."

Amelia laughs. "I think it makes a statement worn independently."

I look back at Amelia. "Is there anything else you liked in here?"

She smirks. "I'm not talking about it." I laugh as she walks to Tierra and Tina.

"Sir, you wanted me." I nod at Steve.

"Rose, box both of those rings as well as this titanium wedding band." I look at Steve. "I need you to handle this purchase. Rose, my driver will wait and collect the items. Put it up for me until I ask for it later."

"Yes sir!" I reach in my pocket, handing him my personal card.

"Would you like to try your band on?" I grin, looking at Rose. I look back at them, they're totally preoccupied with something.

"Sure." I slide it on, it fits perfectly like I knew it would. I smile and give it back quickly.

Rose is beaming as she whispers, "May I offer my congratulations? She will be surprised. You two make a stunning couple."

"Thank you!" I nod walking away.

Chapter 47: Amelia

Pristine beaches stretch as far as I can see. It's literally a picture right of the Travel and Leisure magazine. Subdued shades of white sand … almost like a pastel chalky pink shoreline encompasses the rich turquoise ocean. Breathtaking! This part of the Atlantic Ocean is different than what I'm used to. Fernandina beaches are gorgeous, but this is something everyone should experience in their lifetime. I smile, looking over my shoulder at Quinton. His smoldering eyes were burning into me, I knew he was watching. Tierra is right, they're always watching … gawking. Quinton's life really is like a dream. On the outside he appears perfect … but there has to be something …

"I've been waiting all day to see your beautiful body in that swimsuit." Quinton wags his eyebrows standing … waiting … crossing his arms across his broad chest. I roll my eyes, situating our stuff under our private beachside cabana.

"What? She didn't give you a feel in the limo, when we all got nookie time?" Michael teases. I laugh at Michael, spreading our towels on the cushions. *Honey, Quinton did more than cop a feel.*

Quinton ignores the teasing, obviously waiting for an invite to remove my dress. But I don't cave, just yet. The idea of him ... a man like him ... pining over me, turns me on. Guess Eric was wrong, apparently Mr. Starks does want me!

Shit! Now I've let myself remember him ... Eric! He's probably having a fit about now with worry. I can't believe I've just vanished on him. My lips curl into a halfhearted grin ... he sort of deserves this. No! *No Amelia, no one deserves to be stepped out on.* I look at Quinton grinning, waiting, watching—it would kill me if he stepped out on me! Yep, it's official, I'm a horrible human being. I can't help but enjoy what I'm doing. All while I'm killing someone else. Quinton's voice brings me out of my mental altercation.

"Sweetheart, if you want anything to eat or drink, we have an unlimited open tab at the cabana house."

"Okay." I nod, following his finger. And I still can't believe he bought that necklace!

"What are you thinking?" His question brings me back to the present. I wonder if I was wearing my thoughts on my face.

"That you have to be seriously insane to spend that kind of money on a necklace." He laughs, dismissing my concern.

"Not that big of a deal!" I look at him. He acts like it was nothing. *Then how much were my earrings, really?* I wonder.

"I saw the tag Quinton," I whisper, "it was forty-five thousand dollars!" Who does that? Can do that? That's like a car, and he barely knows me!

"Amelia stop worrying." Quinton clasps his hands around my cheeks, covering my lips with his. "Now this is what I

403

like." He hums a little as he nudges the tip of my nose with his before he covers my lips with an open-mouth kiss, dipping his sexy tongue in my mouth; my tongue is immediately drawn to him like a magnet. His lips are soft and sensual, leaving my taste buds wrapped in desire and gin.

"I love this," I whisper into his neck, dropping little kisses. "I want to see you in your suit." I grab his shorts from the bag. "Here."

"Fine, but I'm stripping off this dress first." I laugh as he unzips and pulls it over my head.

"Dude, you're going to have a fucking hard on the rest of the day." I look at Michael, who is grinning his approval.

"Well, you're not saying anything?" I can't tell what he's thinking.

"I'm glad we had a quickie," he whispers. He nods at Tierra grinning. "Tierra, I owe you a huge thank you gift. Just pick it and it's yours." I laugh at him now visibly gawking.

"Lioness is flawless." Gerry grins. "We love this. I'm helping you shop when we get back to Jacksonville. We can have cocktails and spend Quinton's money." I laugh at him, as I look at Quinton.

"Absolutely!" Quinton smirks holding me.

"Okay you stripped my coverup—go get your suit on," I tease as I push him towards the cabana house. "So we can be graced by the fineness you're hiding."

404

Gerry and Marcus each have an arm looped through mine. "On that note, let's get a rum punch," Gerry sings. We walk to the cabana house for drinks. "Now Lioness, you are sizzling in that bikini." I laugh, dismissing him. "Flaunt it while you got it to flaunt. Boss likes skimpy lingerie and his women hot. The fact he's into you should be a huge ego boost for you." I smirk at Gerry. "Don't look at me like that girl, I know him."

"Three coconuts with rum," Marcus orders as I excuse myself to visit the ladies room. Of course it's nice ... as with everywhere Quinton has taken me. There's a first-class toilet room with a lounge area. I smile as I walk by some chatty cats. I can hear them judging me. Quickly I hang a right into the first stall, just to get out of their sight. Hopefully they'll be gone before I'm done.

One of the girls laugh. "Oh hey Monica did you see who's here this weekend?"

"Shut up!" I hear who I can only assume is Monica. I start to flush, but pause when her friend starts to talk about someone named Quinton.

"What was his name ... Mon ... Quinton something?"

"Starks," she hisses. Then she laughs. "Quinton donkey hung Starks." They're all laughing and making lewd comments. *Well, shit now I've got to stand in the stall and listen.* "He must be here partying this weekend."

"Yeah well, he made it clear when he tossed you out as soon as y'all finished, he doesn't hit it twice!" I gasp into my hands, listening.

"Yeah, that was a real shit move," I hear another friend sympathizing.

"Yeah ... he was hot ... don't get me wrong. But looking back, he was such an arrogant ass. He literally finished with me and went to the next ..."

"He played you like a fine-tuned guitar." I hear them snicker a bit and her friend tells her to shut up as I flush and open the stall door. I'm about to vomit, but I need to see who he hooked up with.

"Not to mention he's seriously rich," another one pipes in. I just roll my eyes, as I walk to the mirror and begin washing my hands. Why are they freaking staring at me? I look at them, at her with almost a growl, and back at myself. *Yep Amelia, you aren't his type. She's model worthy, blond, skimpy and looks easy.* I feel like I'm about to vomit, looking at the sexy vixen in the mirror. That's what he's termed me, after all, *a vixen!* I adjust my suit—the suit he told Tierra I would wear — and run my fingers through my hair.

"Hey!" One of the girls ask, me bringing me from my thoughts. "Why do you look familiar ... are you a model?"

I laugh. "No. Hmm, I'm not from around here. Just visiting this weekend."

"No ... no ... I know I've seen your face ... somewhere ..." I shrug sharing a look between the group. Her friend Mon-

406

ica rolls her eyes uninterested, almost with a growl on her face as she watches me. I can tell she's sizing me up.

Monica pipes up, "If you're not a model ... why the fuck are you in a fifteen-hundred-dollar bikini?" My shock is evident, she bellows out a designer's name, I don't even know what it is at this point, I'm so floored. "Are you hoping to land one of the millionaires who visit the island?" She rolls her eyes. "Sassing your ass around, screaming 'hey look at me.' You trying to get noticed by the guys?" Is this drunk cat serious? I'm stunned by the disgust in her voice.

"Excuse me." I can't even pretend to hide my shock from them as I walk toward the door. Eric's face flashes in my mind as I grab the door, telling me someone like Quinton Starks wouldn't be interested. I pause, looking at the closed door. Here in front of me is one of his past sexual buddies. I'm done being nice and biting my lip where mean asses are concerned! I turn towards this Monica chick. "Are you drunk off your ass or something? Why the hell would you presume I'm the gold digger here?" I start to open the door as one of them pushes it shut.

"You don't know us!" Shit, they're getting loud.

The door swings open and Toni walks in.

"Hey! This is the ladies room," one yells. He has no regard for them.

"Is there an issue?" He trolls the space. Toni grabs his phone. "Yes sir. I have her. Ladies." I look at him. "Mr. Starks is looking for you ma'am." *Thank you, Quinton.* I look at them with the best bitch smirk I can muster.

"Oh for the record, Quinton Starks does hit it more than once if he's interested!" I nod as Toni opens the door for me. My blood is fuming as we walk through the people. My behavior hit juvenile. I'm about to vomit. "Thanks Toni," I whisper.

"Well, Marcus and Gerry went back to the cabana with y'alls drink thinking that you must have walked back with Mr. Starks. Then when you weren't there … you can imagine."

"They were drunk. And apparently formerly entertained by your boss there." My stomach flip flops as I see Quinton coming towards us, at the same time the conversation I just heard floods my mind. "I don't have a good bitch face."

"You did well enough with it." I titter looking at him as Quinton approaches.

"Everything okay?" He looks at me, then Toni.

"Some cats in the restrooms," Toni replies.

"Some gold-digging Quinton Stark admiring cats! You must be well known and your yacht for parties," I quip.

"Did they touch you?" He carefully examines me like I'm a precious commodity.

"No! Of course not …" I look up as I see them walk out. "There they are now," I whisper watching his face.

Quinton looks over at them, and they recognize him. He recognizes her. He looks back at me and slides his hand on my ass, pulling me tighter against him. He's watching my eyes.

"I want to lotion this beautiful body." I don't say anything as I walk ahead. "Amelia ..." I can't be mad, he didn't even know me. And I'm married. *Yes Amelia, married!* "Amelia!" I stop turning towards him. "Don't walk away from me ... what did they say? What has you upset?" I shake my head, ignoring his questions. "Your eyes aren't sparkling ... they only do that when you're unhappy."

"It's just the reality of everything ... my marriage ... your past indiscretions, staring me in the face."

"Amelia ..." He grabs my hand pulling me into him. He's stroking my face looking at my eyes. "Everyone has a past ... I've never downplayed my sexual past to you."

"I know ... I just need to process it." I look down, rubbing across his strong arms. He's holding me tight, like he's afraid I'm about to slip from his grasp. "I must admit I don't feel me around you ... your gang. I feel like I've switched bodies with some high socialite." He chuckles softly listening. "Your arrogance and confidence spills over to the people around you. I've never been as brassy and flirtatious ... definitely never pranced about in practically nothing ... nor had people wait on my every need. And my PDA was in the negative zone."

"Maybe you're just finding yourself ... in different ways."

"Or redefining ..." I huff sarcastically.

"You've been belittled for years ... leashed away from living how you wanted to live life. Now here's an opportunity ... I won't confine you. I won't let you stop living." He coyly grins. "I may show you another way of life. But I'm madly head over heels with the modest innkeeper with a brassy provocative side. It's in you ... it's just been bound and gagged, waiting to come out. I saw a glimpse that day in the Christmas shop."

I purse my lips remembering my brashness with Lori. He grins, covering my lips with his. My libido tingles as I toss caution aside again ... for the arrogant Mr. Starks!

* * *

"Everything okay?" Tierra looks at me, then Quinton. He's not saying anything.

"Yeah." I smile, lacing our fingers. "Your swimsuit almost got me jumped." I take my coconut drink. "Is it good?" I ask Gerry and Marcus. "Oh my god, I think I just found my new favorite drink."

Quinton grins, rubbing lotion around my tits, dipping his fingertips under the skimpy material. "Damn your tits look hot in this suit."

"Yeah they do," Andy chimes, not missing a beat.

I roll my eyes at him. "You all are crazy. I've never seen such ... a friendly, flirtatious group of friends."

"Well, it's not that crazy ... or big of a deal. We grew up together, married our best friends. We're comfortable in our

410

relationships. We know our wives are hot; we know Quinton is philander, but he's our brother! Unexplainable amount of trust here." Michael sips his drink.

"Quinton was a philander." I look at Quinton talking about himself in third person. "I am not anymore." I grin as he grins watching my boobs.

"I've think you've lubed her tits enough boss." Gerry laughs. "I've been watching. Her tits are going to be super brown with the rest pink, if you don't get to other parts of her body." I laugh at him, sipping my drink.

He grins as he adds more lotion, rubbing his hands down my stomach, dipping his fingertips under the small patch of material. I start giggling as he rubs my sides. "That tickles." He's laughing, digging his fingers in as I start twisting.

"Stop it."

"Hold her drink." Marcus takes it from his hands.

"Hey, what are you doing?" Quinton is grinning as he grabs me up in his arms. "Where are you going? Don't you toss me in the ocean." He's walking towards the water carrying me. "Quinton stop, don't throw me. My lotion will wash completely off."

"Is that a big issue?" I laugh at his remark. "I have no intentions of throwing you."

"Oh." I calm down, noticing he's walking us out in the water. I pull his face towards my mouth, covering his lips with an open-mouth kiss. Mmm, he tastes good. I dip my tongue deeper as our tongues dance and massage one another.

"Mmm, I love those lips," he growls as he's dipped us mid-chest deep in water, releasing my legs. I wrap them around his waist. He covers my lips in a deep open-mouth kiss, his tongue taking charge. I just melt into him.

"I'm glad you're here Amelia." He kisses me around my cheek and jaw. "I don't want anyone else."

"I'm glad I'm here too." I wrap my arms around his neck, hugging him.

"Have you enjoyed checking out the island?"

"You know I have. It's been more than anything I could have dreamed." That's the truth, my dreams have never been this lavish. "I'd love to walk this beautiful beach with you."

He laces our fingers, walking us out of the ocean. "Damn, you look hot." He comments as I adjust my suit.

We walk down the beach holding hands, picking up shells just like any regular couple. To the outside world, I'm his and he's mine—only that's not the case. It's sort of depressing to think of reality. My reality is I'm married.

"This is nice." I look at him, waiting for him to say something else.

"Yes, it is." I grin, watching him. Every few steps, he stops to pick up a shell. If I like it, he keeps it, if I don't, he tosses it. "I wish this week didn't have to end," I admit, looking out over the water. "It's been absolutely wonderful."

"It doesn't end." He looks back at me, clasping our hands as we walk. "It's just going to get better." He throws a shell. "You scared?"

"Not of you." I keep walking.

"Of Eric?"

"He's going to flip, Quinton." I watch him smile. "Why are you smiling about this?"

"I am not. You finally used my name." I laugh looking at him. "You called me Quinton last night and once in the jewelry store."

I shake my head. "Mr. Starks." He looks at me grinning.

"It's going to be fine, Amelia." I look down at our fingers laced, nodding with a small grin. *I hope so.* "Now let's talk about what you want to do next."

Chapter 48: Quinton

"Amelia, baby, just jump in." I can't believe she's really this freaked out about snorkeling along the reef. I look back at the others. "I don't know, guys just go ahead. We'll catch up." This is sort of funny, I have a yacht and chartered a snorkeling and dolphin encounter tour for the next two hours and she won't jump in. I look at the guys on the boat, I'm not leaving her alone to snorkel with the others.

"What about barracudas and sharks ... big shit like that?" I laugh. She's cute. The guys on the boat are snickering. She cuts them a serious bitch look. I wonder if that's the look Toni said she gave the bathroom cats.

"I'll punch a shark in the face if it tries to bite those beautiful legs of yours," I tease, watching her smirk and shake her head. "Amelia baby, get in the water. I have you!" Damn I hope she comes the fuck on.

Thank fucking god she's standing up. I watch the guys eyeing my soon to be fiancée like candy. They turned away from my scowling, angry gaze. I walk over to where she's standing and reach for her. "Give me your hands; I got you." She wraps around me like a little octopus. Her legs tight around my hips, her tits tight against my chest. I hold her with one hand under her ass and reach up for them to hand me her

snorkeling gear. "Under other circumstances, I would be enjoying your naked body hung on me." She laughs at me.
Good! I sink us back in the water. "Turn your back to me, bend
those sexy legs." I help slide her flippers on, swimming us on
my back, her back to my stomach. She's starting to kick like I
am. "Here, put your goggles on." Thank god she listens.

"You're going to have to get off my chest sweetheart." She
grabs my hand. "You can stand, see. Why are you so freaked
out?" Now we're both standing together. She looks around; the
others are snorkeling.

"When I was eight, we went on a snorkeling excursion in
Cancun, at a reef. Well, we were all having a great time, then
three barracudas showed up. They started circling one of the
ladies in the group. Within minutes the water was red. I froze
immediately." Fuck, why the hell would she agree to come
then?

"Shit Amelia, that's horrific." She looks up at me, still
holding my hand.

"The lady did nothing to provoke them; there was no
rhyme or reason why she was singled over anyone else that
day. I still remember the sounds of her screams, the fear in her
voice. The sound of the water, splashing … I was so close I
could feel the thrashing of their tails, occasionally the tips hit
my shins. The lady climbed all over the reef cutting her feet
and hands, trying to get out of the water. I don't remember
anyone trying to intervene until they took off." I pull her into
my arms, kissing her on the top of her head.

"Sweetheart why on earth would you agree to come snorkeling? I told you, you don't have to do anything you don't want to do." She shrugs her shoulders.

"I had nightmares for years; I didn't get back in the ocean until I was probably sixteen. I haven't snorkeled since that day. This is the last step to facing that fear. I didn't expect to freeze on you. But I'm ready to take an adventure right?" She's fucking amazing.

"That's right baby, an adventure. We're going to have many." I lean down and take her sweet ass lips into my mouth: our tongues twirl and dance together. Her fingers are twirling the back of my hair. She's putting all her trust in me. She's all in. Maybe I do actually love this woman! *I can't be in love ... not the same depth as my parents' love.*

We adjust our masks and put the snorkels in our mouths. She's so sexy, looking at me with those sapphire eyes. I do want her as my wife. She's looking around. I grab her hand and lace our fingers. "We go at the same time."

She gives me a thumbs up as we swim around reef, pointing out an array of colorful fish, conchs, and shells. She touches a starfish with the tip of her finger; it didn't care to be poked and dives under the sand. I lead her further around, she kicks quickly when a lobster clamps at her. I think she's laughing with the snorkel in her mouth. At least in my mind I can hear that beautiful giggle. She points to a porcupine fish, making a slicing motion at her neck. She's definitely giggling in her head.

I see the others around one of the shipwrecks. I point towards them and she gives me a thumbs up. It's pretty neat with life growing on it. More tropical fish and a fucking shark. Shit, she's going to flip. I look at her. She's calm, sliding her arm around me as we move. She's watching it; hopefully she's breathing.

She stops swimming, snatching my arm. I look towards where she's pointing, she's spotted a turtle. Wow! It's huge. She's got to be old with all the barnacles and shells growing on her. Amelia is having a blast. She's stroking my arm. I can see in her eyes, she wants to kiss me. *Oh, sweetheart so do I.*

Andy points to the timer, to turn back to the boat. We still have a dolphin encounter and some famous pig swimming thing. I shake her hand, getting her attention, pointing to my wrist and pointing back to the boat. She gives a thumbs up and turns. Damn, her ass looks fabulous in that swimsuit. *Oh, sweet Amelia, I cannot wait to dress you.* She will want for nothing.

She doesn't release my hand until we get to the boat. It has been way too quiet of a snorkeling session. We all stand, taking our masks and snorkels off. She kicks her fins off, and so do I. She wraps her arms around my neck and covers my lips in one of our sweet one-lip kisses, she sucks my top lip, letting me get her bottom. She wraps her legs around me. She's lost in kissing me.

"Don't get too hot and heavy, guys on the boat are watching and waiting," Michael whispers. "I want one of us on the boat before the ladies. I think they're creeps." I hear Michael loud and clear.

I break from her beautiful lips. "I'll get on first. Come on sweetheart." I toss our gear up to them, and climb aboard. I help Amelia, then Michael, Tina, Andy, Tierra, Gerry, and Marcus.

"Gerry I've noticed your attire today is, um, very melancholy. Where is my color wheel of life?"

"Marcus didn't want me sporting this bod in a speedo on the island." I laugh. "This sad getup is Marcus's."

I feel Amelia grab my bicep. "Thank you for this." She kisses my muscle.

"Anytime sweetheart." I relax my hand possessively on her knee, making circles with my thumb. I notice a few boat mates checking the girls out. They look like sleaze bags.

* * *

"I don't get it." Andy laughs as I look at him. "She was scared to snorkel, but she jumped right on in with the dolphins."

"She had a horrific event as a child snorkeling. She just froze a bit." I grin as she holds the fin, riding across with the guide. "I hope her swimsuit stays on." I laugh watching her.

"Tierra baby, get some pics of Amelia riding the dolphin," Andy says. I'm sure she would like some pictures of her weekend. She hasn't been able to snap her own because her phone has been off.

* * *

Michael is laughing and snapping pictures. "Tina baby, stop frowning. They're cute."

"It's a pig Michael." I see Amelia laughing, standing next to me. "It's wet and sandy."

"I don't know Tina, they're pretty cute." I laugh at Amelia.

"You want to swim with them?" I ask her. "After all it's a big attraction. I did bring you to swim with them." She has the most beautiful giggle.

"Why Mr. Starks, who would have ever thought you would swim with pigs?" I laugh at her joke. She thinks she's got jokes.

"It's kind of cute," I admit listening to it grunt as it swims. Amelia is giggling because it keeps poking at her with his snout.

"It really is quite charming," she says. "You're just a little charmer aren't you?" She's got her lips poked out, baby talking. I look back and laugh, Michael is getting candid shots. Thank god.

"Really Amelia you're sitting in a designer bikini talking to an actual pig that belongs in the farmyard." Tina is repulsed. "Better yet farm to table," she squeaks, finding a spot to relax on the beach.

"Don't listen to her porker, she's just jealous because you're getting all the attention." I laugh at her.

419

"Did you grow up on a farm?" I sit down next to her. The porker squealed off.

"No." She chuckles watching the pigs and others interacting.

"You're so laid back." I watch Tierra and Tina. "Don't get me wrong, I love Tina and Tierra, but they can be difficult women at times."

"All women can be difficult." Amelia corrects, looking at me. "Tina made a comment about her daddy's yacht, she come from a lot of money too?" I smirk, looking at her.

"Yeah, her dad's a big shot in New York."

"Are you originally from New York?" she asks.

"I am." She's looking out at the view.

"Are you all from New York? I mean you mentioned comments of growing up together and such."

"New York and the surrounding areas. Yes, mostly New York. We met in school. Our families would vacation in the Hamptons. Tina and Michael always had a thing for each other; Tierra and Andy not so much. Originally Tierra liked me." She looks at me, grinning. "But she soon realized that was never going to happen. Andy, now, he was smitten with her from the first time we all met. I don't know what changed, but when we came back home for summer one year, she was hot as shit and she was enamored by him." I look back at the gang. "I think they're ready."

"Yeah." She stands dusting sand off her bottom.

I lace our fingers as we walk towards my gang. "You're as beautiful on the inside as you are on the outside, Amelia."

"Aw Mr. Starks, I'm just a scullery maid smitten with a very sexy hunk of man."

"Are you now?" I grin, sucking her bottom lip. "A scullery maid rocking a fifteen-hundred-dollar bikini."

Chapter 49: Amelia

"Sweetheart, wake up." I jerk awake. I must have dozed off in the limo. "We're at the marina."

"Oh." I smile at him as everyone is stretching.

Steve opens the door. "Sir, your items." Quinton smiles as he accepts the bag. I look around noticing the suits carrying all the bags from our shopping excursions of the day.

"Steve, we'll return in an hour or so. Dinner and clubs tonight," Quinton tells him. He loops our arms together as we walk. "You have a nice nap?"

"So, so." He laughs.

"Sir." I watch him take his shoes off and toss them in the basket. He empties his pockets as well. He grabs my beach bag, and holds his hand out for me to balance to remove my shoes.

I look over the marina. "Do people always stop and stare?" He laughs as he nods.

"Sweetheart I'll only be a few minutes ... I need to speak with the captain." He kisses me. "Then I'm going to strip this little swimsuit from your body."

I walk into our room, all my laundry has been washed and put away. "Son of a bitch," I whisper. The bedding smells fresh. I notice my phone is on. "Weird, I thought Quinton killed it." I pick it up and my voicemail is full; over fifty messages, all from Eric. He has been calling all day from the time he expected me in that car up until thirty minutes ago. I feel sick. He sent over a hundred text messages. I cringe at the visible words … "He's on his fucking way home …" I reread it. "Shit."

"What's wrong?" I turn to Quinton's voice when he walks in the room. I hold my phone up.

"I thought you killed it?" I keep looking at it.

"I did. It was off." He grabs it from my hand. "Was it on when you came in here?" I nod.

"Don't open the texts or he'll be able to tell I've read them." I look up at him with my stomach in knots. "He's been calling and texting all day. He's on his way home." I watch him kill it again, tossing it aside.

"Irrelevant." He grabs my hands, pulling me with him towards the bathroom. How can he say that? I have that worrying nausea in the pit of my stomach. Like something bad is about to happen. He turns the shower on. "Come on beautiful." I watch every muscle flex as he removes his shirt.

"Come on in here." He pulls me into his arms. "Stop being so stiff." I shake my head listening to him … trying to push away my anxiety. He kisses my neck. "Salty." He's unzipping my dress.

"I feel disgusting." I laugh, trying to push Eric out of my mind. I'm a horrible person. He's worried out of his mind, meanwhile I'm having the time of my life.

"Well, you feel wonderful pressed against me." He smiles, reaching around, untying the string around my neck and back, tossing my top to the floor. My hands naturally go up to cover my breasts. He laughs. "Don't be shy. Your tits are beautiful." I smirk, watching him pull my strings from my hips. He holds the itsy-bitsy bottoms up by one string, and he tosses them over his shoulder.

"I can't wait to bury myself in you." He grabs me, kissing me. My sex is tingling from his words. I run my hands down the inside of his shorts, pushing them off his hips, working them down. His cock springs out: hard and ready! He steps out of them, walking me backwards into the shower.

"You're very sure of yourself," I tease bumping against the wall. He nods looking down my naked body. He cups my breasts, passionately kissing my neck, sucking and nibbling my skin. I whimper when I feel his lips suck my nipple. "Ah, shit," I moan watching him move to my other breast swirling and flicking my nipple. I'm biting my lip as he trolls his hand down my stomach, grinning like the devil. He's watching my eyes, as he enters me with his fingers. I gasp, closing them.

"You like this." He growls, sucking my nipple in his mouth and fingering me in that wonderful come-hither motion. He knows how to finger a woman. My legs feel weak.

424

"Yes," I whimper into his ear. He pulls his fingers out and in one movement, he enters me. Hard. "Fuck," I moan. He pulls my leg high around his hip, thrusting deeper. His mouth covers mine with an open-mouth kiss, dipping his tongue deep. Our tongues glide and massage in perfect harmony. Everything is in perfect balance. I'm so lost in him.

My fingers are tugging his hair, bringing his mouth deeper into me. I'm whimpering. He lifts me, wrapping both of my legs around him. He's thrusting harder, heaving my body against the wall. I break our kiss, my insides clutching him tighter. I can't breathe; my toes curl. I silently scream, feeling my release over his big-ass cock.

"That's right baby, I own your fucking comes." He moans in the crook of my neck, "Every. One. Of. Them."

"Yes," I purr squeezing tighter around him. I love to feel his release. He's still pumping into me; we're melted together. "I love this with you." I whimper.

"I love everything with you," he moans releasing my body. "You're all I ever wanted. Amelia, you're it for me." He growls into my neck, becoming flaccid. Our hearts are pounding. He's pinned me against the wall, winded and hovering over my body.

The water sprays my face from his shoulders. I lick my lips, turning away, trying to shield my eyes. He softly chuckles, sucking the water from my neck and shoulders. "God, you taste good ... salty and sexy." He's moaning, loving on me.

I give him little love bites as I stroll my fingers up and down his back. He's so gentle and sweet. My feelings scare me. I've not felt anything real in so long … thoughts of Eric and the bathroom chick flood me … he could just drop me. The nausea is back. I grab him, hugging tight.

"Hey … hey." He wraps his arms tighter around me. "Everything will be fine, Amelia."

"How do you know that?" I whisper against his chest.

"I just do!" He grabs my sponge and body wash. I watch him as he lathers my body, being very gentle watching everything that he does. Like he's worshiping me. I gasp as he washes between my legs. I've never had someone wash me.

I can feel his eyes, as I dry and wrap my body with the towel. He's incredibly sexy lathering his body … I leave him to it as I finish getting dressed. I slip on a blush pink bodycon dress. The silver-ish black beading accents running through make it just sexy. My fingertips are way past the edge of it. *Quinton will like it.* My sun-kissed tan looks good with the black. I look at how it hugs my ass. I do look hot. *Thank god I didn't let my body go the last ten years.*

I walk out of the closet as Quinton is walking out of the bathroom, wearing his pants and a white linen button up shirt. His sleeves are rolled to his elbows. "Damn, you look as handsome as ever!" His hair is freshly styled, his scruff freshly groomed. And oh hell, he smells delicious. I run my hands over his shoulders down to his forearms. I love his forearms.

His lecherous eyes roam my body. "You look absolutely stunning Amelia. Stunning." I thought he was going kiss my

426

cheek, instead he whispers, "You're only missing one thing Amelia." He opens the drawer of his bedside table, pulling out a long jewelry box. He pops the top, and the necklace is as beautiful as I remembered. "Turn around." He drapes it over my neck and fastens it. He kisses behind my ear. "Perfect."

"It's gorgeous." I nervously run my fingers over it, tugging gently and making sure he clasped it tightly. "I'm scared to wear it. I don't want to lose it."

He laughs at me. "You will wear it sweetheart. It has a security latch." He walks up admiring my backside.

"I can see you gawking at me in the mirror," I tease.

"Well, I don't hide my infatuation with you." He's grinning as he buries his face in the crook of my neck. I can't believe I'm this happy. It's everything I've ever wanted. "I want to cover your body in diamonds and sapphires."

I laugh at him. "You're crazy."

"Crazy about you," he teases. "Would you have a problem with that? Me spoiling you with beautiful pieces of jewelry?"

"I only have so many places to wear them." He laughs at me.

"I've never bought a woman jewelry until those earrings. Never in my entire life!"

"Oh, another novelty for you then," I tease.

Chapter 50: Quinton

"Oh … the restaurant, food, and view were just superb." Amelia is beaming. "Thank you." She's so appreciative.

"I'm glad you enjoyed it. It's one of the elite dining establishments on the island. The clubs we're hitting are all exclusive. Lucky for us, I'm a member."

"Thank god we're doing it up Quinton Starks's way," Gerry teases, remembering the tourist death trap.

I've dropped a ridiculous amount of money already tonight; I know she's noticed, but I don't care. I want to share my life with her … my lifestyle. She might as well start seeing it.

We stop at the first club. Steve opens the limo door and camera flashes are already taking flight. I squint, shielding my eyes as I stand. Amelia slips that beautiful ringless hand in mine. She looks at me like I'm her king. *Which I am.* She's fucking gorgeous. Her tits look hot in the extreme v-plunge club dress with thin ass spaghetti straps; the back is completely open and rests just above her hips. Amelia is taking it all in: red carpeted entrances, crowds, and cameras. Her diamond looks gorgeous. I need to rectify that ring situation.

She glides with the perfect amount of sexy and sass; she does look like a model with that face and the way her hips naturally move. She's picking up Tina and Tierra's suave mannerisms perfectly. I like my sex appeal swagger. I'm hot with a fucking hot woman on my arm. She will be my wife.

I stand at the door, talking with the bouncer. I like to watch the gang walk like they own the damn place. She was right, they do give off a certain vibe. *Good!*

"Right this way Mr. Starks, your VIP booth is ready." I watch Amelia take in the surroundings as we walk. It's loud, screams money, and has sex appeal. I like the bluish color that illuminates the joint. There are several levels and bars everywhere. Tables, private lounges, and the VIP areas.

"What would you like to drink, sweetheart?" I yell over the music.

"Surprise me." I grin as I order a tropical coconut rum punch concoction. She loved the rum punch earlier during the day.

She's grinning like a virgin club hopper. "You've never seen anything like this, have you?" Tierra screams.

"No." Amelia is beaming. "This is gorgeous." I grin as our drinks arrive. "Wow, that's fast." She takes her drink. "Mmm … this is good." She's practically dancing.

"Fast because you're in Quinton Starks' VIP section," Michael says, tossing his shot. The lady brings another one immediately.

I don't even try to deny it as I toss my gin. I touch the rim of my glass with my finger, and she returns with a new one. Amelia noticed the subtle gesture with my hand.

"Are you some badass, a big shot yourself Mr. Starks?" she purrs in my ear. I grin, watching her.

"I just like things handled properly and efficiently." I do have a huge ego and am quite arrogant. This is no secret to my sweet Amelia. She's dancing in her seat; that drink must be strong. I point to her drink. "Good?"

She nods, sipping, and covers my mouth. I sip the drink from her beautiful lips. Fuck she turns me on. I lace my hand through her hair, pulling her hard against my open-mouth kiss. My tongue dives deep with passion swirling and tasting her. She moans into my lips … she's falling into me … she's gone. She's like puddy in my hands. I totally consume her lips, her mouth, her senses. She's mine.

I fan the gang to hit the floor. I can hear them laughing as they leave. I curl my body over hers, running my hand up her dress. She gasps, "Mr. Starks."

"Shh, kiss me." I cover her lips, consuming her senses, our tongues are dancing to their own song. I slip my fingers past her lace panties. She's fucking drenched. She's tugging my hair, pulling me deeper into her kiss. She gasps into my mouth as I slip my finger through her wet folds. Our eyes meet. I grin, covering her lips again. She whimpers as I start fingering her with that come-hither motion that drives her insane. I'm totally working her up, she's breathing wild and going insane against my fingers. "Give me your come Amelia," I whisper into her lips. "Scream, no one is going to hear." She lets go of her reserve, and I finger fuck her until she releases her silk

430

over me. Fuck she's hot. I slip my silk-glazed fingers from her sex, pulling her back up to sitting position. Her cheeks are flushed, her breathing ragged and her eyes are sparkling.

I laugh as she looks at me. I touch her thighs, she's holding them tight. "You're horny aren't you sweet Amelia?"

"Yes, for you." She grins, sipping her drink. All in good time sweetheart.

A good grinding song floods the sound system. "You want to dance?" I know she does. I laugh as she jumps up, grabbing my hands. I lead her through the bouncing bodies and I twirl her into my chest. I shift my legs in between hers, we drop and start grinding on one another. Our bodies naturally get lost in the music and we're swaying our torsos front to back, our hips locked; she wraps her leg around my hip for the dips. We look like we just walked off the set of the original *Dirty Dancing* movie. I know she's sensitive, her face is telling me she feels good.

The first song we danced to is now blaring through the club. She grins, remembering. I twirl her back against my chest and spray my big hand across her tight tummy; we start to sway, just like that night. I stroke up and down her sexy body; she leans her head against me, her arms reaching behind my head, lacing my hair with those beautiful fingers. Only now I've had all of her, seen all of her. And I want more, I want all of her. Mine!

I drop my face into her neck, kissing her skin. Damn she tastes good. I look down at her sexy hips rocking into me. The diamond looks fabulous on her. She has her head turned to the side, her eyes watching me. I grin, meeting her gaze. I kiss her soft lips. She smiles at me as she closes her eyes and lets herself get lost in me.

Another song plays, and I wrap my arms tighter around her waist, kissing up and down her neck. I don't see anything other than my beautiful Amelia. She's so perfect. I open my eyes when I feel hands coming up around my chest from behind; Tina is grooving against me. Michael is coming up the front of Amelia.

I laugh, he's making 'she's hot' faces. I don't care, she can dance with anyone in our gang. I release her into his arms. She laughs as Andy comes up behind her. Tierra is climbing my front. "Yeah," she squeals and starts rolling her hips. I grab her waist, she's working it against me.

Amelia is laughing, rolling her hips, breaking it down sandwiched in between Andy and Michael. She looks fucking hot. It's like her and Tierra are feeding off one another. She turns her beautiful hips, shaking and rolling them. She's holding Michael's shoulders as he's working down her body. Her tits are practically in his face. She shimmies her shoulders lacing her hands through her hair. She may be dancing her fabulous body against Michael and Andy, but she never lost my gaze.

I see the bodies moving all around us as we dance that single guy dance, admiring Tierra, Tina, and Amelia grinding on each other.

"Our women are hot." Michael grins.

"Yeah, they are," I agree, watching a group of douches eyeing them. "I knew it would only be a matter of time." Michael and Andy turn. "They've got company."

Andy grins. "I think our ladies can take care of it."

"Amelia isn't as sassy as Tierra and Tina. You forget she hasn't been living for the last ten years." I don't want anyone testing her. I walk towards them as Gerry and Marcus start to move in. I relax, watching Amelia swaying and grinding with Gerry.

"Looks like we got our own company." Andy grins. I turn and we got three ladies, eyeing us like candy. They don't even compare. I turn my attention back to Amelia who is rocking it with Gerry. The douches are still hanging close. I feel hands run up my chest from behind. I look down and turn, about the same time, Amelia is right here. She gave her that 'get the fuck off bitch' look she shot at the guys on the boat. She has the chick's hands in hers removing them from my body. She doesn't say anything, she's watching me—with sultry eyes—waiting.

I wrap her body into mine. "Are you mine?" she whispers, shaking her hips against me.

"Only yours Amelia." I grin at her jealousy.

"I don't want to share you with others." She wraps her body into mine, swaying to the beat.

"I wasn't remotely interested sweetheart." She's laying her cards out there for me.

"Good!" She releases me, trailing her fingers around my hips as she returns to dancing with Tierra and Tina. She's grinning, watching me.

"Looks like the Lioness staked her claim." I laugh at Gerry.

"She certainly did." I'm beaming. She wasn't about to play.

"Looks like you're going to either have to do the same or let some guy think he has a chance." I look at Marcus and follow his eyes. The douche is trying to make his play. He's dancing behind her. Looking like he wants to devour her. I can read his eyes. He's holding two drinks.

"Playing the drink card." I roll my eyes. "I don't think so," I growl, moving in her direction. He whispers to her, she shakes her head and ignores him. Gerry is right behind me. I stop to see if he takes the hint. He grins, watching her, and hands the drinks to some other chicks dancing. He grabs Amelia's hips. Tierra slaps his hands off her.

"Problem?" I was right there, but felt like I couldn't get to her fast enough. The dude meets my chest. *He must be average height.*

"This dick dweeb wasn't getting the hint; Amelia didn't want to dance with him," Tierra yells over the music. Andy wraps his arm around her waist. Michael comes up to Tina.

I reach my hand out, knocking him aside. "Come on sweetheart." She wraps herself around me. "If she doesn't bite with the drink card, all bets are off buddy."

"Yeah," Andy barks.

434

"You mind your manners ... keep your hands off," Michael growls.

"You all ready to hit another club scene?" I look at Amelia, she grins and nods.

Chapter 51: Amelia

Wow this club has the red-carpet entrance too. I look up as Quinton is holding his hand out for me to take. There are flashes and people everywhere. These must be celebrity rich clubs. They don't know we're just regular people. Well, as far as regular Joes go who own yachts and their own corporation.

"You look hot," Quinton whispers, kissing my cheek as we greet the doorman. Same procedure as last time, we're greeted and taken to his VIP lounge.

"Another perk of being Mr. Starks." I grin.

"Now you're getting it," he teases as we sit down. He orders me the same tropical concoction I had at the last dance club.

"Tierra doll." I look to a man's voice. She turns, squealing loudly. I look at Quinton, he rolls his eyes. Andy doesn't look happy.

"Who is that?" I yell in Quinton's ear.

"Her sleaze-ball manager," Quinton quips. "Andy hates him." I remember him telling me that before. I grin as Quinton slides my drink over, sipping it. Tierra is completely lost in her model talk now. She looks over Andy's shoulder and I follow her eyes. A group of girls are waiving and wanting her to join them.

"Andy, some of the girls from the photo shoot are here. I'm going over. You want to come with?" she asks him.

"Nope, think I'll pass." He throws his shot back. I look at Quinton. He's not paying much attention to his friend, who's clearly getting pissed.

"What are you thinking sweetheart?" he asks, looking over the dance floor, his hand taping to the beat.

"Andy doesn't look happy." He doesn't seem concerned with his friend at the moment. "Are you going to ask me to dance or keep scoping the area?" He laughs, standing.

"You want to dance sweetheart?" I nod, taking his hand. I hear him whisper something to Andy.

He twirls me against his chest and we start grooving and swaying. He leans down and covers my mouth with an open-mouth kiss. His tongue is deep and controlling; my tongue glides effortlessly with his and we melt into one. He tastes like gin. I don't know how many songs we danced back-to-back to, but I feel sweaty. His hair is damp around his temples.

"You want to break from dancing?" I nod at him as he leads me to a set of elevators. He punches in the code, and the doors open. I grin, watching him. "They have an excellent rooftop lounge."

"Oh." I welcome his arms wrapping around me. This has been quite the night of dancing. "Gerry mentioned karaoke; are we still doing that?"

He laughs. "There's a little beachfront karaoke hole in the wall. It's a low-key place. We'll hit that next. It's fun."

The doors open and the fresh, cool air is welcoming. He leads me to a white sectional in the corner. We both sit at the same time, and he pulls me into the crook of his arms. There are twinkle lights strung all above our heads. The music is low and relaxing.

He smiles when the waiter appears with a small menu. He orders another round of our drinks and looks over the menu. "Small plates. You have to be hungry, I'm starving." I laugh as I lean over his shoulder, looking to see what looks appealing. "Spinach and cheese empanadas?" I look at him, smiling. "Mediterranean shrimp cocktail?"

"French fries?" I ask.

He laughs looking at me. "You like regular ole French fries."

"Yes! It's my go-to comfort food. I practically lived off them in college. It was the only thing I cooked well. I use to wake up craving them at five in the morning."

"Well, you've certainly surpassed your French fry skills," he teases.

I smile when the waiter returns. "Yes, order of French fries." He looks at me. "Spinach and cheese empanadas, and the shrimp cocktail."

He relaxes back with his hand on my knee. "You're totally chilling out on me?" I stroke his forearms. He's grinning. "Have I worn you out?"

He chuckles. "No! I'm just relaxed with you … happy."

"You best not crash on me," I tease, watching his eyes roll over my body.

"Sweetheart, you've got nothing to worry about. I won't crash until I've made love to you all night." He runs his finger down my neck studying the diamond. "It's beautiful against your skin."

"It's beautiful in general." He laughs taking my hand, rubbing his thumb over my knuckles and fingers. "What are you thinking?"

"About that ring, how gorgeous it was on your finger. You should be covered in diamonds and gems."

"I just want you." I kiss his lips. He smiles as our lips hover for a moment, looking into my eyes then at my lips. He kisses me with a sensual one-lip kiss, loving my bottom lip. I melt into his touch, tenderly stroking my cheek. My fingers lace through the back of his hair, twirling. We sink back into the cushions, kissing. His fingers stroke my leg wrapped over his. My stomach is full of tingles; my mind is all consumed with thoughts of him; I am lost.

We stop kissing when we hear the dishes cling against the table. He grins, looking up. "Your French fries are here."

"Mmm, so good." I do a little happy dance. "Open." He laughs but does. I dip it into some of the spicy aioli sauce before feeding him.

"Good, as far as French fries rank," he teases. He grabs a shrimp, dips and bites it. "Now, you need to try this shrimp."

I laugh, letting him feed me. "I do love shrimp cocktails. I like the zesty cocktail sauce." I think I love him too, but that may freak him out. We've only known each other a few weeks.

"Tell me, what has been your favorite thing thus far?" I laugh, looking at him.

"Being with you." That was an easy answer.

"Specifically." He inquires as he bites the empanada. "Mmm, taste." I hold his hand with mine as I take a bite.

"Oh that's delicious." He laughs and holds it to my lips for me to take another bite. "Specifically, being with you … in the bed … the shower… the limo." His smile reaches his ears as he laughs deep, and he pops the last bite in his mouth.

"Really, so the best part has been making love to me?" He's reeling from that.

I smirk as I eat my fries. "Yes. You know your ego loves that confession. I think I could lay in bed with you all day and do nothing but that and eat."

"I may take you up on that." He smirks with a nod. I shrug, I would totally lay naked in bed with him all day.

Chapter 52: Quinton

She's beautiful, laughing, clapping, and cheering Marcus and Gerry on. "How did you get us a table right at the stage? It was reserved."

"I had Steve reserve us a table by the stage for tonight." She's dancing in her chair. She's never been to a karaoke bar. "You're going up next," I tell her.

"What?" she gasps, looking around the table. We're all grinning and nodding. "No, I don't sing, much less sing in front of people."

"Sweetheart, this is what it's all about. Get that sweet ass up there and sing your heart out. No one cares if you're good or bad. It's just fun." I know she's going to sound beautiful. I still remember the sweetest singing my ears ever heard that night.

"I don't know any songs." She wants to but is nervous.

"You pick the song from the list, then they display it on the prompter." She follows Andy's finger as he's pointing. She nods. "It lights up when you're to sing. If the song has backup singers, you will hear that part, unless you have multiple people singing. They can change it at the DJ system."

441

"Well, I'm warning you all, I suck! You're going to be mortified to have to sit with me." She's cracking me up. She has no idea how beautiful she sounds.

"You've never took voice or singing lessons?" Tina pipes up. Amelia shakes her head, downing her drink. She's nervous as Gerry and Marcus finishes their duet. Everyone is clapping and whistling.

Amelia freezes in her seat when the DJ calls her name over the sound system. "You're up sweetheart." I stand, pulling her up by the hands. She covers her face as I walk with her up on the stage. The crowd is laughing and cheering for her to do it. The DJ jokes with the crowd about her being a karaoke virgin and nerves. "Just have fun sweetheart." I kiss her on the cheek.

"I can't believe you did that to her," Tina spat when I returned to the table. I laugh. She's going to be great.

"She'll be fine. She's just nervous." I watch her pick her song and the DJ talking to her. She's nodding. The lights dim, the room goes quiet. I grin looking at the gang.

"Whoo, you got this girlfriend," Tierra cheers.

I clap my hands. "You got this," I yell. She rolls her eyes at me with a smirk. I laugh, looking at the gang.

The lights fade, and she starts to sing in the sweetest voice I've ever heard. She's singing the first verse to the song "Follow You" by Echosmith. My heart stops as she sings the chorus. Her eyes are closed. She starts to relax by the second verse, and she's opening her eyes. This time on the chorus she's adding her hands.

442

"Damn," Tierra whispers, "she's really good." I grin and nod like I have something to do with it. I don't have anything to do with it.

We're all holding our breaths; hell the entire room was quiet. "She's fucking beautiful," I tell them, "I'm going to marry her."

"We know you are." Andy nods. Michael smiles.

I'm standing by the last verse, the lights go dark and the room erupts with claps and whistles. "Yeah sweetheart," I yell clapping. I'm walking towards her when she comes off the stage.

I swoop her up in my arms, covering her mouth with a full open-mouth kiss, her tongue slides eagerly into my mouth. Our tongues twist and twirl together perfectly. I rake my hand up the back of her head through her hair, holding her to me. She moans into my lips. I start kissing down her jaw, to her ear.

"You sounded beautiful."

"It's how I feel about you," she whispers resting her forehead against mine with her eyes closed. She knocked the wind out me.

"That was amazing," Tierra interrupt us. She's looking at me. I don't have time to respond, Andy and Michael are grabbing me. She laughs as she watches us run to the stage.

She told me she loves me in a roundabout way. I'm reeling. I look at Andy and Michael. "We going to fucking rock this.

Let's drop some male stripper dance moves too, like we use to do in the frat house."

"We're singing, 'The Wolf' by The Spencer Lee Band." Michael grins.

"Sounds good." I nod. "Chorus we all sing, then just take turns picking up the verses. I got the first."

"I got the second verse." Andy grins.

"Leaves the best for last," Michael smarts. "We just keep following this pattern, chorus all." I give him a thumbs up.

The lights fade up, we're pumping and rolling our hips to the beat, I start singing the first verse, looking straight at Amelia. When we start the chorus we look like a set of Chippendales pumping our hips and hopping forward.

Amelia is screaming and dancing, clapping her hands. We're clapping and strutting on the stage, like we own it. Tierra and Tina are screaming and dancing. We're shaking it.

Amelia, Tierra, and Tina jump us as we walk off the stage; the crowd is laughing and whistling. "You guys did awesome." Amelia is laughing. I laugh wrapping my arms around her waist, kissing her lips as we walk back to the table.

"Mr. Starks, are you a strip tease?" Amelia teases. "You got some serious stripper moves."

I laugh. "No. I've never stripped for money." I want to tell her I adore her too, but Tierra snatches her away.

"We're singing next Amelia." She laughs, looking back at me as they haul her up to the stage. I order us all around of shots while we get ready to watch our ladies.

444

"Amelia fits our group perfectly." Michael grins watching them up on the stage.

"Yeah she does." I grin throwing my shot back.

The lights fade up, the music "Happy" by Pink floods the sound system. Tierra starts the first verse. Amelia and Tina are on each side of her, holding their own mics.

"Sing it baby," Andy yells as he watches his wife slink her hips side to side. Her hand slides up and down her body as she sings the first verse. Amelia and Tina are rocking their hips in perfect sync to the beat, they take turns on some of the lines.

"They look hot." Michael grins. He stands and claps as Tina starts singing the second verse, Amelia and Tierra swap a few lines. They're all rolling their hips, looking sexy.

They all sing the chorus together. I laugh as they rub seductively on each other swapping out the center spot.

I stand up as Amelia takes the center of the last verse, she's looking at me. Her voice is beautiful. She closes her eyes as she sings and rocks her hips. "Yeah sweetheart," I yell as she slinks her body, trolling her fingers. The diamond plays the light perfectly. They all sing the last line together.

"It's time to call it a night." I look at the guys. "I'm ready to fuck that fine piece of ass." I can read their thoughts; they're thinking the same damn thing. I just say it. "Gerry, you two ready to head back to the yacht?"

When they don't answer I turn, Gerry and Marcus could be porn stars about now. "I take it they're ready." I look back at Michael and Andy.

Chapter 53: Amelia

Oh god my feet hurt and my voice is shot. I haven't sung that much or hard in my life. I slip my heels off in the limo. Quinton grabs my feet, squeezing and rubbing them between his strong hands.

"Mmm, that feels really nice." I smile at him as he sits back and relaxes. I'm so glad we're heading back to the yacht, I just want to get naked and lay beside him in bed. This has been a long day. I reach up and rub the diamond. He grins, watching me.

"So boss, what's the itinerary for tomorrow?" Gerry grins.

"Freeport ... anything goes. We won't do the nightlife or dinner, we've got to start back before then to make it home by midday Sunday."

"Don't forget you have the black-tie gala Tuesday night." Gerry looks at me. Quinton sits up, still massaging my feet.

"I totally forgot about that event." He looks at me. "It's a charity gala. I want you to go with me." He turns back to Gerry. "Call them first thing Monday and add Amelia as my plus one."

"I don't have a dress for a gala. I don't even know what to buy for one."

"I've got you covered," Tina pipes up. "I'll meet you at Quinton's penthouse Monday, we can do lunch and shopping."

"Don't you work?" They all laugh.

"No! Tina isn't what you would call working material." Michael laughs. "She stays home, plans events, does charity work. Things like that."

"Oh." I smile. "Well, I guess I'll see you Monday then." I look out the window. "If Eric hasn't frozen our account."

"Not an issue," Quinton barks. "I don't want you worrying about that." I look at him in somewhat disbelief. *How can I not worry about these things?* "Steve can drive you two around the city."

"What, in this?" I ask laughing.

"No ... no ... in my Aston Martin DBX or the Bentley." I laugh and look at Tina. She's grinning.

"You're serious?" Why am I even shocked?

"It really depends, do want to use the SUV or sedan?"

"I like the Bentley," Tina pipes up. "It's gorgeous Amelia, top of the line. Silver. It makes you want to have an orgasm."

"No offense Tina, but I don't want you to orgasm on my leather seats." Quinton laughs as he looks at me. I don't laugh, this is too much to process at the current moment.

"Quinton likes his toys Amelia." Andy grins.

"European toys," Michael adds. "The limo in Jacksonville is a Rolls Royce party limo."

447

I look out the window as we stop at the docks. Steve opens the door, Quinton exits first, swooping me up in his arms, carrying me like a baby, with my shoes dangling on his fingers.

I wrap my arms around his neck. "You like being able to swoop me off my feet Mr. Starks?"

"Very much sweetheart." He grins as he carries me all the way to his private cabin. I scoot to the bed's edge. He locks the door and hits the music on low. "I've been waiting all night to get back here." He's grinning as he unfastens his shirt, tossing it from his body.

He's looking down at me wearing nothing but his dress slacks. His body is sexy, tan and hard. He pulls me up and grabs the edge of my dress, lifting it over my head. "Your tits are beautiful." He drops kisses across my chest.

"Damn you're sexy," I breathe. His fingertips glide all around my hips and thighs. He kisses down my body, grinning when I gasp watching him. He taps my legs a little further apart.

"I want you to be mine forever Amelia." He's kissing my knee, sucking and sliding his tongue around to the back of my leg.

"Mmmm." I cradle his head, feeling his heat of his breath cross the outside of my lace panties. He's kissing and nibbling my stomach, his tongue swirling around my belly button. I hold my breath as he loops his fingers in the material, pulling them down, and he taps my ankle for me to step out of them. He strums his fingers across my other calf and taps. I step out.

He runs both hands up the length of my legs, standing. "Now this is better." I moan softly as he starts walking us toward the bed, his hands lacing through my hair, pulling my mouth into sexy one-lip kisses.

My sex aches and feels heavy from my arousal. God his arms feel amazing wrapped around my body. I run my fingers down his chest, toying with the rim of his trousers. I flip the button, unzipping him. He growls as he looks at me. I push his pants down, hooking my fingers through his undies at the same time.

"Amelia," he groans with a smile. "Ever eager are we?"

"Oh you have no idea," I whisper as I drop to my knees, pulling his feet free. His cock is huge, saluting me. I kiss around his stomach, tickling my fingers up and down his sexy thighs. "I must say your quads are very sexy." He nods watching me caress them. I kiss and nibble his hip, working my way towards his belly button. I look up as he sucks in air. I touch his cock, wrapping my hand around him. He's grinning ... waiting. I wrap my lips around the tip, kissing it.

"Fuck." He reaches for my head. I slide my hand down following with my mouth, covering my teeth with my lips, taking him as far as I can. He's very well endowed. I squeeze my hand tighter around his shaft and slide the tip of my tongue back up his shaft sucking; my hand following. I flick my tongue across the frenulum. I look up, his eyes are closed and he's moaning. I grin as I suck the tip, swirling my tongue. I moan deep in my throat and go down on him again, he grabs my head hard ... holding it ... guiding it. I'm giving my first blowjob.

Wow, I can't believe I like doing this. I see his toes flexing with each suck and pull. He likes it. He's so aroused. I taste his cum, sucking him. His essence is slightly salty—delicious. His cock is hard and smooth between my lips, I'm dripping between my legs. God his scent is erotic. I run the tip of my tongue up his length sucking, swirling my tongue around his head. I stand up, kissing over his stomach, nibbling my way up to his pectorals. I suck gently on his nipple.

"Fuck, Amelia," he growls, watching me. Our eyes meet, and I grin as I suck his nipple again, flicking my tongue over the tip. His fingertips brush over my nipples as I crawl on the bed, knee walking. He's following me like a puppy, drooling, rubbing all over my arms, tenderly stroking me ... kissing my neck, down between my shoulder blades. I look over my shoulder at him, and his eyes are full of lust. My breasts swell under his hands, squeezing my nipples between his thumbs and forefingers. His mouth covers mine with a passionate open-mouth kiss, dipping his tongue deep. I break the kiss.

"Oh Amelia sweetheart, what are we going to do now?" He's excited.

"I want to suck you!" He grins roguishly.

"Only if I can taste you." I watch him shift down on the bed. "Straddle my face beautiful." He holds his arms up, to help guide my hips. I'm on my hands and knees, with my junk spread open above his face.

"Fuck," I purr as I feel his first lick. I lift my hips off his tongue, looking down between our bodies, he's grinning. I grab his cock and wrap my lips around his shaft, going down on him.

"Fuck," he growls as he pulls my hips down to his mouth, and licks up my slit. He's swirling his tongue and sucking my clitoris.

I whimper against his cock, squeezing the shaft with my hand as I glide the tip of my tongue down the underside of his cock. Swallowing as my lips sucks on the tip, relaxes my throat, allowing me to take him deeper. Tears push against my closed eyelids I continue my assault. Sucking ... pulling ... coaxing his cum bead.

"Fucking hell Amelia," he growls dipping his tongue deep inside licking, swirling, and sucking my clitoris as I work his cock in my mouth.

Fuck my toes are curling; my senses are in overload, his cock tastes so good, salty. I strum my fingertips over his sac as I suck him. I suck his head, focusing on French kissing his sensitive spot. His hips flex into my mouth.

My hips are flexing into his mouth, he's really good. I can't breathe, my toes curl, and my silk covers his lips. My thighs quiver, trying to support my weight. He's not letting up, using his tongue over my sensitive swollen bud, coaxing another orgasm.

I grab his cock, sucking hard, gagging. He's pumping his hips into my mouth, holding my head in place. His essence hits the back of my throat, filling my mouth. I swallow. His cum turns me on. I lick and suck his cock like it's a cum lolly-pop. God, he tastes good—we're both moaning.

451

I'm too sensitive for his tongue on me. He rolls us. I'm rolling my hips and thighs together as he climbing backwards up my body, kissing and nibbling my skin, my nipples ... until he's kissing me upside down in an open-mouth kiss. Our tongues melt into one.

Chapter 54: Quinton

I lean back on my knees, our fingers laced, stretching her arms above her head. I look down at this beautiful creature writhing in pleasure on my bed, that diamond laying between her fabulous tits. Damn!

Her husband is a complete fucking idiot. I shift our bodies, wrapping my arms around her. "Come here sweetheart." Damn my cock is sensitive.

She rolls into me, running her fingertips across my chest and wrapping her leg over my hip. She looks up at me, then down. I laugh, I think she's shy.

"Hey what is it?" I laugh, she looks like she wants to ask me something. "What's on that beautiful mind?"

"Nothing," she whispers looking down. She's grinning as she traces my muscles. We lay there not saying anything for an entire song. "Was that weird to you?" she finally blurts out.

I laugh. "Was what weird?"

"That? What we just did?"

"What? No ... why do you think it was weird? Have you never done that?" *There is no way she's never done that*. That beautiful damn mouth.

"No."

"No to giving head or no to sixty-nine?" I'm trying to see her face, but she's way too tucked into my body.

"No to both. Was it bad?" Amelia whispers. "Like I know you've probably had it better. I didn't know what I was doing, I just went with it." She's finally breathing after that long-winded statement.

"Impossible." I flip over on my side, rolling her unexpectedly onto her back. I'm leaning over her, looking into her eyes.

"What?" She asks sort of smirking. I can't tell if she's messing with me.

"How have you never given head to your husband in ten years of marriage?"

She looks down. "Our sex life wasn't lecherous." She's toying with the bedding. "I never wanted to." Fuck she's serious. "And he never pushed the issue with me. I've never tasted cum until yours." She looks at me slowly. "Was it bad?"

I laugh, she's fucking adorable. "Bad? You're really serious? You think it was bad?" She shrugs.

"Amelia sweetheart it was ... fucking a.m.a.z.i.n.g! Trust me, I've had plenty of head, and that was the best I've had." I run my hand over my face. "I really don't understand how you knew how to give the perfect head: your pressure ... your suck." I'm strolling my fingertips up and down her arms. "Are you kidding me?"

She laughs. "No. I'm serious. If I should do something different, I want you to be honest."

"Did you think it was weird?" *Please say no.*

"No. I just want you to be satisfied. You know you are Quinton Starks the sex god," Amelia teases as she kisses my pectoral.

"That I am." I smugly laugh. "We're not even close to being done, by the way, for the evening." She laughs glancing down at my cock. "Yeah, it's got plenty to do to this beautiful body."

I stand, pulling down the bedding on my side. "Here, let's get under the sheets." We both jump under the sheets, giggling like teenagers. She's naked in my bed wearing nothing but that diamond and stroking my arm with her fingertips. Her touch is so delicate. My heart is about to rupture. I'm completely and utterly reeling having her here.

Her loving eyes are watching me intently. "Why are you grinning like that?"

I brush the back of my hand over her cheekbone, strolling down, running my fingertips across her jaw. She adjusts her face upward, her gorgeous lips. I want to explore this beautiful orifice. I kiss her, our tongues begin to dance and tingle, tantalizing my senses.

We're lost in each other, kissing and loving one another. She's humming against my lips, rocking her hips. I palm her tit, pulling and squeezing her nipple with my thumb and pointer finger. Her leg wraps higher over my hips. "Fuck, you're making me rock hard."

I stop kissing her. Her sultry eyes are pulling at my lips, my body. I'm the damn putty. She moans, covering my lips with a seeking open-mouth kiss, dipping her tongue deep into me; our tongues massage against each other, twirling and rolling. I reposition myself between her open legs, rubbing her thigh tighter. I thrust my cock against her folds, feeling her heat ... her wetness. She's whimpering. She's a vixen.

Her breathing is ragged. "I want you Quinton!"

"Say it again," I growl. Reaching down I grab my massive cock.

"I want you," she purrs as I tease her opening with the head.

"I want you ..." I coax, sticking in my head and pulling back out, causing her to gasp, "to say my name."

"I want you Quinton," she purrs, as I slide my head in her folds. She gasps as I hold it partially in her. "I want all of you Quinton. I need to feel you all in me."

"That's right baby." I slam into her. She screams, throwing her head back. "I'm all in baby." She's spreading her legs wider with each stroke.

"I love ..." she whimpers in my ear. Holy fucking hell.

"What do you love Amelia?" I growl, fucking her harder. "Tell me what you love."

"You ..." she moans, arching her back, "being inside of me." She's pumping her hips in perfect harmony to my thrusts, grabbing my ass, and digging her nails in, pumping me deeper in her.

"Fuck," I growl. I'm whimpering, sucking air in through my teeth. "I love this," I hiss. "You're mine Amelia."

"All yours Quinton, only yours," she screams, and wrapping her hands around the back of my head, she's watching me thrusting into her. She's whimpering, thrusting her hips hard into mine.

"Fuck Amelia," I whisper. Our eyes are locked while supporting my upper body with my forearms and clasping her head. She grins, nibbling my biceps. We're both whimpering and trying to breath. I look down at her body, her tits are bouncing beneath me. Damn they look good.

I suck her nipple between my lips, watching her arch her back in pleasure, sucking and swirling my tongue. She's going nuts beneath my mouth, thrusting.

"Damn you feel good," I growl, sitting back and putting her ankles on my shoulders.

She screams, clutching the pillows with each deep steady stroke. I open and close her legs some while pounding into her.

She heaves on the mattress below me, her hips riding up. She's holding her breath. I grin, kissing her in a single-lip kiss. I lace her fingers with mine, dragging them above her head.

She's moaning and whimpering, repositioning her legs around my hips. I stroke her deep, watching her; she's loving it. I lean down sucking and flicking her nipple with my tongue. There it is, that sweet spot. I feel her tensing.

"That's right baby, hold it and ride that come out." I moan and whimper as I feel her tense. She's flexing her legs open wider as I keep the pace.

"Quinton," she screams, her breath hitches in her throat, her toes curl and she's holding onto my hands for dear life. She's quivering beneath my strokes.

"I feel your silk all around my cock. I love this," I growl feeling her cinched muscles. "Fuck, you're milking me!" Her sex is sucking me deeper and deeper. Damn I'm seething through my teeth, whimpering as I fill her with liquid heat.

I roll off, collapsing beside her. I look at her, she's satisfied. My chest is heaving. My heart is about to fucking explode.

"Quinton," she purrs, rubbing her face and squeezing her thighs tight. I grin hearing my name on those beautiful lips.

"I hate pulling out of you." I raise the sheet. "Get over here sweetheart," I tell her, holding my arm out for her to cuddle into.

I'm so damn relaxed coming down from my climatic high. She feels perfect laying her head on my chest, my fingers toying with her hair.

"Tell me something about yourself Quinton." She sighs, trolling her fingertips across my stomach.

"You're the only woman I've cuddled with after making love. Hell, you're the only woman I've made love to." She moans into my stomach. "Tell me something."

458

"It's very different being with you."

"How so?"

"You're the only man I've ever wanted to make love to. It's different with you ... to desire your touch ... to want you. Before it felt like an obligation." I hesitate while playing with her hair as I think about what that means. "Tell me something."

"That weekend we spent together at the inn, you completely enthralled me." She kisses my stomach, as she strums her fingertips. "I had no choice, I had to have you. Your turn."

"My feelings scare me ... I'm falling in love with you." I pause. Did I hear her correctly? "Your turn."

"I've never been in love before." I keep toying with her hair. "But being with you has my heart racing, my mind reeling about the possibility of marriage. Your turn."

"I think I would like that," she whispers. I feel a tear on my stomach. I clasp her head in my hands, stroking her hair. "Your turn." She sniffles.

"I wish you had never married your husband." She slowly strums her fingers across my stomach. "Your turn."

Chapter 55: Amelia

With lazy eyes I wake up to the feel of Quinton's chest rising and falling. I roll over, scanning the moonlit room. I peek out the window, we're moving.

He looks so peaceful, stretched out sleeping. Quietly I slip on my silk kimono and sneak out of his cabin. I walk towards the bow of the top deck and relax on the daybed. The crisp sea breeze is refreshing.

Why did I tell him I love him? *Because you do, Amelia, and it scares the living hell out of you,* I tell myself. To have someone who means so much to me. It hurts to think of him not in my life. I finger the diamond on my neck, he has to be in love with me. He's entertaining the idea of marriage. I have no idea why ... *why mess up a good thing?*

My reality, our truth, is just another night away ... I'm already married. I have no right to tell him I love him, just as he has no right to want to marry me. I'm not free to have these choices.

Footsteps pull me from my thoughts, and I see the captain approaching.

"Ah Ms. Amelia, everything all right?" He surveys the area.

"Hello Captain ... yes, I just couldn't sleep. It's a beautiful night."

"Yes, it is. Do you need anything? Perhaps a nightcap?"

"Oh, I'm fine. I don't want to be any trouble."

He smiles. "It's no trouble ma'am. Mr. Starks would have me, if I didn't make sure you were comfortable." He winks. "May I suggest a white Russian?"

"That does sound lovely." I softly smile. "Thank you." Within a few minutes, Toni appears with a blanket and a white Russian. "Oh Toni, I hope you weren't woken for this."

"No ma'am." He waits for me to adjust back on the pillow and hands me my drink. He unfolds the blanket and flaps it out over me. "Let me know if you need another one." Mmm, this is a tasty concoction. The coffee liquor is soothing.

"Amelia?" I turn to Quinton's voice. "What are you doing out here?"

"I couldn't sleep." He walks toward me stark naked. "You may want to get under this cover, Toni and the captain are around."

"I woke up and you were missing." He slips under my blanket and wraps his arm under me. "What are you drinking, a white Russian?"

"Yes, the captain suggested it." He laughs.

"Toni made it and brought you a blanket?"

"Yes." I laugh. "How did you know?" He smirks, like it's his job to know.

"Everything okay?" He's relaxed strumming his fingertips.

I shrug sipping my drink looking up at the sky. "I don't know … it's everything." He doesn't say anything, he's obviously waiting for me to finish. I sigh. "This has been amazing." I smile touching his hand. "You, your life … this trip. But …"

"But what Amelia?" He leans up. "What's bothering you?"

I shrug with a crooked smile. "I'm scared. I'm scared I won't be enough for you once this masquerade disappears. Then what? What if I can't keep up? You'll eventually get bored of me … my body will become bland, and your eyes will wander. I can't handle that. I can't stomach the thought of your mouth on someone else's or these beautiful hands caressing another. I just can't!"

"These are your insecurities talking. I know myself better than anyone—I've had women—tons of them. None of them compared to you. Not even close." He kisses my lips, reading my eyes. "I've never tasted a woman the way I've tasted you. Your taste, your scent remains on me. In me. I can taste you hours after we've been together. You are always in the forefront of my mind and nothing, I mean nothing, will ever change that! Period!"

"Oh, Quinton, I want to believe that."

"I can't tell you enough to make you believe that, but I'll show you in everything I do. I'm not living my life for me— those days left me the day I met you—I live life for us!" I look at him, his eyes are intently watching me.

462

"Come here sweetheart." He sits my empty glass on the table. I scoot down next to him. "I like your wrap ... silk and sexy."

I smirk, he's so cute. "You're a charmer Quinton."

"I like the way you say my name," he whispers, kissing and nibbling my neck.

"Do you now ... Quinton," I tease, rolling on top of him, straddling his waist. His hands and fingers glide with all of my movements.

"We're going to be fine Amelia ... it's going be fine," he whispers tangling his fingers through my hair, covering my lips with his. I playfully dip my tongue in his mouth, barely tracing his. "Yum, you taste like coffee," he whispers against my lips. His hands aggressively cup my face. Our tongues begin to dance the tango, swirling and blending in perfect harmony.

I rock my hips across his length. A mischievous grin reaches his eyes as he unties my sash. He controls our sensual, open-mouth kiss, dipping his tongue deep, exploring. My kimono hangs open. He leans forward, pushing up to a sitting position.

"You are so beautiful." He cups my breast, sucking my nipple in his mouth. I gasp, watching him, lacing my fingers through his hair. "Feel our love ... how perfect your body responds to me." I nod, moaning softly as he swirls his tongue around my areola, sucking my nipple. He massages my other tit, twisting my nipple between his thumb and forefinger. My nipple elongates immediately under his touch.

My sex is aching. I tug his hair between my fingers, guiding that beautiful mouth to my other breast. He looks up, grinning like a teenage boy hitting second base knowing he'll score a home run soon.

The sensations are almost too much for me to bear. I whimper, squeezing him tighter, thrusting harder against his shaft. "You're so fucking wet," he mumbles into my breast.

"Yes, I want you inside of me Quinton," I purr his name. My toes are already curling.

"You never have to ask sweetheart, just take what you want. I'm all yours," he growls, sucking my nipple harder into his mouth. I cry out.

He gasps feeling my hot, wet sex covering his magnificent cock. He moans holding my hips. "Fuck!" His breathing is so controlled, feeling all of me around all of him.

I cry out, welcoming the relief of feeling him inside. He runs his hands through my hair, pumping his hips deeper, as I ride up and down on his cock. My nails leave their calling card over his shoulders. He hisses through clenched teeth, watching my tits bounce in his face.

"Yeah, sweetheart get lost on me. You're so fucking tight," he growls, sucking my neck and rolling his thumb over my hard nipple. "Don't ever doubt this … us!" I nod, whimpering, rocking deeper into him. He grabs both of my tits in his hands, massaging and squeezing them, watching me riding his cock. "You're hot Amelia. I love this body."

I grin listening to his words. He makes me feel sexy. I push him back, his hands slide down to my hips. I lean back, reaching for his ankles, pumping down on him. My wrap slides down my shoulders. "Christ Amelia, your body looks amazing in this light." He presses his finger against the side of my clit.

"Oh hell," I scream in the night. He just set me on fire with his finger. I can't breathe, my toes are curling. "Oh god Quinton," I scream as I feel my release.

"Fuck, you're tightening on me," Quinton growls, wrapping tighter around my waist pulling himself into my chest. He sucks my nipple, whimpering and thrusting harder. I feel his cock explode, his liquid heat rushes through my body. My toes tingle.

He collapsed on the pillows, bringing me with him. His mouth covers mine, our tongues are rolling and twisting in perfect harmony. I feel him all over me, all in me. I'm so lost in love with him.

His pulse sounds like wild mustangs, yet it is soothing to my ears. He gathers my hair, kissing my neck, loving on me. I roll beside him, covering our bodies with the blanket. "I like this," I purr.

He laughs, a deep throaty laugh. "Me too sweetheart … the calmness after the storm."

Chapter 56: Quinton

"Sir." I grumble at the sound of someone waking me. I feel Amelia's body pressed into mine. "Sir, please wake up." I open one eye, the sky is starting to light around me.

"Captain, don't take this the wrong way, but your face definitely isn't what I want this close to me when I wake up." I stretch back making sure she's covered as I hear him chuckle.

"You and Ms. Amelia should really go inside before the sun rises. You wouldn't want onlookers patrolling the docks to see." I grin, looking at her all cuddled into me. Her wrap is at our feet. I look at it.

The captain smirks as he hands it to me. "Thanks. Where is the crew, anyone walking about the cabins?"

"No, not yet sir. You have your privacy." I nod as I watch him leave.

"Amelia sweetheart." I kiss her on the temple. "Wake up."

"No," she moans, snuggling deeper into me. I laugh, she's cute. I stand up naked, looking down my sexy body … even flaccid my cock is impressive … hanging against my thigh. She's whining, reaching for me. I carry her, blankets and all, back to our bed.

I'm awake now, holding her as she sleeps. She slept in her diamond. I grab my phone to check my email and the news feed. I smirk, looking at her beautiful face on my phone. I knew the media would be in a frenzy seeing me out with Amelia.

I power up her phone. He's called and texted all night. I look at his wife, naked and sleeping in my bed. Damn she's gorgeous. The arrogant me wants to take a picture of me grinning next to her and send it to him. It would serve his prick ass right.

His wife loves me. His wife is naked in my bed. His wife sucked my cock and swallowed my cum. She's not his wife anymore. She's mine. She's my girlfriend. She's my soulmate and she will be my wife. I kill her phone, tossing it on the bedside table.

* * *

I sit up, looking around at my empty space. The sheet is pooled around my waist and my feet are poking out. It's bright outside. I can still smell her all over me.

I hear the shower. My morning wood is throbbing. It's a good thing she likes to have sex because I must be a damn debauchee. Just her smell drives my sexual desire through the roof.

She's humming, washing her hair. She's beautiful, absolutely stunning. I wait for her to close her eyes and lean back in the spray, rinsing … the suds washing over her perfection.

I slip in behind her, and she jumps and gasps as I wrap her in my arms. She turns, kissing me. Her tongue is hot and demanding, tracing the shape of my mouth, learning my ridges,

467

and skimming my teeth. She moans deeper into me, our tongues massaging and loving each other. She wraps one leg around me. I shift, and her eyes close as I enter her.

"Mmm." Her breath is breaking and small whimpers are forming. I suck just her nipple, skimming it with my teeth.

"Quinton," she whines, "again." I suck her other nipple and skim my teeth over it. "Do me from behind," she purrs.

"With pleasure." Growling, I drop her leg, pull out and flip her against the wall. She spreads her legs. "Hard?"

"Yes, hard." I grin as slam into her. She cries out, her face flush against the tile, her hands splayed against the wall, her fingers flexing against the tile. *Damn she looks hot!* I yank her hips towards me, thrusting hard into her hot tight sex. "Quinton," she whimpers.

I look down at my massive cock sliding in and out of her. "You're fucking hot like this." I whimper looking at my flexed arms and chest, my abs are flexed and I'm pounding into that firm body. Every thrust lifts her more on her tip toes. "Fuck," I whimper, "you're tightening around my cock."

"Yes," she cries. I reach around and press her clit between my two fingers. *That's right baby, my thrust and that extra friction mean you're about to come fucking hard.* "Oh god." She moans, biting her own fisted hand feeling the pleasure. "It's so intense, you're intense."

"Damn right! I am your sex god," I growl in her ear. She's driving me insane. Her beautiful sex vessel is sucking me deeper and tightening. She's starting to shake. "Breathe sweetheart."

"I can't," she whispers, and her toes curl. I lean down and suck her neck, nibbling and biting across her shoulder as her silk floods over me.

"Amelia," I growl, filling her. Her satisfaction graces her face. "You like this don't you?"

"Oh very much ... Quinton," Amelia purrs. I keep stroking my impressive cock deep in her.

"I want you to have all of me," I whisper, grinding every drop. My heart is vibrating in my ears. No woman has ever left me breathless. I readjust my weight, leaning against the wall above her. She looks over her shoulder as I become flaccid.

Her chest is moving rapidly, like mine. We're watching each other, grinning. She tickles her fingers across the head of my cock. I chuckle and flex at my own sensitivity. She bites her lip, leaving me in the shower.

I grin, shaking my head.

Chapter 57: Amelia

"Earth to Amelia." Tierra snaps her fingers. We can't stop our smiling or petting. "Where do you want to go first?" Quinton laughs as he runs his fingers up my thighs drawing circles. "Well, you two must have had some amazing sex last night, because you've both been ... somewhere this morning."

"Well, since we're already at Port Lucaya, might as well hit the marketplace." Tina pipes up, rolling her eyes and grinning.

"Yeah, let's do lunch at that Cuban beachfront place before we hit the beach." Andy grins. "It has a great atmosphere Amelia, good food and drinks."

"You may enjoy the Garden of the Groves." Quinton smiles all starry-eyed at me. "I know you enjoy your little garden oasis."

"Oh fuck." I look at Gerry. "Casanova's all romance and shit today. Get ready to swelter again in the tourist gridlock." I laugh at him.

"Well, you all can head to the beach, Steve can drop you guys off. We can join you later." Quinton is rubbing his nose on the tip of mine, kissing my lips.

"They have an amazing jewelry store here too, we could check it out." I shake my head at Tina's comment.

"Tina, feel free, but I'll pass." I cut my eyes at Quinton.

"What?" He smirks.

"You're not buying me anything else Quinton. You've spent way too much yesterday." He rolls his eyes as his friends laugh. "I know you bought your yacht with your first million or whatever, but the way your lifestyle is, I would hate for you to run out of dinero in a weekend."

Michael snickers. "That's not going to happen." I look at him and roll my eyes.

"At least you know she's not dating you for your money." Andy chuckles, looking out the window. "You really are re-freshing Amelia."

"Enough," Quinton barks at their remarks, making me jump. "Sweetheart, you don't need to worry about those things. Just know if I want to buy you something I will. Simply avoiding an establishment will not deter me."

I roll my eyes. "Fine, whatever." I look out the window. He laces our fingers, strumming his free fingers up and down my thigh. "You are very charming Quinton," I whisper in his ear.

"Am I now?" He smiles, kissing me in a sweet one-lip kiss.

* * *

Boy, Quinton wasn't teasing ... nothing deterred his spending, because he dropped money constantly. We strolled in and out of all sorts of boutiques featuring some of the most expensive women's fashion I've ever seen in real life. I heeded Tina's advice and just went with it. Tierra told me to relax and let Quinton Starks do it Quinton Starks's way, and he seemed very receptive to the idea. If he found out I liked anything, I'm now the proud owner of it. I really do the love the Gucci perfume he bought me, as well as the Gucci bag. It's quite lovely.

Now we're walking with our arms looped, strolling the streets, and sharing a chocolate chip mint ice cream cone. "You're so cute." I giggle watching him lick the cone like a kid.

"It's melting like crazy." He laughs. "I don't want it to get all over the place." Tierra, Andy, Tina, and Michael are strolling behind us with coconut rum drinks in hand; Gerry and Marcus decided to give the daiquiris a try.

"Gerry this isn't a horrible, sweltering tourist trap now, is it?" Quinton bellows, laughing as he glances at Gerry enjoying his buzz.

"What's not to love about shopping and booze?" I look back laughing, Marcus has his arm looped through Gerry's. They really are quite the couple.

In addition to the high-end boutiques and restaurants, the streets are scattered with crafts and straw vendors, coconut and daiquiri drink carts and Bahamian food fare. There is drumming and dancing in the streets.

"Here it is." Quinton stops walking. "Let's see if we find any artwork for the penthouse."

"What?" I grin looking at the front of the store.

"You're moving in with me. You can add some flare to my penthouse. We can get pieces of art or something to represent our travels. Might as well start with our first trip to the Ba-

472

hamas." He's looking at his hands, holding the melting cone.

"Are you finished?" Quinton asks.

"Yes." I giggle watching him toss it and wipe his finger before lacing our fingers. We walk into the small gallery.

"Good morning," we're greeted by the artist, judging by his painter's smock. "Let me wash my hands. Feel free to look around the studio, prices are on the wall below the pieces."

"Take your time," Quinton replies walking around. "See anything that strikes your fancy?"

"I have no idea. I like the octopus." He looks at me laughing. "I don't know what your penthouse looks like. I can't possibly pick something for it. I didn't think you were expecting me to stay permanently with you."

He looks totally baffled by my comment. "What did you think I meant?"

"I don't know, until I found a place." I touch a piece of art on the table. "This is weird."

"Yeah, it is." He's looking at me intently. "Amelia look at me." He's grinning. "I meant move move in with me. Not just until you found a place. Do you honestly think you're going to spend a night away from me now that we've been together?"

I tittered shaking my head. "No, I don't want to be away from you at all. I actually dread when this trip is over and real everyday resumes."

He laughs, pulling me into his chest. "I adore you sweetheart."

473

My heart skips a beat ... maybe that's his way of saying he loves me too! I wrap my arms around him and cover his lips in an open-mouth kiss, our tongues tease and taunt with desire. It's euphoric.

"Oh hell, Lioness has her lion wrapped up again," Gerry quips, walking around the corner. I laugh breaking the kiss. Quinton is rubbing his thumb over my knuckles, looking at my hands.

"Come on," he teases, pulling me with him.

"Look! It's Porker." He laughs looking at the swimming pigs. "It looks just like Porker."

"Surely you don't want a pig hanging in the penthouse." He laughs. "Tierra and Tina would die." I laugh at the realization of his words.

"I know ... it's cute though." *I like it.* I shrug, strolling around looking. "I like this one."

He stands back and looks at it. "The Reef. We snorkeled there. It has a little octopus in it." He studies it, grinning. "You reminded me of a baby octopus, clinging to my body out of fear."

"Hush." I tease poking him in his side.

"You like this?" Quinton asks.

"Yes, I like it. It's bright." I have no idea if it will work with his penthouse.

"Sir." I hear him getting the artist. "Yes, we will take this piece—'The Reef.'" He looks at me, and exhales. "And the swimming pig one on the other wall."

I grin.

Chapter 58: Quinton

Damn she looks hot in that sapphire bikini. Her ass looks fabulous in that cut. I'm glad she let me slip her white denim shorts off and pull her flowing tank off. At least I got to undress her a little.

"What are you looking at Mr. Starks?" She caught me staring at her fabulous body.

"Just turn your head back and close those eyes," I tease. "I can look at your sexy bod and drool all I want." Damn I want to bury myself in her.

"How did Steve get here and with the limo?" Amelia turns back looking at me.

"He drove down to Fort Lauderdale and took a ferry. That limo isn't mine. He has contacts here on the islands. We use their services when we visit."

"Oh, it looked just like yours in Jacksonville." I laugh at her because it does.

"This is nice, relaxing, doing absolutely nothing." She's beautiful laying there on the beach tanning.

"What would you normally be doing, if you were home?" Her normal is all about to change when we return.

"If I had guests at the B and B, I would be preparing the evening hors d'oeuvres."

"And if not, what would you be doing?"

"Fighting!" I flinch, thinking about his words. "Or listening to Eric yell and cuss about something trivial and completely out of his control."

"That sounds like a miserable day." I run my hand over her ass. "You look smoking hot in this suit."

She's laughs as she rolls onto her back, my hand slides with her body. I tickled my fingers across her sex. "It was miserable. Touch me." She grins looking at me.

I chuckle. "Where would you like to be touched?"

"Anywhere you want to."

"Amelia, are you feeling frisky, dare I say horny?" She leans up and covers my lips with an open-mouth kiss, sucking my tongue. She moans as our tongues start sliding and massaging each other. *Fuck yeah she's horny.* She's kissing me like she does in the middle of sex.

I lace my hand through her hair, keeping her mouth doing exactly what she's doing. I know my hard on is visible, but I don't give a fuck. Her fingers strum up and down my chest, filling every dip and ripple. Her leg slightly rubs across mine. Damn, she looks like a sex symbol. Her tits brush against my other hand, and I finger her nipple through the material. She grins, noticing my subtle gesture.

She leans back as I fold my arm under my head, staring at her. "You want to get in the water?" I ask her looking down at her tits. "Your tits look hot."

"What are you going to do to me in the water?" she teases with curiosity, strolling her fingers around my stomach. I inhale, watching her fingers make a circling motion around my belly button. Her eyes are full of lust.

I lean up and kiss her on the cheek, then nibble her ear. I whisper, "Well I would take you out deep, slide those sexy blue bottoms over and fuck you in front of everyone." I kiss her down her neck as I lay back, watching her.

She contemplates it for a second before leaving me sitting there with my hard on. She dives under the water, and her sexy ass crests the top. That's all I need. I get up and follow her.

"Come on, Quinton and Amelia are getting in." I roll my eyes at Tierra's voice. I'm really starting to regret bringing the gang on this getaway. I knew I didn't want a platonic relationship, why did I think the gang would help me control my debauchee personality? Now our relationship is anything but platonic, and I hate fucking interruptions.

"We should paddle board." Andy comes running up to me. "Think Amelia has before?"

I look at him huffy. "Yeah, we can. I doubt it."

"Come here beautiful." I wrap my arms around Amelia's waist, pulling her to me. Her legs wrap about my waist. She smiles but I can see the disappointment in her eyes.

"Don't look so grumpy," she teases. "It's not a very becoming attribute." I laugh out loud at her. I know she's right. "There's my sexy Quinton." She hugs me tighter against her. "I like this too."

"Oh I do too, sweetheart." I cover her lips in our small one-lip kisses. She gradually sways her hips against my length. Surely, she realizes my hard on from hell will be conspicuous.

"Amelia, you want to paddle board?" Tina interrupts us. Doesn't she see we're busy? I grunt into her lips.

Amelia laughs as she turns to look at Tina. "I've never tried it. It looks fun." She looks back at me, smiling. "Is it fun Mr. Starks?"

"If you say my name, I'll get us a couple." I kiss her lips, tickling my fingertips under her ass cheeks. She's grinning, flexing tighter against me.

"Mr. Starks," she purrs. I laugh shaking my head. "My sex god," she whispers. I smugly shrug ... I like it ... but no not that name. I start flicking my fingers around her bottom. "Quinton," she moans in my ear followed up by a long lick. She sucks my ear lobe as she pushes out of my arms. She spoke right to my cock!

She's grinning, swimming away on her back and watching me. Her tits crest the top of the water. I lunge for her, making her laugh and scream. She's trying to turn to swim faster, but she's not fast enough. I've got her.

I'm tickling her and she's laughing, trying to get away. I grab her hauling her on my shoulders. "Stop it. Don't you dare," she screams. Beachgoers stop and see what is happening. I spank her ass and toss her.

I wait for her to come up, making sure she's okay. She's laughing. I turn around heading back towards Michael and Andy. They're laughing as I act like I just dusted my hands of her.

She pounces on my back, knocking me off balance. *She's trying to knock me down.* "Baby you're trying to take down two hundred and thirty pounds of muscle." She's given up and slid around to my front. I'm carrying her like a baby. Her head is back in defeat, looking at Andy and Michael upside down. Her tits look amazing at this angle.

"Really? You two can't take him down." She's challenging them. I laugh.

"Oh shit." I put her down as they charge me like bulls. One on each of my arms, they push me back. She jumps in the middle, trying push me down.

"Tina baby," Michael calls for backup.

"Tierra," Andy calls too. What the fuck?

"Y'all still can't get me down." I've locked my legs, activated my powerhouse. This is a hell of a sight. I can see people watching and laughing.

Amelia lets go, huffing. She's watching and grinning. "This is insane, to be this big and strong," I hear her yell. Andy and Michael are in agreement. She comes back up to me and dips her hand in my shorts, grabbing me and I drop down. She used sex as her weapon.

She's excited, jumping up and down, cheering for herself. Andy and Michael are dying laughing.

"We always knew your cock was your weakness," Andy chides.

"It's not my cock, it's the vixen who fondled me." I'm laughing as I point at her. "You're mine tonight."

"Can't wait lover," Amelia sasses her ass out of the water. Tina and Tierra follow her.

"Damn." Andy looks at me. Michael's grinning.

"Yeah, you two have no idea." I grin watching that fine ass walk to the paddle boards. "Watch the guys start flexing their muscles and drooling." I laugh looking at them. "See, right on cue."

Chapter 59: Amelia

"How come you're just gliding perfectly across the water, and I'm not?" I suck at this shit. Quinton thinks it's hilarious.

"You have to find your sweet spot on the board. Where you are centered." He's making circles around me. "Maybe you should try it on your knees until you get used to it."

"Oh snap, boss wants her on her knees." Gerry is dying. I smirk, looking at him. Quinton grins mouthing the words, "Oh yeah."

I roll my eyes, stick the paddle in the center, and this time I hop both feet up a little because last time I turned over. "Stop looking at my tits Quinton," I tease.

"I am not." I roll my eyes at him. "Okay, maybe I was." I hear Andy and Michael laughing.

"Tina and Tierra look like freaking paddle board models," I huff getting my balance. "I look like a wet rat looking for a lifeline." The guys are laughing it up. "Oh hey, look, I got my sweet spot." I look at them, grinning.

"Good, now hold one hand in center of paddle and the other at top, for smooth strokes." Quinton is grinning watching me. "See babe you got it."

"So Quinton, an estate in the Hamptons?" I laugh, looking up and focusing.

"Yeah." He nods with a smile watching me, then looks over at the guys.

"I've never been to the Hamptons." I look at him. "You got a staff there too?"

"Yeah." He grins. "Does that estate excite you?"

"Maybe," I tease. "Yes, shit I've got to focus here." They're laughing at me as I almost tip over. "Yes, maybe." He's looking at me grinning.

"I'll take you to celebrate."

"Celebrate what?" I'm getting this paddling down, even over the small waves.

"Your divorce!" I look up. He nods with a roguish grin.

"Any idea how long something like that takes?" I'm curious. "I've heard months and if one fights it, even longer."

"They only fight for marital property," Andy chimes in. I look at him. "Anything you going to fight to keep?"

"Nope!" I casually say looking at Quinton. "Everything is in his name anyway. What if he refuses to sign the papers?"

"You can be a legally free woman in four to five weeks if uncontested. He can refuse, but there are no children or division of property and debts so his grounds for a contested divorce is moot. He may refuse, but the judge will still grant you a divorce." Andy is looking at Quinton.

"Why are you looking at Quinton?" I'm curious.

483

"I told him to find you a divorce lawyer." Quinton casually answers … like it's no big deal.

"Oh." I look at them both. "Hope they're not expensive."

"She's the best in Jacksonville." Andy grins. "You will be divorced probably four weeks after filing. You need to meet with her this week."

"So we can go to the Hamptons in four to five weeks," Quinton quips. "My mom is going to flip. She's been hounding me to find someone." I listen to him and Andy talk. I'm sort of freaked out.

"What about a name change?" I interrupt them.

Andy laughs looking at me. "You can change it. Add it to the divorce papers. Once divorced, it will be filed."

"I certainly don't want to go the next ten years as Amelia Johansson." I'm spinning. Laughing at Gerry. "Don't you turn me over Gerry," I warn.

"You won't," Quinton quips. "What's your maiden name?"

"It's worse than my married name. I'm not telling you. I guess I can make up one." They're laughing at me.

"Now you've got to tell us." Michael is laughing.

"I just can't. It may be why I married the asshole to begin with." I'm laughing about it now. It has been so long since I thought about my maiden name: Amelia Cockburn.

Chapter 60: Quinton

"Boss, what time are we sailing back?" Gerry questions, buzzed, as we're riding back to the Fortuna.

"As soon as we board. Chef is preparing dinner tonight." I look at Amelia, she's so beautiful. "We should be back in Jacksonville tomorrow afternoon."

I watch Amelia grab her new Gucci bag, she couldn't wait to change purses. She dumped her old one in the trash on the street. I'm glad she let me buy her some clothes from the boutique today. She's going to look fabulous in the skirts and dresses.

"Why are you watching me Mr. Starks?" she asks with a grin.

"Because I can, Amelia," I tease. "You like your new bag?" I know she does, she's grinning and admiring it.

"I love it." She leans over and kisses me. "Thank you." I roll my eyes, she's already thanked me. Steve opens the door, and I get out first so I can hold sweet Amelia's hand as we walk to the Fortuna.

"Captain." I smile as we remove our shoes and toss our beach bag into the basket. "Please have our bags brought to my cabin."

"Yes sir. Dinner will be served in an hour sir." I grin and nod as I take Amelia's hand. Well, that doesn't leave us time for anything.

"Do you want a drink?" I ask as we walk by the bar.

"No. I want a bath." She laughs.

"I'm sure that can be arranged."

I watch her as she goes into the bathroom. She fills the tub with jasmine scented water. The aroma fills my cabin and tingles my senses. I nod for our bags to be placed on the sofa.

I lock the door and walk into the bathroom. She's already stripped and is relaxing in the tub. "Join me."

"I don't think we can both fit." I grin, watching her move. "We don't have long."

"Are you making up excuses not to bathe with me Mr. Starks?" Amelia flips on her stomach with her fingers over the edge of the tub. "Please get in with me."

Fuck, she's begging me. I strip and she sits back as I sink down in the tub. Damn it feels good. I bend my knees, pressing my legs against the sides. She turns her body and relaxes back against my chest. Her tits feel good resting on my arms.

"This is nice." She's relaxed with her eyes closed. I rub my thumbs in a circular motion around her nipples. I'm instantly hard. She grabs my hand and slides it down her stomach and releases me. She adjusts her bottom back more against me.

I make small circles around her belly button with my fingers. She closes her eyes, pressing her head into my chest. I keep toying with her hard nipples. I slide my hand lower between her legs. She whimpers, turning her face towards mine. I'm watching her, she can feel my breath on her lips. Her eyes look up at me, she leans over her shoulder kisses my lips.

"What do you want Amelia?"

"I want you to touch me." She whimpers as I enter her sex. Her hands grip the tub. I start fingering her in her favorite come-hither motion.

"You like this?" Oh I know she does.

"Yes," she whimpers. She leans back kissing my lips again. With my other hand, I squeeze and roll her nipple in my fingers.

She starts squeezing her other tit, mimicking my hand. "Oh that's fucking hot Amelia." She's whimpering and leaning back. I lower my mouth over hers, sucking on her tongue. Our tongues dance in perfect harmony. She's panting. She removes my hand from her beautiful tit and pulls my fingers out. I wasn't done.

She turns over looking at me. I grab her tits with my hands shifting our bodies as she straddles me. I watch her adjust herself above my cock and lower down on me.

"Fuck," I growl.

"I want to feel you come," she purrs, rocking her hips. *Oh, fucking hell.* I start pumping my hips. She's holding the sides of the tub and riding me. She's pushing hard up and down. "We don't have long. I don't care if I get off, I just want to feel your heat," she purrs in my ear. She wraps her hands around my face, bringing my lips to hers, covering my mouth in an open-mouth kiss, sucking my tongue deep.

"Shit," I whimper fucking her harder, thrusting my cock. I watch her toss her head back, digging her nails into my shoulders. She's rocking her hips, and water is sloshing in the tub. I suck her nipple, swirling my tongue around the areola. I grab her other tit, squeezing and tugging her nipple.

"Quinton," she cries, lost in the sensations. I know she's getting her clit stimulated. "Oh you're amazing." *Damn right I am.* She cups my face and covers my lips with an open kiss. Our tongues are stroking and massaging one another until we melt into one. I'm lost, thrusting into her holding her ass tight; she's thrusting with me. Her tits are smacking the water.

I can feel her sex tightening all around me. Her toes are curling, she's holding her breath, dropping down hard on me, taking me deep. I feel her silk just before I explode into her, filling her with my cum.

"You feel so good when you release … the force … the heat." She's rocking her hips, sucking all of me dry. "Mmm, it's so sexy."

Fuck me! My Amelia is positively the most alluring woman I've ever known. I cup her face. Grinning, I cover her lips in an open-mouth kiss, dipping my tongue deep. Our tongues dance their own little happy dance. She's moaning into my lips, softly stroking the length of my cock with her beautiful insides.

She climbs off me when I become flaccid, sinking back into the opposite end of the tub. "Maybe you should shower, Mr. Starks, while I finish up bathing in this tub."

Is she really throwing me out of the tub now? I grin, watching her. She flexes her eyebrow up at me. She's serious! "I see how it is, you get my heat and toss me aside," I tease.

"You need to shower and I need to bathe," she smarts innocently enough. "You're wasting precious time, Mr. Starks."

"Yes, my sex goddess," I tease, standing. Her mouth involuntarily opens into a grin looking at my massive cock. I grin following her eyes, *I know sweetheart, it's impressive.* "It's all yours Amelia."

She looks up at my eyes with a grin and nods. "Good," she nonchalantly replies, grabbing her body wash.

* * *

I can't wait, in four weeks she will be divorced from fucktard. When the time is right, I will propose to her. If she wants a long engagement, fine. At least I can call her my fiancée. Although, I'm not that really of a patient man, and I hope she doesn't want it long. Damn, I'm getting way ahead of myself.

When she looks up, I realize I've been watching her, while lost in thought as she looks over her new clothes. She really is like a kid at Christmas with new things. "What are you wearing?" I ask as I open my closet.

489

"I don't know, everything is so beautiful." She beams holding up the pieces. "I still can't believe you bought these. They're so expensive Mr. Starks."

"Wear that," I tell her. I put on my navy button up and white boating shorts. She grins as she drops her towel. She's already wearing the thong I bought her with the matching black lace strapless bra. "Damn," I breathe looking at her.

She giggles as she holds up the dress I told her to wear. We'll coordinate perfectly. She slips on the strapless high-low navy and white striped dress. I walk over and zip her up. "Don't forget this." I grin draping her diamond around her neck as I fasten it. "You looked bare without it today while we were out and about."

She turns around and kisses me softly against my lips. "Thank you again."

"You're quite welcome, my Amelia from Amelia." I'm so enamored by her. "Shall we go to dinner?" I hold out my hand.

"We shall." She grins lacing our fingers.

Chapter 61: Amelia

"Thanks Toni." Quinton nods as Toni serves our drinks.

"Toni really does make the best ones," I tell him.

"I agree." Quinton grins, sipping his gin on the rocks with lime.

"What's on the menu tonight? I'm starving."

"I hope you like it. Pan roasted halibut and scallops over curried cauliflower couscous, glazed vegetables, and wilted greens. Served with a spicy dipping sauce and mango salsa. Chef makes a very delectable halibut and scallops." He relaxes back, resting his hand on my knee. I can feel him making small circles with his thumb.

"Wow! That sounds delicious. I've never tried scallops."

"You should love them. You love shrimp." He's probably right. I sip my cosmo, looking over the water.

"Our last night on the yacht. It's rather disappointing. I've loved every minute being here with you." I smile gently at him. Reality is so close that it makes me nervous.

"We can go out on the Fortuna anytime you would like Amelia." I watch him smile as the others join us.

Tierra turns on some dinner music. "Dance with me." I look up as Quinton stands, holding his hand out. "It's the song you sang at the karaoke bar, telling me how you felt."

Oh I remember, I take his hand as he walks me to the dancing deck. He wraps me in the perfect slow dance stance, and we start to glide effortlessly to the music. I lay my head on his chest.

"These past few days have been amazing. I never thought I would find someone who completes me so perfectly." I grin hearing his words.

"I know exactly what you mean." He tilts my face up towards him and covers my mouth in his sweet single-lip kisses. We keep dancing, lip locked to another sweet slow song.

He grins, twirling me out and then bringing me back in. He glides effortlessly across the deck, leading. I follow, but his footwork is much more controlled, skilled.

"Mr. Starks, you're not just a club dancer."

He laughs. "No. I enjoy many forms of dance, sweet Amelia."

"You're very cultural aren't you?" I grin asking him. He must have always had money.

He laughs. "Cultural." He thinks I'm being funny. "My mother made sure we were both musically inclined in instrument and dance. My sister and I, that is."

"So you've always had money." I'm somewhat curious.

He laughs. "Nothing like I do now, I assure you." He grins, looking up, and notices dinner is about to be served. "Come sweetheart, dinner is being served." I let him lead me back to the table. It does look delicious.

"You two look very graceful moving together." Marcus grins.

"Quinton is a great lead," I confess, looking at him. He grins. His ego likes to be praised.

"So what are we doing tonight?" Tierra asks as we're eating.

"Drinking game?" I laugh, looking at Michael taking a bite of halibut.

"What kind?" I'm curious.

"Strip poker." Michael grins. Quinton looks at him with an 'I don't think so' look. I laugh.

"I've never played regular poker. Somehow, I think I would be the first naked."

Quinton laughs. "Which is exactly why we're not playing it!" I look at him. "If you want to strip, you can strip tease me in my cabin."

Andy laughs. "Bro doesn't want us seeing his prizes." I laugh, looking at him.

"Damn right." Quinton winks taking another bite. "Another suggestion?"

"Kings, spoons, electricity," Andy says. I've never played any of those.

"Fine, cocktails and cards tonight." Quinton shrugs as he finishes his dinner. "I wonder what Chef prepared for dessert."

"I was just going to ask." I grin. "I do have a sweet tooth."

"Your body doesn't show it." His eyes dance with desire, looking at me. I roll my eyes as I watch the steward clear the table. Since he got hung up in my panties, he's very quick about making himself invisible.

"Ah, Chef prepared one of my favorites." Quinton says. My mouth starts to water as the dessert arrives. "It's limoncello dolce."

"Oh ... yum!" The presentation is restaurant quality.

"Do you like lemon?"

"Yes, I love just about any lemon dessert." He's watching me as I savor the tart, creamy lemon taste. "Oh, it's delightful."

"Told you." He hums in appreciation, relishing his dessert.

"Amelia you're so lucky." I look up at Tina. "You get to eat this kind of food every day." I laugh, looking at Quinton.

"I'm sure he has time off, a family," I say, looking up. They're shaking their heads. I look at Quinton, he shakes his head. "He lives at your penthouse?"

"He lives in the building. I typically only drink my power protein shake in the mornings. During the week I'm at work, so he doesn't prepare lunch. He prepares dinner weekdays. Weekends, lunch, and dinner. The rest of the time, he does his own catering and things." He's so laid back talking about it.

"So I guess I can dabble in your kitchen in the mornings," I tease as I watch the steward clean the table.

"Yes, I guess so." He leans over and kisses me. "He will do all the grocery shopping. He keeps a very well stocked kitchen and is very peculiar about how things are kept. So just keep his kitchen the way he has it, and you two will get along just fine." He laughs as I salute him. "It's very functional, I think you two will be just fine sharing the space."

"Okay enough it's a wonderful life chit chat." Tierra stands up walking to the L-shaped sofa lounge. "Let's get the game, kings, set up."

"Instead of beer, we will play with an oversized shot." Andy comments, walking over to Toni.

I take my seat on the end cushion next to Quinton. "So, you ever played before?" I shake my head no. "Each card in the deck is given a rule. You will learn it as we go. Clothes stay on." He reminds, looking down my body. I nod as Tierra picks sexy sounding music.

"Okay, everyone, sit boy girl." Gerry grins and sits next to me. I like him and am glad he's beside me. I watch Tierra set-up the sofa table. She takes the oversized shot glass from Andy and puts it in the center. Next, she spreads the entire deck face down around the glass.

"Quinton you start first. Amelia, you draw next and so on. We flip it over and follow the rule for the card you draw. The person to draw last card takes the shot." Tierra is grinning. "Oh Toni, bring our drinks," she yells. I look at him as he starts preparing them. "Trust me you don't want to mix beer with our liquor drinks. Shots will work just as well."

We all draw, and Quinton gets a five. "Bottoms up fellas." He leans his head back and tosses his shot. Toni starts another round of shots.

I got an eight. "Pick a mate to drink with," Tierra tells me.

"You." I point at her. She grins as we take a sip of our cosmos. Gerry has a five, so all the fellas drink a shot.

Marcus draws seven. "Everyone has to point to heaven." He grins. "Last one drinks." Which is me, so I take a sip. Tierra draws a six, and all the ladies take a shot. I shake from the tequila. Quinton laughs and slips his tongue in my mouth.

"Mmm, I like that," I tease. I'm getting tingly. It must be the drinks.

Andy draws a Jack. "Never have I ever fucked on an elevator. If you have, you're safe, if not take a drink." I smirk as I take a sip. I look around the table—I'm the only one.

Tina draws a queen. "I get to ask a question. If you don't want to answer take a shot, otherwise answer it. Amelia, are you now giving head?" Quinton laughs, looking at me.

"Wasn't that a question I was asked on our last get to know Amelia game?" I tease.

"Either answer or drink." I pause, looking at Quinton, he's watching me; his ear grabbing smile is a dead giveaway.

"I've been told I was good." They start cheering and slapping the table.

"Correction, she was told she was fucking amazing at it," Quinton quips, leaning over kissing my lips. I'm turning red.

496

Michael draws a king. "I get to make a rule everyone must follow until the next king is pulled." I'm dreading his rule. "Ditch the shirts."

"What?" I look at Quinton, he's unbuttoning his.

"Ladies are keeping bras on," Quinton quips.

"Fine," Michael agrees. "Drop your dress top, Amelia." *Unbelievable, I can't believe this.* Thank god I have a bra on with this one. Quinton reaches behind me and unzips it, so I can pull it down.

"Wow, that's a pretty lacy provocative bra there," Gerry growls at me. I look down, checking out my tits.

"She has beautiful tits," Quinton acknowledges, looking at me.

We play this game until all the cards are gone. We're all buzzed and dressed in nothing but our undies. "Drink the big shot Michael, you asshole." Quinton laughs, looking at my tits.

"Quinton, I thought you said clothes stay on."

"I forgot about the king making a rule. Strip poker you would have been completely naked," he teases, looking at me. "You look really sexy."

"I'm really buzzed," I confess looking at him.

"You bored of this game? Because I can think of something I'd much rather be doing right now." The hunger in his voice and the lasciviousness in his eyes make my nipples harden.

"Yes, I am," I purr, dropping my hand slowly over my bra down to my stomach. I lean back, rubbing my foot against his hard cock. He smirks, looking to see everyone else getting more drinks and dancing. I follow his eyes. "Are they going to dance in their undies?"

Quinton shrugs. "No different from dancing in your swimsuit," he reminds me.

I look down at my body. "These pieces are more provocative than my swimsuits." He nods in agreement.

"Have you met your quota for group activities for the day?" he asks, tracing my bra with his finger.

"Have you?" I tease, watching him.

"Here, get your dress back on." I watch him slip his shorts on. "I'm ready for us to retire for the evening." I turn so he can zip my dress. I hold his hand as we walk over to the bar. "Toni, cosmo and gin on the rocks." He's nibbling around my neck as I watch his friends swapping partners breaking it down to the music.

"Have you all ever … you know … swapped partners?" He laughs.

"Why would you ask that?" He's watching me. *Hmm, that's not a no!*

"Have you?" I repeat my question. *Please tell me no.* I don't know how I would feel about Tierra and Tina having fucked him.

"You're cute Amelia." He sips his gin. *Fuck, they have.*

498

"Well, I'm not going to sleep with your friends. I mean if you all get off on that sort of thing, I'm definitely on the wrong yacht." I grab my cosmo and walk off.

Chapter 62: Quinton

"Thanks Toni." I grab her another cosmo and follow her swishing, sassy ass. "See you guys in the morning."

"Really? The party is just starting," Tierra whines, shaking it on Andy.

"He's got him a private party," Michael teases. I grin as I go to find my jealous lover.

"Amelia, I got you another cosmo." I walk into our room. She's sitting on the sofa, looking out the window.

"Thank you." She watches me sit it on the bedside table. I toss my shirt in the hamper, then strip of my shorts and underwear. She looks out the window. She's funny, she thinks I've shared my friends' wives.

"Come here sweetheart." She looks at me, tossing the covers back. Thinking what she does, she still wants to please me. "Turn around." She does without objection. I unzip her dress, letting it fall to the floor. She turns around, looking at my chest. I take her drink from her hands and set it on my bedside table. "Get in the bed." She looks up at me. "Get in the bed Amelia. I want you in my bed."

"Don't you want me naked?"

"Do you want to be naked? I want you however you want me to have you." I strum my fingertips up and down her shoulders. She reaches behind her back and unclasps her bra. I grin, taking it off. I hook my fingers in her lace panties and pull them down her legs. She's holding her breath as I pull them from her delicate ankles. Her naked ass, crawling into bed, makes me rock hard.

"Your tits are fabulous Amelia." I grin, laying beside her, but I don't touch them.

"Why aren't you touching me?" She wants me to.

"Because you think I would actually ask you to sleep with my friends." I watch her look away. She pulls the sheet over her tits. "I would never share you with anyone." I roll over on my side, stroking down her jaw line and neck. "My friends would never share their wives with me or any other man for that matter." I kiss her neck. "I would fucking kill any man who tried to fuck you."

"Good." She exhales. "I'm glad you haven't had sex with Tierra and Tina. Honestly, it was freaking me out."

"It was freaking me out that you think I would ask you to pleasure Andy or Michael." I laugh. "It actually fucking grossed me out. Look, I love them like family, all of them, but I don't want to stick my cock in anything I know they've been shooting their load into."

Amelia laughs. "So poetic Mr. Starks."

501

I laugh shaking my head. "Amelia, yes we're close. We flirt and play, but we don't cross that line. They told you that the first night. You never have to worry about that. Michael and Andy would never, ever force themselves on you. You could be stark ass naked, rubbing that sweet, tight, wet sex of yours on their damn shafts, and they still wouldn't. Tierra and Tina could be dripping wet for me, and I definitely wouldn't."

"Wouldn't rubbing their dicks on me down there count as crossing that line?" She coyly grins.

I laugh cheeky ass. "Yes, yes it would. The point is that would never happen."

She turns her torso into me, running her hands through my hair. "I don't know why … but the thought of you with someone just infuriates me." She doesn't let me respond. Her heated lips cover mine in an open-mouth kiss. Our tongues slide and dance in perfect harmony.

I shift her body beneath me, dominating her kiss. Her legs spread, grinding her heat against my shaft, squeezing her knees against my hips. "Damn you feel good beneath me," I growl, nibbling across her clavicle. Her back arches, her body begging for more.

I shift so I can watch her, running my hands down her body. She gasps as I start caressing her sex, dipping my finger in and out. "You're very beautiful. I want you to be mine," I whisper, kissing her swollen bud.

"I am …" She tosses her head flexing her bud against my tongue. "Yours completely." I steal a glance at her beautiful face, sucking and flicking my tongue over her clit while fingering her with a come-hither motion.

"I want you to be my wife Amelia!" She gasps, wrapping her hands around my wrist and forearm. She's liking this. Her toes are curling and she's tightening around my fingers. She's whimpering biting her bottom lip, flicking her beautiful sapphires between watching my eyes and my hand. "Is that something that might interest you?" I suck her bud. Her hips flex, grinding her hot sex harder against my lips.

"Yes," she cries, "oh god yes ... you're amazing." I tenderly scrape my teeth over her already sensitive core, sucking and pulling her clitoris between my lips, while working my fingers deep inside. "When?" she cries.

"Immediately!" My words vibrate against her, and she tosses her head back. My cock is dripping, watching her.

"I can't," she screams.

"Of course you can," I mumble, flicking my tongue across her clit.

"Quinton." She's tossing her head to the side. Holding her breath.

"I want to hear you say it," I growl against her ravenous clitoris, sucking hard. Her silk squirts, glazing my tongue. My fingers are covered in her creaminess ... she's convulsing hard against my fingers. "Tell me ... tell me you want to be my wife!"

"Yes ..." she cries, digging her nails into my scalp forcing my mouth harder on her, "I want to be your wife." Her hips buck against my lips; she whimpers as I continue to pleasure her. Her fingers lace through my hair as I pull my fingers out. She's tugging me up her body into her mouth, kissing me hard in a deep open-mouth kiss. Her breathing is ragged. She tastes like heaven, love, and lust.

"Quinton, I love you," she purrs against my neck, nibbling, "you've left me tingling ... everywhere!" She wraps her legs around my hips, rubbing her wet, hot sex against me. She still isn't satiated. I stroke my hands all over her perfect body.

"Damn, I adore you. We're going to be one hot couple: my perfection, your perfection," I whisper, smooching our lips together. I really want to blow my load in her. "I liked you riding me last night." I shift indicating for her to ride me.

"What?" She giggles.

"Get on it," I growl, watching her turn her back to me. "Fuck," I hiss, holding her hips as she sinks down on my cock. "Your ass is fucking gorgeous." She leans forward, grabbing my ankles, pumping her hips up and down. Watching her taking my impressive cock is driving me mad. I can't help myself from fucking her from below, thrusting hard, watching my hard cock glisten in her wetness. *We fit perfectly. She feels beyond anything I've known.* "Fuck this is hot," I hiss, running my hands around her body and squeezing her tits. She wraps her hands around mine, sinking back onto my thickness, taking me as deep as possible.

"Is this what you want Mr. Starks?" Amelia asks, toying with her nipples. She's sinking back that gorgeous ass, fucking my cock without inhibition.

I want to control this ... I need to pound her hard! I push up, shifting her forward and yank myself from her; she's confused. I take her hands and press them against the headboard. "Hold on sweetheart," I hiss. I jerk her hips up and slam into her from behind.

"Fuck ... Quinton," she screams, looking over her shoulder at me. She grips the headboard tighter, giving me a salacious smile. *Game on!*

"You're driving me insane Amelia." My voice is distressed. She looks as hot as she feels, gripping the bed for support, on her knees, her ass pulled up and tight against my cock. I slam into her again. Her mouth screams but nothing comes out. *She's unbelievably tight.*

I smack her ass hard. "Ouch!" Amelia cries. I grin, watching her face looking over her shoulder at me. I dig my fingers into her hips before I slam hard into her again, making her scream out. This time her body shifts up the bed. She's pushing her hips deeper into me. I smack her ass. "Again," she whimpers, pushing harder against me. *Damn she likes it rough. Fucking hell, I'm about to explode.* "More," she demands, biting her bottom lip. This time my hand stings against her heated ass. She whimpers, sinking deeper. Her ass has three big handprints. *She has a kink.* I yank myself deeper in her, scissoring her clitoris. Amelia comes immediately. "Quinton!" Her sex tightens, sucking my cock for more. Her toes curl. Her body shakes beneath me. She's holding her breath; her grip is almost as depleted as I feel from my climax. I look at the sweat glistening over my rock-hard body.

I whimper, exploding into her, stroking every drop out into her tight, sweet sex, before collapsing on her back. I'm going to have a heart attack fucking this woman. I can't stop, she just feels like heaven wrapped around me. I kiss and bite her shoulder blades, pulsating deep, trying to collect myself.

"Quinton, you feel amazing," Amelia purrs, "I love you." She's whimpering, her insides sucking me deeper. I stroke her until I'm flaccid. My cum trickles out of her as I pull out.

My chest is about to explode. "You're going to fucking kill me," I gasp.

Chapter 63: Amelia

"I could say the same thing." I grin, catching my breath. My lady parts tingle with twinges of pain. But it's a good pain ... it's his calling card to show where he's been. "I'm not sure I haven't already died. Since you walked into my life, it's been like a dream. Shangri-La perhaps!"

Quinton stretches, his arm rolling me in to cuddle against his chest, pulling my leg over his hip. I love tickling my fingers across his fabulous six pack. His chest is heaving; he's quiet, strumming his fingers across my shoulder while caressing my hip with his other hand.

"Why are you quiet?"

"How long would you want to wait before we got married? It wasn't pillow talk sweetheart."

"I don't know ... I'm married now Quinton."

Quinton softly chuckles. "Why do you think I haven't already proposed?" His admission makes the butterflies increase tenfold. "I want you to know how serious I am about you ... about us."

I nod, kissing softly across his chest. "I do ... Quinton we don't have to rush this."

Our eyes meet for a few seconds before he grabs his phone. "I'll order us fresh drinks. Be sure you cover your tits."

I think he wants to discuss this further, but I don't want to ruin the mood by stating the obvious. I readjust the sheet, noticing the clock. "Where did the time go?" He smugly rolls his tongue, looking down at his cock. I roll my eyes, snuggling deeper into him.

Knock! Knock!

"That was fast." I look at Quinton.

"It's open." Toni sits the drinks on the side table. I sink further down in the bed, not making eye contact. "Here, take these. Sorry we never got to them before they got hot."

"Yes, sir."

"Well, at least Toni didn't fall in your panties sweetheart." He winks as he gives me my cosmo.

"Mmm this is good." I relax back on the pillows. "Why are you watching me?"

"I still can't believe you're actually here, and I like our little talk sessions after we've been together ... I am waiting." Quinton is so cute.

"Oh." I watch him quietly as I sip my drink. He openly rakes his eyes over my body; he really doesn't hide any of his lust. "Normally I'm so sleepy afterwards, we have lazy bed talk before I crash."

"We're not done Amelia. I plan to wear you out, before I let you sleep." I grin as he places our glasses on the bedside table. *Damn he really can go all night.*

"So this talking, not the lazy bed talk, then?" I ask, running my fingers up and down his chest.

"Exactly, more of giving my cock time to reset for another round." I laugh at him.

"I'm going to call Eric tomorrow."

"Well, that should help my cock reset quickly." He sarcastically laughs. "What are you going to tell him?" He nonchalantly nibbles my fingers.

"That I'm not coming back. It's over." I like his hands.

"How do you think that's going to go over?"

I laugh looking up at his eyes. "Really? Probably as well as you would take it, if I told you I've changed my mind about leaving him."

"That bad huh," he teases looking down at me. "Seriously, I know he's going to be livid. I don't want you going to the house alone."

"I'll go Monday, he'll be at the office. I want to get my pictures. I don't really have anything else I can't replace." I can see his wheels turning. "Why are you being quiet?"

"I can't go Monday, I've got meetings all day." He's rubbing my thigh now.

"I can go, I guess Tina will go with me."

"Steve will go, he's going to be driving you two around Jacksonville. If anything does happen, he's protection enough." I nod listening. "I don't want you telling him about us without me there. We will tell him that together."

"Oh I'm not telling him anything about us." I lean up looking at him. "I'm not telling him I left him for you. No way!" *Is he freaking crazy?*

"Amelia, he's going to find out about us." Quinton brings my fingertips to his lips, kissing them softly.

"Quinton, he would be way past livid, way past!" I watch him nonchalantly nibbling about. "You're not concerned at all, are you?"

"Nope!" He grins scooting down. "He's not a threat." I titter at his comment, feeling his soft lips kissing my neck, nibbling along my clavicle. His hand pulls the sheet down. *His sheets feel good sliding across my nipples.* I roll on my back as he continues kissing over my chest, dragging his tongue down my breastplate.

I giggle lacing my fingers in his hair—watching him kiss around my stomach. My breath catches in my throat as he sucks and licks around my belly button. "I love kissing this part of you."

"I love it too," I whisper, watching him, kissing lower and lower.

I gasp, closing my eyes, as he sucks and kisses my swollen sensitive bud. My back arches from the sudden sensation. I feel his lips smiling as he continues to kiss around my pubic mound, blowing on my clit.

"You are so beautiful Amelia." He pushes my legs up, spreading me for his taking, and my toes curl into his shoulders. I whimper, closing my eyes and cradling his head, holding him in place, as he meticulously glides that beautiful tongue. Every titillating lick, swirl, and suck his tongue provides arouses my clit.

"Quinton," My hips are quivering, flexing against his tongue. "Oh … God … you're amazing at that." My delight only comes out as a faint whisper melting under his touch—his hand rubs over my tummy, pressing down as he swirls his tongue, circling my clitoris and sucking the tip. My thighs quiver against his elbows, which have immobilized me. "It's too much," I cry out. He pins my wrists against the mattress, moaning into my center … not letting up. I scream, shivering, bucking my hips. My release is slow and hard at the same time. The sensation is melting over my body. "Quinton." I cry, barely audible. I can't breathe. He's going to kill me by orgasm.

"Damn you taste good," he growls, dropping my hypersensitive bud from his lips.

"I'm too sensitive."

"Oh I know you are." He kisses up my stomach, licking and nibbling up my breastplate. "I love your tits. The way they swell from my sucking and squeezing. How the nipples harden against my tongue with every flick and tug. Mmm, when I get my fill, I'm going to make sweet, slow love to you, Amelia." I gasp, arching my back as his tongue assaults my nipple. He's squeezing my other tit, rolling his thumb over my other nipple. He knows my nipples are directly connected to my core. I feel every sensation down below. And he doesn't even have to touch me there!

511

I'm dying ... bucking against him. "I want you so badly, I hurt," I beg watching him seductively feeding off my body.

"I can feel your wetness on me," he mumbles against my nipple. I whimper, wanting to feel him inside of me. "I can still taste you ... I could live off you." He watches my eyes, stroking his thick cock as he positions himself at my opening. The anticipation is killing me. I arch back, gasping, as he glides his swollen head into my wet folds. "Feel every fucking inch of me. It's all for you."

"Yes," I moan, sucking his neck, "you're huge!" My body stretches for his invasion, the lecherous sensations are immediate ... my toes curl instantly. He's had me so many times already, yet it still feels like the first time every time!

"Damn right I'm huge," Quinton growls in the crook of my neck, "I like filling you with my essence."

"I love to feel you ... your thickness ... pinches me," I whimper adjusting, "I like it. Your cum turns me on."

Quinton grins, bending his legs, pushing his hips deeper. "Keep your knees bent ... legs open ... missionary style." *No worries there!* The mattress dips with his elbows pressed beside me, supporting his weight. He's being gentle ... cuddling me close. I caress his sexy forearms, rubbing my hands over his body of perfection, before cupping his handsome face in my hands. I brush his hair from his face, with each delicious stroke he's giving.

Quinton covers my mouth in a deep lust-filled, open-mouth kiss. Our tongues dance the perfect tango. And he's the

512

lead! His thrust are a slow rocking motion ... like a rocking horse. Controlled and calculated. We're both moaning as I feel my release building again. He's hissing air through clenched teeth.

I run my fingers over his sexy shoulders ... grasping his salaciously delicious forearms. I close my eyes arching my back. "Harder," I beg him, "harder ... Quinton fuck me ... hard!" This sweetness is ... sweet, but I want to feel my hips leave this mattress. I don't want sweetness. I want hard!

"You're greedy sweetheart," he hisses, thrusting hard, with deeper strokes. My hips leave the mattress. He growls as he takes my nipple in his mouth, sucking and swirling his tongue. I scream, arching my chest off the bed, easier for him. He licks his way across, nipping my tit. He laughs when my breath catches. I feel him suck just my nipple, flicking his tongue. My fingers are laced in his hair, holding him in place, as he tortures me.

"I like your tongue." I moan, guiding his head back to my other nipple.

"I like your tits," he growls, biting. I scream, tossing my head back.

He growls, sucking my nipple and letting it pop out of his mouth as he leans back. I reach for him as he moves. He kneels, pulling my calves up over his shoulders.

"I find your forearms incredibly hot." I squeeze them, biting my lip with his first thrust.

"Ah, you're so fucking tight," Quinton hisses through clenched teeth. He feels amazing. I groan, closing my eyes, arching my back off the bed with every thrust.

"Play with my nipples," I purr, pulling him back down. He captures my hardened nipple. I watch him suck and flick the bud. He's caressing my other nipple with his fingers, pulling and tugging.

"Quinton." I lean forward, biting his shoulder. My legs shift a tad down his biceps, as he deepens his thrusts. "Oh god." He's biting my tits—hard! "Ow! Fuck, Quinton."

"Damn, you feel wonderful in this position. So hot!" Quinton thrusts harder, bringing my hips off the mattress ... my knees on either side of my own shoulders. He's relentless, sucking and biting my tits, flicking his tongue across my nipple. My toes are curling; he's whimpering and hissing. *He's getting fucking hard.*

I whimper, closing my eyes. With every bite and suck my body is tightening and shaking beneath him. Now he's screaming. *Who's loud now?* I grin, he's completely lost in me. I feel my release hit, my silk covering him. I can't breathe, I can't think. I can only feel, and I can't get enough of him.

"Amelia," he growls, holding my ankles tight against his shoulders, exploding his liquid heat in me, "god! You're the best fuck I've ever had." He drops my legs and covers my mouth in a deep, open-mouth kiss pumping his hips hard. I've melted.

"I can feel you pulsating in me," I whisper.

"I'm going to stay inside of you, stroking every drop of my essence into you until I'm flaccid." He buries his mouth in my neck and wraps his arms around my body, supporting his weight on his elbows and forearms. His hands cradle my head.

I close my eyes, savoring his attention. I turn my head to the side, so he can suck and nibble down my neck … my body all he wants.

Chapter 64: Quinton

Aw hell ... I'm so consumed by her! She's wrapped all around me, letting me stroke her as long as I want, filling her. Her tits are covered in bite marks, *shit*. I feel like a fucking ass. I stroke her beautiful neck, running my fingers over her jaw, turning her mouth towards me. Her eyes are full of love, trusting me, trusting this. We grin at each other. I lower my lips over hers, smooching her lips to mine in a sweet, open-mouth kiss. Our tongues slide and massage one another. She tastes wonderful. Her mouth is smooth and hot. Delicious! I growl, deepening my kiss, controlling her tongue, leading her how I want her. She loves it. She loves me. I can actually feel her love, her desire, for me!

"Mmmm," Amelia hums into my mouth. I'm so lost in her.

Shit, I'm going flaccid; I roll beside, her wrapping her in my arms and pulling her against my chest. She slides her leg over my hip. Her hand is tracing lazy circles around my six pack, playing with all my dips. I lean up, sliding the sheet over us.

"I'm so relaxed and still tingling," she purrs.

I laugh, strolling my fingers up and down her shoulder with heavy lids. "I hope I didn't hurt you." I gently touch a bite. "I'm afraid I got a little carried away. I've marked your beautiful tits."

"I don't care," she breathes, "you're a fantastic lover. You're gentle, Quinton. You don't hurt me." I hear her words and the underlying meaning. I like her fingers rubbing on my six pack.

"Tell me something," I whisper, kissing her forehead.

"I love your suave walk and mannerisms." She drops little kisses across my chest. *She's so sweet.* "Tell me something."

"You're the first woman I've made love to without a condom." She leans up, looking at me. The disbelief is evident. "I've never blown my load into anyone but you." I grin, watching her settle back beside me. "Tell me something."

"I like to read." She tickles her fingers across my stomach. "Your turn."

"I'm Italian—trust fund baby." I watch her process it. "Your turn."

"I figured you were a trust fund baby," she teases. "I'm not." We laugh. "Your turn."

"I want to take care of you. Your turn."

"You do?" She coyly laughs as she strokes my limp cock. I laugh but I really do want to care for Amelia. I want her as my wife and all the responsibilities that go with it. "I like to watch sunrises." She's getting super comfy in my arms.

"Amelia?"

"Hmm." She stretches and snuggles against me.

"Are you ready to sleep?" She doesn't say anything. I grin. I don't even hear the music playing when we're together; I turn the volume down a tad before I kill the light.

* * *

"Amelia," I call her, but she doesn't answer. The emptiness in the pit of my stomach is almost unbearable. I've not been able to reach her all day. I walk to my window and look at the ants scattering below, she's out there ... somewhere.

Gerry graces my office, wearing black. "What the hell are you wearing?" I snap. My color wheel is ash. I try calling her again, but her phone goes to voicemail.

"Problems on the home front Mr. Starks?" I look at my assistant, he's cold, distant.

Everything in my world is changing. She's gone. My color wheel is gone. She's my purpose. I've got to find her. Even Steve is bleak, my Bentley doesn't have the same pizzazz it once hand. I find it unappealing. I see her naked body everywhere in the back. Her scent is overloading my mind, but I can't touch her nor feel her in me anymore. She's gone.

I have Steve take me to Libation. She loves to move her body. Toni hasn't seen her. What the fuck? I call her again, still she doesn't answer. We've never had an argument. I'm so confused.

I return to our penthouse. It's modern, white and cold. The warmth of those sapphires has burned out. I can feel the emptiness before I swipe the key; she's not home. I walk in-

518

side. My feet crunch on glass. What the fuck? Our place is always immaculate. I flip the switch and I'm standing in broken glass and water. The aroma of flowers fill my senses. I look around, her Gucci purse and phone are on the counter.

Something terrible has happened, my vixen has been stolen from me. I see a wet card, stooping I pick it up, the ink is intact enough to read: 'I told you divorce isn't an option.' Aw, fucking hell, Eric. He's collected his wife!

I don't see any lights on at the B and B. I don't even see a car in the lot. I have no idea where to begin looking. The police are looking now. Steve and Toni are on it. I can't sit back and do nothing.

My phone buzzes, and Steve's face appears on the screen. "Tell me something," I bark getting back into my car. They found something. I'm on my way. He wouldn't tell me shit. I hate this. I can't feel her. She's in a slummy warehouse. He had tied her up and I can't even process what I see. The paramedics are already on the scene. My heart is lurched out and burned. He's laying there bleeding out, unconscious. Toni shot him. Toni and Steve try to pull me outside, but I won't leave. I've got to be here, she's here.

They're yanking me, but I'm too fucking strong for them to move. I see the paramedic take a sheet, what the fuck? She's being covered. I can't breathe, my world has crashed. Utterly crashed and burned. I am dead.

* * *

I lurch up. "Amelia," I scream. My heart is pounding and I feel sick. I think I'm going to die in my skin. I feel clammy, trying to catch my breath.

"Hey." I feel her soothing hands run up my chest. "I'm right here." She has the most beautiful sleepy voice. "Shhh." She kisses my chest. "It was just a dream."

"A fucking nightmare." I relax back down, pulling her tighter. I need to hold her.

"Your heart is pounding," she whispers against my chest. I close my eyes, stroking her beautiful hair. Thank god it was a dream. She completes my world. She kisses my chest more, tickling her fingers over my dips ... tracing my six pack.

I roll us, readjusting my hip and legs between hers. I can feel her sex—hot— against me as she wraps her legs around my lower back. She's hugging and kissing me, making my cock rock hard. I grab my cock and stroke her slit with the head of it. She's slick from her wetness and my cum bead.

"Damn you feel good," I growl, sliding deep into her. We're rocking in a slow lovemaking motion.

She's whimpering, wrapped all around me like a present. She likes this. She's flexing her legs, pushing me deeper. I'm quiet watching her, stroking her. I love being this way with her.

Amelia runs her hands over my hard jaw, lacing her fingers through my hair. She tugs my mouth down towards her, covering my lips in an open-mouth kiss, her tongue dipping and sucking. She's whimpering and quivering beneath me; her toes are curling. Her sex is tightening and pulling me deeper into her. I keep rocking that sweet love motion into her. She's thrusting against me, driving me insane. Her fingers are cinching tight in my hair ... she's holding her breath. I grin as her silk floods over my impressive cock. I keep kissing her.

The whimpers and moaning this time are mine ... she unravels me. I explode into her, kissing her neck. She tosses her head back, grinding harder against me.

My cock is pulsating, buried deep inside of her. "There is nowhere else on earth I would rather be than buried in you, Amelia," I growl kissing down her neck.

"Good because there is nothing I like more than feeling you inside of me, Mr. Starks." I laugh softly, cuddling deep into her neck. We doze back off to sleep, my cock still buried deep.

* * *

I wake up a few minutes before the sun rises. I look at her, her bruised tits exposed against me. "Fuck." I rake my fingers through my hair, shifting our bodies.

"Mmm, I love you," she whispers in a sleepy tone.

I kiss her lips.

She rolls over stretching and blinking her beautiful eyes. "I'm sore," she whispers, looking at me.

I laugh. "Sore in a good way or a bad way?"

"Oh in a very good way Mr. Starks," Amelia teases. "It's still early."

"Yeah." I grin. "You said you like sunrises ... they're spectacular over the ocean. Do you want to catch one this morning?"

"Oh ..."

"Here, put this on." I toss her my shirt. "We don't have much time." I pull on my shorts, watching her slip into it. It's big on her petit frame.

She's gorgeous in this light, relaxed against my chest. Her jasmine-laced hair tickles my senses. The sun dances across the water like the perfect walkway with a panorama backdrop of an amber and gold sky. I look out over the horizon and it's hard to tell where the sky meets the water. The scattered clouds resemble the water. She looks down, intertwining our fingers. "The water looks cobalt blue." I nod, enjoying this serenity.

Chapter 65: Amelia

We sit quietly, wrapped in each other's arms. I'm biting my lip, contemplating the last couple of days. "This has been wonderful." I look over my shoulder at him. "The last couple of days ... here with you." I shrug. "But I'm scared." He wrinkles his brow, watching me. I smile softly. "I know I keep harping on this ... it's just ..."

"I've got you. You will always have me in your corner." Quinton kisses my neck.

I nod, toying with the hem of his shirt. "And you're sure this isn't some infatuation with me ... a married lady?" He sighs and his body stiffens. "What if you get bored, once the thrill of my unavailability is gone?" I tighten our hands. I can't stand the thought of losing this man.

"Is this what you think this is? An infatuation with you? Something like a conquest of a married lady?" I don't say anything, and he rakes his fingers through his hair before clasping our hands. "Sweetheart, I've no shortage of women." *Oh wow, he does have an ego.* "I know how that sounds, but it's the truth." I look down, how can I fit into his life?

"Does that mean you've slept with half of Jacksonville? Am I going to see someone on a daily basis that has had your impressive love making skills?" I flinch at my own words, watching our future approaching, way off in the horizon.

He balks at my words. "I've never made love to anyone but you. All the others were fucks. They knew that. It was just a good time." He watches me decipher his words. "Amelia, I'm a thirty-five-year-old male who, until I met you, had zero interest in a relationship of any kind other than fulfillment of a sexual desire."

"I love you so much Quinton that it hurts." I turn in his arms looking at him. "I've never loved someone or something so much. I've never had something that I actually feared losing." He strokes my face, leans down, and kisses me in a single-lip kiss.

"Well, that makes two of us. Another novelty for me." We both laugh. "Amelia, we both dreamt of each other before we even knew the other existed. When I discovered you were married, I was devastated. I was going to do the honorable thing, and not cross that line. But then everything about you overloaded me. You're my soulmate." I close my eyes, savoring his one-lip kisses. "Why can't you trust this … trust in us?" I sniffle, holding his hands; I want to so badly. "Can you do that? Can you trust us?"

I nod, softly kissing his lips. *I can try.* "You're all I need … all I want, Quinton." I rest my forehead against his.

"Good, you are too, Amelia." I open my eyes; we're staring at each other. "Don't you ever think this is an infatuation?" I nod as he covers my lips with an open-mouth kiss, dipping his tongue deep and soothing. Our tongues say good morning, dancing to their own love song. "You look really sexy in my shirt," Quinton teases, raising his eyebrows. "It looks like a dress draped on your petit frame." I laugh at him, curling his arms deeper around me.

We both turn to the sound of footsteps. "Captain." Quinton grins. I smile, relaxing back in his arms.

"Good morning, sir, ma'am." He has such a friendly smile. "Catch a sunrise?"

"We did, gorgeous as usual." Quinton kisses my temple.

"We're making excellent time, ETA is around three this afternoon. Four if we stop and play a spell." He grins. "Could I get you two coffee?"

"That would be great." Quinton keeps holding me, lacing our fingers.

"Very well, I'll call the galley." We watch the captain leave.

Chapter 66: Quinton

I hear her laughing in the bathroom. Breakfast was delicious. I'm glad she's comfortable around me and the gang. I laugh to myself, thinking about her eating breakfast wearing only my shirt ... with everyone fully dressed around the table. She's definitely lower maintenance than Tierra or Tina. Neither of them would have done that!

"Your love bites are going to be visible in my bikini today," she warns, opening the bathroom door wearing her new Loui Vuitton Bleu Azul Monograph jewel accented strap triangle bikini. The back has the classic clasp. It's sleek and sexy. Her long white, thin linen flowy pants hang just right off her hips, swaying as she walks. She looks like a fucking million dollars. "Breathe," she says as she walks by, grinning.

I didn't even realize I was gawking at her with my mouth open. I wasn't breathing. "You look stunning." I grin following her like a lovesick puppy. "Turn around, let me see your tits." She turns, rolling her eyes. "Shit!" I look up at her eyes, touching my fingertips over her bruised bites. She has several visible on each tit. "It looks like a savage had you."

She shrugs. "They don't hurt." I grin, watching her grab her hat and shades. "You did kind of go all savage like on me," she teases. "You felt amazing." She snakes her arms around my neck, giving me a quick one-lip kiss. I wrap my hand around her hip as we walk to join the others. I literally cannot be next to this woman without touching her. I can only imagine the ragging I'm going to get.

"Jesus Quinton," Tierra barks as she touches the marks. I flinch at her tone.

Amelia removes her fingers. "They don't hurt." Tina is giving me dirty looks too.

"Sweetheart, I'll go get you a drink." I can't sit there anymore watching them judge me.

"Can Toni do a coconut rum concoction?" I grin at her question. *Can he?* "Will you two stop fussing? It's a few love bites. I bruise easy," she tells them as I walk off.

"Toni, gin on the rocks and coconut rum punch." Andy and Michael are walking up to me, smirking. "Don't say a word," I warn before downing my gin.

They laugh holding their hands up. "Wild night," Michael teases. I cut my eyes at him. I've never marked anyone in my life. "It happens to all of us one time or another."

"Some chicks dig it. Tierra doesn't," Andy quips. "You know her model career messes that up."

"I said I'm not discussing it. I don't mark my women. Well, I've never in the past." I grin. "She does have a bit of a wild side." Their faces want more. "That's all I'm saying." I turn, walking back to her. Andy and Michael follow suit. Gerry and Marcus are giving me an approving nod. Sometimes my color wheel is strange. Thank god he's back to normal. "Gerry, what color are you blessing me with today?" I grin, giving Amelia her drink. I relax on the sun lounge beside her.

"Metallic silver." Gerry grins rubbing his hand over his package. "Doesn't this speedo make me look huge?" I roll my eyes. Amelia laughs, sipping her drink.

"I'm not in the market of checking out other guy's packages." I reach over, grabbing Amelia's hand, lacing our fingers. "I'm pretty sure I'm a tit and ass kind of man." Amelia laughs, leaning over and kissing my lips.

"I'd say," Tierra teases, tapping her foot to the beat.

"Music is always around you?"

"Yeah, I suppose it is. Well, not in the office, but my casual life." I grin, sipping my gin. Yep, this is the perfect day. No walking or crowds, just us all relaxing with our drinks, listening to music, and getting some sun.

"Sir ... sir." I turn towards Toni. He looks rather disturbed. He pauses mid-step, flagging me to come privately.

What the hell? "I'll only be a minute." I kiss sweet Amelia's lips as I go see what is so urgent. "What is it?" I follow Toni into the living room. He flips the TV on.

"What is it Toni, what's so urgent on the TV?" I watch him adjust the channel for local news. "What?" I'm not following him.

"Read the chyron when it scrolls again." Toni leans back against the counter, smirking.

"President and founder of Starks Industries and Jacksonville's most eligible bachelor, Quinton Starks, was spotted making numerous appearances with a mystery woman in the Bahamas." I look at Toni. "What the fucking hell?" I pause for a minute watching the next feed. "Well, it doesn't mention who I was with or any pictures ... we should be fine."

"Steve heard about it, and called me immediately." I look at Toni. "There is more sir, your trip to the Bahamas has been a hot topic." I roll my eyes as he flips to a local news gossip channel. "Billionaire Quinton Starks has a love interest. Sources claim the two were traveling with friends on his personal yacht."

"Aw hell."

"May I say those are some excellent pictures of you two?" I laugh at him as he freezes the report. "And your mother keeps calling ... do you want your phone?" I knew it was on the internet, but hell that local gossip channel. "Should I fetch Ms. Amelia?" I lean back looking at our pictures plastered ... *shit*. I nod.

I toss my gin. "I need another, Toni."

I look up hearing them cackling. "No secrets right," I tease as I look at Amelia noticing the group. This could go so many ways. "Sweetheart I need to show you something ... and well ... you just need to sit down." Her tittering laugh as she glances at the group tells me she's already nervous. "Now

Amelia, this is going to freak you out, so just don't freak out."
I laugh on the inside. *Smooth Quinton.*

"What are you talking about?"

Toni brings me another gin on the rocks. "Show her." I watch Toni flip the screen so she can see it. And here it comes ...

"What the fuck?" Panic just hit her. "Shit ... oh shit." Amelia jumps up, looking at herself on the screen. I stand with her on instinct. "Eric!" She's pacing, chewing her thumb nail. "He fucking knows! Oh my god ... I've got to think!" I try to hold her, but she's too freaked out. I look at Tina and Tierra ... to do something.

She stops pacing, looking back at her face plastered on the screen again. "Toni, please unfreeze the TV." I watch her face as she stares at herself on the screen next to me. All the pictures are great of the two of us. She listens to the gossip host, "Well Jacksonville, guess you heard it first here, our billionaire bachelor has a gorgeous mystery woman. But who is this woman? We'll keep digging our noses into other people's business until we get to the bottom of this sizzling relationship."

"Shit! Just shit!" she screams. I flinch, trying to touch her shoulders, but she pulls back. I look at Tina and Tierra for assistance. Hell they're chicks, they deal with female freak-outs. If anyone knows her and watches that stupid gossip channel, they'll be able to connect the two.

Her silence is more piercing than anything. "Amelia, say something."

She exhales in dismay, turning her terrified face to mine. "Billionaire!" She glances back towards the television screen. "Look, I've got to go."

"Go?" Tina jumps up. "Where the fuck do you think you're going?"

"You're on a fabulous fucking yacht, drinking coconut punch with us." Tierra laughs. "You have nowhere to go. You just need to calm down."

"I'm fucking dead … ooh, you just don't understand. He's going to kill me." Her hands are shaking. She's looking around at nothing but ocean. Tina and Tierra are correct, where the fuck is she going to go? "Fuck!" she moans, covering her face in her hands. "I knew I was risking my life to be with you Quinton." She wraps her fingers around my face, kissing me in a quick one-lip kiss, letting me suck her bottom lip. I tighten my grip, holding her hips close to mine. Her eyes are closed, and she's pressing her forehead to mine. "It has been worth everything, but you don't understand—he will kill me. I'm as good as dead. I'll be better off jumping overboard."

I don't release her hips. Tina is rubbing her shoulder. "Don't be ridiculous … you're panicking. Just breathe … it's all going to be all right. Breathe." Amelia turns, watching her breathe in and out. She's nodding and mimicking Tina's breathing.

"Look, he can't touch you." Tierra is rubbing her other shoulder. "He has no idea where you are ... even if he did see that shit." Tierra looks towards the TV. "Look, you need to pull your shit together. Quinton, Andy, and Michael will not let that moron hurt you." She sniffles a little, coming down from her freak out, just nodding. "Now let us lay that cute ass down, you're having a motherfucking fabulous time drinking coconut rum punch on Quinton Starks's yacht."

She gasps again, looking into my eyes gripping my shoulders. "Billionaire!" I grin coyly nodding pulling her tighter ... I have no intentions of letting her go! She plops down on the sofa.

"Toni, get Ms. Amelia a fresh rum punch." I sit next to her. "I'm still the same Quinton Starks."

She looks up at me. "With like what nine digits behind your name." I laugh. She laughs softly, looking at me, like she's seeing me for the first time. "And here I was thinking about how I'm going to fit into a millionaire's world ..."

"She's taking your billionaire news really well," Michael quips. "We told him to tell you." She's just looking at me now.

Chapter 67: Amelia

I've cheated with a damn billionaire. I've had the best sex of my life with a billionaire. I am in love with a billionaire. Everything makes sense with his lifestyle: the yacht, staff, personal chefs, red carpet, suits ... even Trek's comments about Quinton's relationship status, and Quinton wanting to keep my marital status under wraps. *Now I'm cringing inside at the little shot display Tierra wanted to do in front them.*

"Thanks," I tell Toni, taking my fresh drink. Quinton is sitting next to me, relaxing with his hand on my high. I'm looking at it, stealing glances of his handsome face. "Quinton, your money doesn't mean anything to me. I fell in love with you, maybe at first sight."

He laughs. "I know."

My smile is bittersweet. "I'm not able to bring anything to this relationship. Only the baggage of some screwed up marriage. I can see it now, billionaire dates married woman. Won't that just make wonderful headlines?" I hiss sarcastically.

"Amelia, stop talking like that." I look up at him, he's rubbing his fingers across my shoulders. "Look, they print crap all the time, about anything and everything. You've seen media feeds before. They will blow up the tiniest thing into something huge and exciting to make money. I'm rarely in the news. So don't worry about it."

"But you knew … didn't you? What was going to happen while we were on the island, with all the pictures people were taking … the gawking." I huff shaking my head. Why wouldn't he tell me? Why would he know this and risk Eric finding out, unless he wanted it out? I look at his silenced face. "You knew there was a chance Eric would discover the truth, didn't you?"

He nods, watching me intently. "Does it change the way you feel?" He gulps his gin. "I never kept my interest in you a secret … just my full identity."

"No secrets … right!" I huff, looking around at all of them, "The gang's motto."

"Answer me, does it change the way you feel?" Quinton questions as Toni appears with a fresh gin.

"Of course not!" I say as I realize it really doesn't change how I feel about him or see him. "But I don't appreciate being blindsided."

Quinton looks down at his drink. "Look Amelia, the bottom line is this: we're together and we're going to be together, right?"

"I had hoped so," I whisper, looking at him.

"What does that mean?" he quips. The gang slowly slips out of the cabin. "What are you saying, Amelia?"

"It means ... is there anything else that you have failed to mention?" He shakes his head no. "It means if you keep anything from me, we won't be together."

"There's nothing else."

He looks like he is sincere about that statement. "Then yes, I want us. But I'm serious Quinton, don't you blindside me again."

He nods with a soft smile. "I'm sorry I wasn't completely upfront with you. Everything else will work itself out in the wash." He throws back his gin. Toni has him another one within seconds. No wonder his staff are at his beck and call— he expects it. He's right, they know what are expected of them. He's more powerful than I thought ... and he expects certain things ... he's an alpha male billionaire!

"I'm calling Eric."

He nods, grabbing my hand. His thumb lovingly caresses the back of my hand. "Not alone! I told you, we will face this together, phone or in person."

I'm sort of relieved to face this over the phone now. I run down and grab my phone. Quinton is talking with Michael and Andy when I came back up to the deck. I sit down next to Quinton. "If he hasn't seen the news, I'm still not telling him about us." He shrugs with a nod.

"As you wish sweetheart." He leans back, putting his arm around my shoulders. "Put him on speaker ... we'll be quiet." I nod, placing my phone in the center of the table.

I feel like I'm about to hurl my coconut rum punch when he answers. "Amelia! It's about fucking time." I roll my eyes, looking at the guys. "Where the hell are you?" He screams, "Answer the fucking question!" I bite my bottom lip, looking at Quinton.

Taking a deep breath and squaring my shoulders, I try to muster up all the courage I have looking at Quinton, the guys ... *I can be a hard ass.* "That doesn't matter. It's not your concern. Look I ..."

He balks at my comment. "It does most certainly matter and concern me." He huffs. "You're my damn wife or has that minor detail escaped your small mind? So tell me, my sweet little wife, where the fuck are you?" I look up at Quinton. "Amelia!" I naturally jump in my seat at his screams. "Answer the goddamn question. You haven't answered or called since Thursday." He is pissed. I hit the mute button.

"Shit! I don't know what I should say to him." I look at Quinton, Michael, and Andy. "I mean, would you want to hear the truth over the phone or just make it simple?"

"Tell him the truth," Quinton quips, "he's going to find out about us anyway."

"Amelia?" Eric barks. I roll my eyes, hitting the mute button again.

"What?" I hiss back. "Will you stop yelling at me?" I raise my voice. I look at Quinton, he's whispering for me to tell him it is over. Andy and Michael agree with him, to end it over the

536

phone. I exhale. "I am not coming back. It's over. I want out." I take a sip of my drink, waiting for his response. He's unusually quiet. "Eric, are you there?" I can hear him breathing.

"Well ... so there it is," he hisses. "You planned this ... from the beginning. That's why you were adamant you weren't coming on my business trip. Had to make arrangements, did ya?"

I don't confirm or deny his allegations. "I don't want anything. I just want out." I look up at the guys, they're all intently staring at my phone.

"After ten years of marriage, you think you can end things over a phone call." His voice cracks. "Fuck it!" I hear something crash on the other end. I jump but he can't touch me. Quinton touches my shoulder. His tone becomes contentious, "No! Too fucking bad ... you're my wife. You said vows to me, or have you fucking forgot that? Do you think you could spend a weekend away from me and think I'll just let you leave? Just walk away from us, our life, the B and B ... me? Then you really are one fucking crazy bitch!"

"Eric, you can't make me stay married to you," I tell him, but my gut is saying yeah right. "And why in the hell would you think I would want to? Listen to how you just spoke to me, name calling ... really?"

"Amelia, just come home. Stop this shit. You cost me money for that stupid ass ticket. We can talk about it when you get here."

I titter a laugh. "Eric I'm not coming home. Do you understand? I want a divorce." I stand up holding my phone. "You can't make me stay your wife. I'm not going to. So accept it or … or … fuck off!" My hands are shaking. Quinton grabs my phone and sets it down on the table. Andy and Michael give me a thumbs up. Quinton grabs my face in his hands, covering my lips with an open-mouth kiss. His tongue is sweet and soothing.

"Fuck off? You really just went there. Oh Amelia, I'm going to find you and when I do, you will be sorry. It's not over, not from a long shot. I'll never give you a divorce. I told you before and I meant it, divorce isn't an option … and if you think for a second I'll stand by and let someone else have you … I'll kill your fucking ass first. It wasn't a threat, Amelia. You're mine and always will be."

Quinton stops kissing me, looking at the phone. Andy and Michael look at Quinton and then the phone. Andy snatches the phone and Quinton snatches it from him, motioning for him to be quiet.

"Tell him goodbye," Quinton whispers in my ear, holding my phone.

"Goodbye Eric!"

Quinton disconnects it immediately. "I don't want you talking to him or seeing him from this point forward!" Quinton's jaw is hard set and looks seriously pissed off. "I'm going to hang Eric Johansson. He's threatened and belittled you for the last time!"

"He's fucking unstable," Michael quips, "you should have let us say something Quinton."

My phone is ringing again. "It's him." Andy looks at it. "Amelia, you should let us answer it. He has no right threatening you."

I pinch the bridge of my nose. "No, just let him calm down."

"Sweetheart you just told him you're leaving and to fuck off ... he's not calming down." Quinton looks back at my ringing phone.

I grab it hitting the speaker button. "Yes?" I answer calmly. My hands are shaking like a leaf. Toni brings me a shot. I whisper thanks and toss it.

"Where are you at? I want to talk to you in person." Eric is slamming things in the background.

"I am done Eric. I am not talking to you. You just freaking threatened me." I look up, Toni's bringing me another shot. I toss it. "You will be served with papers this week, should I send them to the office or house?" Andy muffles a laugh. Toni brings me a third shot, and I toss it.

"My wife just told me to fuck off and she was leaving. I think I have a right to be pissed," he hisses calmly.

"No, you don't have a right to talk to me that way. That's exactly why this marriage has been toxic!" Toni brings a fourth shot, which I toss. I feel more relaxed.

"Amelia, are you drinking? Talking to me like that?" Eric asks. I look at my punch.

A little giggle slips past my lips. "Yeah, yeah I am, and you can't stop it." Quinton holds his hand up for Toni to stop. "For years you have yelled, stormed around, belittled me, thrown things, hushed me, forced your marital rights. Which by the way makes me want to vomit!" My anxiety is replaced by a warm, tingling sensation. I start giggling at my emotional release.

"Amelia I'm not talking to you drunk. I assume you calling me with this bogus divorce is because you're drunk."

I snicker. "Assume away! You know what they say, assuming makes an ass out of you and me. Trust me Eric, you're the biggest ass I've ever met." Quinton starts kissing my neck. *Ooh I like that.* I look at him. He's grinning.

"Amelia, I'll find you and you're going to wish you hadn't acted this way." I roll my eyes at his threats. Damn those shots are strong … I'm getting so relaxed!

"Right … you do that, Eric. If you touch me again, I will have you arrested. You got that?" I hiss. "Now I'm done discussing this matter."

"Amelia," he barks.

"Shut up Eric. It's over! You can accept it or not. I don't really give a damn. You can't force me to be your wife. I am done. Done! Do you hear me? You will get the papers this week." I disconnect the call.

"Damn … Amelia, lay it down." Michael grins.

"Good job! She just needed a little confidence to get the job done." Andy smirks. My hands aren't shaking now. I feel relieved.

I slide my hand around Quinton's neck, bringing his mouth towards mine. I cover his lips slipping my tongue into his mouth. "Mmm," I moan into his lips; I love kissing him. I hear Andy and Michael walk off, but I don't stop!

"Amelia," Quinton growls kissing across my jaw line, "you were so brave ... strong." His words are muffled against my skin. I smile at his approval, lacing my fingers in his hair, tugging his mouth back to mine. I suck and swirl my tongue deep in his mouth. I can feel his length pressing on me. I stroll my hand down his chest, his six pack.

"I love your sexy body Quinton," I whimper against his lips. I keep trolling my hands down, gripping his cock. He grunts, grinding harder into my hands.

"Is that so?" he hisses, looking at my eyes.

"I want you." Our eyes are locked. "Fuck me," I demand kissing him ... hard. He growls, standing, lifting me with him. My legs snake around his hips. Our lips are glued to each other in a lecherous open-mouth kiss. I feel him open the door to his cabin and kick it shut. He slams me against the wall, thrusting his length up against me. I'm so horny, and my sex is heavy. "I want you Quinton."

"You're horny with your buzz," he growls, looking down my body. His movements are lustful and heady. My hands are pushing his shorts down. I whimper, rolling my head against the wall, his thickness is saluting and ready. In one agile movement, my feet leave the floor and my legs wrap around his hips. It's all happening so fast … his fingers shift my bottoms to the side—I cry out as he propels his thick rod, balls deep into my sex … separating my insides. He's thrusting deep and hard. I grip his powerful shoulders as my body heaves against the wall. I'm so lost in him.

"Ahh," I moan, digging in my nails, hurling myself tighter around him, biting. He's hitting something … just right … "You feel wonderful," I whimper. My toes are curling and I can't breathe.

"I'm going to fuck this beautiful body for the rest of your life." He whimpers, moaning and growling into my tits. "Fuck Amelia," he hisses through clenched teeth. "You're tightening up on me," he screams, "yeah baby … come hard on my cock … thrusting so deep inside your tight pussy!" My release is hard, sending shivers over my entire body as my silk flows over him; I feel him surging through me. He grunts, shaking, pumping his hips deep, hard, and with purpose. He's moaning, sucking down my chest, as his liquid heat fills me.

His strokes have slowed, coming down from our climatic highs. He slips his strong arm tighter around my hips, holding me to him, as he leans against the wall with his other hand. He looks into my eyes, at my mouth before sucking my bottom lip into a one-lip kiss. He doesn't say anything, he adjusts his grip and carries me towards the bed.

His quads and glutes are powerhouses. He had no problem pumping into me against the wall. Hot! The mattress dips beneath our weight. His semi-hard cock slips out of me. But he doesn't roll beside me. I shift my legs open, resting against his hips; his elbows dip into the mattress, cuddled with his sexy forearms wrapped around either side of my body. His fingers are laced through my hair, lovingly touching me. Our tongues have their own song to dance to now. I'm so in love with him.

His body is wrapped around me like the perfect little cocoon. Protecting me. For the first time in a long time I feel content, safe, and truly loved. I left my husband for him. And there is nothing Eric can do to me now ... *right?*

To see what lies ahead for Quinton and Amelia, read Book 2 Forever Captivated.

Author's Note

First, I would like to thank you for taking the time to read this book. When I wrote *Captivated*, I never imagined I would one day publish it. Writing has always been an outlet for me, which even my closest friends were unaware of. That is, until I published *Captivated*.

Captivated is book one of the *Captivated* series. It was originally written as one large book. After working with my editor, we split the book into a series. As I started the editing and rewriting journey, *Captivated* reminded me of the 'honeymoon' phase of a new relationship. You know what I'm talking about: countless hours spent on the phone, every free minute together, clothes on the floor more than on your bodies. But, sometimes, when a person falls in love, they don't think about the ramifications of that love. And that is where *Forever Captivated* begins.

For the best reading experience, read *Captivated* followed by book 2 *Forever Captivated*.

About the Author

JESSICA ROOKER lives in a small town in Northeast Georgia on thirty-acres. She enjoys writing titillating romance novels with erotic intimacy and alpha-male protagonists.
Captivated is her first published novel. For more information, please visit www.jessicarooker.com.

Made in the USA
Columbia, SC
06 May 2023

16092261R00298